C000003157

DIONYSUS AND HESTIA

Rise of the Olympians

Dennis Wammack

DCW PRESS
A Boutique Publishing Company

Birmingham Alabama

Book 3. The Beginning of Civilization: Mythologies Told True

###

Dionysus and Hestia: Rise of the Olympians

©Dennis Wammack, 2022.

Published by DCW Press, Birmingham AL, www.dcwpress.com.
Printed by IngramSpark, Nashville TN.

Book: ISBN 979-8-9860246-2-2
v 221201 pod
v 230228 pod

PUBLISHING HISTORY

Dionysus and Hestia: Rise of the Olympians is the third book in the series *The Beginning of Civilization: Mythologies Told True.*

It was first published as Part III in the novel, *Changed: Chronicles of How and Why.* This version is available in digital format at www.smashwords.com and other digital book providers. The updated, revised, stand-alone version is available only in paperback.

OCEANIDS: Metis, Tyche, Clymene, Eurybia, Amphitrite, Philyra, Rhodos.
TELCHINES: Dexithea, Makelo, Halia.
EAST: Azura, Seth, Typhon, Iasion, Endymion.
OTHER: Centaur Chiron, Charon, Hotep, Petra, Persephone.

###

Jin Jiyan Azadi

Slava Ukraini

Long Live the Titans

###

OCEANIDS: Metis, Tyche, Clymene, Eurybia, Amphitrite, Philyra, Rhodos.
TELCHINES: Dexithea, Makelo, Halia.
EAST: Azura, Seth, Typhon, Iasion, Endymion.
OTHER: Centaur Chiron, Charon, Hotep, Petra, Persephone.

TABLE OF CONTENTS

The Appendix contains a Glossary of referenced names and places.

ELDER OLYMPIANS: Hestia, Demeter, Hera, Hades, Poseidon, Zeus
OLYMPIANS: Apollo, Ares, Artemis, Athena, Aphrodite, Dionysus, Hermes,
Hephaestus, Heracles. LIVING TITANS: Oceanus, Tethys, Selene, Elder Oceanids.
DECEASED TITANS: Queen Kiya, Iapetus/Piercer, Cronus.

OCEANIDS: Metis, Tyche, Clymene, Eurybia, Amphitrite, Philyra, Rhodos.
TELCHINES: Dexithea, Makelo, Halia.
EAST: Azura, Seth, Typhon, Iasion, Endymion.
OTHER: Centaur Chiron, Charon, Hotep, Petra, Persephone.

DIONYSUS AND HESTIA
Rise of the Olympians
1. Hestia
<Year 100, 4th month>

Zeus and his Olympian brothers, sisters, sons, and daughters were in full party mode. Aphrodite was gyrating on the table, her clothes strewn on the heads of her adoring admirers. Poseidon would go first.

Two floors below, his oldest sister, Hestia, quietly stared over the beautiful, peaceful Port Olympus Harbor. She had problems.

-- nothing worked as I planned -- well, no, actually, everything worked as I planned -- it's just the unintended consequences -- I didn't look far enough ahead -- did you know, Grandmother Kiya? -- that I would kill you and your titan children and then I would have it all? -- of course, you did -- you knew it all the time – and now that we Olympians have it all -- whatever shall we do with it and how will we do it? --

She walked to the sofa, sat down, and cradled Philyra's head in her lap.

Philyra murmured, "All right, Chief, you're too quiet. What's our problem?"

"I thought Kiya would have had some kind of retribution planned. She had to have considered that her little Gigante uprising against me would fail. It wasn't like her to not have a backup plan."

"I don't know, Chief. She was grooming you to be Queen of Everything. Maybe she just accepted her death as the way things had to be."

"WHO TOLD YOU THAT?"

"I thought you knew. All the Elder Titans did. Themis and Mnemosyne had better organizational skills than you, but they weren't mean enough to manage this place. By the time Queen Kiya knew how evil you were and couldn't be changed, it was too late. But in the beginning, she was doing everything she could to help you. Feel better, now?"

Puzzled, Hestia asked no one in particular, "She was grooming me?"

She sat thinking. "Find Dionysus. Have him in my office mid-day tomorrow."

Upstairs, Ares joined in.

ELDER OLYMPIANS: Hestia, Demeter, Hera, Hades, Poseidon, Zeus
OLYMPIANS: Apollo, Ares, Artemis, Athena, Aphrodite, Dionysus, Hermes,
Hephaestus, Heracles. LIVING TITANS: Oceanus, Tethys, Selene, Elder Oceanids.
DECEASED TITANS: Queen Kiya, Iapetus/Piercer, Cronus.

~ The Consultant ~

Late the next morning Philyra found Dionysus sitting at his favorite waterside table drinking wine with Heracles. She smiled and said, "Hello. I'm Philyra, Chief-of-Chiefs Hestia's Executive Assistant. She commands your presence in her office immediately."

Excited, Heracles asked, "Can I come, too?!"

Dionysus raised his hand for silence and replied, "Invite your master to join Heracles and me for lunch. Wine and cheese on the dock will do wonders for her disposition."

Philyra replied, "Olympian Hestia doesn't like to mingle with the lower classes nor have her demands declined. Come on, Titan Dionysus! Don't make my life any harder. Go meet with her. Bring your friend."

Dionysus sat silent for a moment and then replied, "Down here! Tell her that I command it."

Philyra laughed. "I didn't become Executive Assistant to the Chief-of-Chiefs of Port Olympus by being stupid, Titan. I will convey your deep regrets of being overly intimidated -- no, that won't work -- how about, you want her to come mingle with the people she is governing so she can get to know them better. That sounds good."

Now, Dionysus laughed. "She doesn't deserve you, Oceanid Philyra. You should have run away with your sisters when you could have."

"I have a physically deformed but otherwise beautiful son somewhere in Tartarus and the psychologically deformed but unbelievably powerful love-of-my-life commands the fifteenth floor of the greatest structure ever built. What's an Oceanid to do? I'll go see if I can convince her to join you."

Philyra left on her new errand.

Heracles stared at her rear as she left. "That's one good-looking Oceanid. I may share my body with her!"

"Hmmph," Dionysus grunted.

The port market bustled with activity. Workers were filtering in for lunch with a view. The gentle wind came off the water and cooled the gathering

OCEANIDS: Metis, Tyche, Clymene, Eurybia, Amphitrite, Philyra, Rhodos.
TELCHINES: Dexithea, Makelo, Halia.
EAST: Azura, Seth, Typhon, Iasion, Endymion.
OTHER: Centaur Chiron, Charon, Hotep, Petra, Persephone.

throng. But there were far fewer people at the port since the war with the Gigantes. The Olympians won an all-out victory but paid a price; there were few Titans left in the city and there was an exodus of most of the Oceanids. The loss of the former was the loss of most upper and mid-management talent. Loss of the latter meant loss of secretarial and temporary jobs plus loss of free childcare at the beaches. Many of the everyday workers had also left with the Titans and Oceanids.

Hestia was prepared to endure these losses until she could recover a viable workforce.

~

Dionysus did not need to look at the ruckus occurring at the patio entrance to know that Hestia was arriving. -- *she can't even be seated at a table with civility -- surely, she let her assistant escort her down --*

He glanced at the commotion. -- *Hestia and two bodyguards -- but no Philyra --*

"Make a place for Hestia," he commanded Heracles.

Dionysus rose and walked to where the Patio Captain was being loudly confronted by Hestia. "Chief-of-Chiefs, how nice of you to join us."

Hestia glared at Dionysus.

He said to the Patio Captain, "Kepten, I will seat our special guest at my table. Find a table where her two escorts can keep watch on her safety. Assign your ablest server to our table. I will be indebted to you."

"Yes, of course. Thank you, Master Dionysus." The captain motioned his best server to attend to every need of Dionysus and his guest.

Hestia huffed beside Dionysus to the waiting table now being prepared for a third guest. The server pulled the chair out for her to be seated. She glared at him for having the audacity to look at her.

Dionysus spoke to the server. "Bring us a flask of the good dry red, bread, cheese, and shrimp with your red sauce to start. Then your fish with the fig sauce and nuts. If we finish that, check back with me. Be prompt and respectful. Bowing and scraping won't hurt, either."

The server said, "Yes, of course. Thank you, Master Dionysus."

ELDER OLYMPIANS: Hestia, Demeter, Hera, Hades, Poseidon, Zeus
OLYMPIANS: Apollo, Ares, Artemis, Athena, Aphrodite, Dionysus, Hermes,
Hephaestus, Heracles. LIVING TITANS: Oceanus, Tethys, Selene, Elder Oceanids.
DECEASED TITANS: Queen Kiya, Iapetus/Piercer, Cronus.

Dionysus leaned back in his chair, lifted his cup of wine, and toasted, "Let us drink to the beauty, wisdom, and charm of Hestia."

"Hear, hear," said Heracles, quickly lifting his cup in salute.

"To what do I owe this attention, my dearest Hestia?" Dionysus asked.

"How can you possibly eat with these people under these conditions?" Hestia said in a voice loud enough to be heard across the patio.

Dionysus laughed. "With a voice like that, I can get you a job selling fish directly off the boats. They need loud obnoxious women to tout their wares. I, however, don't! Nor will I sit with a person without class. Do we have an understanding?" He smiled sweetly.

"Why don't I kill you, now?" she growled, in a softer voice.

"For the same reason I don't kill you now; blood on the table, spilled wine, nothing worthwhile accomplished. You just aren't worth the effort, Hestia. Now, I ask again. To what do I owe this attention? And where is your assistant? She seems nice. She's the only thing that might keep being around you tolerable."

"I have problems, Dionysus. I didn't want her to hear our conversation." She stared pointedly at Heracles.

Dionysus said to Heracles, "Go entertain the two Gigantes, Heracles. Gossip with them. Glean any intelligence they might happen to have."

Heracles reluctantly rose. "Yes, *Master*!" he said as he left to join the two bodyguards.

Dionysus said, "All right, Hestia, keep it business and I will keep it business."

"I have lost half my workforce, the smart half at that. I don't know where workers come from. What port do I raid to capture hardworking subjects to obey the Olympians? What did Titans do to subjugate their workers?"

He stared at Hestia in silent disbelief, then sadness, then anger. "Let's concentrate on your problem. You need to hire more staff. How do you do that? Correct?"

"Yes. We already had too many low-class people working for the port. And now I need to find a higher class of people."

OCEANIDS: Metis, Tyche, Clymene, Eurybia, Amphitrite, Philyra, Rhodos.
TELCHINES: Dexithea, Makelo, Halia.
EAST: Azura, Seth, Typhon, Iasion, Endymion.
OTHER: Centaur Chiron, Charon, Hotep, Petra, Persephone.

"You're too hung up on this class thing, Hestia. Let it go. Your nemesis Titans created a great empire by surrounding themselves with rejects, castoffs, and cripples from other tribes. You have far better talent to draw from. You don't think that you are better than our food server, do you? Never mind! Of course, you do. But know this, it is by accident of birth that I'm not sitting here with the server and you are the one serving. Throw you both naked into a wilderness and I guarantee it will be the server that walks out. Not you. Now, back to the subject that you keep wandering from. You need to hire staff."

"Very well, Dionysus. How do I find these worthy new hires?"

"Oh, I don't know. How about this?" Dionysus signaled his server.

The server hurried over. "Yes, Master Titan -- I mean Olympian."

Dionysus laughed. "You are most attentive and disciplined. What's your name? Are you from around here?"

The server was in an awkward position but responded with false confidence. "I am Charon, Master. I am from Tartarus. My mother was a farmer girl. She told me that my father was Master Outis or maybe even the great Enceladus. But I imagine he was some random metal worker."

"Interesting," Dionysus replied. "What do you do in your off-hours?"

"I am a scribe at the great Library. I teach reading. I also read the scrolls of and about Chief Iapetus, from his boyhood days as Piercer up until his -- last entries."

"Fantastic! And last question. What are your interests?"

"Oh, the metalworking projects they do in the north. I study the teachings of the great Iapetus in the library. I came to the port last season and tried to get work, but I was told that I was not worthy."

"My goodness. An unworthy, studious scribe. How interesting." Dionysus took a small piece of blank parchment from his pocket and scribbled his sign on it. "In five days, take this to Philyra on the thirteenth floor. Tell her you request an internship in upper metalworking management. I make no promises, Master Charon, but I believe Philyra likes me. She will at least listen to you. Be confident, almost arrogant; not subservient."

ELDER OLYMPIANS: Hestia, Demeter, Hera, Hades, Poseidon, Zeus
OLYMPIANS: Apollo, Ares, Artemis, Athena, Aphrodite, Dionysus, Hermes,
Hephaestus, Heracles. LIVING TITANS: Oceanus, Tethys, Selene, Elder Oceanids.
DECEASED TITANS: Queen Kiya, Iapetus/Piercer, Cronus.

Charon accepted the paper with several quick bows. "Thank you, Master Olympian. I will do this. Thank you." -- *master Charon -- he called me 'master' -- he is an Olympian calling me master Charon -- thirteenth floor -- this paper is my way to greatness -- Philyra! -- five days -- an actual job with the port administration! -*

Dionysus cleared his throat and stared at Charon. "Any questions?"

Charon broke from his trance, said, "Oh, none. Thank you, Master," and scurried away tightly holding the parchment.

Dionysus said to Hestia, "He has potential. Philyra can decide. Now, let's go to your fifteenth floor and see what we have to work with."

Hestia nodded with acquiescence.

2. Team Meeting

Philyra met Hestia, Dionysus, and Heracles at the entrance to the fifteenth floor; the executive floor where the Olympian overlords worked. "Did you have a nice lunch, Chief?"

"Exquisite," she replied.

"Sweet, Bitter, or wine?" Philyra asked the three.

"Nothing. We have business to discuss," Hestia replied as she marched toward her desk.

The three sat down at the executive table. "Philyra will join us as an equal," Dionysus told Hestia.

"Join us as an equal?!" Hestia demanded.

"Equal in a business sense. As a matter of fact, in business, she is more equal than either of us. We are discussing business here, Hestia."

Hestia said, "Very well. It's a bad precedent but you may join us, Philyra. Dionysus needs your input."

Philyra hesitated, said "Yes, Chief," and pulled out a chair to sit in.

Dionysus said, "You need to put up a privacy wall, Hestia. Your siblings appear to be interested in what's going on. But then you couldn't watch *them*, could you? No matter. Philyra, what position is most important to fill the quickest?"

OCEANIDS: Metis, Tyche, Clymene, Eurybia, Amphitrite, Philyra, Rhodos.
TELCHINES: Dexithea, Makelo, Halia.
EAST: Azura, Seth, Typhon, Iasion, Endymion.
OTHER: Centaur Chiron, Charon, Hotep, Petra, Persephone.

Philyra looked confused and looked to Hestia for guidance.

Hestia nodded permission to speak freely.

Philyra took a deep breath. "Oh, my goodness. We have been needing someone for Mining, Metals, and Manufacturing for a long time. I'm sure Hades does an outstanding job but no one from that department is ever here to plan and coordinate. Hades is always out in the field. Maybe if he had an administrative assistant, at least on the thirteenth floor, it would help streamline things a little bit. And a coordinator to receive and dispatch port traffic would be fantastic. Amphitrite did an amazing job, but she was retired with all the other Titans. I don't know whose ships to expect or what they carry. That would be a tremendous help. And our internal messaging is almost nonexistent. Nobody knows what they should be doing or what anybody else has done."

Heracles interjected, "Wow, we need those Titans back. They were great at that."

Dionysus said sharply, "Quiet! Dung-head!"

To Philyra, he said, "A candidate for the 3M department will call on you in five days. I don't know if he would fit but he has an interest in the discipline. Do you know anyone who might be a good coordinator?"

Philyra glanced at Hestia. Hestia stared back cold faced. Philyra answered, "Well, yes. There is a young man who worked in Amphitrite's office, Nerites. He's smart and knowledgeable."

Dionysus asked, "Poseidon manages Port Operations well?"

"He's fantastic with the in-the-water part of it. Not so great with the paperwork and managing people part of it. He's seldom here which is probably for the best. Kind of like Hades. Demeter would be a good manager, but she is just interested in grains and harvesting."

"Who is in charge of hiring, Philyra?"

"In charge of hiring? We don't have anyone like that. If a manager needed someone, they went out and found them."

"I've heard enough, Chief Hestia. Can we have a private meeting tomorrow after mid-day meal? Up on the roof? The view is inspiring."

ELDER OLYMPIANS: Hestia, Demeter, Hera, Hades, Poseidon, Zeus
OLYMPIANS: Apollo, Ares, Artemis, Athena, Aphrodite, Dionysus, Hermes,
Hephaestus, Heracles. LIVING TITANS: Oceanus, Tethys, Selene, Elder Oceanids.
DECEASED TITANS: Queen Kiya, Iapetus/Piercer, Cronus.

Hestia considered the request. "Will you have anything worthwhile to bring me?"

"By after mid-day meal, yes. But I need time for it to come together in my mind."

"All right. You and I on the roof tomorrow afternoon. Show them out Philyra."

Philyra rose immediately and motioned Dionysus and Heracles to follow.

As they approached the door, Dionysus said, "Meet me at the cafe after you get off work. All right? I have a problem that I suspect you can fix for me."

"You want to couple with an Oceanid? Sorry, big boy! You aren't my type."

Dionysus laughed. "After work, Philyra! Be there!"

"Maybe. But maybe not."

"Be there, Philyra!"

3. Chiron

She arrived sooner than Dionysus had expected but he had the wine waiting. He poured a cup for her as soon as he saw her approach. It was waiting when she arrived at his table. "Sit, drink this. Let's get you ready for the evening."

"You are persistent, Dionysus, and the answer is still no," she said as she sat down and accepted his wine.

He laughed. "I'm here to negotiate a trade with you, Oceanid. I see the future for your mistress and her Olympian ilk. Plus, for the port and all humanity. Should I sell out my self-respect and tell your chief how to save her butt? I will do it just for you, except, it's what Kiya would want me to do. She's the only reason I'm still in this place. "

"Yes, I would like that. I see a lot of things that need doing but for an Olympian to take suggestions from an Oceanid is unthinkable. You are one of them. She will listen to you. That's why she went to you for help. Yes, I will couple with you if you save Port Olympus from going under."

OCEANIDS: Metis, Tyche, Clymene, Eurybia, Amphitrite, Philyra, Rhodos.
TELCHINES: Dexithea, Makelo, Halia.
EAST: Azura, Seth, Typhon, Iasion, Endymion.
OTHER: Centaur Chiron, Charon, Hotep, Petra, Persephone.

"Sorry, Oceanid Philyra, the price for my self-respect is not your pleasure, it is your pain."

"Ohhh, a spanking beforehand. I can handle that!"

Dionysus became serious. "I have a friend, Philyra. I have heard his story many times. The name 'Philyra' is always there. He is the most noble and worthy human there is. He simply looks different. He needs you." He stared at her.

Her face went cold. "No, Dionysus. I will not see him."

"If I am to sacrifice my humanity for you and your worthless Olympians. I require your humanity in return."

"No. Please, no, Dionysus."

"Have another cup of wine, sweet Philyra. Together, we can do this thing."

After her third wine. He took her hand and led her to the port transportation center. He engaged a carriage and helped her into it. His satchel over his shoulder, he climbed in and said, "900 Pace Path, please."

The carriage arrived at the great path circling the abandoned home of the now dead Elder Titans. It was well into the night when they arrived.

Few people still lived there; some farmer women, animal handlers for the livestock, some stone cutters, and random people. Gone were the Elder Titans, now dead, and the younger Titans, scattered to the high hills of the mainland, and the Oceanids, to waters far from Port Olympus. Gone, too, were the Gigantes. None remained to live in this now accursed place.

"He lives this way, Philyra." He led the reluctant Oceanid up a path bounded by flowers gone to seed. They passed bathhouses and unpruned shrubs on their left. The only light was provided by a quarter moon under slow-moving clouds.

Finally, in the distance were the small fires and torches of the remaining inhabitants. "Halloo," Dionysus called out into the night. A figure appeared. "Dionysus," a female shrieked out, "you have come to see us." Women came running from their homes to greet him.

He removed flasks of wine from his satchel, and said, "I bring you gifts better than I. Here, take these bottles, enjoy the fruit of the grape." They

ELDER OLYMPIANS: Hestia, Demeter, Hera, Hades, Poseidon, Zeus
OLYMPIANS: Apollo, Ares, Artemis, Athena, Aphrodite, Dionysus, Hermes, Hephaestus, Heracles. LIVING TITANS: Oceanus, Tethys, Selene, Elder Oceanids. DECEASED TITANS: Queen Kiya, Iapetus/Piercer, Cronus.

wanted him to join them and provide even more merriment. He declined. "I am here on business. We will have a party next time!"

They retired in sadness, but excitedly, with their four containers of wine.

Dionysus led Philyra past the houses, to the last one, away from the others. He stopped, turned to Philyra, and said, "Not only will you do this, but you will do it well." With that, he walked to the door and knocked. "It is I, Master Chiron, your friend Dionysus."

After the sound of shuffling, the door opened. Chiron stood there with outstretched arms. "My friend, you take time to come see me. Come in."

"I did not come alone, Chiron. I brought someone else."

"To see me, Master? Do they know what I look like?"

"All too well, Chiron. But she sees only the outside. I have brought her to see the real you."

"Oh, Master, I will present myself as best I can."

He motioned to Philyra. "Come here, my dear. You remember Chiron – I believe he is your son."

Philyra stepped forward to face her son. In the darkness looking head-on, he appeared to be a normal man. She took a deep breath. "Hello, Chiron. I haven't seen you in a long time."

"Mother. You honor me. That you will look upon me, brings my heart joy. You need not look more. This moment is more than I deserve." He fell to his knees and prostrated himself before her. The front half, that is. The rear half continued standing.

She choked on a sob.

Dionysus glared at her, daring her not to take his hands and pick him up. She closed her eyes and lifted her son to his feet.

"We wish to visit, Master Chiron. I am here to show your mother the difference between humanity and inhumanity, between grotesque and merely physically different. I bring the mother to face the son. Be patient. This will be difficult for her."

OCEANIDS: Metis, Tyche, Clymene, Eurybia, Amphitrite, Philyra, Rhodos.
TELCHINES: Dexithea, Makelo, Halia.
EAST: Azura, Seth, Typhon, Iasion, Endymion.
OTHER: Centaur Chiron, Charon, Hotep, Petra, Persephone.

"I understand, Friend Dionysus. I will show her my disfigurement. I will suffer the revulsion she will feel. If this is your will, then I shall not try to hide the grotesque shape of my body. I shall trust you to salve the horror that I bring her. Come in, Mother. This is where I live."

Chiron led them into his modest home. He gave them chairs and put another log on the small fire. Illuminated by the firelight, he removed his tunic and stood so she could see the outline of his body. "As you can see, my hindquarters have grown significantly since I became a man. My rear legs are now fully functional. At least, enough that children could ride upon my back. I can gallop, after a sort. Although not as smoothly as a real horse. Friend Apollo taught me the art of the lyre, medicine, and prophesy. Friend Artemis trained me in archery and hunting. Before they left Tartarus, the children would come to the beach to see me. They came to see my grotesque deformity but would deem to ride upon my back, and sometimes let me teach those things which Leto's twins had so graciously taught me. I live in quiet joy. My only regret is the extreme dishonor which my birth brought to my beloved mother and esteemed father."

Philyra threw up.

Chiron hurried away to fetch water and linens to clean her vomit. Philyra remained in the chair sobbing uncontrollably.

While Chiron was away, Dionysus said to Philyra, "Strange, isn't it? Cronus, the only son of Kiya and Pumi, fathered only little monsters. Six physically beautiful but completely inhumane babies by Rhea and one physically deformed but emotionally beautiful baby like Chiron by you. Nature has a delicious sense of humor, don't you think?"

As Charon returned, Dionysus said. "Your mother has a few issues to work through, Chiron. Before you put your clothes back on, there is one last thing to be done." He walked to Philyra, pulled her up, and roughly removed her dress. She stood there in her undergarments, eyes clenched closed, gulping sobs. "Now, Oceanid Philyra, Assistant to Chief-of-Chiefs Olympian Hestia, do as the children of Tartarus have done before you. Ride upon his back!"

She held back as Dionysus pulled her toward her son. He forced her, eyes clenched closed, to touch the deformed growth of her son's extended back. She trembled, vomited again, fell to her knees, and cried out, "Cronus -- Rhea -- Kiya – forgive me." She was silent for a long, long time

ELDER OLYMPIANS: Hestia, Demeter, Hera, Hades, Poseidon, Zeus
OLYMPIANS: Apollo, Ares, Artemis, Athena, Aphrodite, Dionysus, Hermes, Hephaestus, Heracles. LIVING TITANS: Oceanus, Tethys, Selene, Elder Oceanids.
DECEASED TITANS: Queen Kiya, Iapetus/Piercer, Cronus.

and then opened her eyes to stare at her deformed son. She whispered, "Chiron -- my son -- forgive me." She rose, swung her leg over his back, and said "Carry me to Oursea, Chiron. I have not touched Oursea since you were born. Let all people see Philyra with her son."

4. Birth of the Ghods

Noon.

Hestia waited on the Port Olympus building roof.

Dionysus entered and walked over to greet Hestia. "The view is inspiring. You are inspiring. The Olympians are inspiring. I know what you should do. I will tell you what you should do and after I tell you, I will leave. You need not say a word. You need not do anything I tell you. I have told no one what I shall tell you nor will I. This, dear Aunt Hestia, is what you should do."

She stared at him without expression.

He began, "Olympians will no longer see themselves as part of anything. Olympians are above everything. I have a new made-up name for you -- 'Ghods.' You own everything in the world. You don't have to demand anything because you already own it. You are just letting other people use it. You can do and take whatever you want. No one can even aspire to become one of you. And most important, Ghods don't have to associate with the lower classes ever again. Think about that, never again! Do you like that part?"

"Yes, I like that part."

"Well, you won't like this! You will make Oceanid Philyra the Port Olympus 'Chief-of-Chiefs.' You and your brethren are out of day-to-day operations. But you will like this part – you will be the sole chief of Philyra. You can command her what you want to be done, just not how to do it. Your brothers and sisters can tell you what they want, if they really care, and you can command Philyra what her goal is, but the other Ghods will be isolated from Philyra and her staff."

"Hmmm."

"Don't make an immediate decision. Consider everything. You can give out fancy titles like 'Ghod of the Sea.' and 'Ghod of the Sky,' and 'Ghod

OCEANIDS: Metis, Tyche, Clymene, Eurybia, Amphitrite, Philyra, Rhodos.
TELCHINES: Dexithea, Makelo, Halia.
EAST: Azura, Seth, Typhon, Iasion, Endymion.
OTHER: Centaur Chiron, Charon, Hotep, Petra, Persephone.

of the Underground.' But command Philyra to create a Port organization to maximize the reach and power of the port and then stay out of her way except for some petty commands to make you feel good about yourself. She will recruit and appoint based on competence; not on family relations; not on your preferences. When word gets out that Olympians are no longer running -- that is, interfering -- with port operations, old managers will start drifting back in. You and your brethren can party all day on the sixteenth and seventeenth floors. Maybe make some vacation homes in the Graikoi Mountains."

He paused. "That's a lot to absorb. Are you with me so far?"

"Yes."

"There are a few rules. The managers closest to you, the lords of the lower floors, those who actually do the work must all become rich and powerful. But it is not the Ghods they will compete with. It's everybody below them. And everybody below them must have the hope that one day, they, too, can become powerful like your Lords on the high floors. But no one can aspire to ever become a Ghod. The Ghods may look down upon the lower classes like scum beneath their feet if you think of them at all. But you must not look down upon your Lords. They are your top-level managers; the ones who do all the work and are the buffer between the Ghods and the lower classes. You must always, without exception, *always* respect your Lords, love them, and reward them well. They will do everything they can to maintain your favor. Whatever you do -- sear this into your brain -- don't interfere with Philyra. Tell her what you want, then stay out of her way while she does it."

She continued to stare at him, unblinking.

He finished, "I have shown you the way, Aunt Hestia. Now, I am evil like you. Do as you will. I'm going to get drunk. Goodbye."

Dionysus turned and left.

Hestia stared after him. -- *no more dealing with the lower classes – own everything? – I may like this --*

5. Hestia and Artemis

Artemis was thrilled. The great Hestia, herself, had Artemis by the hand pulling her to the rooftop away from the raging Olympian party. This was

ELDER OLYMPIANS: Hestia, Demeter, Hera, Hades, Poseidon, Zeus
OLYMPIANS: Apollo, Ares, Artemis, Athena, Aphrodite, Dionysus, Hermes,
Hephaestus, Heracles. LIVING TITANS: Oceanus, Tethys, Selene, Elder Oceanids.
DECEASED TITANS: Queen Kiya, Iapetus/Piercer, Cronus.

recognition of the highest honor. Even Aphrodite was only allowed here when Zeus required her attention. Artemis wanted to invite her twin brother, Apollo, but she didn't dare suggest it. Hestia seldom paid the lesser Olympians any attention.

They arrived on the roof and sat upon one of the sofas facing Oursea. The view of the port was magnificent. Hestia was uncharacteristically attentive. "My dear Artemis, now that I have made Philyra the port Chief-of-Chiefs, I have time to pay more attention to my dearest Olympian relatives. I have been wanting to show you this view for a long time."

Hestia remained silent as Artemis blathered on about whatever it was she was blathering on about. Hestia finally interrupted Artemis with a drawn-out sigh and the cloying words, "I have not had an opportunity to express my deep sorrow over the unfortunate deaths of your beloved Grandmother Phoebe and our Great-grandmother Kiya. I almost feel responsible. My Hecatoncheire were fighting those dreadful Gigantes, and the Titans were inadvertently caught in the crossfire. It was horrible. I tried to save them, but I couldn't get to them in time. I am so distraught over the incident. But how are you doing, dear? Are you holding up well? You always look so young and beautiful."

Artemis was now even more thrilled. She had known that if she ever brought up the killing of the Elder Titans that she and her brother would no longer be welcomed as Olympians. She had kept her mouth shut on the subject but now she knew the truth. -- *Aunt Hestia tried to save them but couldn't -- I feel so much better about the entire incident -- I will tell Apollo as soon as we're alone --*

She said, "Oh, don't grieve, Aunt Hestia. You did all that you could. I am proud of you for trying!"

Hestia smiled a sad little smile and said, "You are so kind and loving Artemis. I'm glad that you and your brother are Olympians in good standing. Now, tell me, how do you maintain your young girlish features? You don't seem to age at all!"

"Did not Aunt Rhea share the secret of the Red Nectar when she had your Ceremony of Womanhood?"

"Ceremony?" -- *careful, Hestia --*

OCEANIDS: Metis, Tyche, Clymene, Eurybia, Amphitrite, Philyra, Rhodos.
TELCHINES: Dexithea, Makelo, Halia.
EAST: Azura, Seth, Typhon, Iasion, Endymion.
OTHER: Centaur Chiron, Charon, Hotep, Petra, Persephone.

"Oh, no, sweet Artemis. Mother never provided this ceremony, and I was a Titanide after all. Did I miss something?"

"Every Titanide should have received her Ceremony of Womanhood. It was then that we learned the secret of Queen Kiya's Red Nectar which keeps us all so young. We are sworn to share the secret with only our worthy daughters at their Ceremony. Not even the Titanes suspect. We slip it to our males without them ever knowing what it is. I can't believe Aunt Rhea didn't instruct you."

Hestia lowered her head and let out a sob. "No. Mother never like me. I never knew why. I tried so hard to make her like me. I think she was mad at Father for divorcing her and sending us all to that forsaken island where we grew up." She took Artemis's hand in hers and looked deeply into her eyes. "But at least you know the recipe, sweet Olympian Artemis. Sister Demeter and I will simply have to grow too old too soon."

Artemis stared back with concern; unsure of how to respond.

Then Hestia's eyes brightened. She said, "But I wonder, is it possible, under the next full moon, would it be possible for you and me and Demeter, just the three of us, to gather here on the roof and for you, as a Titanide, to give the Ceremony of Womanhood to me and my sister? We are both technically Titanides through Mother Rhea. Is that possible, sweet Olympian Artemis?" Hestia's eyes danced with excitement.

"I am sworn to give the ceremony only to my worthy daughter," Artemis quietly replied.

"I understand." -- *don't rush this – patience -- right, Grandmother Kiya? – "*

Hestia continued, "You think my sister and I are not worthy. But at least consider it. The ceremony would bring the three of us so close together and help salve the horrible loss of our mothers. YOU could be our mother!"

Artemis panicked. "I will consider it, Hestia, but I have no one to turn to for advice."

Hestia smiled sweetly. "Come and see me, anytime, Artemis. My door is always open to a sister Olympian -- who is in good standing."

6. Demeter and Persephone

They sat in a field of flowers. Demeter loved the Elysian Fields. Especially when it was full of flowers. Especially when she sat beside her sweet daughter, Persephone. Persephone would pretend to paint the colors onto the flowers, the yellows, the purples, the oranges, the reds. *-- sometimes, my child looks back over the fields and believes that it was she who had painted the flowers -- she is a sweet, simple child -- so innocent -- but almost a woman -- soon, she will be fodder for rampaging Olympian males who respect no woman -- no decency -- respecting no relation they have with the woman -- they are animals -- miserable male animals --*

She could still feel the repulsive body of her brother Zeus smothering her body, barely allowing her to breathe as he pounded away at her. *-- the sickness of it -- my own brother -- impregnating me -- I will protect my daughter from Zeus at all costs -- my other brothers will at least ask and respect her refusal -- but Zeus won't -- he did not respect me -- he will not respect his daughter -- he made me bear a child -- a sweet child -- a simple, innocent child -- my sweet Persephone --*

Dionysus would sometimes mock her. "You are more Titan than Olympian, Demeter. Runaway with me. Let's escape these monsters."

She would laugh because Olympians were supposed to laugh at everything and have fun and not care about anything other than being an Olympian. Dionysus was an Olympian, but he was the exception, he was more Titan than Olympian. She, however, was more Olympian than Titan. She cared far more about things like power and obedience and fame than about other people. But it was true. She alone of her siblings loved the land, the fields and the flowers, the grains and the harvests.

Hades, too, loved the land. But not the surface. He loved his quarries and his caves. Hades was strange; quiet, serious, and a little scary.

But today, Demeter lay on her back in a field of grass looking up at the clouds, her sweet daughter lying beside her, in a bed of flowers painted by Persephone, on the verge of womanhood.

7. Hades and Chiron

Hades stopped to stare at abandoned Tartarus. *-- the reports must be true -- the titans have been killed -- did Hestia hate them that much? -- master Iapetus - dead?! -- he was the only person to teach me -- to mentor me -- I knew nothing of metals*

OCEANIDS: Metis, Tyche, Clymene, Eurybia, Amphitrite, Philyra, Rhodos.
TELCHINES: Dexithea, Makelo, Halia.
EAST: Azura, Seth, Typhon, Iasion, Endymion.
OTHER: Centaur Chiron, Charon, Hotep, Petra, Persephone.

-- of mines -- of the vast worlds beneath the earth -- he taught me everything -- slaughtered by my own sister's army -- a lot has happened since I was last at the port -- but three months in my mines doesn't feel like a long time --

He walked slowly past the abandoned entrance guest house onto the great patio. He stood looking at the fire pit. He walked on. He came to the great house at the end of the path. *-- Queen Kiya's? --*

He turned right, walked the path in front of the homes of the Elder Titans, and stopped in front of the last home marked with the sign of Iapetus and Clymene. *-- this is where master Iapetus lived! --*

He walked to the door and pushed on it. It opened. Inside were the glories of the greatest metal and stone scholar to ever live, Scholar Master Elder Titane Chief-Research-Chief-for-Metals Iapetus, Piercer the Great.

Hades sank into a chair. He had never cried but now he felt like it. After a while, he composed himself. Being in Piercer's quarters helped focus his mind. *-- if the rumors are true, Hestia has made me some kind of supreme chief of the underground -- all the mines and caves -- but can I still do anything I want and command anyone I want? -- what's that all about? -- what shall I do? --*

Hades had no great love for his fellow Olympians. *-- they look down on me like they are so much better than me -- Aphrodite doesn't even moan when I couple with her -- she thinks she is too good for me -- they are all mean and don't even like the dark -- I hate them all -- Iapetus talked to me like an equal -- even though I am a superior Olympian, and he was only an elder titan -- he taught me everything about metals and rocks and fires and mining but Hestia killed him before he had taught me enough -- without him, I no longer have interest in working with metals -- and there are such wonderful metals I could mine -- find out about -- which ones to combine -- find out what they would do -- we were learning how to make fires bigger and hotter -- that was the key -- hotter fires -- and now I am alone -- after Hestia gave me his job, Iapetus was forbidden to leave Tartarus -- but he would still sneak to see me in the mines to help me -- now I know why he suddenly stopped coming -- the rumors must be true -- and now I am alone --*

He found Piercer's bed and lay upon it. *-- Iapetus -- dead -- I am supreme master of the underground -- but all alone --*

Sunrise.

Hades left the house to the bright sunrise of a beautiful morning. It wasn't that Hades hated beautiful mornings, it was that he loved his cool, dim,

ELDER OLYMPIANS: Hestia, Demeter, Hera, Hades, Poseidon, Zeus
OLYMPIANS: Apollo, Ares, Artemis, Athena, Aphrodite, Dionysus, Hermes, Hephaestus, Heracles. LIVING TITANS: Oceanus, Tethys, Selene, Elder Oceanids. DECEASED TITANS: Queen Kiya, Iapetus/Piercer, Cronus.

subterranean offices more. He continued his walk upon the path that would eventually turn into the road to Port Olympus. He came to 300 Pace Path but continued on. He came to 900 Pace Path and impulsively turned right onto it. There were fields of flowers attended by bees on either side. He came upon small houses. -- *for the workers?* --

Farmer women were beginning to leave for their daily work in the fields. -- *they no longer have masters, but still, they work -- how interesting* --

A man stepped out from one of the houses -- and kept stepping out. Hades stared in disbelief. -- *that is not a normal man -- what is that?* --

Hades shouted at the creature, "What are you? Are you some kind of monster?!"

Chiron smiled at Hades. "Yes, a grotesque monster. I shamed my beloved mother by my birth. Better I had been born dead than live like this. But I am here. Shall I disrobe so that you can stare upon my deformity?"

Hades stared, then said, "Yes."

Chiron removed the tunic which he wore on the human portion of his body. "I would offer to let you ride on my back as the small children once enjoyed, but you appear to be heavy. I'm sorry that I cannot make you this offer."

"Can I touch it?"

"Oh, yes. Please do. It sometimes helps one overcome their repulsion."

Hades walked over and put his hands on Chiron's extended back. -- *he is more grotesque than I am -- how wonderful* --

"You look like some kind of horse."

"Yes. But not a handsome horse. A misshapen, ugly horse. I am the worst of both man and horse. A hideous abomination."

"You take it well."

"What are my choices, Master ..." He waited for his visitor's name.

Hades looked puzzled. No one had ever not known who he was before. Then he realized, this creature did not recognize him. With exaggerated

OCEANIDS: Metis, Tyche, Clymene, Eurybia, Amphitrite, Philyra, Rhodos.
TELCHINES: Dexithea, Makelo, Halia.
EAST: Azura, Seth, Typhon, Iasion, Endymion.
OTHER: Centaur Chiron, Charon, Hotep, Petra, Persephone.

self-importance, Hades said, "I am Olympian Hades, Chief of all Port Olympus Mining Operations. At least, I used to be."

Chiron bowed his front, and rising said, "I am so sorry that I did not recognize you, Olympian Hades. I have never before seen a real Olympian. Iapetus has often told me of your superior knowledge of his mines and your love for all of it. Please forgive me for my shortcomings."

With supreme superiority, Hades replied, "I will overlook your ignorance this time. Pay attention in the future!"

Chiron bowed again. "You are gracious and merciful. Thank you for speaking to one such as me." He backed away, head bowed, expecting dismissal.

"Hmmph! You are respectful enough. You may accompany me on my walk. Advise me on the things I see."

"Yes, Master. It will be my fortunate honor to do so." They continued Hades' stroll up the circular path. Chiron provided a running commentary on the landscape and the things they saw.

They came to a fence. Chiron said, "This fence circles the pastures of the Great Outis. It contains the many beehives which produce our honey plus our aurochs and horses. Over there is a pasture for our Mouflons. Outis tamed them. He called them sheep. Their hair is incredibly soft. Those smaller enclosed places are for our egg-laying birds and our hares. All our animals are raised here. Come, I will show you the small animal section." They entered a gate into the pasture. "Outis was my friend. He was deformed, like me. He had only one eye and it was hard for some people to look into his face. But the Elder Titans took him into their family as one of their own. The great Elder Titanide, Rhea, told me once, in a moment of wine-induced confidence, that her first coupling was with Outis. 'It is the most different who are the most interesting,' she told me. She tilted her head and smiled at me as she said this. In my private fantasies, I pretend that she was inviting me to ask her to couple. I, of course, didn't ask. Any possibility, no matter how small, that I might sire a child must be avoided. But I will confess, many of the older farmer women tell me that they are too old to bear children. I couple with them as best I can. A poor substitute for a real man, I'm sure. Still, they come back to me often."

ELDER OLYMPIANS: Hestia, Demeter, Hera, Hades, Poseidon, Zeus
OLYMPIANS: Apollo, Ares, Artemis, Athena, Aphrodite, Dionysus, Hermes, Hephaestus, Heracles. LIVING TITANS: Oceanus, Tethys, Selene, Elder Oceanids.
DECEASED TITANS: Queen Kiya, Iapetus/Piercer, Cronus.

They saw men and women working in the distance.

Chiron said, "Those are the children and friends of the Great Outis. They continue his work with animals. Come, I will show you everything."

They continued to the area where work was going on. Chiron was greeted by the workers, who glanced at Hades without recognizing that he was an Olympian, but still knew not to speak; this was no friendly Titan master. Chiron continued his monolog.

They came to pens containing dogs. All barked in greeting except one; sitting in the back, a large dog with greatly oversized ears sat staring, unblinking, at Hades.

"What are those things?" Hades asked.

"These are the working dogs. They herd animals and protect them from predators. They provide companionship to those who seek a companion. I have considered taking one, but they don't know that I am different. I feel like that would be a betrayal of trust, so I don't accept one."

Hades returned the unblinking stare of the large dog with its oversized ears. Chiron noticed and said, "That large one in the back seems to recognize you as its master. Do you wish to take him as your own?"

Hades asked, "What's it good for? How does one take a dog? What's involved?" Hades continued to return the stare of the dog as he listened to Chiron's long-winded explanation of everything involved in adopting a dog. -- *the thing likes me -- I can tell -- it thinks I am different from other people -- better - it certainly likes me more than my Olympian kin like me -- will it obey me? — can it bring me things? -- discipline the insolent? -- keep the lower classes away from me? -- does it like darkness? -- what are you good for, dog? -- what is your name? --*

Finally, Hades interrupted Chiron's explanation. "Will it come to me if I command it to? How do I call it?"

Chiron replied, "His name is Cerberus. Call his name and let's find out."

Hades, in his best Olympian voice, commanded, "Cerberus! Come!"

The dog rose, trotted to the gate, and stood waiting for it to open.

Chiron opened the gate. Cerberus trotted through, walked to Hades, and sat down; staring, ears up, waiting for his master's command.

OCEANIDS: Metis, Tyche, Clymene, Eurybia, Amphitrite, Philyra, Rhodos.
TELCHINES: Dexithea, Makelo, Halia.
EAST: Azura, Seth, Typhon, Iasion, Endymion.
OTHER: Centaur Chiron, Charon, Hotep, Petra, Persephone.

8. Hades, Hestia, Charon

Hestia glared at Hades as she demanded, "Where in all of the lands of Hades have you been for over three months? I needed you here!" She then noticed the animal crouching at his feet. She involuntarily gasped and stepped back.

Hades said, "I was busy doing useful things, Hestia. And this is Cerberus. He is a dog. I don't think he likes you because of the way his hair is standing on end. By the way, on the walk from Tartarus, I passed a random woman working in the fields. I pointed to her and said, 'Cerberus! Kill!' He is quite an efficient killer. Would you like to touch him?"

She took another step back and said, "Keep that thing away from me!"

Hades dropped his hand and commanded, "Cerberus! Down!" The dog obediently lay down on the floor at his master's feet alert for any subsequent command. "Now, Hestia shall we continue standing as you tell me why you want me here, or can we sit?"

"Come sit on the sofa. Leave that thing where it is."

"Cerberus! Stay!" He walked to the sofa overlooking the magnificent port. "Where is everybody?"

"Everything's changed. Olympians no longer have to deal with the lower classes. We are a class above all classes. We are greater than Olympians. We are called Ghods. It's all good. We like it. I am the only Olympian who must talk to a lower-class person – Philyra. And she is the only one of her class to whom I must ever talk. We have rules that we Olympians need to observe so that we can keep this arrangement working. Know everyone on the thirteenth floor, always treat them with respect, refer to them as Lords, and never talk down to any one of them. It would ruin everything. They are the buffer between us and the despicable masses. Train yourself to think of them as a high class. We Ghods no longer need to think of ourselves as the higher class. Ghods are above all classes. Just remember to treat the Lords like they are worthy humans. They will obey us out of neediness, not out of fear. Dionysus taught me this. Are we in agreement?"

"That's a lot to consider, Hestia. And what about this 'master of the underground?"

ELDER OLYMPIANS: Hestia, Demeter, Hera, Hades, Poseidon, Zeus
OLYMPIANS: Apollo, Ares, Artemis, Athena, Aphrodite, Dionysus, Hermes,
Hephaestus, Heracles. LIVING TITANS: Oceanus, Tethys, Selene, Elder Oceanids.
DECEASED TITANS: Queen Kiya, Iapetus/Piercer, Cronus.

"Oh, I divided the world into four parts. Poseidon owns everything related to water. Zeus owns everything related to the sky. You own everything below ground. We all share the ground and things on it. I hope you are pleased. By the way, you are no longer 'Port-Olympus-Chief-Research-Scholar-for-Metal-Research.' Philyra replaced that with a Chief-of-Metals, Mining, and Manufacturing position; CoM3 she calls it. Your replacement's name is Charon or something like that. Only Philyra can command him, not me or you. If you want him to do something, tell me and I'll tell Philyra."

"Hmm. I own the underworld, but I must go through you to get anything done. How does that work?"

"You run around doing whatever you want to do. You just don't get to tell other people what to do. The details are being worked out. Now, your relatives are upstairs having a party. You have been away a long time. Do you want to go have fun with Aphrodite or something? I hear there may be a goat sacrifice. Maybe that animal of yours would like to join in."

"That sounds interesting, Hestia. But first, introduce me to this Charon commoner who replaced me. Is he like Titan Piercer?"

"I will ask Philyra to introduce you. He will be like anyone you wish him to be like. Being friendly is not your strong point but you must be friendly to this Charon whoever! And remember, he is a Lord; high class, not a commoner." She paused to let him consider her commands. "All right, Hades, let's go down and meet this Lord Charon person."

Hestia escorted Hades, with Cerberus by his side, to the thirteenth floor. "Chief Philyra," Hestia gushed, "How nice of you to see us on such short notice. Oh, and don't mind the delightful dog. He is quite friendly. You remember Olympian Hades, I trust. He is just in after three hard months in the field. He is just now beginning to catch up on your new organization. I hope Lord Charon can receive him, now."

"Yes, Ghod Hestia. I have a conference room reserved where they can meet. Let me introduce Ghod Hades to Chief Charon and I will return to get an update on your new commands."

As she escorted Hades and Cerberus to the meeting room, Hestia called after her, "Nothing new, Sweet. Just me. I haven't seen you in a long time." Both women smiled.

OCEANIDS: Metis, Tyche, Clymene, Eurybia, Amphitrite, Philyra, Rhodos.
TELCHINES: Dexithea, Makelo, Halia.
EAST: Azura, Seth, Typhon, Iasion, Endymion.
OTHER: Centaur Chiron, Charon, Hotep, Petra, Persephone.

Arriving in the meeting room, Charon immediately jumped up, raised his hands in greeting, and gushed, "Great Olympian Hades, I would recognize your wise counsel anywhere!"

Hades replied, "Lord Charon. It is my pleasure to meet you. By the way, this is Cerberus. He is a dog, a good dog! 'Cerberus! Down!'"

Philyra shut the meeting room door behind her, sighing in relief.

After the cordial meeting, Hades and Cerberus climbed the stairs to the Olympian party which was in full progress.

To everyone's delight, Cerberus got to kill the goat.

9. Poseidon and Dionysus

Dionysus lifted his cup of wine, thrust it toward Poseidon, and toasted, "To the long, powerful, glorious life of Poseidon!"

Poseidon followed his lead, as did Heracles.

Sweeping his arm toward Oursea, Dionysus said, "As I understand it, all this is yours now. What are you going to do with it?"

Poseidon snorted. "Take it away from Oceanus! He may not like that!"

Dionysus almost liked Poseidon. -- *he has all the disgusting attitudes of the other Olympians but at least he doesn't sneer at the servers and the other riffraff -- they may disgust him, but he doesn't throw it up in their face -- he even deems to walk among them -- and drink among them —*

"Probably not, but I thought Hestia wants you to treat your Lords with respect."

"Oceanus and his wife are the last Elder Titans. Hestia agrees that they should bow down before me and acknowledge my natural superiority. After they do that, they will have ground to begin begging for things."

"Yes. I can see that. Oceanus bowing down before his inbred cousin."

"I'm so glad you agree, Dionysus. You can be quite helpful at times."

Dionysus poured more wine -- *dung -- why do I even try? -- the horror is that he's not even in-bred -- that's just the way they are —*

After a while, Dionysus tried again. "You know, Poseidon, Oceanus isn't interested in making storms or controlling the weather or making people

ELDER OLYMPIANS: Hestia, Demeter, Hera, Hades, Poseidon, Zeus
OLYMPIANS: Apollo, Ares, Artemis, Athena, Aphrodite, Dionysus, Hermes,
Hephaestus, Heracles. LIVING TITANS: Oceanus, Tethys, Selene, Elder Oceanids.
DECEASED TITANS: Queen Kiya, Iapetus/Piercer, Cronus.

bow down before him or any of that sort of thing. All he wants to do is increase trade with Port Olympus, raise standards of living, and bring a little civilization to the frontiers. Does that interfere with your view of the way things should be? Maybe he could help you control things."

Poseidon, full of wine, replied, "In the name of Brother Hades, NO! I and Hestia demand Oceanus grovel before me as he does my bidding! He MUST acknowledge that Olympians are superior to Elder Titans!"

Dionysus said, "Yes. Olympians actually believe that." -- *so, is it you or Hestia that demands the groveling?* --

~ Olympian Party ~

The next evening, Dionysus arrived on the roof before the party started. Two goats grazed happily in a corner. Hestia was managing the set-up.

He said, "We need to talk, Hestia. Poseidon intends to humiliate and subjugate Oceanus and Tethys. He isn't getting the message about this Ghod thing. Western civilizations adore Oceanus. If Poseidon can win Oceanus over to the Ghod concept, all of Oceanus's subjects will willingly follow. If he tells Oceanus to bow down and worship the great Poseidon, it will go badly for Poseidon, you, the Olympians, and the port. Of most importance to you, things will go badly for *you*."

She stopped what she was doing. "Hmm. I *had* encouraged Poseidon to make Oceanus bow and scrape; he and that bitch wife *are* Elder Titans, you know. But I suppose I should honor the Lord thing even though Oceanus doesn't work on the thirteenth floor. I got Poseidon excited about humiliating Oceanus, and Poseidon *is* headstrong. He listens to no one; not even me. He will want bowing and scraping from Oceanus regardless of what I tell him. Can you handle this minor problem, Sweet?"

Dionysus considered the problem and asked, "Whatever happened to Titanide Amphitrite? I think she was friends with Poseidon before her early retirement. Wasn't she Oceanus and Tethys's firstborn? With your permission, I will follow up with that. Would you let Amphitrite back in the organization if I can find her?"

She laughed. "My dear nephew, you are the only Titan left of whom I have any fear. Well, maybe except for an angry Oceanus or Tethys. I did kill their mother you know. Hopefully, they don't"

OCEANIDS: Metis, Tyche, Clymene, Eurybia, Amphitrite, Philyra, Rhodos.
TELCHINES: Dexithea, Makelo, Halia.
EAST: Azura, Seth, Typhon, Iasion, Endymion.
OTHER: Centaur Chiron, Charon, Hotep, Petra, Persephone.

Now, Dionysus laughed. "I wonder how many Oceanids witnessed their slaughter. I wonder if any told Oceanus."

He turned to go but reconsidered. "That pretty man I saw on the way up; he was at Amphitrite's old desk. Is that her replacement? Has Poseidon met him?"

"Yes. No."

"Great. I will make a plan and get back to you. By the way, the goats won't fare well, will they?"

She replied, "They seldom do."

10. Amphitrite, Nerites, and Dionysus

Nerites and Dionysus sat drinking wine at the Port Graikoi dockside cafe. The server escorted the attractive, older woman to their table. Dionysus and Nerites rose. Dionysus embraced the woman and said, "You are still beautiful Titanide Amphitrite. Still look only half your age. You are one of the great ones!"

She sat in the chair pulled out by their server. "Dionysus, the flatterer. You never change, Sweet. Sit down. Tell me, whatever are you doing in the hinterlands? And who is this gorgeous man?"

"Great Oceanid, my name is Nerites," he said as he sat back down. "I have the extreme honor of attempting to fill your old job. No one can begin to accomplish the things you accomplished but I work hard and want to be worthy of your old position."

She smiled, "You don't appear to know much about office politics, but your use of flattery is nice. I will simply say, thank you, and I'm sure that you will, Nerites."

Dionysus said, "I am here on Port Olympus business, Amphitrite. Do you hold a grudge, or should I pack up and leave now?"

"And deprive me the company of the two most beautiful men in the world, Dionysus? What kind of an Oceanid do you think I am?"

He returned her smile and said, "Well, then. I am going after a trophy fish that has a penchant for charming women and pretty men. You and Nerites are my bait."

ELDER OLYMPIANS: Hestia, Demeter, Hera, Hades, Poseidon, Zeus
OLYMPIANS: Apollo, Ares, Artemis, Athena, Aphrodite, Dionysus, Hermes,
Hephaestus, Heracles. LIVING TITANS: Oceanus, Tethys, Selene, Elder Oceanids.
DECEASED TITANS: Queen Kiya, Iapetus/Piercer, Cronus.

11. Hades and Persephone

The Great Outer Arc Road connected the Phlegethon northern mines to Port Olympus. This road ran west from Overlook Point, past Phlegethon, arcing through the Gigantes permanent camp, and on to Port Olympus in the southwest. All port traffic to the eastern lands traveled this route. The original road, however, ran south from Overlook Point to Tartarus and then due west to Port Olympus. Most travelers took the direct Great Outer Arc Road, but Hades preferred the longer route through Tartarus. He and Cerberus would spend a night or two in Piercer's home and visit Chiron. Hades had ordered his workers to build a subterranean room under Piercer's home connected by a stairwell. It was nearing completion and was much to his liking. No one would know the room was there. It was only accessible through a doorway built into Piercer's sleeping room; a perfect get-away.

Hades enjoyed visiting Chiron; he felt better about himself when seeing Chiron's misshapen body. Cerberus enjoyed intimidating the other dogs. Hades would command him to kill one now and then to stay in practice.

Hades was on his way to the port for a mandatory meeting. -- *something about Poseidon* –

He and his dog had spent a pleasant night in his home away from home. They rose, ate breakfast, and exited Piercer's home. It was late. The sun shined down brightly upon the Elysian Fields. There were flowers. The man and his dog strolled the fields. Sunlight was fine for short periods, just not entire days of the stuff. In the far distance, he thought he heard singing. Cerberus was interested in the commotion. They strolled that way. It was his sister Demeter and that simple child of hers. -- *she isn't too bad as family goes -- I will deem to speak to her --*

Demeter saw and recognized her brother. She raised her hand and waved.

The child saw him, too. With permission from her mother, she turned and ran toward him with outstretched arms. "Uncle! Uncle! Uncle!"

Hades was strangely moved, a rare emotion for the cold, stern Olympian. The child ran across a field of flowers with arms outstretched. His emotion was not familial love. It was... What? Hades had not seen the child in several years. -- *she has grown up -- a lot -- into a comely young maiden --*

OCEANIDS: Metis, Tyche, Clymene, Eurybia, Amphitrite, Philyra, Rhodos.
TELCHINES: Dexithea, Makelo, Halia.
EAST: Azura, Seth, Typhon, Iasion, Endymion.
OTHER: Centaur Chiron, Charon, Hotep, Petra, Persephone.

The man let the girl embrace him with familial love and then took her hand in his. Demeter came striding up behind her daughter. "Brother Hades out in the sunlight. You look almost happy. What a wonderful day."

Hades smiled his strange smile. "I am on my way to the port. I will see you there but, in the meantime, who is this delightful creature?"

"This is my daughter, Persephone. Say hello to your uncle, Sweet."

She said, "Hello, Uncle Hades. I have been out with Mother. I am painting the flowers. Aren't they beautiful? Do you like them?"

Hades was infatuated. -- *her face is so innocent – so childlike -- not burdened with the cares of everyday people – simple –*

"How old are you, child?" he asked.

"I am twelve years old, Uncle Hades."

"Almost old enough to mate," he said.

Demeter's blood turned cold. "Much too young and innocent to even talk of such things, Brother. You understand what I'm saying, I'm sure!" Demeter removed her daughter's hand from Hade's clasp.

"Yes. This delightful child has not yet reached maturity," he said as he continued to stare at Persephone. "Well, that day is coming soon, isn't it? Have your mother bring you to our Olympian party. We can visit more. Our parties are a lot of fun."

"It was good to see you, Hades. Persephone will not come to the party, but I will see you there. We will talk more."

Hades continued to stare at Persephone. "This is my dog. His name is Cerberus. Would you like to stroke him?"

12. Amphitrite and Dionysus

Back at Port Olympus, Dionysus sat at his usual table, alone, waiting.

She arrived.

The patio captain greeted the attractive, older woman with gushing enthusiasm. She smiled at him. He melted. She had mastered the art of applying subtle colors and powders to her face. She had on her black party dress which accentuated her best features and subdued her worst if,

ELDER OLYMPIANS: Hestia, Demeter, Hera, Hades, Poseidon, Zeus
OLYMPIANS: Apollo, Ares, Artemis, Athena, Aphrodite, Dionysus, Hermes,
Hephaestus, Heracles. LIVING TITANS: Oceanus, Tethys, Selene, Elder Oceanids.
DECEASED TITANS: Queen Kiya, Iapetus/Piercer, Cronus.

indeed, she had a worst. The patio captain, himself, escorted her to Dionysus's table and pulled out her chair. She sat and ordered as she did so. "I will have a cup of dry, red wine from Dionysus's private stock you undoubtedly have hidden away and a bowl of fruit or berries, whichever you recommend." She waved him off and looked deeply into Dionysus's eyes.

"Amphitrite, he doesn't have a chance!"

"He never did, Sweet. A young, determined Oceanid usually gets her way with a male. I am an Elder Oceanid. Shall I have Poseidon jump off this building to please me?"

"How old are you, again?" He asked.

She replied, "How impolite. I am the perfect age to be Poseidon's lover. If I am to capture a new husband and bend him to my will, then I must be perfect, which I am. A daughter of Oceanus and Tethys, the two greatest Titans ever, other than Grandmother. You have given me more than I need to work with. Nerites is the perfect bait with which I can hold Poseidon's interest forever. When he tires of me, I need only bring in Nerites for a change of pace. I can't wait to find out if he wants me to watch him and Nerites or if he wants to watch me and Nerites, or all three of us at one time. I just hope he doesn't bring in that goat I have heard about. I believe I can manage Poseidon's other conquests, of which there will undoubtedly be many. But a patient, understanding, loving wife will always prevail."

The table server brought her wine and a bowl of grapes and wild berries. She sipped her wine.

Dionysus said, "I'm surprised at how quickly and enthusiastically you agreed to enter into this agreement, Amphitrite. And how you intuitively understood the reasons and ramifications."

"Don't be dreary, Sweet. I can prevent war between Oceanus and Poseidon, and I think that I can make Poseidon bow and scrape to Father and Mother. This isn't the way Grandmother imagined things would go, but I will do the best I can to continue her vision. All that, plus I will get to live a life of luxury and get everything an Oceanid could ever dream of having. Maybe, alleviate a little human suffering and advance civilizations as I go. And all I have to do is couple with an Olympian. As disgusting as

OCEANIDS: Metis, Tyche, Clymene, Eurybia, Amphitrite, Philyra, Rhodos.
TELCHINES: Dexithea, Makelo, Halia.
EAST: Azura, Seth, Typhon, Iasion, Endymion.
OTHER: Centaur Chiron, Charon, Hotep, Petra, Persephone.

they are, they are still the most powerful group in the world, and my unknowing future husband may well be the most powerful of them all. Power is an aphrodisiac to a woman. You know that. I will have it all, Sweet. Thanks to you. I owe you forever for this opportunity."

"So, I can now retire from this project and leave it to your capable hands?"

"After you give me a dramatic entrance and hand me off to our mark. Do you like my outfit? The dress was made by Theia, herself. Every stitch designed to make me desirable. My necklace of stones with their color matching my eyes was a gift from Piercer. The great Olympian Bitch Hestia would throw me from the roof if she had the sense to know that I represent the glory of the Elder Titans. You will protect me, won't you, Sweet Dionysus?"

Dionysus leaned back and sipped his wine. -- *protect YOU, Amphitrite?* –

 The on-the-hour bell rang seven times. "They will be gathering, now, Amphitrite. Finish your wine. Then let's go and save the world."

~ An Olympian Party ~

They arrived at the entrance to the rooftop and were met by the Gigante doorman. Dionysus greeted him. "Good evening, Gigante Polybotes." Dionysus leaned over and whispered into his ear.

Polybotes said, "Yes, Olympian Dionysus. Very good." Polybotes escorted them to the party entrance and announced, "Great Olympian Ghods. I present Olympian Dionysus of Everywhere and Princess Amphitrite of Port Graikoi."

The Olympians turned to see who had just arrived. They were impressed with the couple confidently striding in.

Under her breath, Amphitrite said, "I'm a princess, now, am I? I like it!" Her eyes coolly surveyed the mass of people before her; not deeming to acknowledge recognition of anyone. She saw Zeus's eyes widen with excitement. -- *Zeus undoubtedly has a thing for princesses -- sweet Hestia, what do you think of your old port dispatcher, now? -- scared? -- Hades, you still look evil, yet you are the most innocent one here -- Aphrodite, you still have your clothes on -- two goats -- oh, dear* –

Her eyes registered no sign of recognition when she saw Poseidon. -- *there you are new love of my life -- you must come to me -- I shall not come to you* –

ELDER OLYMPIANS: Hestia, Demeter, Hera, Hades, Poseidon, Zeus
OLYMPIANS: Apollo, Ares, Artemis, Athena, Aphrodite, Dionysus, Hermes,
Hephaestus, Heracles. LIVING TITANS: Oceanus, Tethys, Selene, Elder Oceanids.
DECEASED TITANS: Queen Kiya, Iapetus/Piercer, Cronus.

She relied on Dionysus to orchestrate the handoff.

Dionysus said loudly, "Great Zeus -- Dad -- look who I found." He glided Amphitrite over to stand before Zeus. "Dad, this is Princess Amphitrite of Port Graikoi. She is a great fan. Always told her Kingly husband -- he's dead now, tragic accident -- how much she loves you and how she misses seeing your inspiring self. Princess Ampi worked here when she was just a child. She was swept off her feet by a handsome king passing through. You wouldn't pay her any attention, so she went off and married the king."

Zeus stood watching Amphitrite breathe; his wide smile of seduction started to spread over his face.

Poseidon sauntered over to join them.

Dionysus cut off Zeus's coming words with "Poseidon, I miss you down at the cafe. You simply must come down for wine. We can stare out over Oursea and plan your conquests. Speaking of water, do you remember Princess Amphitrite? She knows as much about water as you, maybe more. She worked in port operations back when she was just a young woman."

Amphitrite stared deeply into Poseidon's eyes. Without expression, she extended her hands to him and purred, "The woman remembers the man. A woman does not forget her first experience." Her stare did not waver.

Dionysus grabbed Zeus by the shoulder and led him away. "I love you, Dad. Hades looks so lonely. Shouldn't you go share some love before the party heats up too much?"

Zeus said, looking back over his shoulder at Amphitrite, "A princess, you say? From Graikoi. You were conceived on a beach in Graikoi, you know. So was your sister, Athena. Don't mention that to Hera. They have great women in Graikoi."

The two joined Hades who was standing in a corner with Cerberus sitting by his side. Dionysus said, "Dad is here to spread love, Ghod Hades. Show him some love." Hades was obligated to embrace his younger brother and say, "I love you so much, Brother Zeus."

Zeus happily replied, "Why the sad face, Brother? You are even more dour than usual."

OCEANIDS: Metis, Tyche, Clymene, Eurybia, Amphitrite, Philyra, Rhodos.
TELCHINES: Dexithea, Makelo, Halia.
EAST: Azura, Seth, Typhon, Iasion, Endymion.
OTHER: Centaur Chiron, Charon, Hotep, Petra, Persephone.

"Sister Demeter talked exceedingly mean to me just now. She told me to stay away from sweet Kore Persephone. She talked to me like I am not even an Olympian."

"I will talk to her about that. Who is Persephone?"

Dionysus interrupted, "Why, Dad, if I remember correctly, she is your daughter by your sister, Demeter. As I was told the story, you raped Demeter when she was quite young and demanded that she have your daughter. Persephone is a sweet child but a child by blood-related brother and sister is sometimes different. A little simple, perhaps, like Hebe, but not as much. Ghod Hades, you appear to have met Persephone."

An almost smile came to Hades' lips. "Yes. In the Elysian Fields outside of Tartarus. The maiden was painting the flowers. We had a delightful conversation. She stroked Cerberus on his head. Tonight, I asked Demeter where their quarters are so that I could see Persephone again. Demeter asked me why and I told her so that I could mate with the girl. I like Persephone. I want to mate with her."

"What's wrong with that?" Zeus asked.

Hades answered, "Well, Demeter told me that Persephone has not yet reached womanhood; that she has not been instructed in the ways of a woman. And that, anyway, Persephone was sweet and innocent and would remain chaste her entire life. She actually forbade me to approach her daughter. I, an Olympian. Demeter should be honored. Persephone certainly should be."

Zeus replied, "They certainly should be. I will talk to our sister. Persephone is pretty, you say?"

The hollowness in Dionysus's stomach grew. -- *you start liking these cretins and then they show their true selves -- you should have killed them when you had the chance, Oceanus -- I bring too little, too late -- but it's all I've got —*

Dionysus excused himself.

The music grew louder. Dionysus glanced at Poseidon and Amphitrite talking alone in a corner. She stood close, her hand on his shoulder. Dionysus filtered his way toward Hestia who stood talking amicably to Demeter and Artemis. They all seemed incredibly happy, even Hestia. He joined them. "Alas, there is no beauty left anywhere in the world for all the beauty there is stands before me."

Hestia rolled her eyes. Demeter smiled sweetly. Artemis's heart raced with excitement. -- *he is an Olympian -- talking to me like that! --*

"What do you want," Hestia asked.

Dionysus replied, "You are smiling, Hestia. That can't be good. I come to find out why."

Hestia said, "Shall we tell him, girls? Everybody hates his entrails, but he is sometimes useful."

Artemis looked concerned. "I don't think so, Daughter Hestia. That's to be our secret."

Dionysus processed the statement and went on high alert. He casually laughed. "Secrets among Olympians? I thought it was 'one knows, all know.' Whatever happened to good, old-fashioned family sharing?" He stared expectantly at Hestia, "Well?" — *are these women drunk? --*

Demeter giggled. She said, "No. Mother Artemis is right. It's just between us girls."

Hestia said, "Go away, old man. Leave us girls in peace." They all giggled. As he left, he glanced sideways at Artemis and smiled.

Artemis smiled back. -- I *think he wants to couple with me! --*

Dionysus left the party and ambled down to the port cafe. It was late. The cafe was closed. He took advantage of his status; let himself in, commandeered a vessel of wine, went to his favorite table, opened the flask, and poured wine into his cup. -- *I should be ecstatic -- Amphitrite is going to succeed -- not only that, but she wants to do it -- her mother -- her father -- saved by their daughter -- Amphitrite -- 'power is an aphrodisiac,' she said —*

He smiled. -- *I shouldn't worry about what happens to that little Olympian in-bred girl -- sweet? -- innocent? -- paints flowers in the fields? -- being raped by a monster? —*

Aloud, to no one, he said, "Persephone, my poor child." -- *and you, Artemis -- what about you? -- you told them, didn't you? -- you broke your vow -- only from mother to her worthy daughter -- the secret of the Titanides -- Kiya's red nectar -- secretly served to their brothers — to age at only half the rate of others -- the Olympians now*

OCEANIDS: Metis, Tyche, Clymene, Eurybia, Amphitrite, Philyra, Rhodos.
TELCHINES: Dexithea, Makelo, Halia.
EAST: Azura, Seth, Typhon, Iasion, Endymion.
OTHER: Centaur Chiron, Charon, Hotep, Petra, Persephone.

have the recipe -- Hestia has resources to improve it -- give it to all Olympians -- they will live forever --

His hand played with the small, flat, circular, engraved rock he had laid on the table. He heard the footsteps approaching but did not look up from his reverie. He reached into his satchel, produced another cup, and said, "I am tired, Philyra. I know not to be tired or ask for quarter, but I am so very tired."

"I understand, Dionysus. In a just world, a loving, understanding woman would take your head and press it firmly into her breasts. She would say, 'Poor Dionysus. You try so hard, and you do so well.' She would gently remove your clothes and mount you, taking away the weight of the world, taking you both to the heights of paradise."

"So, Philyra, do that!"

"No, but I will drink your wine. I was watching for you. Did it go well? Will Amphitrite ensnare him? The future of my port depends on it. What is that rock you're playing with?"

"'*My* port?' Philyra, you have become one of them."

She laughed. "No. The port is now my responsibility. It is my duty to keep it operating, to keep it as the Titans envisioned, and to continue its mission. This is what my beloved Cronus would want. What my Queen Kiya would want. Your responsibility is to neutralize the Olympians and keep them from destroying our port under the weight of their greed and self-glory. Did Kiya tell you what to do? Tell me!"

"No. Yes. Maybe. We talked about many things. She liked me. She gave me this rock the night before she died. It was a gift from her friend, Pumi. She told me things. But our first big problem is being handled as we speak. The entire western frontier, everything west of Port Olympus will fall apart if Poseidon challenges Oceanus which, with or without Hestia's encouragement, he was most certainly going to do. But, if Amphitrite succeeds, that part of your empire will be safe and can prosper. She knows what needs doing and why, and she will do it because it is her father and mother that will benefit. That, plus something about an aphrodisiac."

"Amphitrite and Metis are sisters. That will help with Metis. Metis is a big influence in the port cities. The kings or chiefs or whatever they are eat out of the hand of 'Metis, Great Daughter of the Sea.' Hestia doesn't have

ELDER OLYMPIANS: Hestia, Demeter, Hera, Hades, Poseidon, Zeus
OLYMPIANS: Apollo, Ares, Artemis, Athena, Aphrodite, Dionysus, Hermes,
Hephaestus, Heracles. LIVING TITANS: Oceanus, Tethys, Selene, Elder Oceanids.
DECEASED TITANS: Queen Kiya, Iapetus/Piercer, Cronus.

nearly the control she thinks. She wants me to find six more cadres of Hecatoncheires. She didn't say why, but it can't be good." She had picked up Dionysus's flat stone and studied it as she talked.

Dionysus sipped his wine, reflected, and replied, "My will be done or else."

Philyra offered, "This rock is a Winter Solstice Festival invitation. It's what the eastern tribes used in the early days to invite tribes they encountered to the festival. This one isn't well done. Probably a reject."

"Oh."

They sat in silence for a while. Finally, Philyra said, "I think that I have recruited new people and promoted some to fill in the voids, at least for a while. But I need more managers and more brainpower, or I will slowly shrink. I can't grow without new talent."

"Ahhh. Maybe this invitation is Kiya speaking to me. 'Go to Tallstone, Dionysus.' What do you think? Should I go to Tallstone on a recruitment visit? Maybe I can shore up Port relations on the eastern frontier. Rumor has it that Pumi's son is their Grand Master. They have more brainpower than the rest of the world combined. Give me a list of what disciplines you need. Maybe I can convince a few to immigrate. And Urfa has more builders than they need. I suspect Hades needs more builders and scholars; he just isn't smart enough to know it. Maybe I can entice some Oceanids to return. But I don't know if anybody I bring back would be loyal to you, or not."

"Loyal to the company, not to me. The company must own their hearts. They must see themselves as loyal to the company and accept nothing that does not benefit the company. It's up to me to make Lords out of them. I don't want anyone on the thirteenth floor who bows to me; just to Olympians."

They sat sipping their wine, enjoying the stars. Dionysus played with his small, circular rock. The night breeze drifted off the harbor. He said, "Now that that's settled, let's do that thing where you press my head into your breasts!"

"Sorry, Sweet. You are not Rhea or Cronus. You're not even Hestia. I will admit, your friend, Heracles was a temptation but, no. I'm a one-at-a-time kind of Oceanid."

OCEANIDS: Metis, Tyche, Clymene, Eurybia, Amphitrite, Philyra, Rhodos.
TELCHINES: Dexithea, Makelo, Halia.
EAST: Azura, Seth, Typhon, Iasion, Endymion.
OTHER: Centaur Chiron, Charon, Hotep, Petra, Persephone.

13. CoM3 Charon

Chief of Mining, Manufacturing, and Metallurgy Charon sat down for his early morning meeting with Chief-of-Chiefs Philyra. She told him matter-of-factly, "I gave you this job because I thought you would excel. You aren't excelling. You're limping. You handle the scheduling and paperwork well enough, but you know, yourself, you have a dozen people on the lower floors that could do as well. I want the best of the best on this floor. Your evaluation period is now over. Tell me your plans for your, as right now, limited future in this position."

CoM3 Charon leaned back in his chair. -- *here I am -- my only chance at the thirteenth floor – challenged -- fold or triumph -- I don't have a plan -- don't fold -- go for it all – I have always held back – but now, let it flow --* "You didn't offer me a Bitter. That was disrespectful, Chief. Could you instruct your aid to bring me a Bitter? Very Bitter!"

Philyra stared at Charon without expression. "Admete, bring CoM3 Charon a very Bitter."

Charon interweaved his fingers and leaned forward. -- *blank your mind and let it flow -- if I belong here, it will flow –*

"I will speak frankly, Chief. Hades is a corporate disaster. He couldn't survive on the third floor. He has talents. He knows mining and metallurgy basics but when it comes to managing and planning and communicating, he is a complete disaster. That dog of his could manage better. Hades has the most advanced facilities in the world. He could manufacture world-class products, and what does he do with them? Nothing. He won't even manufacture and export spears for trade with the east. 'Let's keep all metalwork for the Olympians,' he says. The potential is overwhelming, just for spears. He could easily manufacture a perfectly balanced integrated metal shaft with spearhead. Who knows what other capabilities he has? I have never seen his facility. You won't even let me communicate with him, 'stay away from all contact with the Ghods,' you tell me. I'm nothing but a caretaker for what Iapetus created years ago. As of right now, I want – demand -- complete access to Hades at any time and any place. Grant me the courtesy of believing I am smart enough not to incur the wrath of the Ghods."

ELDER OLYMPIANS: Hestia, Demeter, Hera, Hades, Poseidon, Zeus
OLYMPIANS: Apollo, Ares, Artemis, Athena, Aphrodite, Dionysus, Hermes, Hephaestus, Heracles. LIVING TITANS: Oceanus, Tethys, Selene, Elder Oceanids. DECEASED TITANS: Queen Kiya, Iapetus/Piercer, Cronus.

He leaned back in his chair as Admete handed him his Bitter. -- I *think that came out all right* --

Philyra leaned back in her chair staring at him. Finally, she said, "He left three weeks ago for the Phlegethon site. He has not made contact since."

"I will take Acmon with me. He is bright and eager. Get me a meeting with Hestia so that I can receive her approval directly. I must have both your and Hestia's approvals. Let me know; her place or mine." -- *it flowed -- by the ghods -- it flowed--*

That afternoon, the call came from Hestia, "Send CoM3 Charon to me!"

Philyra replied, "Yes, Ghod Hestia. Immediately." She walked to her door, called Charon, and said, "All right, CoM3, you have been summoned! Her Place! Five minutes ago! Do well!"

Charon stood, walked to the elevator, and pulled the red cord for the 16th floor. -- *as few words as possible – direct -- to the point --in and out -- don't tarry –*

The elevator came. He entered it. He was carried to the next floor, got off, and said to the waiting Gigante, "Lord Charon to see Olympian Hestia." He was escorted to her office and waited just inside her door.

Hestia glanced once more at the plaque Philyra demanded that Hestia keep on her desk: "!!! RESPECT THEM !!!" Hestia looked at Charon and, with her head, motioned him to come stand in front of her desk. "Yes?"

He began. "Great Olympian Hestia, CoM3 is in urgent need of decisions that can only be made by Olympian Hades. Rather than requesting through Chief-of-Chiefs Philyra that he return to headquarters, I requested her permission to seek your advice on whether it would be prudent for me to travel with an assistant to the Phlegethon site and meet with him there. Meeting a superior Ghod outside the workplace would be highly unorthodox and certainly requires a decision from the highest levels. I seek your counsel." He stepped back, arms at his sides, and waited. -- *I think that came out all right --*

She leaned back in her chair and stared out her window. -- *cheeky bastard -- wasting my time on this -- of course, I would have had him killed if he went behind my back -- Hades return here? -- I would have to visit with him? -- I think not -- better the 'lord' visit Hades -- that might be a fine idea -- have company meetings at his sites -- not at headquarters -- I wouldn't have to deal with Hades again –*

OCEANIDS: Metis, Tyche, Clymene, Eurybia, Amphitrite, Philyra, Rhodos.
TELCHINES: Dexithea, Makelo, Halia.
EAST: Azura, Seth, Typhon, Iasion, Endymion.
OTHER: Centaur Chiron, Charon, Hotep, Petra, Persephone.

She looked up at Charon and replied, "Very well. Check-in at Port Transportation at sunrise, tomorrow. A chariot will be waiting to take you to Phlegethon."

"Very good. I understand. Thank you."

"You may go."

Charon walked immediately to the elevator, stopped in front of it, and said to the attendant, "Thirteenth floor, please."

The attendant pulled the cord for the floor below.

Charon entered the elevator, rode down one level, got off, and walked toward his desk. Without turning to look at Philyra, who stood watching him from her doorway, he merely jabbed his fist to the front of his stomach with his thumb pointing up.

14. Charon, Acmon, and Hephaestus

CoM3 Charon and Acmon arrived at Port Transportation as the sun rose. "I am Lord Charon. I was told that you would have transportation for me and my associate to Phlegethon this morning."

The dispatcher replied, "Yes, Lord Charon. Olympian Hestia ordered a nice chariot for you. I have a driver if you require one. I am commanded to tell you that Olympian Ghod Hephaestus will be traveling with you."

An expression almost came across Charon's face, but he suppressed it. He said, "Very good."

Acmon did express shock. "An Olympian, Chief? A Ghod? We are going to meet a Ghod with another Ghod with us? I have to go defecate."

Under his breath, Charon said, "That was lower class, Acmon. Never let them see you display emotion. It shows weakness." To the dispatcher, he said, "Wonderful! Do you have any tips on traveling with an Olympian?"

The dispatcher looked around and softly replied, "Great Lord, order a driver, save my horse. Olympian Hephaestus loves to drive, and he would run my horse into exhaustion."

"Thank you, Dispatcher. I do require a driver. Your most useful driver. I don't know what 'useful' means but you do."

ELDER OLYMPIANS: Hestia, Demeter, Hera, Hades, Poseidon, Zeus
OLYMPIANS: Apollo, Ares, Artemis, Athena, Aphrodite, Dionysus, Hermes, Hephaestus, Heracles. LIVING TITANS: Oceanus, Tethys, Selene, Elder Oceanids. DECEASED TITANS: Queen Kiya, Iapetus/Piercer, Cronus.

"Yes, Lord. Thank you. I do and I will provide a driver who knows how to talk to Ghods."

They waited. And waited. Charon said to Acmon, "Go strike up a conversation with the dispatcher. Learn what you can."

Acmon did. Charon waited.

After two hours of waiting, Olympian Hephaestus strolled into the transportation center. Acmon briskly walked past Charon and whispered, "I will get us loaded up, Chief." Acmon kept walking to face the Olympian, stopped, and bowed deeply. "Great Ghod, I am commanded that you wish to ride standing up beside your driver so that you feel the wind in your face and thrill to the excitement of the vigorous ride. I will direct Lord Charon to sit facing the back with me, Acmon, your lowly servant."

Hephaestus looked at Acmon, nose in the air. "Is it a fast horse?"

"The fastest, Ghod Hephaestus!"

"Is it a fast driver?"

"The fastest, Ghod Hephaestus!"

"Lord who?"

"Lord Charon, Ghod Hephaestus! Your brother Hade's best employee. He works two floors directly below you. We go to meet with your fabulous brother." Acmon pointed and began walking to the waiting chariot as he said, "This way to the absolute best chariot ever made."

The driver greeted Hephaestus with a mighty, "Are you ready to ride the high winds, Great Ghod Heph?"

Acmon seated Charon in the back seat and then sat down beside him. "I had a good conversation with Abas. He is the transportation dispatcher. He gave me a lot of great tips on dealing with 'difficult things,' from one working-class man to another. Abas deals with 'difficult things' all day long. He knows his way around."

The driver began their journey north up Great Arc Road with a fast trot, then built up speed, then slowed to let the horse cool down. During the cool-down periods, the driver entertained Hephaestus with ribald songs

OCEANIDS: Metis, Tyche, Clymene, Eurybia, Amphitrite, Philyra, Rhodos.
TELCHINES: Dexithea, Makelo, Halia.
EAST: Azura, Seth, Typhon, Iasion, Endymion.
OTHER: Centaur Chiron, Charon, Hotep, Petra, Persephone.

and sexual jokes. After almost an hour, they came to the way station serving the city of the Gigantes. "Ghod, Lord, and other person, we will stop here so that you can relieve yourselves and take nourishment." To Hephaestus, he said, "You don't want to use the common toilet, Ghod Heph. Too disgusting. Let me take you to my sister's house. You will find it much more to your liking."

Charon and Acmon relieved themselves in the nice, clean facility. Then they sat down on the patio with a glass of wine and a bowl of fruit. Acmon said, "Abas was a wealth of information on how to deal with the Olympians. Are you taking notes on our driver? Don't give them a chance to think about anything. Keep talking, keep them distracted. That doesn't work with Hestia or Poseidon. With them, keep quiet. Abas was not given a reason why Hephaestus was sent along. Do you want me to talk to him and try to find out?"

Charon said, "No. I have been listening to our driver while considering an appropriate time to engage our guest."

After a while, the driver, Hephaestus, and a young Gigante woman entered the patio. The driver signaled for wine for his important client and sat him down at Charon's table. The woman touched Hephaestus's shoulder and said, "I enjoyed your visit, Great Olympian Ghod Hephaestus. You are every woman's dream. She then curtsied, glanced at Charon, then the driver, and discretely disappeared. "

The driver said, "The women are always thrilled to see this particular Ghod come through. Take your time gentlemen. I and Horsefly are ready to go when you are." The driver left them and went to tend to his horse.

Charon said to Hephaestus, "I go to Phlegethon to discuss important mining issues with Hades. Are you interested in the mining process?"

Hephaestus turned up his nose to ignore Charon but then Hestia's admonishment flowed into his brain, "Charon is a Lord. You WILL respect him. If you do not respect him, I WILL have Athena cut off your testicles and give them to Aphrodite to play with. AM I UNDERSTOOD?!"

Hephaestus understood. He believed. "Why, I don't know. I have never seen a mining process. Is it interesting?"

ELDER OLYMPIANS: Hestia, Demeter, Hera, Hades, Poseidon, Zeus
OLYMPIANS: Apollo, Ares, Artemis, Athena, Aphrodite, Dionysus, Hermes,
Hephaestus, Heracles. LIVING TITANS: Oceanus, Tethys, Selene, Elder Oceanids.
DECEASED TITANS: Queen Kiya, Iapetus/Piercer, Cronus.

Charon said, "Your brother seems to think so. He stays at his field operations all the time. There must be something to keep his attention. Consider signing on with him. He could probably use the help of another Ghod."

"My brothers and sisters say that Hades is stupid. They say the only thing he can do is work in his mines and isn't smart enough to stay with us on the seventeenth floor and party."

"That's an interesting observation. Has anyone gone out to see if Hades has a better thing going on than his brothers and sisters do?"

Hephaestus's eyes widened with indignation, but he remembered. -- *you WILL respect them or... –*

He calmed himself and replied, "Better than the seventeenth floor, is that even possible?"

"No. The seventeenth floor is the best place ever. Do you have suggestions on how I can please Ghod Hades?"

"Yes. Bring him maiden Persephone to couple with. Hades talks of nothing but the girl. She isn't a woman yet, but Zeus told him to go ahead and mate with her. Ghod Demeter is livid. They have exchanged harsh words. Zeus listens with disbelief. None of us understand. If Hades wishes to mate with her, then he should mate with her."

"I thought Persephone was not yet a woman"

"She isn't. What difference does that make? But Sister Demeter says that her daughter will never be known by any man, especially her own uncles. Can you believe that kind of talk?"

Charon could not conceive of an answer which Hephaestus might consider to be correct. He said, "You are the wisest of the Ghods."

Hephaestus seemed pleased with the response.

Charon suggested that they continue their journey to Phlegethon.

~ Dactyl Celmis ~

The chariot arrived at Phlegethon where they were met by Dactyl Celmis. Celmis was a metal specialist, a dactyl, and titular chief of Phlegethon, after Hades, of course. Celmis took Ghod Heph to find Hades, who was

OCEANIDS: Metis, Tyche, Clymene, Eurybia, Amphitrite, Philyra, Rhodos.
TELCHINES: Dexithea, Makelo, Halia.
EAST: Azura, Seth, Typhon, Iasion, Endymion.
OTHER: Centaur Chiron, Charon, Hotep, Petra, Persephone.

wandering around in the mines. Celmis returned to properly introduce himself to Charon and Acmon. He then gave them a comprehensive tour of the mines. After the tour, the three went into the dining hall.

Celmis asked, "Well, what do you think of our mines?"

"Fascinating," Charon replied. "I did not realize the mining capability we have. So little ore is delivered to the port."

"Chief Hades doesn't have the same interests as Great Chief Iapetus. We don't do that much mining anymore. I had men sitting around doing nothing. Now I send them to the Metals Workshop to make things from the processed metals Master Iapetus had stockpiled. The Workshop is the last stop on our tour. As a thirteenth-floor Lord, you may see some things of interest, things to trade. We are overflowing with trade items. Chief Hades isn't interested and I'm not sure what is valuable to the outside world, but we are overflowing with items. I asked Chief Hades for another building to store the overstock."

"Trade items that aren't in the system? How long has this been going on?"

"Pretty much as soon as Chief Iapetus was kicked -- I mean -- as soon as Chief Iapetus retired."

"I look forward to seeing these items. Our metals trade is far below historical numbers. I may be finding the reason why. By the way, what does Chief Hades actually do?"

"I'm not sure. He enjoys walking around inspecting and walking through the mines fingering everything. Giving me and the men direction is not his biggest interest. If you are ready, Lord, I can continue your tour. I will find Chief Hades and Olympian Hephaestus whenever you tell me to."

Charon said, "Let's let them do their own tour. We are getting a lot accomplished on our own. Let's continue our tour."

Celmis led Charon and Acmon outside, through a wooded area, down a little-used path. They came to a small, abandoned fire pit in a clearing. "This is the first fire pit Master Iapetus built when he settled in Tartarus and was learning 'how to melt rock.' He and Master Littlerock worked here long hours experimenting. They, of course, eventually realized that hotter fires were needed which led to the kilns I am about to show you. Let's walk this way."

ELDER OLYMPIANS: Hestia, Demeter, Hera, Hades, Poseidon, Zeus
OLYMPIANS: Apollo, Ares, Artemis, Athena, Aphrodite, Dionysus, Hermes,
Hephaestus, Heracles. LIVING TITANS: Oceanus, Tethys, Selene, Elder Oceanids.
DECEASED TITANS: Queen Kiya, Iapetus/Piercer, Cronus.

They walked back toward the mountain into an open area containing progressively larger and more sophisticated kilns. "This kiln opened things up for them," Celmis said, as he pointed to the smallest of the three. "It's hot enough to melt Tinom ore. They tried to make daggers and swords by General Porphyrion's orders. But Tinom wasn't strong enough to be useful. Besides, they didn't have much ore to work with. What they had plenty of, on the ground and, as they later discovered, inside the mountain was Kopar ore. They called it 'colored rock' back then. 'We need hotter fires,' they decided. So, they built a bigger, more efficient, and hotter kiln."

He took them to the next kiln.

"Ahh," Celmis said. "Here we have the great kiln we still use today. This one is hot enough to control the melting of the Kopar ore. Still not strong enough for daggers and swords. But it is a metal that can be used for many things, especially jewelry and decorative items. Master Iapetus mastered this art and then turned the entire Kopar and Tinom manufacturing responsibilities over to me. He took Damnameneus to a Winter Solstice Festival to find a source for Tinom; which they did. But when Chief Hades took over, he wasn't interested in continuing the trade, so what we have is all we are going to have. That's a shame because Master Littlerock's last great discovery was that if you mix Tinom and Kopar you get the metal of all metals: Orichalcum, a miracle metal. General Porphyrion would be beside himself with all the swords and shields and armor we can make, plus untold useful things. I'll show you when we get there."

Charon looked at Acmon. -- *this isn't happening -- these things exist, and I didn't even know about them? -- I had no idea!* --

Charon wanted to get to the Metals Workshop, but first, they came to the third kiln and stared at it with wonder.

Celmis said, "It's beautiful, isn't it? Never been fired up. Chief Iapetus and Master Littlerock put everything they knew and suspected and hoped into building this one. It's got a curved top, real special design. They hoped it would produce temperatures twice as hot as number two. All the holes pull air through the kiln. It was ready to fire up. Chief Iapetus had a plan on what ores to melt and combine in different mixtures. He thought they were on a great breakthrough, but Chief Hades was not interested. Now, most of our research people are gone to Port Spearpoint. They left when

OCEANIDS: Metis, Tyche, Clymene, Eurybia, Amphitrite, Philyra, Rhodos.
TELCHINES: Dexithea, Makelo, Halia.
EAST: Azura, Seth, Typhon, Iasion, Endymion.
OTHER: Centaur Chiron, Charon, Hotep, Petra, Persephone.

the Elder Titans were removed. So now you have had the kiln tour. Let's go on to the Metals Workshop."

Acmon said, "Chief, I'm getting overwhelmed. I don't know if I can absorb much more information."

Celmis laughed. "Son, there's much more to see in the workshop."

~ The Metals Workshop ~

"By the Ghods, it's huge!" Acmon said as the workshop came into view.

"Yes. Twenty paces wide, eighty paces deep. Constructed out of strong wood with clay covering the insides. They didn't want a fire breaking out and burning the place down. Two Orichalcum working kiln's inside. We can work with any metals we want. We mine whatever Kopar we need, and we still have some Tinom stockpiled, but we need a source for it if we want to make Orichalcum in quantity." He stopped at the door. "Well, let's go in, and let me show you things we could make if anybody cared." He opened the double doors leading into the workshop and they stepped inside. "We store the finished colorful Kopar and gray Tinom items on this end and the shiny Orichalcum items on the other end. The tables are holding examples of Orichalcum products we are trying to create. As I said, the artists have mostly left, so none of the Orichalcum items are especially fine. See anything you like?"

The three men walked past bins of colored Kopar jewelry and ornaments and past the plates, utensils, and failed weaponry fashioned from the pure Tinom. Almost everything was ready to be delivered to Port Olympus for trade if anyone outside of Phlegethon had known it existed.

Acmon took notes on the parchment he carried. "We can triple last year's trade in just one month with these items, Chief."

"Yes, Acmon. Yes, we can," Charon answered without apparent emotion.

Halfway down the building, they arrived at the tables containing the proven and experimental items made of Orichalcum. Charon gasped at what lay before them. -- *impossible! -- this is not possible!* --

There lay cups, bowls, vases, caldrons, cooking utensils, farming shovels, hoes, scythes, small chains, and jewelry, and then came the musical instruments, cymbals, drums, bells, statues; large and small. And then the weapons of war; swords, shields, spears, helmets, body armor, large

ELDER OLYMPIANS: Hestia, Demeter, Hera, Hades, Poseidon, Zeus
OLYMPIANS: Apollo, Ares, Artemis, Athena, Aphrodite, Dionysus, Hermes,
Hephaestus, Heracles. LIVING TITANS: Oceanus, Tethys, Selene, Elder Oceanids.
DECEASED TITANS: Queen Kiya, Iapetus/Piercer, Cronus.

chains. There was a standing flat plate in which one could see oneself clearly. An unimaginable collection of bright, shiny, useful things.

Celmis ran his hand through a bin of small, thin, round pieces of a different metal, one of golden color. Celmis said, "Master Piercer named this particular metal 'Gold' because of its color. He designed these pieces with an engraving of Queen Kiya on one side and Port Olympus on the other. The design is based on Master Pumi's stone invitations for the Winter Solstice Festival. Piercer called these things 'coins' and thought they might someday have value as collectible pieces but, again, his retirement was forced upon him before anything came of it."

Acmon offered, "We can have quite a display table at the Festival."

"Yes, we can," Charon answered as he took a handful of coins.

They spent an hour inspecting and discussing the treasures in the Workshop. Acmon dutifully recorded all in his notes.

The three men left the building in late afternoon. As they walked past the number three kiln, they came upon Hades and Hephaestus with Damnameneus trailing dutifully behind.

Charon thought -- *take control -- give them only choices that work in my favor* –

He said, "Great Ghod Chief Hades, what a magnificent facility you have here. We need to have our meeting. Do you prefer to meet before we eat, while we eat, or after we eat?"

Hades looked at Charon with disinterest. – *'treat them with respect'* – *'take an interest in them'* – *'the lords are the only thing between us and the lower classes'* –

Hades softened his response, "Before dinner, Lord Charon. That way you can be about your business as Ghod Hephaestus and I dine together."

Charon replied, "Excellent, Chief Hades. Acmon and I will be waiting in the dining hall. There is much we need your wisdom and approval for."

Hades replied, "Very well." He and Hephaestus then continued their walk to show Hephaestus the Metals Building.

Acmon said, "I need three months to prepare for this meeting, Chief."

OCEANIDS: Metis, Tyche, Clymene, Eurybia, Amphitrite, Philyra, Rhodos.
TELCHINES: Dexithea, Makelo, Halia.
EAST: Azura, Seth, Typhon, Iasion, Endymion.
OTHER: Centaur Chiron, Charon, Hotep, Petra, Persephone.

Charon laughed. "You have thirty minutes." He looked at Celmis and said, "Master Celmis, let's take the next thirty minutes and advise me on what you would do to get this place up and running to its full potential."

Celmis's eyes brightened. "You want my advice? Really? You won't have me killed, will you? Or worse, tell Chief Hades?"

Charon chuckled again. "No. Your guidance will be our secret. We both want what's best for Phlegethon and its people. Let's make it happen."

"Well," Celmis began. "If you really want to know what I think..." He was talking when they arrived at the dining room, as they entered, found an appropriate meeting table, and still talking as they sat down. Fortunately, it was much later when Hades and Hephaestus entered the dining room. Celmis knew to cease talking. Charon motioned him to stay, but behind him, away from the table.

Charon was surprised to see Hephaestus excited and animated. He was talking without slowing down. Hades was feigning interest.

Charon rose to greet them. *-- let it flow -- maintain control -- make it easier to agree than disagree -- I need three days to prepare -- not three seconds -- I don't know where to begin -- why is Hephaestus so happy? –*

He said, "Great Ghods Hades and Heph, welcome to our meeting." *-- abas called him Heph and got away with it -- dangerous -- be careful -- Heph was dour in front of the kilns -- he saw something in the workshop –*

Charon said to Hephaestus, "Ghod Chief Hades has many wonderful bright and shiny objects in his workshop. What did you find most exciting?"

Hephaestus began. "Did you see all of those things? Did you see the armor? It was so bright and everything. I could have one made that fits Athena perfectly! She would be so excited! She could replace that old leather thing she is always wearing with bright, shiny armor. She would look so grand!"

Charon broke in *-- they have the attention of a small child -- they are small children -- mean, arrogant, little children -- just know how to handle them -- be careful -- let it flow --* "And a helmet. She would look good in a shiny helmet with big feathers on it, made just for her. And Heph, *you* could make it. I'm sure Damnameneus could teach a brilliant Ghod like yourself how to make one in no time at all! You could make Athena a breastplate and a helmet and arm guards and everything. By your own hand. By your very genius. Can you do it? Do you *want* to do it?"

"Yes, yes. Can you begin teaching me right now 'what's-your-name?'" Heph turned around looking frantically for Damnameneus, who stood frozen with confusion.

Charon said, "Of course, he can. He would love to teach you." Charon turned and spoke to Celmis, "Celmis, take Damnameneus outside right this minute and explain to him what he shall do. Help him understand!"

Charon then spoke to Hades, "Chief Hades, this is so exciting! You and Heph are going to make Athena so excited. And make something for Zeus to show your love, Something bright. He will love it. Like this coin," he said, as he handed one of the golden coins to Hades. "But place Zeus's image on it instead of that woman. Chief, with a few responsibility changes in your organization, you could be free of all the overwhelming management requirements Olympian Hestia laid on you. You would have time to pursue that little Persephone girl. I have some great ideas on how you can make that happen. We just need some organizational changes. I'll send the paperwork to Celmis. Just sign your approval. Celmis will make a great point of contact for you. Olympian Ghods Hades and Hephaestus are going to liven up the grand Olympian parties. All the gifts and pretty things Heph is going to be able to make. You two are going to knock Chief Hestia right out of her clothes."

Hephaestus laughed. "Hestia, out of her clothes! That's funny. Nobody has seen Hestia naked except Lord Philyra. Hestia naked! That's funny!"

"Lord Philyra and Ghod Hestia -- naked?" Charon asked with surprise.

"Yes. I hear them get together a couple of times a week. I bet they are both naked. They have a lot of fun. They think I can't hear them."

Charon was stunned but he said, without emotion, "Well, let that be our little secret, shall we? Nothing we need to repeat. Now, shall we all go to the workshop and get started on making some amazing things for the amazing Olympian Ghods?" He began herding the men outside to meet with Celmis and Damnameneus, the two soon-to-be top-ranking managers in the Department of Mining, Manufacturing, and Materials. -- *Philyra and Hestia – of course! -- how could I have been so blind? --*

OCEANIDS: Metis, Tyche, Clymene, Eurybia, Amphitrite, Philyra, Rhodos.
TELCHINES: Dexithea, Makelo, Halia.
EAST: Azura, Seth, Typhon, Iasion, Endymion.
OTHER: Centaur Chiron, Charon, Hotep, Petra, Persephone.

15. Charon and Philyra

CoM3 Charon was already at his desk, head down working when Philyra arrived a little after sunrise. He gave her a thumbs-up when she walked in but made no effort to engage her. CoC Philyra gave him the day at his desk to get his report in order but sent him a note that said, "My office, after closing, business only."

Charon waited until only her assistant remained and then walked into her office with no papers. "Are you ready for me?" he asked.

"Yes." To her assistant, she said, "Two very Bitters, Admete." To Charon, she asked, "Were you successful?"

"Yes. I will give you the short report. Oh, and will you be seeing Hestia this evening?"

"Yes, to give her my daily report."

"Tell her that Hades cordially received me and answered all of my questions. He agreed to meet me whenever I come up and if he isn't available, his aide, Celmis, can officially answer in Hades' absence. I will want paperwork authorizing this. I'm not going to be brought down by acting on something Celmis said was all right and Hades then said wasn't. Hephaestus showed a great interest in the manufacturing side. I will ask that he, and his aide Damnameneus, be spun off and have their own responsibilities. And without fail, tell her the new organization would not necessitate either of these two coming into headquarters. All company matters would be handled in the field." He accepted the Very Bitter drink from Admete. "Is that enough of a report for now?"

"You have more?"

"It is beyond belief, Chief. Trade is about to explode. But before we discuss trade issues, let me attack the organizational changes. That's the key to success. The rest will be joy and profits. Oh, you don't need Admete as a chaperone. I am a loyal employee. I will tell you if that changes."

"You may go, Admete." She then asked Charon, "What should be my concerns when I present your report to Hestia?"

Charon answered, "None based on what I just told you. Your concerns don't start until you present the new organization chart for Hestia to sign off on. But she is going to be so eager to keep Hades away from headquarters that she won't read what she signs. It involves demoting Hades to assistant to Celmis. Celmis was a protégé of Iapetus and Littlerock, you know, or maybe you didn't. I will be technically reporting to Celmis, but I may never mention that to him. I'll go over the reorganization line by line tomorrow and lay out possible issues. After you get it signed off by Hestia, we take Acmon to the patio with a couple of bottles of wine and share the joy."

He hesitated. "And for your personal information only -- cover your ears and don't listen -- I am in Hade's good graces because I suggested he take his chariot filled with flowers to Elysian Fields and accidentally find Persephone playing there. If she happens to be alone, I'm sure Persephone would love to go on a chariot ride with him back to his place without her mother knowing where she went. Hades would be quite persuasive with a little girl."

"You are playing with fire, Charon."

"There's more. Keep your ears covered. If Queen Kiya had the weapons stored at Phlegethon, she would have dispatched both Hecatoncheires and gone out looking for more. After Athena finds these things and trains hunters from the frontiers, Hestia will have more than she needs to enforce her demands. But everything will be in Acmon's report tomorrow evening."

"You are about to get me into deep trouble aren't you, Charon?"

"If I belong on this floor, it will work. If I don't, have her throw me off the roof. I will scream all the way down. That will more than satisfy her."

"I will be the one to throw you, Charon. Thank you. That's all."

He rose, walked to the door, stopped, and turned to face her. "Chief, we are all in this together. It is the Lords of the thirteenth floor against the Ghods on the fifteenth floor with little help from those beneath us. I am loyal to us. If you need a third when you 'discuss' things with Hestia, I will volunteer, if it would help you."

She stared back at him coldly and did not speak.

He smiled, nodded, and returned to his desk.

OCEANIDS: Metis, Tyche, Clymene, Eurybia, Amphitrite, Philyra, Rhodos.
TELCHINES: Dexithea, Makelo, Halia.
EAST: Azura, Seth, Typhon, Iasion, Endymion.
OTHER: Centaur Chiron, Charon, Hotep, Petra, Persephone.

16. Clymene: Elder Oceanid
< Year 100, 6th month >

On the road to Riverport, old man Seilenos held the reins to the donkey, Onos, which pulled the wagon in which Dionysus and Marsyas lay in the back each playing their double aulos. Seilenos sometimes dropped the reins to keep time with his tambourine.

Riding in his wagon under the gentle sun playing his aulos, Dionysus remembered what his life had always been about and almost rued the day that he and Heracles set out to find their father and become entangled with their insane Olympian brethren. But he had discovered Kiya and the Elder Titans. For a short time, his life had meaning. He was surrounded by a Titan family that sincerely cared for him and who understood and appreciated the gift of wine he had given them. They respected him for who he was and did not lay guilt or expectations or insecurities or sheer mindless stupidity onto his being. They embraced his wine into their sense of warmth, love, and well-being; not into a frenzy of suppressed sexual libido. For the first time, Dionysus belonged and was respected for who he was. *-- now they are dead -- I can run away -- leave this path-of-the-titans nonsense -- the world is full of people eager to party -- I can make them dance -- throw off all inhibitions -- is that what I want? -- am I stupid enough to think that I can save the world from the ghods? -- Kiya could not -- I certainly can't! -- what's that?! -- shut up, Queen Kiya -- I will not listen to you! -- shut up! -- you are dead! -- I have nothing left to give! -- Philyra is fighting for a cause she cannot win! -- the ghods will win! -- the ghods will always win! --*

Dionysus sat up. "Stop the wagon, Seilenos! I've got to urinate. Break open more wine, Marsyas! Life is short! Let's get on with the drinking. They are all dead, you know! Dead!"

~

The wagon arrived at Riverport in the early afternoon. The Port Master saw them, assessed what need be done, and dispatched an Oceanid with a wagon-carrying barge to transport the visitors across.

The Oceanid sailed the barge across the river, pulled into the landing, lowered the back of the barge, and led the donkey and wagon on board. She raised and secured the back of the barge and cast off toward Riverport. She then greeted the three men. Her gaze held on Dionysus.

ELDER OLYMPIANS: Hestia, Demeter, Hera, Hades, Poseidon, Zeus
OLYMPIANS: Apollo, Ares, Artemis, Athena, Aphrodite, Dionysus, Hermes,
Hephaestus, Heracles. LIVING TITANS: Oceanus, Tethys, Selene, Elder Oceanids.
DECEASED TITANS: Queen Kiya, Iapetus/Piercer, Cronus.

"You're somebody, aren't you? Are you important? Shall I raise the important-visitor-on-board flag?"

Dionysus was infatuated. His wine-mellowed mind loved this Oceanid creature. "Yes! I'm a man of great importance. I am an Olym... I mean, I am a Titan!"

She raised her eyebrows, turned toward the docks, and shouted, "Port Master Clymene, one of your relatives is onboard!"

The woman on the dock heard, dove into the water, and swam out to meet the slow-moving barge. She arrived and pulled herself on board. The Elder Oceanid, with her linen tunic clinging to her full, fit body, looked at him and said, "Great Titan Dionysus. I am thrilled to see you again. I am Clymene, daughter of Oceanus and Tethys. Welcome to Riverport."

Dionysus's eyes grew large as he took in the vision before him. Two disparate replies formed simultaneously in his mind -- *Clymene, let's get in the back of this wagon, get that tunic off, and spill some wine on that body of yours -- Marsyas can play a wild song as you and I celebrate you being an oceanid –*

And, too, this -- *Clymene, your family was kind to me -- they gave me hope in a hopeless world –*

Knowing he had drunk too much wine, he compromised. "Clymene, I am delighted to see you. Let's visit this evening and reminisce."

Clymene recognized the flash of lust that blew through his brain and was impressed that he behaved like a Titan rather than an Olympian. "Grandmother thought you a superior person, albeit young, Titan Dionysus. I will prepare a proper reception for you and your friends. Perhaps you could spend the night at our guest house. I will have an Oceanid tend to your poor donkey. It could stand a nice rubdown, proper food, and a good night's rest. And an Oceanid to tend to you and your guests, too," she laughed.

The dock was filling with young Oceanids wishing to find out what was causing the excitement. Wherever there was excitement, there should be Oceanids. Dionysus looked out over the dock with an appreciation of what lay before him. "Yes, we would be delighted to visit overnight. I will supply the wine." -- *dozens of waiting, willing oceanids -- I should be ecstatic -- but I'm not! -- what is the matter with me? --*

OCEANIDS: Metis, Tyche, Clymene, Eurybia, Amphitrite, Philyra, Rhodos.
TELCHINES: Dexithea, Makelo, Halia.
EAST: Azura, Seth, Typhon, Iasion, Endymion.
OTHER: Centaur Chiron, Charon, Hotep, Petra, Persephone.

They arrived at the dock, debarked, and were shown to their guest quarters as Onos was led to his stable by a dozen young girls.

After refreshing and before the evening meal, Marsyas and Seilenos began serving wine to all who wished to experience their gift; and Oceanids were always open to new experiences. A full flask was dispensed. Normally outgoing and happy Oceanids became even more outgoing and happy. Dionysus, mostly recovered from his 'too much' wine, and Clymene sat at a table and looked over the festivities.

Clymene said, "You should not have introduced them to wine, Dionysus. They are too young and aren't experienced enough to properly handle it."

An unfamiliar emotion flashed through his mind. -- *what was that? -- guilt? --regret? – naaa –*

Dionysus pulled his Aulos from his bag and began to play. The Oceanids began to dance with one another. Then they pulled Marsyas and Seilenos into their midst to dance with them. -- *so easily corrupted -- regret? – perhaps –*

After a while, Dionysus stopped his play and said, "That's all, my friends. It is time to cease drinking and dancing and take some food into our bodies. Thank you all for the good time!" The Oceanids were seriously disappointed. They were having such a grand time! Both Marsyas and Seilenos looked at their leader with surprise. They had expected a wild night of drinking, dancing, and music to ensue. The party disbanded after the evening meal of fish, roots, and berries were served to their revered Elder Oceanid Clymene and her guest, Dionysus.

He asked Clymene, "Will you return to Tartarus with me and help us protect the world from Olympians as best we can?"

"You mean the place where I watched my beloved husband die? Where I watched my aunts and uncles slaughtered? Where I saw the head of my beloved Grandmother removed from her body? That accursed place where evil replaced goodness upon the face of the earth? *That* place, Cousin Dionysus?"

He sat in silence, wishing he had a cup of wine. Finally, he said, "That place, Clymene. You may sit here doing nothing wrapped in hatred or do whatever you can to keep civilization moving forward. Your choice."

She considered his words. "What would you propose I do?"

ELDER OLYMPIANS: Hestia, Demeter, Hera, Hades, Poseidon, Zeus
OLYMPIANS: Apollo, Ares, Artemis, Athena, Aphrodite, Dionysus, Hermes,
Hephaestus, Heracles. LIVING TITANS: Oceanus, Tethys, Selene, Elder Oceanids.
DECEASED TITANS: Queen Kiya, Iapetus/Piercer, Cronus.

"Well, *not* return to Tartarus, it appears. But consider this, the Olympians will undoubtedly send messengers, or come themselves, to this year's Festival. They will demand tribute from every source they see. They will come through Riverport and demand the Port meet their demands, or else! You need a plan on how to handle them then and for all days in the future. You need the port to look poor and useless, 'no tribute here.' Their first impression is important. It is the one they will remember."

"When the time comes, I can have the Oceanids retire downstream with all but our most decrepit craft with them. They love to play-act. I can have a few pretend to be diseased and needy. Beg for food. That sort of thing."

"You're better at this than I, Clymene. Queen Kiya would be proud!"

"She is," Clymene replied without expression.

"Well, plan on this. They will be all bluster this year because they are Olympians and truly expect their every command to be obeyed. But when their demands are not obeyed, Hestia will figure out how to enforce them. Right now, she is trying to find more Hecatoncheires to control the lower classes. She doesn't know it yet, but she can recruit lowly hunters, train them, and provide them with armor and weapons she will soon discover she has. Had the Elder Titans had this armor, they would have defeated the Hecatoncheires. Long term, Clymene, things will get quite bad."

"It will be easy enough to take the first wave of these armored hunters halfway across the river and then let the river take them. But they will be wiser with the second trying. We would probably be killed, and the dock burned. I will think about this, Dionysus. Now, let's finish our meal, then slip us each a cup of wine. I will show you the Reflection Pond where I and my sisters met our Titan family. There is a tree where, as a child, I learned to hang upside down. After I became a woman, I learned some interesting things that I might share with you."

The next morning, the men rose late. They dressed and walked to the dock where Onus was hitched to his wagon and awaited them. He wore a straw hat with flowers and colorful ribbons braided into his mane and tail. He smelled of wild jasmine. His coat glistened.

Dionysus walked over to the animal and put his forehead against Onos's. "You are prettier than I, old friend. You bring me joy."

OCEANIDS: Metis, Tyche, Clymene, Eurybia, Amphitrite, Philyra, Rhodos.
TELCHINES: Dexithea, Makelo, Halia.
EAST: Azura, Seth, Typhon, Iasion, Endymion.
OTHER: Centaur Chiron, Charon, Hotep, Petra, Persephone.

Clymene watched from her table on the dock. She laughed and called to him. "Come say goodbye to an Elder Oceanid. You have brought *her* joy."

He walked over to join her.

She said, "But far more important, you have brought me knowledge. Perhaps I will allow some Oceanids to return with you. We have our own private communication network which could keep me up-to-date on my despicable brethren, who Grandmother Kiya commands me to love."

He laughed. "Know yourself. Know your enemy!"

"Grandmother was wise, wasn't she? You have shown me that I have been remiss in my responsibilities. Hatred accomplishes nothing. Knowledge and planning are so much more useful in accomplishing our goals. We will never rid the world of these abominations, Dionysus. Each generation must deal with them as best they can. If we become complacent, they will have their way. Opposing them? Well, we will see. Thank you for opening my eyes. I will not close them again."

"When they come marching in, which they will surely do, it will be here that they enter the eastern lands. It will be you who will face them, as did Kiya and her children. I will provide whatever small help I can."

"Give my regards to Azura. Tell her that we must establish closer relations. Maybe she will allow some of my Oceanids to reside in her city for communication purposes. I will have them promise to not tempt her precious male citizens too much. Oceanids are extremely disciplined you know. We just need to know why."

He laughed as he rose to leave. "You give me hope, Clymene. May your kind live forever."

17. Azura: Great Mother of Urfa

Impressive fountains greeted them as they entered the gates of Urfa. Across the plaza, the two-story government building faced them. The city bustled with activity.

Dionysus dismounted and dismissed his two companions. "There should be an outdoor cafe around here somewhere. I will find you there for our evening meal."

He walked to the two-story building, through the double doors, surveyed the scene, walked to the receptionist, and announced, "I am Titan Dionysus of Tartarus. I wish to meet with Great Mother Azura."

The woman raised her eyes and looked him up and down. "Many wish to meet with the Great Mother. What business does one so young have with one so important?"

Dionysus closed his eyes, composed himself, and replied, "I can cover your land with water. I can bring fire from the sky. My command can bring endless hordes of locusts over the land. I am feared by kings and the Olympians themselves. I can make your citizens dance naked through your streets. I assume that even *you* have heard of Titan Dionysus, confidante of Queen Kiya, whose counsel is sought by all who know him. Or had you rather I continue my journey to counsel with Master-of-Masters Seth of Tallstone without paying my respects to Azura?"

She hesitated, unsure how to proceed, but finally rang a bell. An attendant appeared immediately. "Is Great Mother Azura available for an unscheduled, somewhat young, visitor? A 'Titan Dionysus of Tartarus.'"

The attendant scurried to the second floor, entered a room, stayed, and scurried back down. "Yes, our Great Mother is finishing her mid-day meal and can meet with him shortly."

The receptionist said, "Very well, show this young man to her office and have him wait."

"You are kind and merciful," Dionysus said, as he left.

He climbed to the second floor and sat down in the outer office. Soon, a tall, dynamic middle-aged woman strode from her office, hands extended in greeting. "You are Titan Dionysus, a friend of Queen Kiya?"

"Yes. I am told that she thought quite highly of me, albeit I am on the young side." They both laughed.

"Come, we will sit at the table near the window," she said as she led him toward a large table. Dionysus glanced at the administrative assistant sitting at her desk by the door.

OCEANIDS: Metis, Tyche, Clymene, Eurybia, Amphitrite, Philyra, Rhodos.
TELCHINES: Dexithea, Makelo, Halia.
EAST: Azura, Seth, Typhon, Iasion, Endymion.
OTHER: Centaur Chiron, Charon, Hotep, Petra, Persephone.

He followed but said, "Great Mother, my beloved Queen Kiya commands me from her grave to say this to you: 'Mother Azura, these are dark days. Dionysus will say words which only your ears should hear.'"

They stopped at the desk.

Azura glanced at the aide, her ears already homing in on the upcoming conversation. "Noam, you are my assistant because of your attentiveness, loyalty, and discretion but you heard that your ears should not hear this."

Noam said, "Yes, Great Mother," rose from her desk, left the room, and closed the door behind her.

"Sit," Azura said. "Of what shall we talk?"

Dionysus talked of dead Titans, of living Olympians, of new Ghods, of terrible weapons of war, of Clymene and her words, of despair, of hope, of how Urfa should prepare for the coming days of darkness.

Azura listened without expression or interruption. After he finished, she merely said, "It will be difficult for Urfa to make a poor first impression. Provide me with the names of all the Ghods and their nature, especially their weaknesses." She then asked, "Can Clymene assure me that her little Oceanids will conduct themselves like proper young women?"

When their discussions were finished, she bid goodbye with, "When you meet with my husband and son, tell them that I miss them, and I send them my constant love."

Dionysus shook his head in affirmation. He did know if it was with resignation or with hope.

18. Seth: Master of Masters

The road from Urfa to Tallstone was well-established and beautiful. It was lined with trees with a way station every thirty Stades. Onos contently pulled his wagon.

Dionysus announced, "No more wine for those in the east. Let someone else corrupt them. It will not be me."

Old man Seilenos laughed. "Have I taught you nothing, boy? Wine does not corrupt. It merely allows corruption to expose itself. But, have your way. No more wine for the locals."

ELDER OLYMPIANS: Hestia, Demeter, Hera, Hades, Poseidon, Zeus
OLYMPIANS: Apollo, Ares, Artemis, Athena, Aphrodite, Dionysus, Hermes,
Hephaestus, Heracles. LIVING TITANS: Oceanus, Tethys, Selene, Elder Oceanids.
DECEASED TITANS: Queen Kiya, Iapetus/Piercer, Cronus.

"And me, Dionysus?!" Marsyas exclaimed. "I'm already corrupted. At least let me sip wine. I won't share!"

Dionysus did not speak but took out his Aulos and began to play. He stopped, hesitated, and put it away. "If nothing more is accomplished, at least Clymene and Azura have seen their enemy. Let them do as they can. But I promised Philyra I would bring her a least a dozen port management candidates and maybe some metal department field people. In the meantime, let's find out if these scholar people can maintain any kind of resistance to the Olympians. It will be interesting to see if Hestia sends the Ghods themselves, or just sends emissaries to this Festival."

They soon came to obelisks on either side of the road with intricate markings representing the various guilds of learning that resided within these boundaries. They traveled on. On their right were tables that would be filled with bread and items for trade during the increasingly popular Winter Solstice Festival. On their left were dozens of long houses where the scholars resided and studied. They came to a great hall fronting an impressive patio, the apparent center of Tallstone activity. They stopped there and exited the wagon.

Directly in front of the patio was a table of stone surrounded by sitting rocks. From there, the land gently rose into a small hill. Twelve stone monoliths surrounded the hill. And on top -- the tall stone. Beneath the obelisk, due east, at the foot of the hill, sat the great stage from where, in six more months, the chiefs would meet, and three proper young women from Urfa, dressed in red, would loudly proclaim in unison, "Let's go have ourselves a festival!"

A young man came from the building and said, "I am Enosh. Welcome to Tallstone. Come inside for refreshments. The road from Urfa is pleasant but still, relaxation after a journey is also pleasant. I will have a docent attend to your donkey."

Enosh led them into the welcome center which was also a meeting area which was also a dining area which was also a library containing scrolls and other documents. He pointed out large, cushioned chairs circling a table where they could sit. He sat them down and said, "I will bring you refreshment. Sweet or Bitter?"

Marsyas replied, "Thank you, but I brought my own."

OCEANIDS: Metis, Tyche, Clymene, Eurybia, Amphitrite, Philyra, Rhodos.
TELCHINES: Dexithea, Makelo, Halia.
EAST: Azura, Seth, Typhon, Iasion, Endymion.
OTHER: Centaur Chiron, Charon, Hotep, Petra, Persephone.

Dionysus shot him an angry glance and said to Enosh, "Three Bitters, please." He glared at Marsyas, who simply shrugged.

Enosh left and then returned with their Bitters. He sat down and asked, "Gentlemen, how can I help you? What is the purpose of your visit?"

Dionysus replied, "I am not at all sure how the scholars can help. I come to tell you of the imminent end of the world."

"Oh, should I summon Master Seth or are you being melodramatic?"

"Why, both. I am Titan Dionysus of the late Tartarus, and these are my companions, Seilenos and Marsyas. I seek a meeting with Master-of-Masters Seth. I wish to discuss the Olympians of Port Olympus and the coming sad times they will bring. Is such a meeting possible?"

"Of course. He is in his study. I'm sure he will find your visit most enlightening. Let me announce you. I will return shortly."

Enosh left. Dionysus looked at his companions and took a deep breath.

Enosh returned and escorted Dionysus to a side room.

Middle-aged, distinguished, charismatic Seth greeted Dionysus at the door of his study. "Come in, Titan Dionysus. I have asked Typhon to join us if you don't mind. Typhon is our Master Scholar in the Art of War. From what I surmise, war will be our topic of conversation, today."

"It will be of war, Master Seth. The Olympians will attend this year's festival and make unreasonable demands for tribute. If refused, they will return with weapons you cannot defeat. I fear the worst for you and all the eastern tribes."

"I see. But before you begin my education, you introduced yourself as Titan when, in fact, you are an Olympian. Why is this?"

Dionysus was taken aback. -- *that's brazen! – but reasonable, I suppose –*

He answered, "The Elder Olympians are all Titans through their father Cronus. I am a son of Olympian Zeus who now considers me to be an Olympian but who, upon our first meeting, dismissed me as unwanted and unworthy. Titan Queen Kiya accepted me with graciousness and, I believe, with love. Such is my heritage. 'Titan' is my preference."

Seth asked, "You saw Kiya and her children die?"

ELDER OLYMPIANS: Hestia, Demeter, Hera, Hades, Poseidon, Zeus
OLYMPIANS: Apollo, Ares, Artemis, Athena, Aphrodite, Dionysus, Hermes, Hephaestus, Heracles. LIVING TITANS: Oceanus, Tethys, Selene, Elder Oceanids.
DECEASED TITANS: Queen Kiya, Iapetus/Piercer, Cronus.

"I did. I begged her to let me stay and fight alongside her and her children but her last words to me were, 'You have your orders, Titan. Execute them!' She turned from me and took her position near their fire pit. I mounted my pony and retired into the darkness to see -- it." He stared coldly at Seth.

Seth leaned back in his chair, clasped his hands together, and said, "Ahhh. So that is what you are doing here. Executing your orders." He stared at Dionysus without expression.

--- you arrogant, obnoxious, all-knowing pond-scum -- I should leave now! -- leave you to the coming darkness --

Seth said, "I now understand, Titan Dionysus. Tell me your story."

Dionysus calmed himself and glanced at the man sitting against the wall.

The man nodded in recognition and merely said, "I am General Typhon, Master Titan."

Dionysus told his story.

Seth listened without interrupting. When Dionysus had finished, Seth and Typhon exchanged glances and imperceptibly nodded to one another, as if they had heard what they had expected to hear.

Seth leaned forward and said, "You bring interesting news and much new information, Titan Dionysus. It will take me several days to understand the implications of what I have just heard and formulate a response. In the meantime, I will assign Typhon to be your host during your stay. You have brought us your gift of wine, I trust."

Again, Dionysus was taken aback. "What? Wine, Master Seth? I have wine in our wagon, but, I mean, I had decided not to dispense it in the eastern lands. I mean, I decided not to lead your people into the abandonment of their dignity. I mean, wine is both a blessing and a curse. It is a curse to far too many people. I did not want to bring a curse to your people. They are decent people, I mean."

"You do not want our scholars to test themselves? To learn about themselves? To gain knowledge of themselves and their peers? How interesting that you think so little of us." He rose in dismissal of Dionysus.

OCEANIDS: Metis, Tyche, Clymene, Eurybia, Amphitrite, Philyra, Rhodos.
TELCHINES: Dexithea, Makelo, Halia.
EAST: Azura, Seth, Typhon, Iasion, Endymion.
OTHER: Centaur Chiron, Charon, Hotep, Petra, Persephone.

Dionysus continued to sit -- thinking. He then rose, smiled, and said, "For this evening's meal, wine for all. And I shall have Marsyas and Seilenos play music for your entertainment."

Seth replied, "Excellent!"

Typhon also rose, walked over, and introduced himself. "Master Titan Dionysus, the concept of creating a caste above all others -- 'Ghods' as you have them calling themselves -- is extremely novel and interesting. Isolating them in this manner has great possibilities but there will be unforeseen unintended consequences. Let us attempt to foresee them as best we can. You have the potential of becoming a great general. I look forward to showing you Tallstone and discussing the art of war."

Dionysus was disgusted that he was pleased with himself. -- *have I just passed some kind of test? -- they aren't as terrified as they should be -- like they are already planning --*

Typhon escorted Dionysus to the building entrance, joined the two men waiting there, and began their tour of Tallstone.

Later, at the evening's meal, there was wine and music.

19. Enosh: Shaman

Several days passed. Dionysus was passed from guild master to guild master and joined in discussions of their interests.

Then one afternoon, Enosh found Dionysus and announced that he had been assigned to expose Dionysus to the knowledge of Enosh's discipline of study. "You will find it interesting enough, I believe. Come, let us sit at Grandfather Pumi's Rock Table where he, himself, sat. That would be appropriate." They walked to the table of rock which sat unobtrusively midway between the main building and the tall stone. They sat across from one another as Enosh asked, "Will you provide wine for us?"

Dionysus shook his head in acquiescence and signaled to Seilenos, who sat on the entrance porch of the building across the patio between them, "bring us wine."

Enosh began, "I believe you will pass, Master Dionysus. We shall meet after evening's meal, and from what I ascertain, you will be found worthy. You will not be introduced into our brotherhood because you never asked. But Father Seth and any of us will share our knowledge and plans with you freely."

"All of this was nothing but a test?"

"Oh, no! We obtained a great deal of information. About your character, your desires, your associates, things you know that we did not, things of that nature. And the only knowledge we shared with you is what we would share with anyone who comes seeking knowledge. But we are not without our secrets. Typhon, especially. Our Guild of Metal scholars, too. But wait, I should not yet be telling you these things." Enosh laughed. "And here comes our wine. Joy! Now, tell me, judge us on how we faired with wine night at Tallstone? Myself, especially."

Dionysus sat thinking. -- *they were using me to get information! -- I told them everything without even thinking about it -- they were judging my character? -- me?! -- a titan and an Olympian -- what arrogance! -- I will be found worthy?! -- am I happy or enraged? --*

"How interesting," Dionysus finally said as he accepted the cup from Seilenos. "Most did well with the wine. The older scholars, anyway. The younger ones? Well, if I had brought in a few Oceanids, I could have made things get out of hand. Out of hand by eastern standards, anyway. So, the scholars of Tallstone pass. You, too. Happy?"

"Ecstatic, actually," Enosh replied, relieved.

"So, what is your 'interesting' discipline, Master Enosh?"

"I am not a master, yet. But I continue my quest to understand the nature of death. Can we bring the dead back to life? Can the dead communicate with us? Where are the dead? Questions of this sort. Once, long ago, children of Tartarus visited and received knowledge on these matters. They were serious and insightful. I am hopeful that the seeds of knowledge will grow in their fertile minds. But in your case, the question I believe to be is if Queen Kiya continues to give you guidance from her grave. If so, how? What do you think? Does she?"

"I sometimes remember words she has spoken to me. Hardly new words spoken from her grave." -- *these people are strange -- easier to understand the mind of an Olympian -- even an oceanid --*

OCEANIDS: Metis, Tyche, Clymene, Eurybia, Amphitrite, Philyra, Rhodos.
TELCHINES: Dexithea, Makelo, Halia.
EAST: Azura, Seth, Typhon, Iasion, Endymion.
OTHER: Centaur Chiron, Charon, Hotep, Petra, Persephone.

"We have been with our brothers many times as they lay dying. Agreements had been established to send communication back after they die. No one ever has. We shall continue to try, of course. We have only one possible occurrence, from Grandfather Pumi. He, himself, would not verify that it was truly his dead son who spoke to him. It could have been a dream, a hallucination, an imagination from an overtired, overstressed mind. But still, I, myself, believe the dead still live. My quest is to find where they live. How to speak to them. Let me ask you this, do you believe yesterday still exists?"

"I have never in my life given that particular question a single thought."

"Think upon it. Let me know your thoughts. You are quite clever. You have seen many people with minds altered by wine. Perhaps the secrets are inside their altered minds. Perhaps they see worlds that I cannot see. Maybe travel to yesterday."

Enosh laughed. "Grandfather Pumi lived his last day believing he would be reunited with Grandmother Valki in death. Wishful thinking? An old man's hopes? Possibly. Probably. But he was our best. From rock, will, and earth he built Tallstone from nothing to the centerpiece of modern civilization. Before Pumi and Valki, our civilization did not exist. Does he look down upon us, now? Does she look up at us? The dead may know these things, but the living must search further. Pumi's scroll on the subject is in our library. It is the basis from which Shaman thought begins. If you find the time, consider reading it. Maybe learn how to hear the words Queen Kiya says to you."

Enosh rose and said, "You will be dining alone tonight as all the brothers meet to decide your fate. Rest well. Your tomorrow may be busy." He smiled and left Dionysus alone at the stone table.

-- *are you sitting here with me, Pumi? – do I just have to open my eyes to see you?* --

20. Typhon: Scholar of War

Dionysus rose at sunrise and walked out of the guest quarters, stretching. In the distance, on the hill, in front of the tall stone, he saw the mass of scholars doing morning exercises, performing movements in unison. They appeared to be defensive maneuvers; agile, evasive, thrusting, all in perfect unison. -- *do they do this each morning? -- maybe I should always rise at sunrise -- I don't want to miss anything –*

ELDER OLYMPIANS: Hestia, Demeter, Hera, Hades, Poseidon, Zeus
OLYMPIANS: Apollo, Ares, Artemis, Athena, Aphrodite, Dionysus, Hermes,
Hephaestus, Heracles. LIVING TITANS: Oceanus, Tethys, Selene, Elder Oceanids.
DECEASED TITANS: Queen Kiya, Iapetus/Piercer, Cronus.

He took dried fruit and nuts from his traveling bag, walked to Pumi's stone table, and sat down to watch the scholars. *-- they are more physical than one would suppose -- a little muscle to go with big brains -- no -- not muscle -- fluid agility -- defense against an attacking force – 'we are not without our secrets' -- apparently so -- today is to be my big day? -- and I thought that it was me who would bring you information to shatter your hopes --*

The scholars responded to commands given by Typhon. Upon one command, all scholars crouched into a ball. Upon the next, they sprang to their feet holding a curved cutting blade in the attack position. More commands, more choreographed moves. Finally, Typhon issued a great bellow. The scholars held a fist in the air and returned the bellow in kind. They then dismissed themselves and turned with laughter to their brothers and drifted toward the great building for morning's meal and talk.

"Well," said a voice standing behind Dionysus, startling him to the point of jumping, "what do you think?"

Dionysus rose and turned to face Seth.

Seth said, "Sorry. I didn't mean to startle you, but you were so lost in thought that I thought it best not to speak."

Dionysus composed himself. "Impressive. I thought I came to tell the lambs to prepare to be eaten. The lambs appear to be preparing to eat."

Seth laughed. "Yes, you came thinking we were simple, innocent folk. A perception we encourage. But I come to ask you to join us in brotherhood, not as a scholar but as a dear, trusted friend. One who will never betray the secrets we share with you. If you are unsure, tell me 'no,' there will be no adverse effect on our relationship. If you tell me 'yes,' then Typhon wishes a long conversation with you today and then, tonight, there will be a little ceremony of brotherhood. We will invite your two companions to visit Urfa for the evening while we initiate you. If you wish time to consider your answer, I will leave you alone to consider it."

"So, I am to make a solemn vow to those whom I do not know, nor know their aims and goals, nor know what they wish of me, nor what they will ask of me, and what I get for this is to know some of their secrets?"

Seth stared at him. "*All* of our secrets. Shall I leave you to consider?"

"What are the scholars' attitudes toward Olympians?"

OCEANIDS: Metis, Tyche, Clymene, Eurybia, Amphitrite, Philyra, Rhodos.
TELCHINES: Dexithea, Makelo, Halia.
EAST: Azura, Seth, Typhon, Iasion, Endymion.
OTHER: Centaur Chiron, Charon, Hotep, Petra, Persephone.

"The Ghods, as you call them?" Seth stood silent, then turned toward the building, blew loudly upon a whistle, and shouted, "Position to Defend!"

In a moment, the building boiled forth scholars running to take positions on the patio, in formation, crouched, blades in hand. Seth inspected them and proclaimed, "I am well-defended! Dismissed!"

The scholars rose from their crouch, looked around, and returned to their morning meal inside the building.

To Dionysus, Seth replied, "Our attitude is one of love. It is necessary to love all things, all people, even those who despise you, even those you must kill. Pumi taught us that. I believe he learned it from your Queen Kiya. Consider your answer; let me know your decision." Seth turned and walked away.

Dionysus called out after him, "You know my answer, Master Seth. You have always known my answer. I look forward to counseling with General Typhon. I have much to learn."

That afternoon, Typhon and Dionysus strolled the grounds of Tallstone.

Hands clasped behind his back; Typhon talked. "Your moves against the Olympians are extremely interesting -- isolating them as a caste above all classes -- they no longer compete with their lower classes – extremely interesting tactic -- That Philyra woman -- we knew her name but still do not know her nature -- and it was you who maneuvered her into becoming the Port Olympus Chief-of-Chiefs -- no small accomplishment -- and if not your ally, she at least appears not to be a blind disciple to her masters -- what motive drives her? -- love? -- hatred? -- lust for power? -- She is an Oceanid, as the Great Metis is an Oceanid -- which, by the way, is of grave concern -- why has Metis not contacted you? -- does she believe you to be her enemy? -- why? -- why not? -- a consideration to watch closely -- Is Philyra bound to Kiya in some way? -- she was consort to Cronus after Rhea divorced him."

Typhon continued, "All in all, you have made several significant tactical moves to alleviate the coming impact of Olympian lust -- Although, your decision not to seek qualified metalworkers for Hades' department is a miscalculation on your part -- you, yourself, told us that Hades had been neutralized in his own department -- an occurrence not of your making -- Philyra's doings? -- if not, then whose? -- Regardless, the replacement of

ELDER OLYMPIANS: Hestia, Demeter, Hera, Hades, Poseidon, Zeus
OLYMPIANS: Apollo, Ares, Artemis, Athena, Aphrodite, Dionysus, Hermes,
Hephaestus, Heracles. LIVING TITANS: Oceanus, Tethys, Selene, Elder Oceanids.
DECEASED TITANS: Queen Kiya, Iapetus/Piercer, Cronus.

Titan Iapetus by Olympian Hades has been neutralized -- disciples of Iapetus and Littlerock appear to be in a position of power -- many who left the department when Hades took over, were scholars in the metals before they immigrated to Tartarus -- those that did not immigrate to Port Spearpoint simply returned to Tallstone -- then, there was a mass return of metal and stoneworkers when the Elder Titans were slaughtered -- We can supply Philyra with whatever talent her mining and metal department might need -- just don't mention our names -- or where the talent comes from -- they will happily work away creating whatever the Olympians require -- I might mention that we have over a hundred Orichalcum swords tucked away courtesy of our friends at Phlegethon -- amazing instruments of battle -- we don't wish the Orichalcum helmets or shields because I rely on speed and mobility rather than brute strength -- Kiya and the Elder Titans did quite well against the Hecatoncheires with this tactic -- you need all this information for your planning and your dealings with Philyra.:

Typhon continued, seemingly without end, "I embrace your Ghod isolation tactic -- there will be unintended consequences -- we must identify the possibilities and take corrective actions -- you remain an Olympian in good standing -- how is Hestia using you? -- of what good are you to her? -- you appear to have the love of your father and know how to keep that love strong -- how strong is the bond between you? -- your bond with Kiya appears to be the stronger of the two -- but when the time comes, who will you betray, and when and why? -- Hestia looked to you for advice and you gave her Ghods -- interesting that she would have called upon you in the first place -- why? -- the Oceanid Clymene -- there is hatred in her heart -- I must counsel her -- hatred is a weakness -- she must love those to whom she will bring death -- your tactic of preparing her for the initial onslaught by Olympian troops was wise -- a tactic which I had completely overlooked -- I must plan with Clymene -- give her resources -- I envisioned all battle occurring here at Tallstone -- a blunder on my part -- you saw farther than I on that issue -- our first goal is always to prevent war -- but to prevent the war, we must be prepared for war -- my strategy is to make the Olympians look to the west for their spoils -- not to the east."

Typhon became silent, then looked at Dionysus, and asked, "So, what do you think?"

OCEANIDS: Metis, Tyche, Clymene, Eurybia, Amphitrite, Philyra, Rhodos.
TELCHINES: Dexithea, Makelo, Halia.
EAST: Azura, Seth, Typhon, Iasion, Endymion.
OTHER: Centaur Chiron, Charon, Hotep, Petra, Persephone.

"I came here thinking you knew nothing; that I had all the answers. I now know that I know little; that you have all the answers. What is it you expect me to say? This is all interesting, extremely interesting."

21. The Book of Pumi

Dionysus completed his initiation by walking between the two lines of scholars, each in their auroch robes and wearing the necklace of their guild. Each reached out to touch his extended hands.

-- have I been somehow cleansed -- somehow better than I was -- I have been washed in -- purity? -- family? -- I did not come seeking this thing -- they found me -- they think I am worthy of their brotherhood -- am I? -- will I be? -- no matter -- I came without hope -- I have been given hope – perhaps --

The lines ended with Seth standing in front of Pumi's stone table. Seth embraced him and said, "Welcome, my son. Now, do as you will." Seth waved the lines to disband and all left Dionysus standing at Pumi's table, alone with his thoughts.

Dionysus sat down on the stone upon which Pumi had once sat. He felt the weight of history. *-- it's no longer a game we play, Philyra -- we have purpose – we have allies -- Kiya's will be done -- we shall do it -- you and me and all the others -- life after death, Kiya? -- I am told Pumi recorded his thoughts on that subject -- let's go read it -- maybe I can learn how to talk with you once more.*

He rose, walked to the great building, entered, and looked around for an attendant.

Master Shaman Teumessian greeted him. "Searching for the answers, Titan Dionysus? I fear you must learn to look beyond this world."

Dionysus laughed. "Is Queen Kiya around someplace where I can talk with her? I'll bring the wine!"

Teumessian was not amused. Teumessian was never amused. "Do not jest of the dead. They are not of this world and are beyond our power!"

"My apology. I mean no disrespect but there is much I do not yet understand about this world. I seek understanding."

Teumessian motioned Dionysus to sit at his table. The two men sat and engaged in a long conversation discussing abstract concepts of life and death. Teumessian, with self-important, self-proclaimed wisdom,

ELDER OLYMPIANS: Hestia, Demeter, Hera, Hades, Poseidon, Zeus
OLYMPIANS: Apollo, Ares, Artemis, Athena, Aphrodite, Dionysus, Hermes,
Hephaestus, Heracles. LIVING TITANS: Oceanus, Tethys, Selene, Elder Oceanids.
DECEASED TITANS: Queen Kiya, Iapetus/Piercer, Cronus.

dismissed any control that Kiya might have in this matter. "Power in death must lie beyond our natural world."

Teumessian was much more interested in the Ghods than the Titans. He asked about and listened with great interest as Dionysus described the nature of the Olympians.

"My father, Zeus, is extremely transactional. You express love to Zeus; he loves you back intensely." He talked of Aphrodite and her insatiable appetites; of Hestia, as she sat in front of her endlessly burning fire pit; of the vicious wrath of Ares toward any real or imagined slight; of Demeter and Persephone and their innocent love of field and flower. "I don't wish to make them seem unnatural, but they are not like you or me."

"Yes. I understand. You have been most informative. Now, come with me, I will show you the scroll where your journey begins."

He led Dionysus to the back wall and removed a large, elegant gold-covered chest from a shelf. He sat the chest upon the table, removed a scroll, handed it to Dionysus, closed the chest, and returned the chest to its shelf.

Teumessian said, "Our knowledge begins with this writing, but the answer is lacking. I feel it to be my destiny to someday provide the correct answer. Leave the scroll on the table when you are finished. I must retire and reflect upon what I have learned tonight." With that, Teumessian left Dionysus alone with Pumi's scroll.

Dionysus sat down at the table, rolled open the scroll, and read the primitive writing.

"I am Pumi, a stonecutter. I write to answer a question once asked of me which I did not answer. Valki and I had buried our son, Breathson, in the year of the twentieth Winters Solstice Festival. His older brother murdered him in an act of passion. After the grave was closed and all other mourners were gone, Valki attacked me screaming in pain and fury. We fell to the ground and lay there together, exhausted and in emotional turmoil, beyond tiredness. She then slept. I lay there with her in my arms, void of all emotion, staring into a brilliant, moonless firmament. I then remembered that I had never answered Breathson's question. He had witnessed the death of a hare by a wolf. He asked me: 'Father, can something come back to life after it is killed?' I replied, 'I know of nothing

OCEANIDS: Metis, Tyche, Clymene, Eurybia, Amphitrite, Philyra, Rhodos.
TELCHINES: Dexithea, Makelo, Halia.
EAST: Azura, Seth, Typhon, Iasion, Endymion.
OTHER: Centaur Chiron, Charon, Hotep, Petra, Persephone.

that has returned to life after being killed. That is a good question. I shall ask someone far wiser than myself.' As I lay there, near oblivion, I wondered, 'Well, Breathson, are you now far wiser than I? Do you now know the answer? Does the rabbit live?' Tears leaked from my eyes. Exhausted, with a blank mind, I fell toward unconscious sleep."

Dionysus read on, "Breathson then said to me, 'The rabbit lives. I live. We are the light. We are free from the burden of the flesh that carried our souls which records the history of all we have ever experienced, all we have ever known, all the joy and sorrow and pain we have ever felt. I now know my soul. I now know the soul of the rabbit; experienced its joy of life, its fears, its death. And, to the limit of its comprehension, it knows mine. Once we were bound and blinded by the flesh. Now we are no longer bound. Now we are no longer blind. Now, not only are we alive, at last, we live.'"

The writings continued, "My last thought before my deep sleep was this — 'We have so much to learn.' Whether he spoke to me, or I dreamt it, or it was a hallucination, I will not say. But if he did speak then this I know: All days which have ever been -- still are. All days still exist and those that lived in those days still live in those days. We cannot go there because, in our bodies, we cannot travel from today to yesterday, only from today to tomorrow. Our souls form at our birth and end at our death. Our soul cannot travel into tomorrow after our body dies. Upon death, the soul remains in all the days it once lived -- released from the passion and weakness of its body -- joined to all it has ever encountered -- sharing the experiences of all it has ever known. Death is only a transition. To join them, to speak to them, we have only to die. This, then, is my answer."

For reasons he never understood, Dionysus, overcome with the weight of civilization, wept.

22. Return to Tartarus

The group left Tallstone and set off to Urfa. Typhon rode with Dionysus in the back of the wagon drawn by Onos. Seilenos and Marsyas sat in the front. Marsyas played his aulos. Three dactyls -- Paionios, Epimedes, and Lasios -- walked behind the wagon. They had been the first three M3 research managers to leave Phlegethon when Hades replaced Iapetus as chief. Dionysus had assured them they would be free to perform their research free of interference by Hades if they would return to Phlegethon

ELDER OLYMPIANS: Hestia, Demeter, Hera, Hades, Poseidon, Zeus
OLYMPIANS: Apollo, Ares, Artemis, Athena, Aphrodite, Dionysus, Hermes,
Hephaestus, Heracles. LIVING TITANS: Oceanus, Tethys, Selene, Elder Oceanids.
DECEASED TITANS: Queen Kiya, Iapetus/Piercer, Cronus.

and would probably report to Celmis. They would miss the intellectual comradery at Tallstone, but Phlegethon had massive research and manufacturing facilities along with their deep Kopar mines. Plus, they would have educational leave to return to Tallstone four times a year with updates on the work they were doing to share with the scholars.

They arrived at Urfa where Dionysus and Typhon went to call on Azura. The others left to sight-see. Azura met with the two men. She and Typhon gossiped for a while and then broached the possible coming dark days.

Azura then said to Dionysus, "I visited Clymene at Riverport. We had a nice conversation and talked about many things. She assured me that Oceanids always wear proper clothing except when at the beach or in the water. Several have agreed to split their time between Riverport, Urfa, and Tallstone. All three centers can coordinate information and stay informed. I am told that Oceanids love intrigue, and this arrangement speaks of intrigue. I am delighted that Typhon, himself, is involving himself in these discussions and will, I'm sure, develop plans for future contingencies. You are to be congratulated Titan Dionysus for alerting us and bringing our communities closer together."

"Bring a little wine, bring a little joy, help save the world. It's what I do."

Azura laughed. "There is one more courtesy you might extend. I wouldn't mention it, but Typhon said that you were recruiting workers for Port Olympus. Is that true?"

"Yes. The recent unfortunate events drove away most Titans, almost all the Oceanids, and many of the competent workers and farm people. Anyone I can convince to return to the lands of Tartarus will be welcomed. Do you have candidates?"

"Why, yes I do. Three delightful young women who, we all agree, would be more fulfilled away from our little staid Urfa community. Will you interview them?"

"I don't need to. The lands of Tartarus were built on accepting any immigrant of any nature who sought a new life. I'm sure these three women will work out well."

OCEANIDS: Metis, Tyche, Clymene, Eurybia, Amphitrite, Philyra, Rhodos.
TELCHINES: Dexithea, Makelo, Halia.
EAST: Azura, Seth, Typhon, Iasion, Endymion.
OTHER: Centaur Chiron, Charon, Hotep, Petra, Persephone.

"Excellent. The three gravitate toward excitement. I suspect they have already discovered your men, but I will send my assistant, Noam, with you in case you have to track them down." The three bid their goodbyes.

Dionysus, General Typhon, and Noam walked toward Onos happily munching wheat stalks at his wagon. Their men stood facing the back of the wagon where-on sat three young women merrily entertaining the men with stories and banter.

Noam approached the back of the wagon, looked at the three women, and barked, "Ladies!!!"

The three hopped off the wagon, looked at the dactyls, said, "Oh-oh, we got to go, bye-bye," and began rapidly walking away.

Noam called after them, "Telchines, a moment, please. Would you like to go on an adventure?"

The three turned in unison, marched to Noam, and replied, "Yes, please."

The assistant introduced everyone, explained the proposal, and asked the women, "So, are you interested in immigrating?"

They squealed. "Wait here! We will go pack!" and ran off. The leader turned and ran back to speak to Seilenos, "Now, you don't let them go anywhere without us, you hear?!"

Seilenos obediently nodded affirmatively as the girl ran to catch up with her sisters.

Noam told Dionysus, "They were traded to us by the elder woman of the Telchine tribe from the extremely far east. They were toddlers. Three girls born to one woman at the same time. The elder woman seemed a little frightened of them for some reason. We exchanged grain and bread for them. The tribe was far from their normal hunting grounds and was not faring well. The three young women were never 'conventional girls' and are somewhat a disruptive influence on Urfa's other fine young ladies. I wish you well with them." Noam smiled and returned to her office.

Dionysus said to Seilenos, "Here they come. Let's get packed up and head for Riverport."

The loaded wagon headed to Riverport.

Again, Dionysus and Typhon rode in the back casually watching the three dactyls and three Telchine sisters walking side-by-side behind the wagon.

The dominant sister appeared to be named Dexithea; she had latched onto Paionios and was telling him, "So, after we have tilled the fields and planted the seeds, we like to go back under the full moon and dance naked because that makes it rain for the seeds to grow and make the fields muddy so that we can roll around in it and get muddy and wrestle with each other. We had rather wrestle boys, but I guess boys aren't allowed to play in the rain or something. Do you like to play in the rain, Paionios?"

"I love it!" he replied. "One time, when I was just starting as a dactyl, I was moving raw ore to be washed. A big storm came and between the dust, the ore, and the mud, I was covered with stuff. It was great! But manager-trainees aren't supposed to get naked in the rain -- I don't think."

She said, "Oh, it's easy. I'll teach you the next time we make it rain! Ore? What do you do with ore?"

"We refine it, melt it, and eventually turn it into Orichalcum. That's an extremely bright and shiny metal."

Dexithea exclaimed, "I love bright and shiny things. What kind of things?"

Their banter went on all the way to Riverport.

That night at Riverport, Dionysus and Typhon sat with Clymene at a table on the dock eating fish and roots with herbs. The three dactyls sat at another table: each with a Telchine on their lap. The women were enthralled by dactyl talk. Oceanids hovered about, taking care of their guests.

Typhon and Clymene talked of gathering intelligence, disseminating it, quick response times, guerrilla warfare, conserving assets, and the like. Dionysus listened to both conversations absent-mindedly playing with his small, circular engraved rock.

Finally, her conversation with Typhon completed, Clymene turned her attention to Dionysus. "The three young women you recruited from Urfa once discovered Riverport. They were young girls looking for adventure. They loved the independence here but hated the water. They had rather roll in mud than swim in water. Our loss, your gain, I suppose."

OCEANIDS: Metis, Tyche, Clymene, Eurybia, Amphitrite, Philyra, Rhodos.
TELCHINES: Dexithea, Makelo, Halia.
EAST: Azura, Seth, Typhon, Iasion, Endymion.
OTHER: Centaur Chiron, Charon, Hotep, Petra, Persephone.

Dionysus gave a half-hearted chuckle and sipped his wine.

Clymene asked, "Where is your mind, Sweet? It is not here."

Dionysus glanced at her. "You said I might recruit some Oceanids. Is that still a possibility?"

"Yes. I have a dozen eager to join the Port Olympus team. Eager to discreetly feed me constant information on those delightful people who butchered our people. *More* than a dozen if you need them. Just mention to any one of them, how many Oceanids are requested. They are packed and ready to go."

He asked Clymene, "Can the Oceanids be served wine tonight? Should I ask the Portmaster?"

Clymene stared at him for a moment and raised an eyebrow. She nodded and said, "The Portmaster would be delighted if you provided wine to her Oceanids this evening. Just don't push it on them. Let them enjoy it."

Dionysus quietly said, "I would like that." He so ordered, filled his cup, and walked by himself southward, where he sat in the night on a bench by a beautiful pond.

Later that evening, Portmaster Oceanid Clymene quietly joined him.

Sunrise.

The troupe rose and ate a light morning's meal. Dionysus bid Typhon and Clymene farewell, crossed the river, and set off on their return trip to Tartarus. Dionysus sat in the back of the wagon, playing his Aulos, followed by three dactyls, three Telchines, and more than a dozen Oceanids. All singing the walking song.

In five days, the troupe arrived at Overlook Point. The dactyls wanted to return to their old workplace at Phlegethon. But Dionysus was adamant; they would have to reapply for their positions at Port Olympus. For now, they would continue to abandoned Tartarus where they would spend the night and discuss their options. The thought of gathering his companions around the patio fire pit appealed to Dionysus's ongoing melancholia.

They continued to Tartarus where some of the Oceanids ran to Oursea, some set up camp in the guesthouse, and the others camped on the ground. Seilenos built a small fire in the fire pit. Everyone gathered an

ELDER OLYMPIANS: Hestia, Demeter, Hera, Hades, Poseidon, Zeus
OLYMPIANS: Apollo, Ares, Artemis, Athena, Aphrodite, Dionysus, Hermes, Hephaestus, Heracles. LIVING TITANS: Oceanus, Tethys, Selene, Elder Oceanids. DECEASED TITANS: Queen Kiya, Iapetus/Piercer, Cronus.

hour after sundown for their evening meal. Wine was served. They dined. They talked. Dionysus played with his circular rock.

Finally, Dionysus gave them their orders. "Dactyls and Oceanids will go with me tomorrow to Port Olympus to request jobs at the Port. If you happen to cross paths with a Ghod, do not look in the face and never speak to them unless they require it. They had rather throw you off the Port Building atrium and listen to you scream than they had look at you. If they speak to you and are charming, be afraid, it is only so that you will scream all the louder on your way down. When you apply for your work, be honest, but don't volunteer that you may be reporting information back to the east. Remember, Chief-of-Chiefs Philyra demands what is best for the company. Your duties will always be to do what is best for the company. Any questions?"

Dexithea asked, "What about us, Chief? Where should we Telchines go?"

"On our way to the Port tomorrow, we will cross 900 Pace Road. Asphodel Meadows lays there. Farmer women live there, and ranchers grow animals there. Something on that road will attract your interest. They have a lot of meadows and fields for you to bring rain to. Plus, you can easily find your way to Phlegethon dactyls, if you grow bored."

The Telchines were visibly delighted. After more banter, Dexithea asked, "What is that thing you keep playing with?"

Dionysus looked at the rock he had been absent-mindedly fingering. "Oh, this?" He handed it to her as he told her its story.

"Can I have it?"

"Have it! Queen Kiya gave it to me! Of course not!" Dionysus surprised himself with his terse response. What was the emotion he had just felt? -- *why not give it to her? -- it's only a stone -- one should not refuse a request -- if asked, one gives -- the Telchine admires it -- why not give it to her? --*

He continued, "I apologize. I meant to say, yes, someday. Just not today."

Dexithea examined both sides intently and replied, "Never mind. I think I can make one. What do you call this thing?"

He laughed, "A rock!"

OCEANIDS: Metis, Tyche, Clymene, Eurybia, Amphitrite, Philyra, Rhodos.
TELCHINES: Dexithea, Makelo, Halia.
EAST: Azura, Seth, Typhon, Iasion, Endymion.
OTHER: Centaur Chiron, Charon, Hotep, Petra, Persephone.

An Oceanid interrupted, "Titan Dionysus, I and my sisters have been talking. It would be best if at least three of us stayed in this place. Nature is reclaiming its land. We need to prune, weed, and clean and can only imagine what the insides of the buildings are like. Will this be permitted?"

"No, you must apply for positions at the port. They understand that Oceanids require time to attend to their sea and are well structured to grant you working hours as flexible as you wish. Accept employment at the port with the agreement that you will have at least one quarter moon each season away from the port. Make whatever rotations among yourselves you wish. Philyra should have completed her project to add a room at Port Reception that contains a description of each position available. If you can't read, I'm sure scribes will be there to read it to you."

"Of course, we can read, Master Titan!" an Oceanid snapped. "We are Oceanids!"

"You can read?!" Telchine Makelo exclaimed. "But you are not a scholar!"

The Oceanid, at first annoyed, took a second glance at the Telchine and reconsidered. "Yes, we sisters teach one another all that we know as soon as one joins our sisterhood. Reading is taught first. If you wish to learn, join us here when we return. It would be our delight to teach you."

Makelo, unaccustomed to politeness, was humbled by the generosity of the unknown woman. Without bravado, she meekly offered, "We could teach you how to make rain."

"That knowledge would be of interest," the Oceanid replied.

All were excited. Tomorrow, they would complete their journeys. Tomorrow, they would begin their new lives.

23. The Abduction of Persephone

Hades spent a great deal of time at Tartarus. There wasn't that much to do but he did enjoy rummaging through the homes of the Titans and visiting Chiron. That, plus he had commanded Chiron to watch for Ghod Demeter and Persephone. "I would love to surprise my sister and her lovely daughter when they visit Elysian Fields."

Today, Hades rose early and walked with Cerberus from Piercer's home, now his, to visit Chiron. He found Chiron tending animals near the barn housing Hades' chariot and black stallion, Alastor.

Chiron saw Hades' approach and prostrated his front half, eyes down, in subservience.

Hades called out, "Greetings, horse-like Chiron. Rise and speak."

Chiron rose, bowed to Hades, and said, "Good morning Great Olympian Ghod Hades. A farmer woman informed me the two women which you asked about passed by not too long ago."

Hades became excited at the thought but was confused, "What farmer women?"

Chiron laughed. "Oh, Ghod Hades, there are many women nearby who tend the fields and animals. A Ghod would never see one of them because if a Ghod ever sees a common person, then that person would burst into flames. I am the only person to look upon a Ghod and then only upon you. We all disappear whenever anyone we don't know from the Port comes."

Hades, lost in thought, replied, "Oh." He hesitated and then asked, "My relatives, you say they passed by recently?"

"Yes, Ghod Hades. They walked the road from the Port toward Elysian Fields. I am told they do this once every quarter moon. They will stay the day and return in the evening."

Hades said, "Farmer women, nearby, many you say? Can you command they harvest flowers and place them on my chariot? Make the chariot festive? Something to delight the eyes of a young maiden?"

"Certainly, Ghod Hades. But they will not appear if you might see them. They certainly don't want to burst into flames."

"Yes, yes. I understand but tell them that I'm not that kind of Ghod. Now, Cerberus and I will continue our walk and return after the mid-day meal. Have my chariot festive and Alastor ready. I wish to look impressive when I greet Persephone and Demeter."

"Yes, my Ghod. It shall be done. And you will be impressive, indeed."

OCEANIDS: Metis, Tyche, Clymene, Eurybia, Amphitrite, Philyra, Rhodos.
TELCHINES: Dexithea, Makelo, Halia.
EAST: Azura, Seth, Typhon, Iasion, Endymion.
OTHER: Centaur Chiron, Charon, Hotep, Petra, Persephone.

Hades smiled his smile and set off with Cerberus to consider his coming day. They returned in early afternoon and found Alastor and his chariot waiting.

Chiron rushed to meet him. "Great Ghod Hades, one of the farmer girls insisted that flowers be woven into his mane. She said that any woman would be delighted to see a horse decorated like this! I will remove the flowers immediately if you dislike them. "

"No, no. All is perfect. The lower classes sometimes surprise me. I am well pleased." With that, Hades entered his chariot and set off without further comment to the Tartarus-Port Olympus Road.

He soon came to the road, turned left, and slowed Alastor to a trot so that he could scan the horizon. In a few minutes, he saw a figure walking in the Elysian Fields. He drew closer. It was her.

Persephone looked up from her walk and saw a vision. She stopped and stared at the vision coming down the road. *-- what is that? -- it is beautiful -- like a painting in a dream -- it has flowers in its hair -- it pulls uncle Hades in a beautiful chariot -- a chariot overflowing with beautiful flowers -- flowers as pretty as the ones I paint -- Uncle Hades -- a painting in a dream -- it is all so beautiful --*

Hades stopped his chariot, got out, faced her, knelt, and held his arms out to Persephone.

She walked to him slowly, eyes wide, lips parted, the whole time blankly staring at the image before her. *-- a painting within a dream --*

Persephone walked into his open arms still staring at Alastor and the flower-bedecked chariot. He embraced her, more tightly than she had expected.

"Is that a horse, Uncle Hades? It is the most beautiful horse in the world."

"Yes, sweet Persephone. This is my horse. His name is Alastor. Where is your mother?"

"Mother is at the beach. She likes to sit there after our mid-day meal. May I touch Alastor? Will he bite me?"

Hades stood and scanned the horizon. "Of course, you can touch him, Sweet. Here, let me pick you up so you can scratch his ears." He took her in his arms and held her close to Alastor. *-- I don't see Demeter --- she can't see us*

-- the beach is over the horizon -- Persephone is here alone -- lord Charon knew the flowers would enchant sweet Persephone -- he suggested taking her on a chariot ride to my place --

He asked, "Do you like Alastor? Would you like to go on a chariot ride?"

Her eyes grew even larger with excitement. "May we? Oh, Uncle Hades. That would be so grand!" *-- a chariot ride -- pulled by a black horse from a dream -- a dream filled with beautiful flowers --*

She asked, "Can we go fast?"

He carried her in his arms and placed her in the chariot between himself and Cerebos. "Yes. We will go fast. Stand close and hold on to me. Tightly. We will go fast." He commanded Alastor toward the road back to Phlegethon. They went fast. Oh, so very fast.

--- this is like a dream -- I am living in a dream -- I can paint the wind -- Uncle Hades is the greatest ghod of all -- mother -- can you see me? -- I wish you could see me -- I wish you were here with me, mother -- riding on the wind -- I am a flower on a black horse -- surrounded by flowers -- riding on the wind --

Hades and his chariot approached Phlegethon immediately before the evening meal. Celmis saw them arriving and summoned Idas. All Dactyl jobs included distracting their once-supervisor, Hades, and never mentioning that Hades had been promoted out of the organization. The two standing orders were, "Let him have whatever he wants. Keep him distracted and away from the real work."

Dactyl Idas was assigned to keep Ghod Hades happy at all costs. Idas was Hade's personal assistant aka employee aka servant aka slave. Idas knew, "Whatever he wants, do it!" Idas arrived just in time to take Alastor's reins. "Welcome back, Ghod Hades. Your quarters are clean and waiting on you. Will you take your evening meal in your quarters, or should I empty the dining room for you and your guest?"

Hades replied, "In my quarters, Dactyl. A delicious meal for my young guest. I will also want her to sample my delicious cave mushrooms. And an Aulos player playing in my quarters. Take care of Alastor. And take the flowers on him and my chariot to my quarters. What are you waiting on?"

Idas had extensive training from Lord Charon in dealing with Ghods. Idas replied, "I was lost in your radiance, Ghod Hades. Your will shall be done immediately. Do you wish wine with your meal?"

OCEANIDS: Metis, Tyche, Clymene, Eurybia, Amphitrite, Philyra, Rhodos.
TELCHINES: Dexithea, Makelo, Halia.
EAST: Azura, Seth, Typhon, Iasion, Endymion.
OTHER: Centaur Chiron, Charon, Hotep, Petra, Persephone.

Hades replied, "Of course, I want wine, idiot!" Idas bowed and led Alastor away. He called for a cook to join him and plan Hades' evening meal.

Hades led Persephone down the long stairsteps to his subterranean quarters. The door opened into a massive room containing all manner of geodes, colored rocks, bronze statues, bronze vases, bells, and other decorative objects. An attendant hurried in to light enough oil lamps to illuminate the room. Fans circulated air through inlet and outlet vents. "Come over here, Sweet Persephone. You can remove your garments and I will wash the dust from your body."

Persephone was overwhelmed by the beautiful objects in the room. She stared at everything with wide-eyed amazement. "Thank you, Uncle. But I know how to wash my body." She walked toward a stand-up shower area. "How do I operate this?" she asked as she began innocently removing her clothes.

"Oh, I will show you. You will find the experience entirely enjoyable." He studiously watched her remove her clothing piece by piece as he started the flow of the water in the shower and helped her step into it. He stared at her not-yet-mature body as she used the linen cloths to wash herself; then helped her out of the shower and used large towels to dry her body for her. "I don't have a tunic to fit you. Just wrap this blanket around you while we eat and drink tonight. You do drink wine, don't you?"

She shook her head, "No."

"Wine is delightful. A perfect way to end our day. It frees your mind of all care. And I have a delectable mushroom you must enjoy. It will take you places you simply can't imagine. We are going to have such fun tonight. This can be our wedding night!"

The cook entered the room bringing their evening meal and a small cask of wine. An Aulos player also entered, stood near the table, and began to play. Idas brought the flowers, placed them in containers of water, and arranged them. He discretely stood by the Aulos player awaiting orders.

Persephone asked, "Are we getting married, Uncle Hades?"

He replied, "Yes! Let's! This very night! Your mother will be so pleased! It will be a surprise! I shall name myself King and make you, my Queen. You will be responsible for painting all the flowers! It will be such fun!"

ELDER OLYMPIANS: Hestia, Demeter, Hera, Hades, Poseidon, Zeus
OLYMPIANS: Apollo, Ares, Artemis, Athena, Aphrodite, Dionysus, Hermes,
Hephaestus, Heracles. LIVING TITANS: Oceanus, Tethys, Selene, Elder Oceanids.
DECEASED TITANS: Queen Kiya, Iapetus/Piercer, Cronus.

"But I have not yet become a woman, Uncle. I have not been instructed in the art of mating! I must ask Mother!"

Hades smiled his smile. "Whatever you wish, Sweet Persephone. Let us eat and drink and you can make your final decision then."

They sat at the table; her large towel still wrapped around her. They dined. They drank wine. The wine made Persephone disoriented, but a warm feeling enveloped her mind and body.

"Here is our wonderful dessert, Sweet Persephone. It is called a cave mushroom. You will find the effect to be exquisite." He watched her nibble on the mushroom, smiled, stood, retrieved her discarded clothes, handed them to Idas, and told him, "Clean these. Bring back more clothes to fit her and fit for a Ghod."

Idas took the clothes and scurried off to consult with Celmis. The Aulos player continued to play. The cook continued to stand beside the Aulos player awaiting instructions. Hades returned to the table, took Persephone's hand, pulled her to her feet, and walked her to his bed.

Already her mind was beginning to hear colors and she could feel the color red. She felt the towel being removed from her body. She felt her body being lowered onto a bed. *Everything is so beautiful -- I hear flowers singing -- I feel the walls hugging me -- Everything is so wonderful -- Mother -- are you near?*

He asked, "Are you ready to marry me, Sweet Persephone? Are you ready to mate with me?"

I see words hovering -- flowing into me -- words asking me things -- what things do you ask me words? -- I don't understand the words I see -- are they nice words? -- I don't know how to hear any more -- just feel -- just see — just feel beautiful colors.

Hades said, "Rather than telling you, Sweet Persephone, let me show you."

Hades entered her. Persephone began foaming at her mouth. Hades licked the foam from her face. The cook gagged. The Aulos player closed his eyes and played on.

~

In the Asphodel Meadow, in the intermittent silence of the dark of the night, the farmer women huddled together, afraid, not daring to approach a Ghod lest they burst into flames, listening to distant screams coming

OCEANIDS: Metis, Tyche, Clymene, Eurybia, Amphitrite, Philyra, Rhodos.
TELCHINES: Dexithea, Makelo, Halia.
EAST: Azura, Seth, Typhon, Iasion, Endymion.
OTHER: Centaur Chiron, Charon, Hotep, Petra, Persephone.

from Elysian Fields. Screams of a mother who has lost her child. Screams of a woman who has lost the only person to ever love her. Screams of Olympian Ghod Demeter screaming for her lost, innocent daughter. Her lost, innocent daughter, Sweet Persephone.

24. The Seduction of Poseidon

Exquisitely dressed Elder Oceanid Amphitrite, looking half her actual age, sat on the sofa on the sixteenth floor overlooking the beautiful Port of Olympus. She sipped her superior wine as she watched Poseidon couple with Nerites. She would reach down periodically to stroke Poseidon. Poseidon finally threw back his head and released himself. Amphitrite slid onto the floor beside the two, put her free hand on Nerites' naked rump, pushed him away, and said, "Good work Nerites. You were fantastic. Now, go stand by the window so that we can admire your superb body."

She pulled Poseidon backward to lean against the sofa beside her and handed him a cup of wine. She purred, "My hot, dripping Ghod Poseidon, you need no mere woman to tell you what you already know, but I am overcome with pure desire for you. You are the greatest lover to ever live. You transcend all men, all Ghods. You stand alone at the height of all sexuality, all power. You are beyond even the Ghods. I must have you!"

Gently leaning against him, she glanced to see if he was rising. -- no? -- She kept purring, placed her free hand on his inner thigh, squeezed it, and began whispering in his ear. "All power resides in you. You control the seas, the ocean, you need no Ghod or man to bow down before you. You are above all these things. To bow before you would be to say 'I bow to you because of your power; not because you are better than I.' You are above those common needs, my great Poseidon."

She saw him twitch and began stroking him. He responded.

She then stood, removed her blouse, walked to Nerites, leaned her back against him, took his hands, and placed them on her breasts. "Dear Nerites, show my great Ghod Poseidon what he misses by not coupling with a woman who craves his magnificent body inside hers. Don't be timid, Sweet, feel my body, all over. Show Poseidon what he misses."

Nerites began squeezing and kneading her body. She closed her eyes, threw her head back, began breathing laboriously, raised her skirt, and

ELDER OLYMPIANS: Hestia, Demeter, Hera, Hades, Poseidon, Zeus
OLYMPIANS: Apollo, Ares, Artemis, Athena, Aphrodite, Dionysus, Hermes,
Hephaestus, Heracles. LIVING TITANS: Oceanus, Tethys, Selene, Elder Oceanids.
DECEASED TITANS: Queen Kiya, Iapetus/Piercer, Cronus.

began fondling herself. She did not need to open her eyes to know that Poseidon was coming for her.

25. Debriefings
< Year 100, 7th month >

Dionysus arrived early so that he could get his favorite table at the dock cafe. "Good morning, Kepten. Is my table available this morning?"

"Yes, Titan Dionysus. Your usual?" the captain asked as he led Dionysus to his table next to the water.

"Please. Has my friend Heracles been around lately?"

"No, Master Titan. But Chief-of-Chiefs Philyra and Elder Oceanid Amphitrite took their evening meal here, late, three nights ago. The Chief-of-Chiefs inquired about you. I am to notify her when you come in. Should I do that, or should I notice that you are not here?"

Dionysus laughed. "By all means, tell her that I'm here and shall be so until she joins me or until Poseidon brings forth the sea; whichever occurs first."

"Very good, Master Titan. I will see that you are served promptly and notify the Chief-of-Chiefs." Kepten left to attend to his instructions.

The wine arrived; his wine cup filled. Dionysus took the cup, leaned back in his chair, looked out over the bay, sniffed his wine, sipped, and relaxed into his old self for the first time in months. -- *life is good -- so good -- why cannot we all enjoy this good life -- why must we make it so hard? --*

He sipped his wine. He savored life.

One always knew when a Lord was nearby. The atmosphere changed. Dionysus did not even look up. He filled the second cup and sat it on the table across from him, then again looked out over Oursea.

Kepten pulled the seat out for her. She sat. "Thank you, Kepten. Fruit, please." She took the cup, sipped, sat it down, and said, "I am all business, Titan Dionysus. I am sure you understand."

"Oh, yes, I understand, Sweet Thing. You are always business!"

"I demand respect, Titan. Here or falling down the atrium. Your choice."

OCEANIDS: Metis, Tyche, Clymene, Eurybia, Amphitrite, Philyra, Rhodos.
TELCHINES: Dexithea, Makelo, Halia.
EAST: Azura, Seth, Typhon, Iasion, Endymion.
OTHER: Centaur Chiron, Charon, Hotep, Petra, Persephone.

He laughed. "Of course, Chief-of-Chiefs. But I must test the limit. It's the only way that I know where the limits lie." He sipped his wine. "I report success on my mission. Twelve Oceanids and three Dactyls are inside reading job descriptions as we speak. I promised the Oceanids that the company would respect their need for water time. I trust that will be acceptable."

"Of course, Titan. The well-being and satisfaction of my Port employees are second only to their excellence in performing their duties. Dactyls, you say? Are they accomplished?"

He replied, "I believe so. They were advised to speak only the truth to you even if they find it uncomfortable to do so. They worked at the highest levels of Phlegethon before the late unpleasantness."

She replied, "Excellent. Good work. You may be interested to know that the restructuring of M3 goes well. My managers are slipping into their new roles quite nicely. There are no more questioning, upper egos to address. And you will be delighted to know that Ghod Poseidon and Oceanid Amphitrite have a torrid relationship going. He appears to be enjoying his new position that does not need to impress anyone or demand anyone's subservience. She and I had a private meal a few nights ago. She is pleased with their progress 'as a couple.' But...," she stopped to sip her wine, "... there is a crisis on the floors above me and there is nothing I can do to resolve it. I would be thrown down the atrium if I became involved."

He asked, "Anything I can do to help you?"

Philyra said, "I don't think so. Persephone is missing. She has been missing for two quarter moons. She and Demeter were on their quarter moon excursion to Elysium Field so that Persephone could 'paint flowers.' The girl simply disappeared from the face of the earth. Demeter spent the afternoon and night looking for her. She found no sign of her. All the Ghods are at Demeter's throat because she won't make any more of their precious Ambrosia, whatever that is, until she finds Persephone. She is the only one that has the recipe, and she is in no mood to make it. My problem is that it's CoM3 Charon who told Hades how to simply 'take' the girl. The thirteenth floor is in a precarious position. To tell Hestia what I know or not tell her. Both are bad choices."

Dionysus held up his hand for silence, took his wine, leaned back in his chair, and stared out over Oursea.

ELDER OLYMPIANS: Hestia, Demeter, Hera, Hades, Poseidon, Zeus
OLYMPIANS: Apollo, Ares, Artemis, Athena, Aphrodite, Dionysus, Hermes,
Hephaestus, Heracles. LIVING TITANS: Oceanus, Tethys, Selene, Elder Oceanids.
DECEASED TITANS: Queen Kiya, Iapetus/Piercer, Cronus.

"You know something, don't you, Dionysus? Am I free to worry about other things, now?"

He was somber. "Yes, to both, Philyra. Don't worry your pretty little -- I mean don't concern yourself with it. This is what I do."

They sat together in silence, looking over the harbor, and sipping wine.

26. A Party of Ghods

Dionysus stopped in front of the door to the Port roof. He stared at it, closed his eyes, took a deep breath, and knocked. The door opened.

"Good evening, Master Gigante. Am I still allowed to join Dad's parties up here?"

The Doorman-Guard Gigante replied, "Of course, Olympian Dionysus. Come in. Shall I announce you?"

"No. Just let me slip in and get a feel for what's been happening the last month." He entered and quickly surveyed the room, identifying who was where and with whom. He retrieved a cup of wine from an attendant. He chose Athena and Hephaestus and walked toward them; arms outstretched. "Sister Athena! Come hug your beloved brother! You look fantastic, girl. Where did you get that stunning outfit?!"

Athena recoiled in disgust until she heard the words 'stunning outfit,' and then became exuberant, holding out her arms and accepting his embrace.

"Wait!" he said as he jumped back and stared at her Orichalcum form-fitting chest armor. He reached out to pinch her breast. "Wow! That's harder than a rock! You are protected on battlefield and in bedroom. It's so bright and shiny and it matches your helmet. It's gorgeous! Where from Hade's lands did you get it?"

She leaned over and embraced the arm of Hephaestus who stood beside her. "This wonderful man made it just for me. No one else can wear it! It fits only me. My beloved brother Hephaestus made it. Isn't my little brother wonderful?! Am I not wonderful?!"

Dionysus replied, "Yes, you both are! So wonderful! Now, tell me about this thing you have made, Ghod Heph. It's so -- impressive!"

OCEANIDS: Metis, Tyche, Clymene, Eurybia, Amphitrite, Philyra, Rhodos.
TELCHINES: Dexithea, Makelo, Halia.
EAST: Azura, Seth, Typhon, Iasion, Endymion.
OTHER: Centaur Chiron, Charon, Hotep, Petra, Persephone.

Hephaestus replied, "Yes, it is, isn't it? I thought of it myself and I MADE IT MYSELF. I saw all that Orichalcum metal just sitting there in blocks and thought to myself that an Orichalcum chest plate and helmet would look so Ghodly on Athena. Did you see the sword? Show him the sword, Athena."

She held out the Orichalcum sword for Dionysus to admire.

Hephaestus did not slow down. "Hestia saw the outfit and immediately ordered ten more. She was so excited. That is until she found out that Hades didn't have enough Orichalcum. He mines all the Kopar he needs but he needs to mix Tinom with the Kopar to make Orichalcum and we don't have any more Tinom. It's extremely complicated. I told Hestia to go scream at Philyra for not having enough."

Athena interrupted, "And look at this, Ghod Dionysus. Look at what I'm drinking my wine out of. It's a cup made from Orichalcum. Isn't it shiny? I love it so."

"Incredible!" Dionysus replied. "You two are wonderful. I love you both so much! Can I get one of those shiny cups to remind me of you two when I drink wine?" Athena presented him with an Orichalcum cup of his own. He thanked her profusely and, with a broad smile, disengaged himself and drifted toward Demeter, Hestia, and Artemis. -- *I can't deal with the three of them at the same time* --

He shifted his path toward Zeus, Heracles, Ares, and Aphrodite. He held out his arms. "Dad! I love you so much! You are the greatest! Let your favorite son embrace you and bask in your radiance!"

Zeus's face brightened. He extended an arm for Dionysus to slip in under.

Dionysus continued, "Heracles you have abandoned the street life for the world of glamor and power and wonderfulness. I miss you in the cafes, my old ex-friend."

Heracles shrugged. "Oh, well."

Dionysus looked at Aphrodite and widened his eyes. "The love of my life! The love of everyone's life! My sweet, exceedingly beautiful, unbelievably desirable, Aphrodite. We simply must couple sooner rather than later. Many different positions. Start planning right now!"

Her eyes widened, her breath quickened, she smiled back at him.

ELDER OLYMPIANS: Hestia, Demeter, Hera, Hades, Poseidon, Zeus
OLYMPIANS: Apollo, Ares, Artemis, Athena, Aphrodite, Dionysus, Hermes,
Hephaestus, Heracles. LIVING TITANS: Oceanus, Tethys, Selene, Elder Oceanids.
DECEASED TITANS: Queen Kiya, Iapetus/Piercer, Cronus.

Ares interrupted, "I live for the day we find ourselves on the opposite side of a field of battle. I shall take great pleasure in disemboweling you and then cutting that chattering throat of yours!"

Dionysus reared back with a wide grin. "Ares, you useless bag of dung. How are you? I haven't seen you torturing animals in a long time. We must simply fight to the death over who gets to couple with our little Aphrodite all they want to. Look at her, she is already excited about the prospects. Your death will be a frenzied joy for both of us! But enough about the lesser Ghods. I want to talk to the King of the Ghods, himself. My beloved Dad."

Dionysus turned his attention to Zeus, but first moved to stand beside Aphrodite, cupped his hand on her butt, and pulled her body to his. She pressed her body firmly against his. He glanced at Ares, smirked, looked back at Zeus, and said, "Dad, who I love so much, tell me about this tragic incident with Persephone."

Aphrodite disengaged herself, took Ares by the hand, said, "You boys enjoy your talk," and led Ares away. Heracles followed.

"Is it too painful, Dad? I don't want to cause you any pain. Let's talk about naked women instead."

Zeus chuckled and looked around "Well, I need someone to confide in that really loves me. I know everybody really loves me, but they get upset sometimes."

"Some people are just ingrates, Dad. I don't know how you put up with it but maybe I can smooth things over. What do you need doing?"

Zeus lowered his voice to a conspiratorial level. "Demeter is really mad at everybody because that daughter of hers is missing. I think maybe Hades took her because I told him it was all right if he wanted to couple with her. Demeter is going to be furious with Hades if he took her, and she is going to be furious with me, for no reason, because Hades will tell her it's my fault. I don't like people being mad at me, Son, you know that. I can't have Demeter killed to keep her from being mad at me -- can I?"

"No, Dad. And you do have a horrible problem, but you don't worry about it. I will visit Ghod Hades and make your problems go away. Maybe you will turn out to be everybody's hero just like you already really are. All

OCEANIDS: Metis, Tyche, Clymene, Eurybia, Amphitrite, Philyra, Rhodos.
TELCHINES: Dexithea, Makelo, Halia.
EAST: Azura, Seth, Typhon, Iasion, Endymion.
OTHER: Centaur Chiron, Charon, Hotep, Petra, Persephone.

right, Dad? Now, let me send that little Artemis girl over to visit you. She will be thrilled if you pay her some attention. Will you do that just for me, Dad? You wait here. I will send her over!"

With put-upon resignation, Zeus shook his head, "Yes."

Dionysus breathed deeply and made his way over to Hestia, Demeter, and Artemis. "There is no beauty left in the world because it all stands here before me!"

Hestia rolled her eyes, Demeter smiled, Artemis embraced his arm.

Artemis said, "Ghod Dionysus, you look so enticing tonight."

He leaned over and whispered into her ear. "And evidently, so do you Olympian Artemis. Ghod Zeus just told me that he is infatuated with your desirability and must have you! It would please him no end if you joined him right now. Literally!"

Her eyes widened, she looked at Zeus, then at Dionysus, and without a word, scurried over to join Ghod Zeus.

"Such a nice girl," Dionysus said as he turned toward Hestia. "Hephaestus was telling me about some kind of shortage of something called Kopar. I have just gotten back from the eastern frontiers. That's a word I overheard. Would it help you if I could find a source for this stuff?"

Hestia coolly replied, "I have instructed Philyra to resolve that issue, Dionysus."

He replied, "I understand. But it serves me no purpose to please Philyra; only you. I won't interfere."

"And why should Lord Titan Olympian Ghod Dionysus of Everywhere wish to please little ol' me?" she asked, raising an eyebrow.

"Oh, come on, Hestia. You rule this place. I enjoy this Ghod thing even if I would never claim the title. It's good to move around in the center of world power. You hate my guts, so I need to keep myself useful to you."

Hestia chuckled. "Good boy! Find Philyra a source of Kopar. I will order her to reward you handsomely."

"Oh, Sweet Hestia. I simply want to please you! Now, please excuse us. I just heard the horrifying news." He turned his attention to Demeter. "How you are holding up, poor Demeter?"

Demeter suddenly remembering to look distressed, said pitifully, "Not well, Dionysus. I have lost my precious child. I have no hope. I shall try to exist until I find her."

He replied, "I have never experienced the pain of losing a child. I don't know how you bear it."

Hestia, hearing enough, excused herself to go join anyone else.

Dionysus continued. "I know the Elysian Fields area well. That is where it happened, isn't it?"

Demeter forlornly shook her head, "yes."

"I will leave before dawn in the morning to find her. What is your greatest hope for her situation?"

"Maybe some of those awful Oceanid creatures found her and are taking care of her."

"Yes, that would be good. I understand that Hades has a lot of people working in that area. Maybe she wandered into a camp of his. That would be better."

Demeter shuttered at the mention of Hades. "That Hades is disgusting. He said that he wanted to mate with my precious daughter. He is disgusting!"

Dionysus took her by her shoulders, stared at her, and said, "Look at me, woman. ALL men are disgusting! You know that! Raped by your brother! Living with the likes of Ares and Hades! Disgusting, Demeter. Live with it! All women must live with it! But we must do the best we can for sweet maiden Persephone. Do you think you can always protect her from the world?! You have done all a mother can do. She is sweet and unspoiled. She will always be so. If I am to help you, then you must trust me to advise you. You are too close to the situation. You have too much love in your heart. You must trust my advice when I find your daughter. Can you do this?"

She forlornly shook her head, "Yes."

OCEANIDS: Metis, Tyche, Clymene, Eurybia, Amphitrite, Philyra, Rhodos.
TELCHINES: Dexithea, Makelo, Halia.
EAST: Azura, Seth, Typhon, Iasion, Endymion.
OTHER: Centaur Chiron, Charon, Hotep, Petra, Persephone.

He pulled her to him and embraced her. She sobbed. He said, "Hades is no more disgusting than any of the others. Less disgusting, really. In his way, he is an honorable man, the most honorable man in this room. You should judge him by how he feels about your child, not how you feel about him. Besides, maybe she is out with Oceanids learning how to swim. They swim naked you know."

Demeter choked back a laugh. "Right now, that would please me a great deal."

Dionysus squeezed her. "Be brave, Demeter. I will fix this thing. Now, let me give my regards to Poseidon."

He released her, turned, and walked to the group surrounding Poseidon. He held out his arms to Amphitrite, said, "Oceanid Amphitrite, you look stunning," and walked to embrace her.

She looked, tensed, and embraced Poseidon's arm, pulling herself close to him. She made not the slightest motion of accepting his embrace.

Dionysus shifted direction, slightly. *Oops.* He walked to face Poseidon. "Great Ghod Poseidon, you are looking much more powerful since I last saw you. You are certainly growing into this Ghod of the Sea responsibility. You're exceptionally impressive." Dionysus made no motion to look at Amphitrite.

Poseidon replied, "Thank you, Ghod Dionysus. The sea is a mighty adversary. I shall endeavor to be worthy to be its master." He had placed his arm around Amphitrite's waist as if to protect her. She clung to him.

"I won't interfere with your meeting. It was so good to see you, Ghod Poseidon; Amphitrite." He nodded farewell to both and began easing toward the door. He glanced at the long dining table where Aphrodite was on her back entertaining Ares but staring directly at Dionysus. She wore nothing but a smug look of satisfaction.

Zeus and Artemis were nowhere to be seen.

27. Dionysus and CoM3

Dionysus walked down the stairs to Philyra's twelfth-floor apartment. He knocked on her door. The door cracked open. She saw Dionysus standing there and opened the door. "It's late, Dionysus. How can I help you?"

"I'm leaving at sunrise to find Persephone. I want Charon to go with me."

She stood there in silence, then said, "All right. Wait here. I'll get dressed." She closed the door.

He waited, patiently sipping his wine.

The door opened, and Philyra stepped out dressed in full business attire. "All right, his apartment is two floors down. We can walk." She strode into the hallway and began walking.

She glanced at the cup holding his wine. "Is that an Orichalcum cup? They are described in my reports, but I have never seen one. May I?" she asked as she held out her hand to accept it.

He handed it to her. She hefted it as she considered its texture, balance, and weight. "Nice. I could make a fortune trading these to Graikoi. Is wine better from this?" she asked as she lifted the cup to her lips.

"Much, don't you think?" he replied as she handed the cup back and they continued walking. "Those things are all over the place upstairs. Hera has a special one, three times normal size. Hephaestus made them all as gifts for his brothers and sisters. They love him, now. Have you seen Athena's outfit?"

"No. Is it a suit of armor?"

"Yes, complete with helmet and sword. The combination is deadly, but they don't have the stuff necessary to make more. I understand that's your problem. You are to be screamed at until you correct the problem."

She chuckled. "Yes. CoM3 is working on it. Can any of your dactyls help?"

He hesitated. "I think so, and I suspect my search for Persephone will lead me straight into the lair of Ghod Hades and the dactyls. That's why I want COM3 with me. Will he be helpful?"

"Charon thinks on his feet. He is good at presenting a plan as it's forming in his mind. Good intuition. Too clever, maybe. But I own him, at least until he owns me."

"Charon? Is that the server from the cafe I sent up to you?"

"Yes. I owe you. I gave him an opportunity at the thirteenth floor because his name reminds me of my son. It has worked out well."

OCEANIDS: Metis, Tyche, Clymene, Eurybia, Amphitrite, Philyra, Rhodos.
TELCHINES: Dexithea, Makelo, Halia.
EAST: Azura, Seth, Typhon, Iasion, Endymion.
OTHER: Centaur Chiron, Charon, Hotep, Petra, Persephone.

"Your son Chiron is a great resource, Philyra. You should be proud. CoM3 Charon will probably meet Chiron in the morning. Shall I mention that Chiron is your son?"

She considered. "Charon will certainly find a way to use Chiron as leverage over me but I shall never again deny or be embarrassed that Chiron is my son. I visit him each quarter moon. He carries me on his back to Oursea. I owe you much. Do as you will."

They reached the door to Charon's residence. She knocked. In a moment, the door opened -- a little too wide. CoM3 Charon was only half-dressed. Three women sat on the floor, saw who was at the door, and scurried out of sight. "Chief-of-Chiefs, I was not expecting you. I am embarrassed. Step inside while I properly dress. I am having some friends over. I will only be a moment."

She held up her hand for silence. "I would be remiss if I interfered with your well-deserved personal time, CoM3. I will be brief. You know Titan Dionysus, I trust."

"Yes, of course, Great Titan Dionysus of Everywhere. Good evening, Master Titan." From behind the door, a woman's arm handed Charon a large robe which he hastily put on.

"Hello, CoM3 Charon. I am leaving at sunrise on a matter of urgent Port business; potentially M3 business. If you are available, your presence would be a significant help."

"Of course. I will be honored. Sunrise? At Port Transportation?"

"Yes. I will arrange for horses. I believe they will be better than a chariot or wagon."

"Excellent Master Titan. I look forward to serving the company."

Philyra said, "Thank you CoM3. If there is one person I know the Company can depend on, it is you. Continue entertaining. Good evening."

Before Dionysus turned to go, he said to Charon, "Give my regards to Dexithea and her sisters."

Philyra and Dionysus turned and left.

ELDER OLYMPIANS: Hestia, Demeter, Hera, Hades, Poseidon, Zeus
OLYMPIANS: Apollo, Ares, Artemis, Athena, Aphrodite, Dionysus, Hermes,
Hephaestus, Heracles. LIVING TITANS: Oceanus, Tethys, Selene, Elder Oceanids.
DECEASED TITANS: Queen Kiya, Iapetus/Piercer, Cronus.

As Charon closed the door, a Telchine squeal of delight was heard. "Both Philyra and Dionysus! At the SAME time! And he remembered my name!"

Dionysus smiled. -- *bring a little joy!* --

28. Persephone Reborn

Dionysus thought he was arriving early, but Charon was already there talking with his old friend, Port Transportation Manager Abas.

Charon saw Dionysus arrive and said, "Titan Dionysus, you caught me! Abas was instructing me in the art of pony riding! 'Show no fear! Then get on.' I am sure I can do it, especially since Abas handpicked Ponywalk to be my ride. I'm ready to go!"

Dionysus laughed. "Something slow, steady, and capable of carrying my large pouch, Abas."

"Yes, Titan Dionysus. Horsetrot fills the description. She will be a good match with Ponywalk. They like each other."

Dionysus chuckled, "Well, by all means, let's have our mounts like each other."

Abas prepared the two horses, including packing the large traveling pouch on Horsetrot. Business and pleasantries out of the way, the two men rode toward Elysian Fields. "How much do you know about this Persephone business?" Dionysus asked.

Charon replied, "Well, in the interests of serving the Port as best I can, and at the risk of being thrown down the atrium, then I caused it."

"Oh? How is that?"

"I suggested to Hades that he abduct Persephone and told him how to do it. I did it to gain his trust and with it, power. I didn't tell this to Philyra. Not exactly. She can justifiably feign ignorance if asked."

"Hmm."

They talked on about Hades and Persephone, about Elysian Fields, about Asphodel Meadows, about the farmer women and men unknown to most Olympians, about Phlegethon, about ores and metals and smelting, about the potential of Orichalcum for good and evil, about the western frontiers,

OCEANIDS: Metis, Tyche, Clymene, Eurybia, Amphitrite, Philyra, Rhodos.
TELCHINES: Dexithea, Makelo, Halia.
EAST: Azura, Seth, Typhon, Iasion, Endymion.
OTHER: Centaur Chiron, Charon, Hotep, Petra, Persephone.

about the eastern frontiers, and about their new mutual friends, the Telchines.

Charon chuckled. "All three are so innocent, or devious, I can't tell which. They don't actually work for me. They drift between Asphodel Meadows and Phlegethon. They are attracted to dactyls because they love bright and shiny things and Dactyls deal in bright and shiny things. They latched onto me yesterday when I was leaving my meeting with Celmis because 'I'm tall and handsome and look like somebody really important.' How could I resist them?"

Dionysus asked, "Nobody mentioned Hades and the child?"

"No, but neither did I ask. Celmis would not volunteer such information. Hades wasn't around, which I took to be a good thing. Based on what you told me, it looks like Hades was at Asphodel Meadows when your friend Chiron told him that Persephone had passed by. Hades filled his chariot with flowers, found Persephone alone, seduced her into his chariot without Demeter knowing, and away they went. To his lair, as it were. Just like I told him to. I will be his best friend, now, if he remembers me."

Dionysus said, "Yes, now we only need to find the lair, I mean bridal suite. I believe that everything we do and say from this point forward is to establish that Hades is the best possible match for Persephone."

They rode by Asphodel Fields and saw the women working. Dionysus waved, stopped his horse, and took a large flask from his riding pouch. The women recognized him and ran to the fence to greet him. He gave them the flask and hugged the women. Rather than raucous double-entendres, he spoke to them with seriousness. "You have provided significant assistance in this Ghod matter. Thank you."

The women were flattered and made no suggestive comments. They talked together for a while and then Dionysus bid farewell, mounted his horse, and continued on.

Dionysus said, "No need to visit Chiron. The women said they have seen no one since the disappearance. Let's go search Tartarus and then on to Phlegethon."

When they arrived at Tartarus, three Oceanids were busy cleaning the grounds. The two men dismounted and walked to the patio. One of the

ELDER OLYMPIANS: Hestia, Demeter, Hera, Hades, Poseidon, Zeus
OLYMPIANS: Apollo, Ares, Artemis, Athena, Aphrodite, Dionysus, Hermes,
Hephaestus, Heracles. LIVING TITANS: Oceanus, Tethys, Selene, Elder Oceanids.
DECEASED TITANS: Queen Kiya, Iapetus/Piercer, Cronus.

three walked over to greet them. "May I bring you a Sweet or Bitter, Titan Dionysus?" She glanced at Charon and added, "And your friend?"

He answered, "A Bitter for both of us, please. There are flasks of wine in my traveling bag, take one for your future guests and one for the enjoyment of you and your sisters in the evenings."

She thanked him and left to mix their drinks.

When she returned, Dionysus asked her, "We are looking for a man traveling with a young woman, maybe in a chariot. Have you seen anyone like that?"

She replied, "The sisters we replaced mentioned a man and a girl arriving in a chariot a few days ago. They ignored my sisters; not even speaking. They spent the night in Titan Piercers' old dwelling, walked in the fields the next morning, and departed toward Overlook Point in the early afternoon. They were somewhat strange. The girl's mind may not yet have grown to her age. The man was extremely attentive to her. They thought it might be a father with his special child."

Charon asked, "So the child was not distressed in any way?"

She replied, "I didn't ask but my feeling is that they were having a wonderful overnight outing together. Do you wish me to summon my sisters who were here?"

Charon said, "I think I have enough information. What about you, Dionysus?"

Dionysus agreed and turned the conversation to what an outstanding job the current Oceanids were doing both at the Port and here at Tartarus. "The beach to the east is Metis's favorite beach in the world."

The Oceanid's eyes widened. "You know Metis, personally?!"

"Why, yes, I do! Personally!" -- *bring a little wine* -- *bring a little joy* -- *it's what I do* —

They continued talking for a while, then bid farewell.

Dionysus and Charon continued their journey to Overlook Point and then on to Phlegethon. And a lair. They talked as they rode.

OCEANIDS: Metis, Tyche, Clymene, Eurybia, Amphitrite, Philyra, Rhodos.
TELCHINES: Dexithea, Makelo, Halia.
EAST: Azura, Seth, Typhon, Iasion, Endymion.
OTHER: Centaur Chiron, Charon, Hotep, Petra, Persephone.

Charon said, "Well, she's happy, he's happy, everybody's happy except Demeter, she's livid. As I understand it, Demeter is withholding some kind of drink they crave, and she is the only one who knows how to make it. She is making their lives miserable. She doesn't care. She wants her daughter back!"

"So it seems."

"How does this thing play out? What's your plan?"

"I don't know. What's best for CoM3?"

"Things are going well enough. Hades isn't doing much more than wandering around looking at his lands. Hephaestus is a real asset. His metalworking skills improve daily. He is really good and innovative. The new organization chart makes Celmis 'Permanent Temporary Chief' of M3 and Hades his 'Supreme Advisor.' Celmis is actually my direct supervisor. I suppose I should mention that to him, someday. If we could crown Hades king of the underworld and Persephone his queen, we would probably never see him again. He would just wander around and rule with Persephone."

Dionysus muttered, "A wedding? A royal wedding for the King of the Underworld to the Queen of the Colored Fields. Hmm. It's only Demeter that's the problem. Her daughter could be a queen. That might make things more palatable. What do you think? A royal wedding?"

"That works for me."

"Then that's the plan!"

They arrived at Phlegethon in mid-afternoon. Celmis greeted Charon. "CoM3 Charon, you were here only yesterday. Is something wrong?"

Charon replied, "Not at all, Master Dactyl Celmis. I wanted to show my associate, Titan Dionysus, what wonderful work we now do here. He is interested in finding more Tinom for us and he is widely traveled. He would be delighted to assist us." Charon introduced the men to one another, waited while they exchanged pleasantries, and asked, "Is Ghod Hades around? I never see him anymore. I need to pay my respects."

"I believe he is in the mines showing his young friend the colorful stone formations. He takes pleasure in impressing her and making her smile. He takes little interest in our operations and doesn't interfere with our work in the least. Shall I send Idas to find them?"

"No. I don't want to interrupt them. I will see him after the evening meal. You say he treats the girl well? Tell me about them."

Celmis launched into a dialog on Hade's infatuation with Persephone. "She is quite young, but Idas tells me that they mate every day. She seems happy enough. Hades is certainly happy enough." He talked on and on.

Charon said, "Excellent. All seems to be going well under your direction, Celmis. But now, my friend would like to see the Orichalcum workshop and what you do there."

"Of course, CoM3 Charon. Damnameneus is there working with Ghod Hephaestus. Those three young women who were working with Hephaestus disappeared two days ago. They are great when they are here, but they are not at all reliable. Hephaestus prefers the women because they are so creative in fashioning Orichalcum into useful items. They don't really work here but they took up with Hephaestus and know all the words to keep him happy. Damnameneus must step in when the three disappear like this. Ghod Hephaestus is easier to get along with when he has the three women helping instead of Damnameneus. He gets fussed at a lot."

The three walked to the Metals Workshop building, speaking to dactyls and support workers along the way. They entered the building as Hephaestus fussed at Damnameneus about a statue they had cast. "The Orichalcum was not the correct temperature when we poured it. This statue lacks detail. Melt it down, clean the mold, and re-pour it."

Dionysus stared at the contents of the building with wide eyes, absent-mindedly listening to the chatter of the other men. The works of Iapetus and Littlerock lay before him. Bright, shiny unimaginable riches ignored and unappreciated by Hades but prized by Hephaestus. The men talked at length as they fed off the excitement of Dionysus.

Evening mealtime was approaching as the three Telchines ambled into the workshop. "What's going on?" Dexithea asked. Their appearance added to Hephaestus' excitement as he dove into an explanation of the ruined statue of Hades they had all been working on. Makelo examined the statue in question. "Yes, bad casting. No detail. I can't even tell that it's supposed to be Ghod Hades."

OCEANIDS: Metis, Tyche, Clymene, Eurybia, Amphitrite, Philyra, Rhodos.
TELCHINES: Dexithea, Makelo, Halia.
EAST: Azura, Seth, Typhon, Iasion, Endymion.
OTHER: Centaur Chiron, Charon, Hotep, Petra, Persephone.

This encouraged Ghod Hephaestus to once more fuss at Damnameneus.

Finally, Dexithea said, "We're hungry. It was a long trip back from the Port. Are you going to feed us, or what?"

Celmis laughed and said, "May we go to evening meal, Ghod Heph?"

"Yes. I'm hungry, myself. I'll go with you," Hephaestus said, forgetting that he was a Ghod among the lower classes.

They were almost to the dining hall when Hades came running up in a panic. "My Persephone! My beloved Persephone is bleeding to death! Help her whats-your-name! Right now! Help her!"

Idas ran to him and asked, "Is she in your quarters, Ghod Hades? What was she doing?"

Hades answered. "The cave mushrooms were taking effect! We were about to mate, and she started bleeding from between her legs. I couldn't stop it! It's horrible! Somebody save her! Save her right now!"

The three Telchines looked at one another. Dexithea asked, "Is that the little girl I have seen you running around with, Ghod Hades? You were about to couple with her?"

"Yes. Yes. She's dying! Save her!"

Dexithea commanded Idas, "Take us to her! We will take care of this!"

As they hurried away, Makelo said to Charon, "Keep the men calm, Chief. We will send Idas back when we have things under control."

Dionysus took Hades by his left arm and nodded to Hephaestus to take his right. They led the distraught Hades back toward the workshop where they continually consoled him.

Several hours later, Idas hurried into their presence. He pulled Dionysus aside and spoke to him in confidence. "Great Lord Titan, Persephone is being counseled by the Telchines, but I fear there will be a disturbance. The Telchines are piecing together the story of her abduction and the cave mushrooms and the fact that Hades mated with her while she was still a child. Persephone does not fully realize that she has coupled with a man. All three Telchines are furious. Dexithea is enraged. She has a hammer to beat Ghod Hades to death with. I couldn't calm her. Her sisters force themselves to remain calm so that they can continue to explain things to

ELDER OLYMPIANS: Hestia, Demeter, Hera, Hades, Poseidon, Zeus
OLYMPIANS: Apollo, Ares, Artemis, Athena, Aphrodite, Dionysus, Hermes,
Hephaestus, Heracles. LIVING TITANS: Oceanus, Tethys, Selene, Elder Oceanids.
DECEASED TITANS: Queen Kiya, Iapetus/Piercer, Cronus.

Persephone. They are taking her to their camp tonight and counsel her on mating and being a woman, but Dexithea is not fa..."

Dexithea burst into the room carrying a large hammer. "Where is that worthless pond scum-sucking, spawn of a filthy water-dwelling ..."

Dionysus commanded, "CHARON, TAKE HER AWAY! NOW!" Then he took Hades firmly by the arm and said, "Ghod Hades, let us walk in your mines until your precious Persephone can join us."

With both arms, Charon picked Dexithea off the floor and carried her from the building. She spewed words no gentlewoman would know.

Hades blathered in confused distress. "WHAT IS SHE SAYING? WHO IS SHE TALKING TO? WHERE IS MY PERSEPHONE? IS SHE DEAD? WHAT IS A WATER-DWELLING POND ...?"

Dionysus said, "Great news, Ghod Hades! The girl just reported that Persephone is safe and doing well. Did you not hear the excitement in her voice? She was so excited to tell you this good news."

Hades stared blankly at Dionysus. "My sweet Persephone did not bleed to death? She is going to live?"

Dionysus spoke with jubilation. "Oh, much better than that, Ghod Hades. This is wonderful news! This is a wonderful night! Your sister Demeter is going to love you! All your brothers and sisters are going to love you! The path is now clear! I can make everything wonderful with Demeter. She will joyfully serve Ambrosia to all the Ghods. I need only meet with her and explain how overjoyed her sweet daughter Persephone is that she has now become a woman and can be married to Hades. Hades will be King of the Underworld and Persephone will be Queen of the Colored Fields. How did you make these joyful events take place, Ghod Hades? What a genius you are to make all of this happen. Come, let's inspect the beauty of your mines as we rejoice." Dionysus walked Hephaestus and the confused, muttering Hades toward the Phlegethon mines.

Meanwhile, Charon, with both arms wrapped around her, carried the screaming Dexithea from the building. To quieten her he used his only available resource. He kissed her. Forcefully. She tried to shake her lips loose from his, but they seemed to be stuck in some way. She tried to break loose for a few seconds and then accepted what was being forced

OCEANIDS: Metis, Tyche, Clymene, Eurybia, Amphitrite, Philyra, Rhodos.
TELCHINES: Dexithea, Makelo, Halia.
EAST: Azura, Seth, Typhon, Iasion, Endymion.
OTHER: Centaur Chiron, Charon, Hotep, Petra, Persephone.

upon her. She settled down. He removed his lips but kept carrying her in a bear hug.

"Bastard!" she said.

"Me or him?" Charon asked.

"All of you!" she said quietly. "Every last worthless pond scum son of ..."

Charon gently placed his lips on hers as he continued their walk back to where she had come.

The Telchines had made their camp out of sight but near the Phlegethon kilns. This was the crossroads of Dactyl's daily activities. Something exciting was always going on.

It was here that the Telchines took Persephone. Charon and Idas were allowed to stay nearby, but out of sight. This was a night of woman talk in a language unknown to men. Persephone was welcomed into the company of women; with laughter, giggling, and sharing of ancient, secret knowledge known only to women.

It was late in the evening before they allowed themselves to sleep. All but Dexithea. With crossed arms, she walked to the embers of the small fire which Charon and Idas had made nearby. She sat down. "Bastards."

Charon quietly said, "That's well established, Dexithea. What remains is, what do we do now?"

She stared at the embers and then looked at him without expression. "You're CoM3. You tell me."

"We are going to do what's best for Persephone, the absolute best thing that could ever happen to her. But tell me, is she ready to mate? Does she dread it or look forward to it? Does she like Hades or not?"

She considered the questions. "The girl understands her new bodily functions and how to handle all the issues. She understands that her body can make babies whenever she mates. Halia explained the basics of mating. Persephone listened with wide-eyed disbelief, but Halia made it sound wonderful. Halia didn't mention that Persephone had probably been raped every time she ate a cave mushroom. Halia made Persephone promise not to eat a cave mushroom and make Hades mate with her until Hades performed to her satisfaction."

ELDER OLYMPIANS: Hestia, Demeter, Hera, Hades, Poseidon, Zeus
OLYMPIANS: Apollo, Ares, Artemis, Athena, Aphrodite, Dionysus, Hermes,
Hephaestus, Heracles. LIVING TITANS: Oceanus, Tethys, Selene, Elder Oceanids.
DECEASED TITANS: Queen Kiya, Iapetus/Piercer, Cronus.

"Perfect. The pieces are coming together nicely. And Dexithea, don't think of these people as being like you or me. They are different. All of them, including Persephone. They live in an alternate reality. They were born into privilege, wealth, and power and they believe it to be their birthright; that they are better than the lower classes because they are entitled to all they have and everything they want. The Port Olympus Lords, Dionysus, and some others do what we can to insulate the world from these Ghods. But the way is dangerous and never-ending. This whole Hades-Persephone exercise is just one more way of distracting these people. You like excitement, woman. Well, here you are in the center of it! The Ghods don't yet know, but there is to be a royal wedding. King Hades will marry Queen Persephone. It will be grand. We will make it so."

29. Demeter

Dionysus was granted entrance to the floor by the Gigante Guard. He walked to the door of Demeter's apartment, took a deep breath, and knocked. He heard her approach the door, crack it, and then open it wide.

She said, "Hello, Ghod Dionysus. Do you bring me good news?"

Dionysus looked at her and smiled. -- *great ghods, Demeter! -- I have never seen a more pathetic expression -- do you just roll around in self-pity all day?* --

He handed her a package and said, "Good news and my best wine for our celebration! May I come in?"

She forced an 'I hope you can make me happy' smile onto her face, leaned into an embrace he had not offered, and pressed her poor put-upon body against his. He returned the embrace. A Gigante attendant came and took the wine. She led him into her sitting area, and they sat down as the Gigante poured wine into Orichalcum cups. "Now, what good news do you bring me?"

Dionysus leaned toward her, reached out, and took both her hands into his. "Sweet Demeter, imagine a world with me. A world in which your daughter is a grown woman, fulfilled, with place and purpose, ecstatically happy. A world where she is in control; no longer a sweet child to be protected. A world where she is looked up to. A world where she is Queen. Can you imagine this Demeter? Can you make a mother's ultimate sacrifice where you release your child into this world, giving up the

OCEANIDS: Metis, Tyche, Clymene, Eurybia, Amphitrite, Philyra, Rhodos.
TELCHINES: Dexithea, Makelo, Halia.
EAST: Azura, Seth, Typhon, Iasion, Endymion.
OTHER: Centaur Chiron, Charon, Hotep, Petra, Persephone.

completeness that her dependency gives to you? Letting Persephone become independent of you?" He looked deeply into her eyes as he spoke, with compassion, with love, with understanding.

She fell to her knees, placed her head in his lap, and whispered "You have found my daughter, Dionysus. You found her safe?"

"Safe and well-protected by the one you abhor, Demeter. Hades found Persephone wandering around in Tartarus crying her eyes out. She was terrified. She was in the process of becoming a woman and did not know what was happening to her. Hades, of course, had no idea, either. All he saw was the blood. He panicked, placed her in his chariot, and rushed her back to Phlegethon where his staff was. His female staff members quickly assessed the situation, calmed everyone down, and took Persephone to counsel her. It was well into the evening before things returned to normal. The next morning, they ate their morning meal together. Each enchanted with the others' conversation. He took her on a tour of his mines, which she found fascinating, and then on a chariot ride, which she found exhilarating, and then on a tour of the flowers and plants on the mountainside, which he encouraged her to color. By then another day was over and they were both still laughing and talking. Hades may have a strange appearance and strange mannerisms, Demeter, but he is captivated by your daughter. He is a worthy Olympian Ghod. Let your daughter find true happiness. Let her become Queen to King Hades of the Underworld. Please, for her sake."

"He asked her to marry him?"

"He did."

"What did she say?"

"That it would be her joy to marry him if..."

"If I approved?"

Dionysus rose to his feet pulling Demeter with him. He stood her back at arm's length, with his hands on her shoulders, and stared deeply into her eyes. "Yes, Demeter. If her beloved mother will approve."

She choked on a sob and fell into his arms. "I must approve of this Dionysus. It hurts me so much, but I must approve of this." She made no move to do anything more until he removed her clothes.

ELDER OLYMPIANS: Hestia, Demeter, Hera, Hades, Poseidon, Zeus
OLYMPIANS: Apollo, Ares, Artemis, Athena, Aphrodite, Dionysus, Hermes,
Hephaestus, Heracles. LIVING TITANS: Oceanus, Tethys, Selene, Elder Oceanids.
DECEASED TITANS: Queen Kiya, Iapetus/Piercer, Cronus.

He held her tightly and whispered, "You are so brave, Demeter. You are so very, very brave." He then proceeded to reinforce her decision. *-- bring a little wine -- bring a little joy -- it's what I do --*

30. The Wedding

Dionysus stood where Kiya had once stood; on Overlook Point looking south toward Tartarus. The male Ghods stood upon the overlook; save Hephaestus, who commanded the great black stallion, Alastor, who was pulling the chariot in which Hades was standing; waiting for the great wedding procession to begin. Hades was ecstatic because, as he understood it, this would be the most exciting day of his Queen-to-Be's life. Her wedding day! To him!

Beneath Dionysus, on the slope leading to the plains below, stood the lords and their guests. Philyra stood alone on the incline, a few feet below him. On the other side of the sloped road, honored dactyls and Phlegethon workers stood. Behind them stood the hundred-voice choir from Graikoi along with players of musical instruments, and behind them the Briareos cadre of Hecatoncheires. The road up the slope was lined on both sides. Facing Tartarus were two dozen alternating Graikoi nude male and female statues. On the plains below, all the lower-class inhabitants of the island gathered waiting for the procession to begin. Waiting on the pageantry of the glory of the Ghods.

Dionysus heard the great horn sound from distant Tartarus. Too, the sound of drumbeats was heard. *-- it begins -- I am pleased -- everyone wins -- the child, the ghods, the lords, civilization itself -- glory be to the ghods on the highest -- but a world at peace, working together, is an illusion -- the winter solstice festival is next month -- Olympian greed and scorn will rise again -- Hestia will demand large tribute from the east -- from the west -- impose back-breaking trade regulations on them -- not yet a time of war but it will come when Hestia grows her army -- what can I do, great Queen Kiya? --*

In the far distance, the procession could be seen. Three men on hidden wooden stilts twelve feet tall led them. They were followed by jugglers juggling fruits, knives, and axes. Then the drummers came, drumming the cadence. And then the glory of the great black stallion Alastor, prancing, pulling, assured that he was the star of this show. Ghod Hephaestus, stone-faced, looking straight ahead commanded the chariot. Standing

OCEANIDS: Metis, Tyche, Clymene, Eurybia, Amphitrite, Philyra, Rhodos.
TELCHINES: Dexithea, Makelo, Halia.
EAST: Azura, Seth, Typhon, Iasion, Endymion.
OTHER: Centaur Chiron, Charon, Hotep, Petra, Persephone.

beside him, dressed in black but covered with colorful jewelry, the 'is-that-a-smile?' Hades waved to the adoring lower classes. And behind them, to the gasps of the crowd, six matched white horses pulled a white wagon decorated in white material in which rode the Olympian females; all dressed in white. They deemed to wave to the lower classes. With magnificence.

And then came Dexithea, in her flaming red dress, prancing, throwing flowers upon the ground.

At last, in a chariot pulled by four sheep -- flowers braided into their wool -- garlands around their necks -- harnessed in colors pulling on reins of color -- with delicate bells that rang with every step – and, too, with deep ringing bells -- led by Makelo, in her bright yellow dress -- and Halia, in her deep purple dress -- waving to the masses with overwhelming excitement -- Persephone came.

She stood erect in her chariot Her tall headpiece of bright, sparkling Orichalcum was woven with wisteria. Her gown was of endless pieces of Orichalcum cut like flower petals. It glittered and shined in the afternoon sun. It was knee length in the front and segued into a twelve-foot train trailing behind her chariot.

And last, holding the train, came Chiron. He was formally dressed in front, his rear half festooned with flowers and colorful ribbons. He nodded to the crowd, most of whom had never heard of a Centaur.

They each thought -- *what an interesting way to end the procession* --

Dionysus watched as the procession drew closer. He looked to where they had started: Tartarus. -- *Kiya, you built Tartarus because your children had no place to go -- you outgrew it and then had them build you another place -- a mountain – Olympus -- this kept you, your children, and your people happy, content, and fulfilled for all of your lives -- and made the world a better place –*

He thought again, -- *'happy, content, fulfilled?'* –

And then -- *Demeter, how do you and your ilk live and work on three floors of a building? -- why don't you all go insane? -- you don't know any better -- it's all any of you have ever known -- we could build you a new place -- bigger -- better -- gaudier -- away from those you despise -- you would be distracted for years -- kept away from this year's festival -- maybe forever –*

ELDER OLYMPIANS: Hestia, Demeter, Hera, Hades, Poseidon, Zeus
OLYMPIANS: Apollo, Ares, Artemis, Athena, Aphrodite, Dionysus, Hermes, Hephaestus, Heracles. LIVING TITANS: Oceanus, Tethys, Selene, Elder Oceanids. DECEASED TITANS: Queen Kiya, Iapetus/Piercer, Cronus.

He stared toward Tartarus and visualized a tall building rising out of the flat plains. *-- Zeus will be on the top floor, in the sky -- Hades will be on the ground beneath the building, in Tartarus, itself -- Poseidon and Hestia can be in the middle --*

He saw a perfectly circular man-made canal encircle the building with a canal going to the sea for Poseidon. *-- they will be isolated from all mankind -- and love it -- and not even know that it is they who are the outcasts -- the future unfolds before me -- Kiya, you have shown me the way! --*

The procession exited the road at the foot of the hill so that the wedding party could walk the last leg of the journey. Chiron alone noticed that the Graikoi statues slowly turned to follow Persephone up the hill to her wedding place. Centaur Chiron would stand with his mother, Philyra, to watch the ceremony. The three Telchines to stood with the Dactyls. The ceremony was beautiful. It was Halia that first noticed, during the ceremony, that the Graikoi statues were slowly assuming various positions of sexual intercourse.

As the ceremony neared its end, Dionysus took a few steps down the slope to stand beside Philyra and her son.

It ended. The couple turned to face the adoring crowd. The Master of Ceremonies, Ghod Zeus, announced to the world, "I introduce to you Hades, King of the Underworld, with his wife Persephone, Queen of the Colored Fields."

The Graikoi statues had completed their transfigurations. They now modeled the various positions the newlyweds might want to sample.

Dionysus and Philyra applauded with the rest of the crowd.

Dionysus leaned over and said, simply, "Philyra, build me a mountain."

31. The Plan

Kepten seated the four people as the sun appeared on the horizon.

Philyra complimented Charon in front of their peers, "You handled the Persephone kidnapping with great delicacy and effectiveness, Charon. I'm impressed. A Titan could not have done better." She paused, "The wedding removed pressure off Hestia, but she is again demanding I obtain large trade concessions from our partners."

OCEANIDS: Metis, Tyche, Clymene, Eurybia, Amphitrite, Philyra, Rhodos.
TELCHINES: Dexithea, Makelo, Halia.
EAST: Azura, Seth, Typhon, Iasion, Endymion.
OTHER: Centaur Chiron, Charon, Hotep, Petra, Persephone.

Amphitrite produced four Orichalcum cups and an Orichalcum flask from which she filled the cups. "Do not speak of this. Hestia will throw me down the atrium if she finds out that I have it or even know of it. It's from Demeter's newest batch of their secret concoction they call Ambrosia. The Ghod's only whisper of its existence among themselves. Drink it and live forever." She held up her cup to toast.

Dionysus frowned. "Sweet Aunt Amphitrite, you reveal family secrets somewhat loosely."

She laughed. "I have been receiving Grandmother's Red Nectar all my life and you, I suspect, along with Philyra, have been given the formula. The only new ears here belong to our newest best friend, CoM3 Charon. He, as I understand it, has proven his worthiness several times over."

Charon knew well when to look discreet and keep his mouth shut.

The remaining three held up their cups. Amphitrite lifted hers and said, "To long life!" She then sat back and said, "All right, Dionysus. You called this meeting for this unghodly hour. What are we to do?"

Dionysus described his vision of the building dedicated only to the Ghods rising over the plains of Tartarus. "Philyra would have to use her resources in actual design and building this project but this I believe, if the Ghods can be convinced of their glory in this project, it will distract them from interfering with Port negotiations and operations for years. Maybe forever. I propose that we casually ask our personal Ghod friends what they think of such a project and make sure that they believe that it was their idea. I can handle Dad and Demeter. Charon is comfortable with Hades and Hephaestus. Amphitrite can influence Poseidon. The only major person left would be Hestia. She has the most to lose and will be the toughest to convince. I suggest that we three begin influencing our Ghods before Philyra officially hears of this concept. If our Ghods start after Hestia to build such a thing, then she will have to go to Philyra for advice. Philyra can play as dumb or as smart as needed."

Dionysus looked at Philyra and said, "Chief, I know you have your hands full. You just came off this wedding thing and your office is still overrun with Graikoi officials and guests, and you have to negotiate everybody's trade negotiations, and you have to entertain the western world next month at the Winter Solstice Festival. Should we move with haste, slowly, or forget the entire concept as a bad idea?"

ELDER OLYMPIANS: Hestia, Demeter, Hera, Hades, Poseidon, Zeus
OLYMPIANS: Apollo, Ares, Artemis, Athena, Aphrodite, Dionysus, Hermes,
Hephaestus, Heracles. LIVING TITANS: Oceanus, Tethys, Selene, Elder Oceanids.
DECEASED TITANS: Queen Kiya, Iapetus/Piercer, Cronus.

Philyra replied, "The trade negotiations last year were an unmitigated disaster. We lost respect and influence. None of the western ports are eager to go through that again and I don't want to promise what I can't deliver. Hestia still doesn't accept the fact that trade is a partnership. Port Olympus connects the eastern and western worlds. Trade through us is beneficial to all concerned. But when we become a liability instead of an asset, it's all over for the port. Hestia thinks she can enforce her will on the world with a war machine. Maybe she can but the Port will not be part of that. I will play dumb until Hestia calls me in. I say, go as fast as you can with your little project."

"May I see you after hours, Chief Philyra?" Dionysus asked.

"No, you may not. Work on this great plan of yours! And now, give my kindest regards to Kepten for the courtesies he extended us. I need to get to work. Thank you all for the meeting and your excellent drink, Oceanid Amphitrite. Charon, do you wish to stay or ride up with me?"

Charon hesitated.

Dionysus stood and said, "Thank you for coming Charon. We work well together."

Amphitrite stood and announced, "I can't let the love of my life hear that I was sitting alone by the sea with a tall good-looking Titan." She touched Dionysus on the shoulder, looked at him with an odd intensity, and said, "Grandmother is proud, Dionysus. By the way, you usually come alone to the Olympian parties, but it would be helpful if you escort an attractive young commoner next time. It's such fun to play with men's combative instincts."

They then left Dionysus alone at his favorite table. -- *bring a little wine…*

32. The Olympians
< Year 100, 12th Month >

They arrived at the entrance to the rooftop and were met by the Gigante doorman. Dionysus greeted him with, "Good evening, Gigante Polybotes," then leaned over and whispered into his ear.

Polybotes walked to the entrance of the party and loudly announced, "Great Olympian Ghods, I present Olympian Ghod Dionysus of Everywhere escorting Telchine Dexithea of Phlegethon Mines.".

OCEANIDS: Metis, Tyche, Clymene, Eurybia, Amphitrite, Philyra, Rhodos.
TELCHINES: Dexithea, Makelo, Halia.
EAST: Azura, Seth, Typhon, Iasion, Endymion.
OTHER: Centaur Chiron, Charon, Hotep, Petra, Persephone.

Dexithea trembled with excitement. She curtsied to the Olympians. -- *how can this be? -- I am here at the pinnacle of all things – me – Dexithea -- they know that I am lower than pond scum -- that I am disgusting -- but here I am -- Dexithea of Phlegethon -- if I die now -- I die happy -- I HAVE LIVED! --*

Several Olympians nodded a welcome. Several turned up their nose. Queen Persephone started to run over and embrace her friend, but King Hades took her arm and nodded for her to wait beside him.

Dionysus extended his arm to Dexithea and escorted her toward the King and Queen, discretely tracking to see if any of the Ghods might try to physically interfere with a lower-class commoner approaching a Ghod. But even Athena and Hera were accepting. This woman, they knew, had been the flower bearer in Persephone's wedding and it had been her that had excitedly brought the wonderful news to Ghod Hades that his beloved Persephone was indeed safe.

Dexithea arrived, curtsied before the Queen, and removed a small bouquet of narcissus from her purse along with a small, flat, circular piece of Orichalcum. She handed them to Persephone. "For my Queen," she said as she curtsied again.

Persephone was delighted. She accepted them and looked around for her mother who hurried over. "Will you put these flowers into water, Mother? They are from a friend." She then asked, "And what is this?" as she examined the piece of Orichalcum.

Dexithea replied, "I call it a 'Ghod Coin.' My friend Ghod Heph gives me leftover Orichalcum from his creations. Another friend carved a likeness of you and a likeness of narcissus out of wood. I made impressions of each out of clay and poured Orichalcum into each impression. I pressed them together and after it cools, I have a Queen Persephone Ghod Coin. I made many to give to my friends and everyone who is nice to me. Would you want some of these for yourself?"

Persephone stared at the coin with wide eyes, "Yes. Many."

Demeter exclaimed, "I want one, too. I want many!"

Dexithea took two from her little black purse, handed one to Demeter, one to Hades, and said, "I will send you many."

Dionysus watched and listened to the exchange intently and with amusement. *-- your 'coins' are better than my little circular engraved rock, Telchine -- much better -- you have outdone yourself -- and the ghods are infatuated with them -- you have created something new and desirable -- good work! --*

He spoke to Hades, "Marriage becomes both of you, Ghod Hades. I have never seen either of you so radiant or so happy."

The four talked on for a while and then Dionysus bid them both "unending happiness." He took Dexithea's arm, tugged on it, and pulled the reluctant Telchine away.

He quickly surveyed the room. Amphitrite made no motion of welcome. *--- Aphrodite would love to do battle with this young, upstart, outgoing, self-confident Telchine -- but no good could come of that -- where to, Dionysus, where to? --*

Dexithea saw Hephaestus alone and they walked to him, "Ghod Heph, you old metal-master you. How are you?" She handed him a Ghod Coin. "Look what you can make out of your Orichalcum!"

Dionysus relaxed. This evening will go all right. He excused himself and left the two talking.

He saw Demeter standing alone. He walked to her, embraced her, and kissed her on the cheek. "I had a lovely time the last time we were alone. Are you doing well?"

"Well enough; for a woman without husband or child. I, too, enjoyed your company. Call me again. Anytime."

"I shall. But you need to get out more. You stay in these cramped quarters surrounded by no men but your brothers. Disguise yourself. I will take you into the planting fields. You love the earth, the harvests. I will get a little wine in you. Many men would fight for your company in a plowed field."

She laughed. "I see that you are a dirty old man, too, Titan. But at least you amuse me."

"Resign yourself to traveling with low-class people, Demeter. Dress in inferior clothes. You are no longer tied down here. I will send you home with my new friend over there. She is intelligent, talented, and can always find excitement. Go with her. It will do you good. You have lived in your

OCEANIDS: Metis, Tyche, Clymene, Eurybia, Amphitrite, Philyra, Rhodos.
TELCHINES: Dexithea, Makelo, Halia.
EAST: Azura, Seth, Typhon, Iasion, Endymion.
OTHER: Centaur Chiron, Charon, Hotep, Petra, Persephone.

cramped, isolated quarters for far too long. Get out. You might even have fun. I will call you. Let me go say hello to Dad."

She tightly embraced him goodbye. Again, she said, "Anytime."

Dionysus walked to disengage Dexithea who was now in animated conversation with Athena. It had been Dexithea who had helped Hephaestus fashion Athena's suit of armor. She could point to every detail and was actively interested in Athena's every comment and criticism. The three of them fed off each other. Dexithea said, "You two are going to need a much larger space to display all the wonderful things that Ghod Heph is going to make for the Olympians. Much more space."

Concern flowed through Dionysus. -- *much more space? -- where did that come from? -- Charon? --*

Aphrodite sidled up and took Dionysus by the arm, pressing her breasts into his arm. "Introduce me to this sweet young thing, Dionysus. Do you find her talented?"

Dionysus replied, "Hello, Aphrodite."

Dexithea turned and looked at Aphrodite with wide eyes. "Aphrodite? Ghod Aphrodite? The most beautiful and desirable woman in the world? I would give anything to be like you! Would you teach me things?"

Aphrodite had expected disdain, not adulation. She laughed a sincere laugh of merriment. "Dear, you must join me tonight on the table. I usually prefer males, but you are quite lovely and interesting. Do join me."

Dionysus said, "No! Dexithea came with me. She will stay with me, and she will leave with me."

Aphrodite said, "Ohhh! Jealousy raises its little head. You must have something special, Dexithea." As Aphrodite turned to leave, she turned back toward Dexithea, smiled seductively, winked, and said, "Come to me tonight. I will teach you things." She looked at Dionysus, smirked, and ambled off.

From the corner of his eye, Dionysus noticed the stares of Ares, Poseidon, and Zeus. "Excuse us from this delightful gathering but I must say hello to Dad. Say goodnight to your friends, Dexithea, and come with me." He took her hand and pulled her toward Zeus. She turned back toward Aphrodite and with her free hand, waved goodbye.

ELDER OLYMPIANS: Hestia, Demeter, Hera, Hades, Poseidon, Zeus
OLYMPIANS: Apollo, Ares, Artemis, Athena, Aphrodite, Dionysus, Hermes, Hephaestus, Heracles. LIVING TITANS: Oceanus, Tethys, Selene, Elder Oceanids. DECEASED TITANS: Queen Kiya, Iapetus/Piercer, Cronus.

They approached Zeus's gathering. Dionysus stopped suddenly, crouched down, held out his arms, and said "Dad. I love you. Do you love me?" He then scurried to Zeus for his embrace and exchange of declarations of love. Ares looked disgusted; Poseidon bored; until Dexithea walked up.

She looked up wide-eyed at Zeus and said, "Is this your father, Dionysus? He is even more handsome and desirable than you said. I see why the women can't keep their hands off him. May I have him?"

Zeus was at a momentary loss for words.

She continued, "Your brother Hades is King of the Underworld and has a big, wide world for his kingdom. You are King of the Heavens. You need a great big, huge castle high in the sky where everybody can see you and you can see everybody." She looked at him with wide eyes.

Dionysus said, "Humph. Dexithea, you now know my father. This is his brother, Poseidon, and his son, Ares." -- *more space?* -- *still at it, Dexithea?* --

Dexithea smiled politely at Ares but went into full, "I am woman -- you are MAN," mode with Poseidon. Her breasts actually heaved. "Ghod Poseidon, King of the Ocean, the unbelievably large, unending ocean. Oh my, what a large castle you will need. It will be so big I will wander in it for days and never find you. Maybe don't build one quite that big. All right?" She stared at him with wide-eyed adulation. He stared back.

She handed each of them a Ghod Persephone Coin as she said, "I simply must make these with your likeness engraved upon it."

Amphitrite came walking over. "My manly-men. It looks like this sweet young thing could stand some reinforcements." She squeezed in beside Poseidon and took his arm. "Right, dear?" The two women exchanged long, hard stares.

Dexithea answered, "Riight."

Dionysus said, "I need to get my friend home. Aphrodite appears to be warming up the table. Dexithea has never beheld these things nor should she. Good night, all." He pulled Dexithea away by her hand.

Dexithea turned to look longingly at the action now starting on the table and said, "No. I haven't, but I would love to." But she obediently followed Dionysus toward the exit.

OCEANIDS: Metis, Tyche, Clymene, Eurybia, Amphitrite, Philyra, Rhodos.
TELCHINES: Dexithea, Makelo, Halia.
EAST: Azura, Seth, Typhon, Iasion, Endymion.
OTHER: Centaur Chiron, Charon, Hotep, Petra, Persephone.

Near the exit, Hestia drifted from the shadows, wine cup in hand. "Hello, Dionysus, who is your pretty little friend?" -- *be careful, Dexithea -- this is the enemy -- THE enemy --*

He replied, "Hello, Chief Ghod Hestia. This is my friend, Dexithea. She works with Ghod Hephaestus at the Phlegethon site. She is talented and creative. One of the forces driving the production of Orichalcum products. She is a commoner but an especially useful commoner for the company." -- *are you drunk, Hestia? -- not tipsy -- drunk! --*

He glanced at Dexithea for her reaction to Hestia's over-familiarity.

Dexithea stared at Hestia as a professional, valued employee being introduced to her respected supervisor.

-- you know, don't you, Dexithea? -- you know office politics right down to who to smile at and who to ignore -- Charon has trained you, hasn't he sweet? -- he briefed you on every one of us -- including me -- in great detail -- you can play each one of us like an aulos. --

He said, "Dexithea has my utmost confidence and respect." *-- you flinched, Telchine -- did that comment catch you off guard? -- you are on the top floor -- to stay here, never be caught off guard -- never flinch --*

Hestia said to Dexithea, "I'm glad to hear that. We need only the best people working for us. Join me for a cup of wine. I would enjoy your company."

Dionysus said coldly, "She came with me, Hestia. She leaves with me."

Hestia shrugged and said, "As you will, Sweet." Hestia then looked at Dexithea and said, "A pleasure to meet you, pretty Dexithea."

Dionysus turned to leave but Dexithea had locked her eyes with Hestia's and made no motion to join him.

Dexithea finally said, "Actually, Dionysus, I would like to stay with my new best friend, Hestia -- for a cup of wine."

Dionysus looked at her, then at smug Hestia. He nodded acquiescence. *-- be careful, Dexi -- you are on the top floor -- there are monsters here --*

He left the party and slowly walked down the many flights of stairs.

ELDER OLYMPIANS: Hestia, Demeter, Hera, Hades, Poseidon, Zeus
OLYMPIANS: Apollo, Ares, Artemis, Athena, Aphrodite, Dionysus, Hermes,
Hephaestus, Heracles. LIVING TITANS: Oceanus, Tethys, Selene, Elder Oceanids.
DECEASED TITANS: Queen Kiya, Iapetus/Piercer, Cronus.

33. Black Underwear

The cafe was closed but Dionysus took advantage of his status and let himself in. He commandeered a flask of wine and sat sipping for a long time. -- I *left you at the party with Hestia – it's getting late – still no sign of you --this can't be good!* --

He heard familiar footsteps approach but did not look up from his reverie, He reached into his satchel, produced another cup, and said, "Are you tired Philyra? You know not to be tired or ask for quarter. But are you very tired?"

"Yes, Dionysus. In a just world, a loving, understanding man would take me into his arms and hold me tightly. He would say, 'Poor Philyra. You try so hard, and you do so well.' He would gently remove my clothes and mount me, taking away the weight of the world, taking us both to the heights of paradise."

"So, let's do that!"

"I will drink your wine, Dionysus, and I will consider the other."

"It always ends, Philyra. Are you upset? I mean, *really* upset or just upset?"

"You mean about me and Hestia? How did you know?"

"Kiya once told me, 'Listen quietly and the stars will tell you everything.' So, now I listen to stars."

"Did the stars tell you why she was so furious with me?"

"Ahh, so this is only a lover's quarrel, not the end of a romance. Good. And no, she told me nothing, but I suspect she has been telling my friend, Dexithea, quite a bit the last few hours."

Philyra sipped her wine. "I think I shall be cast off soon enough. Hestia has been fuming ever since the wedding was announced. It took the Ghod's attention off the upcoming trade demands and focused it on a 'useless, dung-filled wedding between idiots.' Her fury came to a head last week when I suggested she go easy on demands this year and give the Port time to recover from last year's disastrous negotiations. I have been expecting the Atrium every day, since. I had a wonderful time as Chief-of-Chiefs, Dionysus. Thank you for making me so."

OCEANIDS: Metis, Tyche, Clymene, Eurybia, Amphitrite, Philyra, Rhodos.
TELCHINES: Dexithea, Makelo, Halia.
EAST: Azura, Seth, Typhon, Iasion, Endymion.
OTHER: Centaur Chiron, Charon, Hotep, Petra, Persephone.

"It's not over, Philyra. We don't yet fully understand the enemy, even who the enemy is. There is still the matter that Dexithea knew things that she should not have known. Hestia was drunk. I have never seen her drunk. And one of Charon's most faithful friends just happened to be available for seduction. How can Charon benefit from all of this? The answer is obvious, he would be your replacement!"

"I trust Charon. He would not betray me. Your Telchine women are extremely intelligent, quick, and seek all things exciting plus they have ongoing access to Hades in general and Hephaestus whenever they want. Therein lies their source of knowledge. They play their own games of intrigue. They may be thirteenth-floor material. Who appears to be coming out on top of this chaos? Telchines."

"Yes, that's all true. But tell me, Sweet Philyra, exactly how did you know about the Telchines?"

"Amphitrite told me. We gossip all the time. We are the only confidant each other has. She met them at the wedding and adopted them. She said, 'They are so like Sister Metis but more earthy, more full of life, more ambitious.' She meets them at Gigante City Cafe for lunch each quarter moon."

They stared at one another and said simultaneously, "Amphitrite!"

Dionysus said, "It is not yet time to take you to paradise. You are still standing. The stars have told me so! Here, have more wine! And no, you may not yet have me!"

~ Reconciliation ~

With hope, fear, resignation, and the setting sun, Philyra entered the Fifteenth floor. Her only guidance for the upcoming meeting had been a cryptic note from Amphitrite, "We are winning! Check the sofa for underwear!"

Philyra announced to the doorman, "Chief-of-Chiefs Philyra to see Ghod Hestia." She was immediately escorted into Hestia's office.

Hestia looked up from her desk, smiled broadly, rose, walked to Philyra with outstretched arms, put her hands on Philyra's shoulders, and said, "Philyra, how wonderful to see you." She moved her fingertips down Philyra's shoulders. "Come, let's sit on the sofa this evening. Our workday

ELDER OLYMPIANS: Hestia, Demeter, Hera, Hades, Poseidon, Zeus
OLYMPIANS: Apollo, Ares, Artemis, Athena, Aphrodite, Dionysus, Hermes,
Hephaestus, Heracles. LIVING TITANS: Oceanus, Tethys, Selene, Elder Oceanids.
DECEASED TITANS: Queen Kiya, Iapetus/Piercer, Cronus.

has almost ended, and I have so much to command you to do. I hope that it meets with your approval, but regardless, the other Ghods and I have discussed it all day and this is what I command you to do." Hestia launched into her list of demands.

Philyra listened intently. -- *what happened last night? -- she is demanding more than I ever dreamed of asking for -- this is unbelievable -- be careful -- I am on shifting ground --*

Hestia finished. "Do you fully support the demands of the Ghods?"

"The wisdom of the Ghods is greater than all things. Of course, all Lords will support this and make it happen to your satisfaction. Thank you for your wisdom, Chief Olympian Ghod Hestia."

Hestia said, "Don't be so formal, Philyra. The workday has ended. Everyone has gone but us. Perhaps we can have a cup of wine and relax."

Philyra reached between the sofa cushions and pulled out a strip of black leather underwear. She held it up for Hestia to see. "I don't seem to remember this."

Hestia snatched it away, laughed, and said, "Let's don't worry about that meaningless little thing."

Philyra stared at Hestia, made a split-second decision, gently kissed her, and said, "Bribe me with a glass of wine."

Hestia laughed with relief.

~ Port Olympus Memorandum ~

From: Port Olympus CoC Philyra

To: All Lords of Port Olympus Departments

Subject: Expansion Building Project

Port Olympus Building overcrowding has reached unsustainability.

Effective immediately, dedicate your department to conceptualizing, designing, building, and furnishing a new building to provide office, residential, and entertainment space for the Olympian Ghods.

This will free the three entire upper floors they currently occupy for expansion by the Lords and their subjects.

OCEANIDS: Metis, Tyche, Clymene, Eurybia, Amphitrite, Philyra, Rhodos.
TELCHINES: Dexithea, Makelo, Halia.
EAST: Azura, Seth, Typhon, Iasion, Endymion.
OTHER: Centaur Chiron, Charon, Hotep, Petra, Persephone.

The new building will be named "Olympus Towers" and be built at the abandoned Tartarus location.

It will be twice as high as the Port Olympus building which is already fourteen floors higher than any building known to exist.

The building must be suitable for Olympian Ghod Zeus, "King of the Heavens," so that he may observe birds flying by.

The needs of Olympian Ghod Poseidon, "King of the Sea" must also be met. This will include, but not be limited to, a circular canal surrounding the building with sea-going access.

The building will include ample residential space for each current Ghod with consideration for expansion.

A glorious entertainment space must be provided for their relaxation away from the day-to-day demands inherent with their responsibilities of being Ghods.

Consideration for large support staff and guards must be met.

This important project supersedes all other projects and commands your total attention. Lessor projects including, but not limited to, upcoming trade negotiations, Winter Solstice Festival representation, and hosting tasks will be relegated to our lower managers, as is befitting their relative importance. This will be a good training experience for them.

Our first planning meeting will be held at sunrise in two days. You will spend the next quarter moon in meetings and have a draft plan by the new moon.

Everyone will spend the entire month of the Winter Solstice Festival here, working non-stop, to finalize our plan, and, after approval by the Ghods, begin implementation.

This project is of such importance that the Ghods, themselves, have graciously agreed to meet with us on an as-needed basis to guide our thoughts and plans, and to provide inspiration.

Your immediate and dedicated attention to this urgent matter is expected and required.

s/ CoC Oceanid Philyra

ELDER OLYMPIANS: Hestia, Demeter, Hera, Hades, Poseidon, Zeus
OLYMPIANS: Apollo, Ares, Artemis, Athena, Aphrodite, Dionysus, Hermes,
Hephaestus, Heracles. LIVING TITANS: Oceanus, Tethys, Selene, Elder Oceanids.
DECEASED TITANS: Queen Kiya, Iapetus/Piercer, Cronus.

34. Gossip

It was late, extremely late.

Philyra knocked on the door to Amphitrite's apartment. She was surprised when Amphitrite answered. "I thought you would be sleeping with Poseidon," Philyra offered.

"No, no, come in, Sweet. I took the night off. I left him with Nerites. Too much of a good thing is destructive. I must maintain a balance with my availability. I received your memorandum. It was written more for the Ghods than for your staff, but everyone will get the picture. It's a rather ambitious schedule. Can it be accomplished?"

She led Philyra to her sofa, sat her down, and then retrieved a flask of wine and two cups. She sat down beside Philyra.

"Oh, my, no! There is no way any of that will happen. The Port doesn't have any of the design resources, more or less the building resources but we have bought six weeks. So, how did you do it?"

Amphitrite laughed. "I'm supposed to say, 'Do what, Sweet?' and then we banter back and forth until we get to the truth of it. But first, let me ask you, what made you suspect that I might have a hand in it?"

"Dionysus, of course. His new friend was simply too aware of everything going on; too briefed on the situation. He wanted to blame Charon, but I didn't think so. I then told him of your friendship with the three Telchine women. Dexithea's source of information was then obvious. You had already set things up so that Dionysus would be inclined to bring an attractive escort, a commoner exactly like one of the Telchine sisters. Hestia was drunk and susceptible. Most uncommon. Black leather underwear? How did you arrange all that? Plus, over one night, Hestia changed her mind completely and passionately about the building project. And so, the question remains; how did you do it?"

Amphitrite leaned back, sipped her wine, and was silent. They both drank in silence for a long time.

Amphitrite began. "Know yourself -- know your enemy -- gather information -- plan for all things -- be good -- be wise -- bring hope to all

OCEANIDS: Metis, Tyche, Clymene, Eurybia, Amphitrite, Philyra, Rhodos.
TELCHINES: Dexithea, Makelo, Halia.
EAST: Azura, Seth, Typhon, Iasion, Endymion.
OTHER: Centaur Chiron, Charon, Hotep, Petra, Persephone.

-- be prepared for victory -- be prepared for defeat --accept either with grace and dignity."

She was silent for a while longer. "There is a direct line from Hestia's mouth to my ear. Its name is Poseidon. You were close to being thrown down the atrium, Philyra. It was my Poseidon who saved you. He told Hestia, 'Let them have their puny little wedding. We have a lifetime, a long lifetime, to bend the savages to our will. Life is better for you and me when our brothers and sisters are happy. This wedding dung makes them all happy. It entertains them.' Demeter is back to making Ambrosia. That was a big issue, now solved because of a wedding for her simple daughter. I hate that she had the three chemists killed so that it would be only Demeter who knew how to make Ambrosia. Hestia realized quickly that she, too, must learn the recipe rather than just relying on Demeter. Encourage Demeter to teach it to her worthy daughter so you can trick it out of Persephone like Hestia tricked the Red Nectar recipe out of Artemis."

Amphitrite continued. "Hestia and Poseidon went on and on, but you get the gist. Besides, Poseidon likes you and doesn't want you dead. You best be prepared to surrender your virginity to him; maybe to both of us at the same time. Be prepared if the time comes. He wants Dexi, too, but he doesn't want to annoy Hestia by taking her."

She sipped her wine and continued. "At the least, Hestia was going to remove you the day after the Olympian party. She intended to promote Nerites to your position; a tragedy on so many levels I don't even want to discuss it. Didn't Dionysus wonder how the three Telchines happened to be at the Port Cafe on the afternoon of the Olympian party that night?"

"No, he didn't."

"You should review your port transportation reports. A fast chariot was sent to Phlegethon three nights ago. The chariot returned with three excited Telchines who spent the night in my apartment. I told them the plan we wished Hestia to command, the reasons she should command it, and how to drive home their demands. They came to me as wild but innocent young women embracing life to its fullest. They left me as weapons of war."

"Oh."

ELDER OLYMPIANS: Hestia, Demeter, Hera, Hades, Poseidon, Zeus
OLYMPIANS: Apollo, Ares, Artemis, Athena, Aphrodite, Dionysus, Hermes,
Hephaestus, Heracles. LIVING TITANS: Oceanus, Tethys, Selene, Elder Oceanids.
DECEASED TITANS: Queen Kiya, Iapetus/Piercer, Cronus.

They sipped their wine.

Amphitrite said, "I went to Hestia's office early. I engaged her in sparkling conversation and shared my exquisite flask of wine. To be an engaging conversationalist simply say, 'Your conversation is so interesting. I can listen to you talk for hours; here, have some more wine.' Even I was a bit tipsy when I left, and I had drunk only half of what Hestia had drunk plus I left her with a full cup. I peppered the conversation with variations of my rather sensuous adventures with Nitrates and Poseidon, which she enjoyed."

Amphitrite paused, provided wine refills, then continued her story. "Rule Number Two: 'Know your enemy.' Do you know everything about Hestia? If you did, you would know that she is tormented with guilt. She comes to you for love and adoration. Where does she go for the punishment she so desperately wants and deserves? I said to Dexithea at the party, 'Right, Dear?' It was my signal that if she could become involved with Hestia and inflict maximum pain. Dexithea responded 'Riight,' meaning, 'I understand.' A person wanting punishment appears to adore skimpy black leather underwear and leather whips. I happened to have these things; I don't remember exactly why. But I gave them to Dexithea, along with instructions, before she met Dionysus."

She continued, "Hestia didn't question why Dexithea happened to have a little black whip and binding rope in her purse along with a blindfold. When Dexithea came to my apartment early yesterday morning after laying with Hestia, she told me that getting the hang of the whip wasn't that difficult and it was all much more fun than one might think. She told me that Hestia was punished severely for her coming betrayal of her faithful lover, Philyra, and for not providing her siblings with the magnificent living quarters they all deserved but weren't smart enough to know it. The callous killing of her grandmother wasn't even addressed."

"If you had miscalculated, Dexithea would have been tortured before she was thrown down the atrium. Probably limbs pulled off one at a time."

"That is exactly what I told the girls during their training. Do you know what they all three said? 'What a way to die!'"

OCEANIDS: Metis, Tyche, Clymene, Eurybia, Amphitrite, Philyra, Rhodos.
TELCHINES: Dexithea, Makelo, Halia.
EAST: Azura, Seth, Typhon, Iasion, Endymion.
OTHER: Centaur Chiron, Charon, Hotep, Petra, Persephone.

35. The Port Graikoi Delegation

Nerites led the visiting Graikoi wedding performers to the docks to greet the ship bringing in the Graikoi dignitaries and trading staff. Nerites had been charged with entertaining all who had performed at the wedding, and he understood full well, that he was performing damage control from last year's disaster. These were low-ranking entertainers, but Graikoi leadership valued their entertainers and would want to know how they were treated. Nerites' nightly reports were read and reread by every Lord to glean every possible bit of information they could before sitting down with the Graikoi trade negotiators.

The trade delegation debarked and was met with carriages, wagons, and chariots to transport them to guest houses. They were served wine and other drinks by young port staff women wearing short, lightweight dresses even though the air was cool.

Dionysus took note that among the delegation were two sons of Titans Iapetus and Clymene, named Atlas and Meoetius. -- *they may be of use -- but titans can't be overjoyed to be in the land of Olympians -- why did they come? --*

Loaded, transported, and checked in, all were informed that they would be fed and entertained on the Port Cafe outdoor patio that evening.

They began arriving early that evening. Kepten was in his element as he commanded his staff to their peak performance of attentiveness, responsiveness, bottomless wine cups, and endless food trays. Talented Oceanids harmonized to upbeat sounds of musical instruments. Two Graikoi 'statues,' courtesy of negotiations by Nerites, stood motionless in the middle of the patio frozen into positions of a nude couple displaying obvious remorse over some unknown disagreement. A cool, gentle wind blew in off the moonlit sea.

Dionysus, too, was in his element. Flitting from table to table, bringing laughter and joy to all.

Kepten signaled Amphitrite that Prince Periphas and his party were arriving.

Amphitrite nodded. -- *Father, I hope to make you proud -- let me do well -- Mother, I am a common whore -- but I shall do what I must do -- I shall do what is right --*

She with her back to Oursea. On her far left sat Philyra. The chair between them was for Dionysus. They looked down the long table which formed a tee with their own table. The prince and his dignitaries would be seated there. They would all have residual indignation from their treatment at last year's meeting. Trade with Graikoi had fallen to nearly nothing. This night was dedicated to re-establishing positive relations.

Kepten began seating the guests at the table, seating the prince and his consort last. Dionysus appeared from behind and seated the consort with his most charming smile, greeted the prince, moved to stand behind his own chair at the head of the table, and made an eloquent welcoming speech. Wine was served before he was finished; a toast to past and future friendships made.

Everyone chatted away with official cordiality. The prince spoke. "You know of our difficulties last year. We would not be here this year were it not for my once-dearest friend Oceanid Amphitrite. I sneered when she came to my court asking for our wedding planners to stage a great wedding between two of your Olympians. This, after she had left her place at Port Graikoi to take up with an Olympian. It was a great deal to ask of me, even from a once-dear friend. I denied her three times. Did she tell you that she fell to her knees and begged me, in front of my court, in front of her once-admirers, to help her with this wedding, to send this delegation to these trade negotiations? Did you tell them those things, Oceanid Amphitrite? Did you tell them that your sister, the Great Oceanid Metis, looked upon you, spat out, 'Whore,' and left us? Did you tell them that the only reason these things came to pass is that you begged me, on your knees, in front of my court?"

Amphitrite laughed. "I did NOT tell them, sweet Periphas. I would never take away your joy in sharing these things. And, you are correct, my beloved sister Metis is angry with me. Yet, here you are, enjoying the hospitality of Olympian Dionysus and Chief-of-Chiefs Philyra. Oh. Look! I think those statue things have moved."

All, except Dionysus, turned to look at the Graikoi statues which had imperceptibly shifted their pose and position to create various poses of supplication toward the Graikoi prince. Dionysus kept eating and drinking as if he had heard nothing. Finally, he stood and said, "Well, that was delicious. I trust everyone enjoyed it. Now, I must excuse myself. I have

OCEANIDS: Metis, Tyche, Clymene, Eurybia, Amphitrite, Philyra, Rhodos.
TELCHINES: Dexithea, Makelo, Halia.
EAST: Azura, Seth, Typhon, Iasion, Endymion.
OTHER: Centaur Chiron, Charon, Hotep, Petra, Persephone.

things to attend to." -- *you will find me -- you bottom-feeding, scum-dwelling, son of a mindless slug -- I know you will!* --

He left but whispered to a statue in passing.

Philyra took over the conversation as hostess.

They finished their meal with cool, but official, cordiality. Philyra announced that there would be music, dancing, and drinks on the dock until no one remained. They rose to leave and noticed that the statues had imperceptibly shifted their pose to one of retreating defeat.

Dionysus stood sipping fine wine leaning against a rail at the edge of the dock directly beneath the patio. He was surrounded by three weapons of war, each with a different plan. The band was playing a fast song and the singers were singing. The guests began drifting down. Dionysus and his weapons did not look at the guests but continued to stare out over the bay, ignoring the crowd. After a while, the drummer inserted an unexpected riff into their song. Dionysus said, "He is on his way. Improvise as you go. I hope you find this exciting!"

The prince and two of his chief negotiators ambled toward them with a cup of wine. "Olympian Dionysus! May we join you and these three lovely creatures?"

Dionysus turned, smiled professionally, and said "Please do!" He introduced the Telchines; each of whom assumed their pre-planned personalities.

Prince Periphas and Dionysus talked for a while, then Periphas said, "You seemed offended when I told of Amphitrite. Were you offended?"

Dexithea jumped into the conversation. "Dionysus told me that you were a bad boy. Were you a bad boy?"

Periphas looked at her with surprise.

"Ignore my sister, Great Prince Periphas," Halia said. She does not appreciate the great pressures of leadership. The need for compassion and understanding." Halia dripped with a sweet, understanding, hidden desire.

Makelo said, "Quiet, Sisters! Two chiefs of state discuss the course of countries. Give them your utmost respect and allegiance. Act as if you belong in their presence!"

ELDER OLYMPIANS: Hestia, Demeter, Hera, Hades, Poseidon, Zeus
OLYMPIANS: Apollo, Ares, Artemis, Athena, Aphrodite, Dionysus, Hermes,
Hephaestus, Heracles. LIVING TITANS: Oceanus, Tethys, Selene, Elder Oceanids.
DECEASED TITANS: Queen Kiya, Iapetus/Piercer, Cronus.

Dionysus laughed. "My heart went out to Amphitrite. You humiliated her. Apparently for a second time. I thought it a strange negotiation tactic; certainly not one you learned from Queen Kiya or any other of your past Titan benefactors. Perhaps you learned it from the Olympians. Strange that you found it to be a successful technique considering their results. By the way, I prefer the title Titan instead of Olympian. My Olympian brethren are not as noble as Titans, and certainly not as noble as Amphitrite."

"He needs to be punished," Dexithea said.

Periphas glanced at her.

Dionysus ignored the interruption. "I assume you have an intelligence system to keep up with what is happening in Port Olympus. I'm sure you do. You would be remiss if you didn't. But you will want to know..."

Makelo interrupted, "Titan Dionysus! You allow the prince to continue to drink the common wine. Stop, while I throw that out." She took the cup of wine from the prince and replaced it with a cup from Dionysus's private container. "Here, Great Prince Periphas. You will find this much more agreeable."

He took the cup, nodded to her, and smiled.

Makelo moved to the center of the group making everyone step back. She signaled for a passing server to bring fruits, nuts, and sweetbreads, which he did, forcing the group to separate even more. The group reformed but with the three women now standing mingled within the circle of men.

Dionysus continued. "You will want to know these things for our meetings tomorrow. We have scheduled three days for negotiations but hope to finish within two so that we can provide a leisurely trip to the Festival. But mostly because the Olympians -- we now refer to them as Ghods for reasons you should already know -- will be tied up all day tomorrow presenting their demands to Philyra concerning their new home we will soon start building."

The three women were somehow standing slightly closer to the three men than they had been a few seconds ago.

OCEANIDS: Metis, Tyche, Clymene, Eurybia, Amphitrite, Philyra, Rhodos.
TELCHINES: Dexithea, Makelo, Halia.
EAST: Azura, Seth, Typhon, Iasion, Endymion.
OTHER: Centaur Chiron, Charon, Hotep, Petra, Persephone.

Periphas said, "Yes, that is all well and good Titan Dionysus but tell me, are these three delightful young women special friends of yours, or are they free to mingle?"

Dionysus scoffed. "These three? Special friends? I apologize. I did not make appropriate introductions. These are three senior trade negotiators. We were discussing tomorrow's goals. They are their own persons!"

Halia purred, "We may be sitting across the table from each other tomorrow morning. I think that it might be beneficial to both sides if we give you a tour of our docks. They are intensely interesting, all the unloading facilities, all the little hidden rooms. We could discuss our goals for a trading agreement and things."

Dionysus rebuffed, "This night is for pleasure, not for business. I doubt that these men wish to see the working parts of our docks."

One of the negotiators, the most formal, offered, "Quite the contrary, Master Titan Dionysus. It would be most helpful for my understanding of Port issues if one of your senior advisors could show and explain the intricacies of your operations." He glanced at Makelo, who smiled graciously but said to the prince, "Would that be your wish, Great Prince Periphas?" One had the impression she was hoping that, perhaps, she could be the prince's guide rather than the negotiator's guide.

The prince hesitated, glanced at Dexithea who coolly returned his gaze, and said, "An excellent suggestion!"

Halia, seeing and understanding the glance, quickly moved to brush up against the younger negotiator, and dripped, "May I show you the glory of the port, all the hidden places for experiencing the excitement of trading?" She softly pulled him away without waiting for an embarrassed response.

Dexithea said, "And, so, Chief Dionysus, you appear to be the only obstacle keeping me from hearing how this prince humiliated my beloved mentor and teacher. Twice!"

Dionysus held up his cup of wine, raised it to the prince, and said, "Let him tell of again, then, Chief Negotiator Dexithea. Let him relive his tasteless victories!" -- *you have too much makeup around the eyes, Dexi -- at least for my taste --*

ELDER OLYMPIANS: Hestia, Demeter, Hera, Hades, Poseidon, Zeus
OLYMPIANS: Apollo, Ares, Artemis, Athena, Aphrodite, Dionysus, Hermes,
Hephaestus, Heracles. LIVING TITANS: Oceanus, Tethys, Selene, Elder Oceanids.
DECEASED TITANS: Queen Kiya, Iapetus/Piercer, Cronus.

She put her arm around the princes' and said, "Come with me Great Prince Periphas, I will show you the deepest, darkest secrets of Port Olympus." The prince happily went with her with the confidence of his kind. She carried, on her shoulder, the cutest little black leather bag.

36. Olympus Towers

The next morning, Dionysus awaited the Graikoi trade delegation with sweetbreads and a special mixture of wine and fruits perfect for starting a day of intense negotiations. The Telchines and Graikoians were late. A dozen lower-level Port employees sat waiting and looking important. They were window-dressing. They knew little about negotiation. It would be he and the three Telchines who would do the talking and forge whatever agreements could be forged. Amphitrite had given the three women a comprehensive course in negotiations, and they had been well briefed on the goals set by Dionysus.

Actually, any agreement would be a triumph. It was a triumph simply to get them to the trading tables and try to reestablish some degree of goodwill. They were no longer simple, needy people. They had taken the concept of Titan civilization and were not only approaching Port competence but were also developing an artistic and cultural sense that surpassed the Olympians. To come to an agreement as close as possible to the old, standard Titan agreements was the optimistic goal. The Telchines knew what Dionysus wanted and were to lay whatever groundwork they could in last night's private meetings. Dionysus was resigned to whatever walked through the door.

Dionysus heard the prince laugh long before his party and the Telchines arrived. -- *that's got to be a good sign* --

The six walked through the door bantering and laughing, followed by a half dozen lower-level scribes.

"All right, everyone. Settle down. This is a business meeting," Makelo commanded the group.

Halia said, "Let's get business over as quickly as possible so that I show my friend the loveliness of our port city and start our trip to the Festival."

Dexithea said, "So sorry, Halia. I'm going to escort the Graikoi group. You are escorting the Kemet group. My good fortune. Be more aggressive

OCEANIDS: Metis, Tyche, Clymene, Eurybia, Amphitrite, Philyra, Rhodos.
TELCHINES: Dexithea, Makelo, Halia.
EAST: Azura, Seth, Typhon, Iasion, Endymion.
OTHER: Centaur Chiron, Charon, Hotep, Petra, Persephone.

next year. Prince Periphas is going to have an exciting time if I have anything to do with it, which I do." She looked at the prince suggestively.

Dionysus said, "Get some sweetbread and a wine-drink and let's get started. We are going to have a long three days."

Prince Periphas laughed. "I want this signed before this afternoon so that Telchine Dexithea can show me your local sights. She can arrange for our group to leave in the morning so that our journey will be leisurely. You need to teach your negotiators how to be more demanding. It slipped out during last night's tour that you wanted to meet us halfway between what the Olympians wanted and our traditional contract, but your loss of our business presented you with hardship. I am fairly certain that after three days of talks, you will be willing to accept reinstituting our old agreement. We can argue about it for the next three days or just sign the agreement this morning and enjoy the next three days. This is your choice."

Dionysus considered the proposal. "You know that I not only want your trade but that I wish to re-establish your goodwill?"

"Yes. I know that. That's why I hold the superior position."

"One should never mix personal feelings with matters of state, but you treated my friend, the most honorable Oceanid Amphitrite, with a great deal of public disrespect and humiliation." He left the statement hanging.

"Yes. I understand. I will not publicly apologize but I will reconcile with Oceanid Amphitrite in a private setting."

Dionysus hesitated, but begrudgingly said, "That will be satisfactory. I will accept whatever trade agreement terms my negotiators agree upon." Dionysus stood, picked up his wine-drink, looked at the chief scribe, and said, "Record that which the six agree upon." He walked over to the scribe and asked, "Where do I sign?" He signed the blank paper, looked at the prince, held up his cup, and drily said, "To the glory of the Graikoi people and their prince," drank, forcefully sat his cup on the table, and disgustedly left the room. -- *wonderful work, Telchines – Amphitrite* --

~ Ghod Meeting ~

Meanwhile, Philyra's day began with a meeting with twelve mid-level managers with aspirations of moving up. "I promise you nothing but an opportunity to spend a day with the Ghods. They will find associating

ELDER OLYMPIANS: Hestia, Demeter, Hera, Hades, Poseidon, Zeus
OLYMPIANS: Apollo, Ares, Artemis, Athena, Aphrodite, Dionysus, Hermes, Hephaestus, Heracles. LIVING TITANS: Oceanus, Tethys, Selene, Elder Oceanids.
DECEASED TITANS: Queen Kiya, Iapetus/Piercer, Cronus.

with you disgusting and talk to you as if you are lower than dung. Deal with it! If you irritate one, they may well have a Gigante throw you down the atrium. I'm sure you have all heard the screams. You may NOT pass yourself off as a Lord because you aren't. Yet. You are lower class. You will flatter them, praise them, and record their every word. If you can improve their words by repeating them more coherently, then do so. But never, never take credit for anything. All credit is theirs alone. I have tried to match you as best I can. You have been briefed on the personality and idiosyncrasies of your assigned Ghod. Give constant, unending praise of both what a glorious thing they are building and how glorious it will be. We will gather on the roof and wait for them there. You will be following them around on the fifteenth and sixteenth floors. Do NOT embarrass me by getting thrown down the atrium and do NOT disappoint me. Any questions? No? Let's get up there, team! Excellence is expected."

Philyra led them onto the roof.

Their excitement was palpable. -- *opportunity!* -- *risk!* -- *associating with the ghods!* -- *even the lords have limited exposure to the ghods* --

At last night's planning and familiarization meeting, each had put money into a pot. It would be divided by those that survived this assignment. They had all agreed to scream extremely loud if they were thrown down the atrium. This might make it easier for the survivors.

Hestia arrived mid-morning with her Gigante attendant. She spoke to Philyra, looked down her nose at the twelve mid-managers, and asked, "Are these the ones?"

Philyra announced, "This is Chief Olympian Ghod Hestia. Do as she commands immediately!"

A woman stepped from the twelve and announced, "Great Olympian Ghod Hestia, I am Creusa. It is my high honor and privilege to be called to serve the most powerful and glorious of all the Ghods. I carry your favorite food and drink in my bag so as you become weary of dealing with the lower classes, you can demand sustenance. Your every desire and command will be faithfully recorded and sent to Chief-of-Chiefs Philyra for her report to you. If I fail you in any way, tell me so that I can include my failure in my report."

OCEANIDS: Metis, Tyche, Clymene, Eurybia, Amphitrite, Philyra, Rhodos.
TELCHINES: Dexithea, Makelo, Halia.
EAST: Azura, Seth, Typhon, Iasion, Endymion.
OTHER: Centaur Chiron, Charon, Hotep, Petra, Persephone.

Hestia looked at her, smirked, looked at Philyra, and asked, "She knows about the atrium?"

Philyra coldly replied, "My people are driven by their desire to achieve excellence in all things; not fear, Ghod Hestia."

Hestia commanded, "All right, then. The others will be arriving shortly. Come with me to the sixteenth floor, Creusa. We will start there!"

Philyra watched Creusa obediently follow three steps behind Hestia on their way to the sixteenth floor. -- *do well, my child -- you have it within you --*

Poseidon and Apollo walked in. Philyra announced, "This is Ghod Poseidon and Ghod Apollo. Do as they command immediately."

The day had begun. Eventually, the lessor Ghods became excited and enthusiastic about designing their new house and forgot they were talking to a lower-class person.

Hestia and Poseidon, however, did not forget.

~

The next morning, Hestia sat on her office sofa reading Philyra's report. Philyra blankly stared out over the port far below.

"Good, good. You recorded all my requirements and Poseidon's, too. And most of Zeus's and all the other mindless chatter. I think we are off to a good start. You look like dung, Philyra. You need to take better care of your appearance."

"I will go and clean up but I'm glad you like the report. The Ghods had such wonderful suggestions, it was easy to write the report; just consolidate everyone's ideas. There was just so much of it. I didn't finish until a little after sunrise. There is still a great deal to do simply to initiate the plans, but CoM3 Charon is working on implementation requirements. Now that we have the concept, I will take a quick nap and meet Charon at mid-day meal to firm things up a bit."

"Oh. All that exciting design talk about the Ghod's new house has me excited. I planned on you and me taking this morning off for a little well-earned relaxation. What do you think?"

"Well, if you are happy with the report, I can certainly put Charon off a few hours. What relaxing technique would please you?"

ELDER OLYMPIANS: Hestia, Demeter, Hera, Hades, Poseidon, Zeus
OLYMPIANS: Apollo, Ares, Artemis, Athena, Aphrodite, Dionysus, Hermes,
Hephaestus, Heracles. LIVING TITANS: Oceanus, Tethys, Selene, Elder Oceanids.
DECEASED TITANS: Queen Kiya, Iapetus/Piercer, Cronus.

Hestia rose and walked to Philyra.

~

Meanwhile, on the street below, Dexithea arrived as Amphitrite organized the Graikoi caravan. The procession would be led by a two-level chariot driven by Dexithea. The prince and his consort would ride on the higher level and Amphitrite would stand with Dexithea on the driver's level. A carriage would follow carrying the two chief negotiators followed by a wagon carrying the twelve statue performers and then seven more wagons carrying the remaining personnel.

The caravan would stop at Gigante Settlement for mid-day meal and sightseeing and then on to the Phlegethon camp for a tour of the facilities. Neither Hades nor Hephaestus could join them because they were attending a mandatory meeting of all Olympians. The caravan would end the first day with a small party at historical Overlook Point. Dionysus had made it a point to ensure more than a sufficient supply of wine was available.

The party members began arriving as the wagons were loaded. The prince and his consort arrived and were seated. Amphitrite had arranged for drummers to drum and bystanders to cheer and wave goodbye.

Dexithea took the reins, stood up, turned to look at her caravan, held her whip high in the air, and shouted, "All right, everybody, we are going to have ourselves a wonderful time!" She waved the whip in the air with confidence, glanced at the prince, and said, "If you need anything at all, just ask me." She cracked the whip, and they were off!

~

And on the sixteenth floor, as Philyra dressed, she noticed the Graikoi caravan far below depart but her attention remained on Hestia. "That was unbelievable and refreshing, Hestia. I felt your excitement about your great new project; the most glorious project anyone has ever attempted. You lie there and rest while I get back to work. I'll borrow your copy of the report so that I can have scribes make additional copies. Can I bring you anything before I start making your great project happen?"

Hestia continued to lie on the sofa and contentedly shook her head, "No."

OCEANIDS: Metis, Tyche, Clymene, Eurybia, Amphitrite, Philyra, Rhodos.
TELCHINES: Dexithea, Makelo, Halia.
EAST: Azura, Seth, Typhon, Iasion, Endymion.
OTHER: Centaur Chiron, Charon, Hotep, Petra, Persephone.

Philyra made it to her thirteenth-floor office, decided that was far enough, and entered. She told Admete to assemble yesterday's Ghod team and for her to read the report to them while each recorded an additional copy. "I am going to sleep in my office for a few hours. No interruptions, please." She entered her office, removed her outer clothes, lay on her sofa, and fell into a deep sleep.

When she awoke it was dark outside. Admete had put her head on a pillow and had covered her with a blanket. A reading candle was burning. Philyra's suit had been cleaned and pressed. The original manuscript was on her desk plus a copy for Philyra and a note saying that she had given Charon a copy and that ten additional copies were filed in the outer office.

Philyra demanded excellence but, still, she was moved by Admete's care and diligence. Philyra wrote a note thanking her and left her office to place it on Admete's desk. She turned to reenter her office and saw a reading candle burning on the other side of the office.

A voice called out, "My eyes do not deserve to behold such beauty."

She looked down at herself standing there in only her underwear. "Don't be a butt-kisser, Charon. I'll get my clothes on. Let's meet."

She dressed and went to Charon's desk with her copy of the report. Charon sat with his copy opened a third of the way through. Two cups of a dark wine-like drink sat on his desk. "Don't speak. Sip this. It's a major new drink from Dionysus. It is aged beyond wine. It is what wine wanted to be." He handed her the cup, and both sat in silence, sipping the aged brown-wine.

She exhaled a long sigh. "That's sooo good. It's been a difficult three days. What do you think of the report?"

"It's a work of genius. Restating their words so they sound wonderful, praising their suggestions, affirming that this is the greatest project ever undertaken, that they must dedicate all their energy to nothing other than making this happen, and how glorious it will be when they finally move in. As a plan, it's dung. I mean 'I want my apartment to be wonderful and extraordinary,' a requirement by eight of them for Ghod's sake; 'I want my apartment to be really high so I can look out and see birds flying by;' and on and on. But the report is still a work of genius. It will keep them distracted for years. I suggest you assign someone to provide them with a

ELDER OLYMPIANS: Hestia, Demeter, Hera, Hades, Poseidon, Zeus
OLYMPIANS: Apollo, Ares, Artemis, Athena, Aphrodite, Dionysus, Hermes,
Hephaestus, Heracles. LIVING TITANS: Oceanus, Tethys, Selene, Elder Oceanids.
DECEASED TITANS: Queen Kiya, Iapetus/Piercer, Cronus.

progress report that vomits this dung back to them daily. Control their wants and demands."

She considered his suggestion as she sipped. "Excellent suggestion. We can distract them from our problems and redirect their demands by controlling their thoughts. I will assign Creusa to provide a daily progress report to Hestia. What else?"

"I have read the demands of the Big Four. Consider this. Build this thing directly over Tartarus. It should have an atrium like the Port building. Place the four foundation columns at the four corners of the patio with two smaller support columns between each column. These columns will rise to the top. Build the first floor one hundred twenty paces square centered on the columns. The first floor will be the grand entrance and it will make the existing Tartarus a basement to the building. The basement will be the realm of Hades and Persephone. Leave Iapetus's residence and let Hades claim it as his own. The basement will have egress designed to give Persephone maximum delight when she leaves for her Elysium fields. Am I boring you? Shall I go on?"

"I'm intrigued. Go on."

"The second level will be three paces smaller on each side. The roof of the first floor will then provide a walkway three paces across around the second floor. The walkway will contain hanging gardens, water features, sitting areas, and whatever else. One side will contain a stairway or an incline to the next level. The third level will be three paces smaller on each side than the lower floor and so on to the top floor. I figure this would give twelve floors, one in honor of each of them. The height of each level should be as high as possible so that the building is much taller than the Port building. An elevator up the atrium along with a water supply and waste disposal will have to be designed. The upper room should be their party room with really high ceilings. The building must be tall enough 'to see birds flying by.' That's as far as I am right now."

"We have a plan, Charon. I am relaxed for the first time in months. Maybe it's the brown-wine but I think not. I think it is your concept. It's certainly enough to buy us time."

"How shall I proceed?"

OCEANIDS: Metis, Tyche, Clymene, Eurybia, Amphitrite, Philyra, Rhodos.
TELCHINES: Dexithea, Makelo, Halia.
EAST: Azura, Seth, Typhon, Iasion, Endymion.
OTHER: Centaur Chiron, Charon, Hotep, Petra, Persephone.

"I will call CoRO Petra tonight and have him meet you mid-morning at Transport. Between you and the Chief of Rock Operations, maybe you can get an idea of the scope and placement of the building. Place spears in the ground to identify the corners and atrium placement. I can lead the Ghods there whenever you think it's ready to show. I love the Hades concept and the Ghods will love it too. Zeus will be excited because his quarters will be up high. We still need a grand concept connecting Poseidon with the sea and we need to decide what would excite Hestia most. Although, the concept of Tartarus being below her in the basement may be enough to take care of that. Maybe have the waste empty into Kiya's house."

They sat quietly as Charon refilled their brown-wine.

"You have made significant contributions to the Port and the world, Charon. You are invaluable."

"May I suggest how you can repay me?"

"Only if it does not involve giving you my job or my body."

Charon laughed a somewhat bitter laugh. "Never mind. It is my pleasure to be of some small assistance to you and the port."

37. Port Kemet and Kaptara Delegations

Dionysus sat at his cafe patio table awaiting Makelo and Halia. They were to finalize their negotiation plan for the Port Kemet delegation which was expected to arrive in the early afternoon. Port Kemet was not as developed, nor was Chief Kemet as sophisticated, as the Graikoi delegation. Chief Kemet had to accept last year's trade demands to the severe detriment of Port Kemet. Their trade had fallen but not drastically so. Dionysus wanted to get resources flowing back into Port Kemet without infuriating Hestia. What to do?

He was staring out over the water when the two Telchines walked up with Charon and another manager in tow.

"Look who we found at the transportation center," Makelo said excitedly. "Can we keep them?"

Dionysus stood, greeted Charon, and introduced himself to the manager.

The manager said, "Great to finally meet you, Olympian Dionysus. I am Petra, Philyra's Chief of Rock Operations. I was apprenticed to Piercer back in his day. His interests shifted to metals later in life but mine stayed with rocks, especially Marmaros as a building material. I was involved in building the Library of Olympus and several other Marmaros buildings. Charon has got a major project on his hands. This will be exciting."

Dionysus looked at Charon and said, "Have you made progress? Sit, join me and bring me up-to-date."

They sat. The server brought them fruit and nuts.

Charon said, "Admete has your copy of the Olympus Towers Report on her desk. Read it and learn what Philyra is feeding them. Use the same language. Petra and I are on our way to Tartarus to mark off the building. You don't want to know what we are going to do. It will break your heart."

Dionysus chuckled. "It's been broken before. Not anything Makelo, Halia, and little wine can't mend."

Charon said, "This is the initial plan; subject to change every moment." He described the concept.

"Destroy the fire pit and patio? Construct a building over the home of the Titans? You were right. This will take a lot of wine and sympathy."

"You'll recover! But now, we must get to the site. We have a long day ahead."

The five bid farewells leaving the two Telchines sitting with Dionysus. "We need a plan for tomorrow's negotiations. Suggestions?" They talked through the morning.

The ship from Port Kemet arrived in the early afternoon. Philyra joined the three to officially welcome the delegation as they debarked. Dionysus presented Chief Kemet with three large containers of honey. The chief was happy with his reception. A feast was held that night in the chief's honor. There was adequate entertainment. The delegation, still provincial by Port standards, was unfamiliar with wine and its effects. The chief's grandson, dark-skinned Hotep, drank far too much. Halia spent much of the evening fending off Hotep's aggressive attention. "I build great buildings of stone," seemed to be words that Hotep expected to impress her since he whispered this to her three separate times.

OCEANIDS: Metis, Tyche, Clymene, Eurybia, Amphitrite, Philyra, Rhodos.
TELCHINES: Dexithea, Makelo, Halia.
EAST: Azura, Seth, Typhon, Iasion, Endymion.
OTHER: Centaur Chiron, Charon, Hotep, Petra, Persephone.

Negotiations began in the early morning. The chief was resigned to failure, but he would make his case as best he could. Dionysus listened with interest through the chief's lamentations and a long list of hardships. He finally asked, "Great Chief Kemet, the Port requires a twenty-five percent increase in trade. What must I offer you to get this increase?"

The chief was distressed. "A twenty-five percent increase? I cannot sustain the trade we have under the terms of your agreement! Certainly, there can be no increase!"

"I understand. Twenty-five percent is what the Port wishes. What new terms do you require to achieve this increase?"

"New terms? I can relieve your onerous terms?"

"Yes. What new terms do you require?"

The chief considered this new opening. He calculated what would work for him and stated numbers twice the amount he hoped he might obtain.

Dionysus stood and said, "Done! Scribes, draw up the agreement for our signatures. Great Chief Kemet and I are going out to celebrate." To the chief, he said, "You drive a hard bargain, but I must increase our trade position with you. Our future is too important to argue over details. Shall we go drink a little wine? Do you want my traders to join us?"

The triumphant chief said, "Yes. The music of a woman's voice will brighten our meal. Does Great Oceanid Metis still visit your port?"

Dionysus escorted the two Telchines, Chief Kemet, and Hotep to the private dining room at the Port Cafe. Musicians and singers entertained them as they ate. Hotep refused wine and said to Halia in broken common language, "This drink made me speak to you in a swinish way last evening. I am more respectful toward women than I behaved last night."

Halia acknowledged Hotep's apology with, "A builder of great buildings of stone should be allowed to have fun now and then."

Dionysus overheard Halia's comment and became alert.

He later told the two Telchines, "Whoever escorts the Kemet delegation to the Festival, take them through Tartarus to sightsee the old Titan home and the outline of the Olympus Towers. Encourage the Hotep boy to stay behind and offer his services to Petra. He might be of use. We are going to need a lot of good people for this project." He paused, thought, and said, "At every opportunity, turn your excursions to the Festival into recruiting trips for builders of the tallest and grandest structure ever built, the glorious Olympian Olympus Towers."

Halia and Makelo had decided between them that Halia would be the official escort for the Port Kemet delegation's trip to the Festival. Both the chief and especially Hotep responded more warmly to Halia's sweet, assumed persona than to Makelo's official, no-nonsense persona.

~ Kemet Caravan ~

Abas and Halia had the caravan prepared and waiting at the transportation center. Halia would command the carriage carrying Chief Kemet, Hotep, and his senior staff. A mid-level manager would drive the wagon carrying junior staff and ceremonial trade goods.

Additionally, a large carriage commanded by Nerites would join the Port Kemet group. It would carry Demeter, Apollo, and Artemis to the Festival. They had never been and had heard how disgusting but wonderful it was. Demeter had pouted, "Yes, I know I will be submerged in a sea of lower-class people. But great suffering is sometimes necessary. I am no stranger to great suffering, and I want to see this Festival." Demeter wanted Artemis to go with her to keep her company. Apollo, twin brother to Artemis, volunteered to go and protect the two high-born women from the lower classes as best he could. Hestia and Poseidon were unsure of the wisdom of this trip but relented if Poseidon's friend Nerites would be their driver, host, and attendant. "At least Nerites is a Lord and knows how to treat Olympian Ghods."

The Port Kemet contingent and Nerites arrived for departure but there was no sign of the Olympians. Halia and Nerites agreed to take the Tartarus route. Halia would leave with her group now and stop at Tartarus to sightsee and wait on Nerites' group to join them.

The Port Kemet delegation pulled out for their grand adventure. There were drummers and a recruited crowd to excitedly cheer them away.

~ The Kaptara Delegation ~

Dionysus and Makelo met with Philyra to bring her up to date on the plans for the next, and last, delegation scheduled to arrive -- the Port

OCEANIDS: Metis, Tyche, Clymene, Eurybia, Amphitrite, Philyra, Rhodos.
TELCHINES: Dexithea, Makelo, Halia.
EAST: Azura, Seth, Typhon, Iasion, Endymion.
OTHER: Centaur Chiron, Charon, Hotep, Petra, Persephone.

Kaptara delegation. The Kaptara frontier was midway between Graikoi and Kemet in development. Oceanus and Metis were encouraging them to build a sea-going civilization, but they were hampered by limited trading opportunities. Graikoi, Kemet, And Olympus were the only major ports with only small, unorganized ports springing up along the coast. Kaptara leaders longed to have access to the higher sea to the west of Port Spearpoint but the high, sheer cliff dividing the higher western sea and the lower eastern sea blocked their vessels. Port Kaptara sent a great deal of trade through the Port Spearpoint deep-wells, but efficiencies were reduced.

Philyra said to Dionysus and Makelo, "We are doing well! Two down, one to go. I have shown Hestia the numbers. She ranted about what a weak negotiator you are and how you are failing the Ghods. I pointed out the twenty-five percent increase that you demanded and how they eventually angrily capitulated to your demands. She is happy enough for now."

Dionysus was elated. "Great! By the way, I told Makelo and Halia to turn this into a recruiting trip for the Port. If you have any specific requirements, tell Makelo before she leaves in the morning." He paused. "I agree. We are doing well. Let us hope the Ghods remain on our side!"

That afternoon, the delegation from Port Kaptara arrived. Old Chief Aeolus and his General Achaeous led them. They were all to be feted but Aeolus said, "I do not need mindless festivities. Let us instead sit together and talk about the needs and requirements of our countries. Entertain my staff, instead."

Makelo turned out to be the perfect all-business, no-nonsense, representative for Port Olympus. The four principals retired to the dock-side patio to negotiate while the remainder of the Kaptara delegation was entertained and fed.

Chief Aeolus explained the hardships the current trading terms presented and requested reasonable concessions to alleviate the hardships.

Makelo listened intently and responded, "I cannot speak of last year's terms or even what terms may be requested from you next year, but this year it is my responsibility to increase our trade with you and to increase your profits for you to reinvest and grow richer. I also request your goodwill and relations such as you had with Queen Kiya. What terms do you suggest, in order for me to achieve this?"

ELDER OLYMPIANS: Hestia, Demeter, Hera, Hades, Poseidon, Zeus
OLYMPIANS: Apollo, Ares, Artemis, Athena, Aphrodite, Dionysus, Hermes,
Hephaestus, Heracles. LIVING TITANS: Oceanus, Tethys, Selene, Elder Oceanids.
DECEASED TITANS: Queen Kiya, Iapetus/Piercer, Cronus.

"Would you consider a return to the historic terms?"

"Is that sufficient?"

Aeolus laughed. "We all know that these terms were always favorable to Port Kaptara. Those terms are more than acceptable."

Makelo said, "Done!" She raised her cup to salute them.

Dionysus laughed. "I should at least have gotten to say something during these intense negotiations. Chief-of-Chiefs Philyra may figure out that she doesn't need her chief negotiator, anymore."

Aeolus said, without amusement, "It was you who trained this young woman, wasn't it?"

Dionysus became serious. "Yes, Great Chief Aeolus. And I trained her well. It appears to me that women make better negotiators than men. A man hears only the words you say and understands the resources you have backing you. A woman hears the words you don't say and sees what concessions work to her benefit in the future."

Aeolus looked at Makelo and said, "Well, then. Could you remove the wall which Port Spearpoint sits upon separating Oursea from the great western sea? It would certainly benefit Port Kaptara although, admittedly, it would be an inconvenience to the other settlements on the coast of Oursea."

Everyone laughed.

Dionysus said, "That would be a problem!" -- *remove the wall?* -- *raise the level of Oursea?* -- *destroy civilization?* -- *that's what Kiya commanded Oceanus to do* -- *to kill the Olympians* -- *he wouldn't do it then* -- *would he now?* --

~ Tartarus Stopover ~

Halia pulled into Tartarus about the same time Nerites and the Ghods were leaving the port transportation center. Halia had given a running commentary of the countryside. What she didn't know, she made up. Halia had not seen it in its prime, but Tartarus was the stuff of legend. This was the home built by Queen Kiya and her children. This, Halia did not have to make up. Ask, and any Oceanid would share the story in detail. Everyone walked the grounds and wound up at the fire pit on the great patio. They sat at the tables as Halia dramatically -- Telchines love drama -- told stories of local legend.

OCEANIDS: Metis, Tyche, Clymene, Eurybia, Amphitrite, Philyra, Rhodos.
TELCHINES: Dexithea, Makelo, Halia.
EAST: Azura, Seth, Typhon, Iasion, Endymion.
OTHER: Centaur Chiron, Charon, Hotep, Petra, Persephone.

Chief Kemet was awe-struck. "This is the place of Starmaster and Oceanus and Great Oceanid Metis. This is where they lived!"

Hotep, much younger and not impressed, asked, "What are these spears driven into the ground for?"

Halia hesitated and said, "I'm not sure, but two Lords came yesterday to lay out the corners for the Olympus Towers they are going to build. Maybe the spears mark the corners."

Now it was Hotep that was awestruck. "The spears are corners for a building?" They are at least 150 paces apart. There cannot be a building that size!"

"Well, I don't know about that, but I know it's supposed to be tall; much taller than the Port Olympus building."

"Taller than the Port Olympus building? Impossible."

"They are going to start recruiting builders and designers soon. If you are interested, you could be first in line. Go to the port receptionist and ask for Petra. Tell him Halia sent you. He can give you all the details. Now, everybody. Let's all have an early mid-day meal and eat at the same tables where Queen Kiya and the Elder Titans ate and entertained!"

~

Meanwhile, the Ghod caravan, hosted by Nerites, had finally left the port and was passing 900 Pace Road.

Apollo became animated. "Artemis, isn't this the road where Chiron lives? He was a great student. Ghod Demeter, can we stop and see our old protégé, Chiron?"

Demeter sniffed, "A commoner? I didn't know anyone lived here anymore. Beautiful, sweet Persephone and I passed this place every time we walked to Elysium Fields. I'm so glad that we were never accosted by him."

Artemis joined in, "Oh, Ghod Demeter, Chiron was such a good student. He learned archery, music, medicine, hunting, and everything. He taught these things to the young children and let them ride on his back. We haven't seen him in ages. Can we stop and see him? Please!"

ELDER OLYMPIANS: Hestia, Demeter, Hera, Hades, Poseidon, Zeus
OLYMPIANS: Apollo, Ares, Artemis, Athena, Aphrodite, Dionysus, Hermes,
Hephaestus, Heracles. LIVING TITANS: Oceanus, Tethys, Selene, Elder Oceanids.
DECEASED TITANS: Queen Kiya, Iapetus/Piercer, Cronus.

Demeter relented. "I suppose so. Sweet Persephone will someday make her home at this Tartarus place. Perhaps I can instruct him and make sure he never comes around to bother her."

Apollo said, "Go back, Lord Nerites. I'll show you the way to Centaur Chiron's house."

Nerites turned around and then turned right onto 900 Pace Road. The farmer men and women had not noticed that the carriage carried Ghods. Demeter was surprised to see them working in the Asphodel fields. "Hmph, there are commoners everywhere. Be careful, Nerites."

The carriage eventually approached the last house on the path. Apollo said, "Stop here, Nerites. I will find out if Chiron is home!"

Artemis jumped down with Apollo; they walked to the door and knocked.

Demeter looked around, sniffing the air with disdain.

The door opened. Chiron answered, stared at Apollo, and then fell to a knee. "Great Titane Apollo, my mentor! My friend! You honor me greatly! Welcome to my poor house!"

Apollo pulled Chiron to his feet. "It's good to see you again, Centaur Chiron."

Chiron then saw Artemis. "Titanide Artemis. You, too, have come! What a glorious day!"

Artemis stepped forward and embraced Chiron who was still standing half-hidden in the doorway. "You are as gracious as ever, Chiron. I miss that. We aren't Titans anymore, though. We are Olympians. We are allowed to associate with the Ghods. They even sometimes consider Apollo and me one of them. It's all so exciting. But I do miss you and your friendship."

Chiron asked, "Can you stay? Shall I invite you in?"

Artemis replied, "We can't stay. We are on our way to the Festival. We are escorting the Great Ghod Demeter there; she has always heard of the festival but has never been to one. Ghod Demeter is an especially important Ghod; she is the mother to Persephone, the Queen of the Colored Fields. Persephone will soon move to Titan Piercer's old home

OCEANIDS: Metis, Tyche, Clymene, Eurybia, Amphitrite, Philyra, Rhodos.
TELCHINES: Dexithea, Makelo, Halia.
EAST: Azura, Seth, Typhon, Iasion, Endymion.
OTHER: Centaur Chiron, Charon, Hotep, Petra, Persephone.

with her extremely important husband, Ghod Hades, King of the Underworld."

Chiron said, "Ghod Hades is my friend. I did not realize how important he was. He is kind to me. And maiden Persephone! She, too, is my friend!"

Overhearing, Demeter glanced toward Chiron still standing half-hidden in the doorway. "You know King Hades?" she sniffed. -- *he knows my beloved daughter?* --

Chiron asked Apollo, "Am I allowed to address the Queen Mother?"

"Yes, you may," Apollo replied.

Chiron looked up at Demeter sitting in the chariot beside Nerites. "I know Ghod Hades well, Great Queen Mother. It was I who adorned his chariot and his horse Alastor with flowers to impress the young maiden he sought. He was most pleased with me."

Demeter was puzzled. "Adorned his chariot with flowers? When was this? Step forward so I can see you more clearly."

Chiron stepped into the open, his hindquarters included.

Demeter put her hand to her mouth and gasped, staring at Chiron's misshapen body.

Apollo offered, "Chiron has a birth defect, Ghod Demeter. He has the body of a normal man but also a growth from his back that has the appearance of a horse's hindquarters. But he is well adjusted and extremely learned in all the arts. Artemis and I have both taught him. And he is an excellent teacher of young children. They all love him. He is an excellent companion to Queen Persephone. He was in her wedding bringing up the rear."

Artemis added, "Chiron is patient and kind, Ghod Demeter. And humble. He doesn't even pretend to be as good as anybody else. Queen Persephone really likes him."

Demeter mumbled, "I see. He was in Queen Persephone's wedding, you say? I didn't see him. Are you sure that he isn't dangerous?"

Chiron took a step toward Demeter, looked up at her, and said, "Great Ghod, sometimes it helps one to overcome their revulsion by laying their hand upon my deformity. As disgusting as this sounds, it may be of help."

ELDER OLYMPIANS: Hestia, Demeter, Hera, Hades, Poseidon, Zeus
OLYMPIANS: Apollo, Ares, Artemis, Athena, Aphrodite, Dionysus, Hermes,
Hephaestus, Heracles. LIVING TITANS: Oceanus, Tethys, Selene, Elder Oceanids.
DECEASED TITANS: Queen Kiya, Iapetus/Piercer, Cronus.

He bowed his head, knelt his front knees to the ground, and waited for her decision.

She was aghast, "Touch it?!"

Apollo walked to the carriage and held his hand up to Demeter. "Most of the children from the old days delighted in riding upon his back after they had completed their lessons. They were not disgusted at all. Touch him. Persephone was not frightened."

Demeter hesitated and stared at the misshapen figure before her. -- *a safe companion for Persephone? -- young children love him? -- humble? -- patient? -- a teacher? -- actually touch him?! --*

With hesitation, she took Apollo's hand.

~

Meanwhile, at Tartarus, Halia understood the reverence which had overwhelmed Chief Kemet. Playing the situation, she sat the chief at the foot of Kiya's table where the guest of honor would have sat. Hotep rambled on about the impossibility of the building project Halia had described but was ignored by Halia and Kemet. Halia remained uncharacteristically silent as she served lunch. After they were served, she sat at the head of the table and only then, with a somber voice, addressed the chief. She began her dramatic soliloquy. "I sit in the exact spot Queen Kiya sat. You, Chief, sit where every honored guest sat as they dined with the Titans. Great Oceanid Metis would have sat over there." Telchines love drama. Halia had an appreciative one-man audience.

They finished their lunch with still no sign of Nerite's party. -- *oh, well -- too bad -- I will just have to go on without them --*

Halia began loading her wards into their carriage and wagon with Hotep still talking non-stop about the building project. A melancholy Chief Kemet took his talkative grandson by the shoulders, gave him a bear hug, and said, "Hotep, if these Lords are to be successful, they certainly need your assistance. Return to the port and offer your services in their building project. Learn all that you can for the future benefit of our land. Stay safe until we meet again. Now, go in peace!"

OCEANIDS: Metis, Tyche, Clymene, Eurybia, Amphitrite, Philyra, Rhodos.
TELCHINES: Dexithea, Makelo, Halia.
EAST: Azura, Seth, Typhon, Iasion, Endymion.
OTHER: Centaur Chiron, Charon, Hotep, Petra, Persephone.

Hotep was delighted, his decision made for him, he returned his father's hug, and said, "I shall make you proud, Grandfather." He then turned toward the port and began his walk back.

Halia almost made it away, but just then Nerites Carriage could be seen arriving in Tartarus. She pasted a smile on her face and waited for the carriage to draw even with hers.

Nerites greeted her. "The Ghods don't want to stop here. They had a nice visit back up the road. Let's just keep going!"

Halia said, "Wonderful! We have a long five-day journey ahead of us." She looked for but did not see, Demeter. "Nerites! You lost Ghod Demeter!!"

"Oh, yes. Wait a few minutes. They are catching up. That Chiron fellow is going to be tired. "

"What? What's going on?"

Nerites nodded his head toward the figures now pulling into sight.

In the distance, Chiron came; Ghod Demeter riding upon his back.

~ The Kaptara Caravan ~

Sunrise.

At Port Dispatch, Makelo loaded her carriage and three wagons with her Kaptara guests, and the final western delegation set out to the Winter Solstice Festival.

Both Dionysus and Philyra were there to bid them good travels. After waving goodbye, they went to the dock patio for a morning meal where Charon, Petra, and Hotep, were already sitting drinking fruit-wine. The three rose to greet Philyra who used hand motions to quickly reseat the men. Kepten arranged the table to accommodate the new arrivals ensuring that all had fresh plates of fruit with their fruit-wine drink.

All were quiet. Hotep started to speak but remained silent after Petra kicked him under the table.

Philyra sipped her drink, leaned back, breathed deeply, and said, "Outstanding work, Team. Excellence every step of the way. I am proud of the entire organization. Creusa is developing a relationship with Hestia nicely. She is an expert at keeping Hestia engaged in our Olympus Towers project and out of our way. Dionysus and his Telchine team have given us outstanding trading agreements. The Telchines are transporting our dignitaries to Festival Seventy-Five as we speak. Amphitrite will be there to observe and command. Petra and Charon are getting the physical plans for Olympus Towers under control."

She paused to look at Hotep and asked, "Is this our new architect, Hotep?" She did not wait for affirmation. "Hello, Builder Hotep. I am Chief-of-Chiefs Philyra. Thirteenth floor. I am there for you if Petra fails" She looked at Petra and said, "Which you won't, will you, Lord Petra? And, Lord Petra, let's plan an event at Tartarus to show the Ghods how well they are guiding us. Give me a time and a plan." She held her cup up to transfer the conversation to him.

Petra was caught off guard. He stammered, "Well -- I guess -- I need --"

Charon interrupted. "Chief Philyra, Petra is a thorough planner. I am a 'say it first and think about it later' planner. May I speak?"

She asked, "Do you have any idea what you are about to say?"

"None."

"Go ahead."

Charon began, "They like to see and touch things. We need an expert wood craftsman to build a scale model of Olympus Towers for them to keep on their roof and keep them excited. He can build a second one for us to keep at Tartarus as a reference. They can inspect the site after we complete the main structural Marmaros columns defining the infrastructure and get flooring on the first floor for them to walk on and look down onto the patio. That will excite Hestia. I need a least a month to prepare. Our trading partners will be returning from the Festival around that time. Whether it's beneficial to mix the Ghods and our trading partners in an Olympus Towers unveiling ceremony is questionable but you could if you wanted to. It would give you a reason to delay showing them any progress at the site." He stopped talking.

Philyra said, "Comments, Lord Petra?"

Petra said, "One month? One month!"

OCEANIDS: Metis, Tyche, Clymene, Eurybia, Amphitrite, Philyra, Rhodos.
TELCHINES: Dexithea, Makelo, Halia.
EAST: Azura, Seth, Typhon, Iasion, Endymion.
OTHER: Centaur Chiron, Charon, Hotep, Petra, Persephone.

No one responded. All looked at Petra. Petra looked at Hotep and said, "We have one month, Builder Hotep. We will go through Tartarus for a quick look and continue to the stone quarries to enlist builders. Maybe there is a master wood artist still there. We need to assign a liaison with the Gigantes. They provide the muscle. We can talk on the way. May Builder Hotep and I be excused, Chief Philyra?"

"Of course, Lord Petra." Petra and Hotep rose to go. Philyra added, "Oh, and Lord Petra -- I love your plan!" Petra nodded and hurried to the transportation center to obtain two fast horses.

Charon thought, rose, and said, "I will go with them. We can get a carriage and a driver and have planning meetings as we go. I know the dactyls well and they have good relations with the wood craftsmen and the Gigantes. Tell Acmon to handle any problems while I'm gone," He walked away but then stopped, turned, looked intensely at Philyra, and said, "Thank you, Chief. You are a good leader. I hope to know you better one day." Once more, he turned and left them.

Caught off-guard, Philyra smiled and, with embarrassment, cut her eyes toward Dionysus.

Dionysus raised his cup toward her and said, "True is the path of Queen Kiya. Long live those who walk it!"

Then they drank.

38. Riverport

Melia, dressed in rags, pulled herself onto the dock to face Port Master Clymene. "A large contingency will be arriving soon. Two carriages, six wagons. Many people. They are the best the west has to offer. Their host is Telchine Dexithea plus a port Oceanid. The chief dignitaries are Prince Periphas of Graikoi and his consort."

Clymene replied, "That's too large for us to host overnight."

To Doris, standing next to her, Clymene said, "Prepare a standard short reception for important people. Volunteer to lead the party into Urfa."

Melia stared at Clymene. "There's more. Sit down."

"There is always more. Why should I sit down?"

"Sit down."

ELDER OLYMPIANS: Hestia, Demeter, Hera, Hades, Poseidon, Zeus
OLYMPIANS: Apollo, Ares, Artemis, Athena, Aphrodite, Dionysus, Hermes,
Hephaestus, Heracles. LIVING TITANS: Oceanus, Tethys, Selene, Elder Oceanids.
DECEASED TITANS: Queen Kiya, Iapetus/Piercer, Cronus.

"You are too melodramatic, Melia," Clymene said as she pulled out a chair and sat in it. "Yes?"

"The port Oceanid host is," she paused, "... Amphitrite!"

Clymene gasped, then smiled broadly. "I haven't seen Sister in years. How wonderfully exciting! Does she know that I am Port Master?"

"I don't know. Your name was mentioned." Melia hesitated. "There's more."

"More?!"

"Yes, there are two older men in the delegation." She paused again. "Atlas and Meoetius."

Clymene froze, lowered her eyes onto her upturned hand, released an audible sob, and looked at Melia through red-rimmed eyes. "My sons... "

Doris took over the situation. "Port Master, retire to the Reflection Pond. I will take over your duties. I and Melia will convince Amphitrite and the two Titans to remain here overnight. I will replace Amphitrite as host for the group and get them settled in at Urfa. Melia can lead your family to the Reflection Pond after the delegation is on its way. That is a command, Port Master Clymene!"

Clymene said softly, "You are acting Port Master, Doris. I am going to the Reflection Pond."

And so it was that Clymene sat on a bench near Reflection Pond. In the distance, she heard Melia and Amphitrite approach as they happily bantered of meaningless things. Melia entered the clearing and then became silent and stopped. This took Amphitrite by surprise. She looked at Melia and then followed Melia's gaze to the seated Clymene. Amphitrite registered no recognition but turned to the two men following her and said, "Nephews, I believe I see your mother."

The two men now stopped, looked at one another, walked past Melia and Amphitrite, saw the woman at the table, stopped again to stare, ran toward her, and arriving, simply said, "Mother," and sat beside her to lay their heads in her lap.

She leaned her body over to cover them and, with tears, said, "My sons!"

OCEANIDS: Metis, Tyche, Clymene, Eurybia, Amphitrite, Philyra, Rhodos.
TELCHINES: Dexithea, Makelo, Halia.
EAST: Azura, Seth, Typhon, Iasion, Endymion.
OTHER: Centaur Chiron, Charon, Hotep, Petra, Persephone.

Melia said to Amphitrite, "I will go prepare the evening's meal. It will be ready when you are." She left the reuniting family.

The family laughed, cried, and reminisced for hours.

The day began to fade, Amphitrite said, "All right Titanes, let me conduct some Titan business. I haven't had the opportunity to talk privately with either of you, but I assume that you are both spies for Mother."

Atlas and Meoetius glanced at one another.

She continued, "You are in luck, nephews. I am whore to Poseidon, the strongest Olympian of them all. And I am confidant to Titan Dionysus. If I don't know of it, no one knows of it." Amphitrite looked at Clymene and said, "Please Sister Clymene, don't be angry with me! Sister Metis is furious with me! I could not bear it if you are angry with me, too." She paused, then continued, "I decided to become Poseidon's loving wife because he was going to openly challenge Father's right to manage the waters of the world and humiliate Father in front of all of his subjects. To prevent this, I have cultivated my husband's love – whatever -- carefully. He has grown to rely on my counsel. I told him to win the love of all those on the western frontier he need only allow Oceanus to pledge his allegiance to Ghod of the Sea Poseidon; that Oceanus hates adulation, that he runs from fame, and that it would be to his relief and good fortune if Poseidon would agree to take on these responsibilities." She grew silent.

Atlas volunteered, "You have saved us much work, Aunt Ampi. You have just written our report to Aunt Tethys for us. Those are the unknowns Aunt Tethys is concerned with. With this knowledge, she can make a plan for when Poseidon enjoins Uncle Oceanus."

Atlas added, "My brothers and I should come to visit you at Port Graikoi more often, Aunt Ampi. We have been remiss in our duties."

She laughed. "It is good that you weren't there to witness me humiliate myself in front of the prince."

It was now Meoetius who laughed, "We heard of the incident, Aunt Ampi. I was on my way to kill the scum, but Brother Atlas intervened. I went instead to Port Kaptara to see Aunt Metis and get her version of the story. I promised to hold off killing anyone until we got back from the festival with more information. We saw the prince belittle you at the State Dinner. I believe the scum needs killing! Don't you agree?"

ELDER OLYMPIANS: Hestia, Demeter, Hera, Hades, Poseidon, Zeus
OLYMPIANS: Apollo, Ares, Artemis, Athena, Aphrodite, Dionysus, Hermes, Hephaestus, Heracles. LIVING TITANS: Oceanus, Tethys, Selene, Elder Oceanids. DECEASED TITANS: Queen Kiya, Iapetus/Piercer, Cronus.

"No," she laughed. "Prince Periphas came to me the next day and apologized. He may be useful to us someday. Let him live. Remember, Grandmother said to love those that despise you."

Meoetius said, "I would most certainly love Periphas as I cut his throat!"

Clymene said, "Children, behave!" They returned to the dock for their evening meal.

~

Meanwhile, the Kemet-Demeter caravan continued their journey to Riverport. Halia and Nerites had traveled together for five days. Halia was exhausted keeping the two delegations happy. Her group was easy enough to entertain but Nerites insisted the two delegations make a common camp at night, "leopards and bears, you know."

Demeter was terrified but Artemis assured her that both she and Apollo were expert marksmen and, too, any predator would probably take Chiron first and leave the Ghods alone. Demeter insisted Chiron stay nearby because he told the best stories and was not at all lower class. And in case a leopard dashed in.

Finally, the caravan came to the final way station before Riverport. Halia called for a rest stop.

The wagons were accosted by five women in rags begging for food. "Food! We will do anything for scraps of food." The women raised their tunics to their waists for the men. To the women, they pleaded, "Food, Sister. Please."

Halia charged Nerites with taking care of both delegations while she took care of the beggars. She took them away from the delegations and sat them down. "You will all be fed. Remain here and DO NOT ACCOST my guests. Understood?"

Out of hearing of the main group, the oldest beggar woman matter-of-factly asked Halia, "What is the nature of your travelers? Are any of them Olympians or Ghods? Do they come in peace and with goodwill?"

Halia, taken aback, hesitated, thought, and said "Dung! You're Oceanids, aren't you? You're good!"

OCEANIDS: Metis, Tyche, Clymene, Eurybia, Amphitrite, Philyra, Rhodos.
TELCHINES: Dexithea, Makelo, Halia.
EAST: Azura, Seth, Typhon, Iasion, Endymion.
OTHER: Centaur Chiron, Charon, Hotep, Petra, Persephone.

The Oceanid replied, "Thank you. Now, I need a report before your friends return. I must brief Port Master Clymene on what to expect so proper protocols can be implemented."

Halia talked rapidly. When finished, the Oceanid instructed her to ensure that Nerites would be the first to be transported across the river.

Halia told Nerites to go on ahead while she took care of the beggar women.

After a while, Halia loaded her people and continued their journey. Kemet looked back with pity at the four women sitting there devouring their food. -- *weren't there five women when we arrived?* --

~

Melia and four more Oceanids, clothed in dirty rags, were waiting with a decrepit barge when Nerites and the Ghods arrived at the dock across from Riverport. The carriage, with a horrified Demeter clinging tightly to Artemis, was transported across the river. The barge master suggested they be careful what they touched because there was so much disease going around but they would be safe enough once they left for Urfa. Melia reached out to touch the hem of Demeter's cloak, but Demeter screamed and jerked away. Nerites debarked his carriage as soon as he could and hurriedly continued their journey to Urfa. No one was concerned about the whereabouts of the wagons behind them.

Clymene told Melia, "You and your sisters gave an outstanding performance. Now, change clothes and follow the Ghods to Urfa. Try to become their servant or guide or something.

When Halia's caravan arrived at the river; a luxury-sized barge was waiting. A cheerful Oceanid greeted Halia. "Let's get your honored guests across and properly greeted."

Halia and Chief Kemet, with their horse and carriage, were transported across the river, docked, unloaded, and greeted by Clymene. "You and your people simply must spend the night with us, Great Chief Kemet. We are so excited to have such a distinguished visitor. My Oceanid sisters wish to dance and sing for you at this evening's dinner. Sister Doris will take good care of you. She is a senior Oceanid, well-versed in hosting important people. Now, let her show you to your executive quarters until we get your staff settled and the next delegation on their way to Urfa. Doris and I are excited to share you. Anything you wish will be provided."

Doris took the excited chief by the arm and led him away from the dock area as his staff, wagons, and horses were tended to.

Halia walked to join Clymene. Clymene asked her, "Are these the last of the Port's delegations?"

"There is one more behind me probably arriving tomorrow or the day after. It will be hosted by my sister Telchine Makelo. As far as I know, it will be a small delegation, and everyone will be an honored guest of the Port."

"Excellent! So far, so good. Now, what sleeping arrangements would Chief Kemet enjoy?"

"Chief Kemet is an old, overweight, outgoing, world-loving, passionate kind of man. I, myself, am too sweet to be of interest to him. Do you have dancers? He loves watching, as he says, the 'fluid poetry of the female body moving in concert with sensuous sounds of flutes and drumbeat.' Perhaps one might be willing to be his bed companion."

"Passionate, you say? I miss the loving, eager embrace of my murdered, sweet Piercer. He loved life! Dionysus is the only male I know that has that thirst about him. Do you think an older Oceanid might interest him?"

As it turned out, the chief was interested and delighted.

39. The Ghods Entry into Urfa

Meanwhile, as Nerites' group hurriedly left Riverport, their carriage was passed by a woman riding a galloping horse. Chiron looked upon the passing horse with quiet pride. *What a beautiful horse.*

The carriage eventually arrived at the gates of Urfa and was met by a young woman. "Greetings! I am hostess Melia, a person of high rank. You bring Ghods, do you not?"

Nerites said, "Yes," and introduced each member of his delegation.

"Wonderful! I am to take you directly to your quarters so you can avoid mingling with the lower classes. Urfa's Great Mother Azura wishes to be notified any time someone as glorious as a Ghod arrives. She will want to

OCEANIDS: Metis, Tyche, Clymene, Eurybia, Amphitrite, Philyra, Rhodos.
TELCHINES: Dexithea, Makelo, Halia.
EAST: Azura, Seth, Typhon, Iasion, Endymion.
OTHER: Centaur Chiron, Charon, Hotep, Petra, Persephone.

meet and escort you to our executive dining room for the evening's meal." She spoke each of their names, "Ghods Demeter, Apollo, and Artemis, Lord Nerites and commoner Centaur Chiron, follow me to your quarters. I will tell Mother Azura of your glorious arrival." She turned and strode toward the most impressive guest house.

"Well," said Demeter. "At least they know how to show proper respect in this place."

Everyone muttered agreement except Chiron, who was lost in thought. *- - that is the woman who rode past us on the pony -- she looks exactly like the barge master in the ragged clothes who ferried us across the river -- maybe they're sisters --*

Melia checked them in and said, "I will have refreshments sent to your quarters. Do you require wine?" She completed her tasks and then hurried to obtain an audience with Azura. She entered the building and with the words, "I am Oceanid Melia. I come with Ghods," received an immediate audience with Azura. The two studied the personality dossiers of their visiting Ghods. Ghod Demeter was the Ghod of consequence, her history rich and interesting. The other two were young and more Titan, at least more Olympian, than Ghod.

Azura said, "Titanide Selene is a resident of Urfa and cousin to the two young ones. She may have a deep-seated hatred for Olympian Demeter and complete disdain for her traitorous cousins."

Melia said, "All the better to enlist her help, Mother Azura. She has powerful motivation."

Noam was dispatched to summon Titanide Selene, daughter of slain Elder Titans Hyperion and Theia, to the office of Mother Azura of Urfa.

When the Ghods arrived at the executive dining room, they were met by a manager who knew how to entertain important guests. The three Ghods and the Lord sat at the fine table near the entrance so that everyone entering would see them and undoubtedly be impressed by their magnificent presence. They were serenaded by two aulos players.

Melia stopped by the table. "Are they treating you well? Is the service tolerable?"

The twins were enchanted with their reception, but Demeter sniffed, "It's all right, I suppose. It's just so lonely being a Ghod, sometimes."

ELDER OLYMPIANS: Hestia, Demeter, Hera, Hades, Poseidon, Zeus
OLYMPIANS: Apollo, Ares, Artemis, Athena, Aphrodite, Dionysus, Hermes, Hephaestus, Heracles. LIVING TITANS: Oceanus, Tethys, Selene, Elder Oceanids. DECEASED TITANS: Queen Kiya, Iapetus/Piercer, Cronus.

The twins repeated in unison, "So lonely."

Melia said, "Lonely? I will see what I can do. I will be around, call me if you need anything." Melia hurried away.

After a while, a small murmur ran through the room. Others of consequence were arriving; a striking young woman about the same age as the twins escorted by two men; all of great beauty. The three were seated several tables away from the Ghods. Melia drifted back in and unobtrusively took up a position to eavesdrop on both tables.

"Hmph. Who were those people?" Demeter inquired of her table attendant.

The attendant replied, "That is Titanide Selene. She is of high rank and much loved by the citizens of Urfa."

Artemis squealed. "Cousin Selene? Here? How exciting. May I go speak to her, Ghod Demeter?"

Demeter sniffed, "I suppose so, but be careful. There are so many lower-class people here."

Artemis rose, hurried to Selene's table, and said, "Cousin Selene! I am Leto's daughter, Artemis."

Selene glanced up, stared, smiled widely, rose, as did the two men, and embraced Artemis. "Titanide Artemis! How are you? It's been forever since I last saw you! Is Apollo here?"

Artemis looked over her shoulder and nodded toward Apollo. Selene gave a big smile and waved to him.

Artemis said, "But I am an Olympian now, you know! A Ghod, actually!"

Selene, who had been extensively briefed on the situation and was inwardly fuming, graciously replied, "How nice for you. We simply must get together sometime."

One of the males cleared his throat. Selene said, "Oh, yes. This is my friend Endymion and one of his managers, Iasion."

Endymion nodded his head in recognition and said, "How nice to meet you, Ghod Artemis. Welcome to Urfa. We have a nice outdoor patio here. Let's meet after the meal for drinks and maybe some dancing. Iasion, here,

OCEANIDS: Metis, Tyche, Clymene, Eurybia, Amphitrite, Philyra, Rhodos.
TELCHINES: Dexithea, Makelo, Halia.
EAST: Azura, Seth, Typhon, Iasion, Endymion.
OTHER: Centaur Chiron, Charon, Hotep, Petra, Persephone.

needs to visit with beautiful women. He's too tied to his work and needs to socialize."

Selene said, "Master Shepherd Endymion oversees Urfa animal management. Shepherd Iasion is his master of horses."

Artemis flashed her sexiest little smile toward Iasion. "How impressive!" Her smile cooled a bit when Iasion replied, "Thank you. Who is that lovely older woman with the interesting sad smile?"

She glanced at Demeter with her eyes downcast and perpetual sad little put-upon smile. "That is Ghod Demeter. She is really important, but she doesn't like to associate with commoners."

Iasion said, "I understand. The high-born are often the loneliest people. But I would be honored to meet her if she wishes to join us after dinner." He smiled across the room to Demeter and nodded his head to her."

Demeter quickly looked away and pretended not to have noticed.

Melia strolled to Demeter's table, told her that her evening meal was ready to be served, and inquired if Artemis should return to her table.

Demeter snapped, "She most certainly should!"

Melia left and returned with Artemis. Melia said to Demeter, "It appears that you have an admirer at the other table."

"Oh," sniffed Demeter.

"Yes. Iasion, the pretty one. He wants to know 'who is the lovely, lonely woman with the sad, haunting eyes?' He would like to meet you on the patio after the evening meal."

"Oh, no. I could not possibly meet with a commoner," Demeter said as she cut her eyes to survey Iasion.

"I will convey your rejection. He is, of course, a man of high rank in Urfa."

"High rank? I don't know. I will consider it. Perhaps I will." -- *he is handsome -- more so than both Nerites and Dionysus — 'sad, haunting eyes?' -- no one appreciates how much I suffer -- other than Dionysus -- would Iasion? -- high rank? -- he is handsome --*

Melia left the table but remained within earshot of her seven principals.

ELDER OLYMPIANS: Hestia, Demeter, Hera, Hades, Poseidon, Zeus
OLYMPIANS: Apollo, Ares, Artemis, Athena, Aphrodite, Dionysus, Hermes, Hephaestus, Heracles. LIVING TITANS: Oceanus, Tethys, Selene, Elder Oceanids. DECEASED TITANS: Queen Kiya, Iapetus/Piercer, Cronus.

Selene was the only one who had received a briefing on their four out-of-town guests. She had invited Endymion to dinner without sharing her ulterior motives. He was sweet and highly intelligent, but otherwise uncomplicated, as was his best friend, Iasion. She had said, "Oh, and invite Iasion. You sometimes enjoy his company more than mine."

Melia had suggested that Iasion might be a perfect companion for Ghod Demeter. -- *we will find out* -- Selene sometimes grew impatient with Iasion because he was so concerned with others 'feelings.' -- *that's fine and good, Iasion -- but you are a man -- not some weepy-eyed woman!* --

The meals neared completion. Melia went to Selene and said, "Titanide Selene, Mother Azura would be thrilled if you and your company could ensure that our Olympian friends have a delightful evening. Ghod Demeter is shy but expressed an interest in your friend Iasion."

Selene looked at Endymion and asked, "Endy, do you think Iasion can seduce Ghod Demeter? If he can, I will give you a special treat later."

Iasion blushed. "Titanide Selene, I would never take advantage of a vulnerable woman like Ghod Demeter!"

She replied, "I understand, Iasion. But Endy won't get his treat, either. Come on, you two. Let's entertain our self-important out-of-town guests!" She rose and led the two men to Demeter's table. "Cousin Apollo, I demand that you dance with me! My dull and dreary Endymion does not even pretend to dance. Command your Nerites friend to dance with my beautiful cousin. They will be the envy of the dance floor. Now, come. Let's dance!"

She pulled Apollo up and led him toward the dance floor. She glared back at Nerites and snapped, "Dance with my cousin!" Nerites had no choice but to stand, extend his hand to Artemis, and say, "We are in a land of commoners, Ghod Artemis. Let's humor them. May I have this dance?"

Artemis stared at the extended hand. -- *Nerites* is *a lord -- a handsome lord, at that -- and a favorite of ghod Poseidon* –

She stood, took his hand, and decided to flash him her sexiest little smile. They left to join the others on the dance floor leaving Endymion and Iasion standing awkwardly at Demeter's table. Demeter was busy studying something, anything, other than the two men standing before her.

OCEANIDS: Metis, Tyche, Clymene, Eurybia, Amphitrite, Philyra, Rhodos.
TELCHINES: Dexithea, Makelo, Halia.
EAST: Azura, Seth, Typhon, Iasion, Endymion.
OTHER: Centaur Chiron, Charon, Hotep, Petra, Persephone.

Endymion understood Selene's instructions. "I will leave you two sensitive people alone to explore all the suffering and sadness in the world. I will be at the bar, drinking wine, and watching Selene heat up. I, too, will be suffering." He laughed, stared at Iasion, and said, "I expect Selene to give me a special treat later," winked, and left Iasion alone with Demeter.

Iasion, almost trembling with fear, ventured. "You have a lovely smile. I understand that you have suffered a great deal."

His introductory line was perfect. She engaged.

And so...

Iasion sat beside Demeter on the bench overlooking the original einkorn field. The moon approached its fullest. "How you have suffered, Ghod Demeter. You have been through so much. Yet you go on, head held high, with hope in your heart. You are an amazing woman."

"I try. And my sweet daughter is a queen, you know -- Queen of the Colored Fields."

"That is why I brought you to this place, Sweet Ghod Demeter. This place is the most honored in all of Urfa. Here is where Great Mother Valki lies in peace. It was here that Mother Valki took wild grains of einkorn and learned its secrets. Now we grow fields of endless golden tasseled wheat. It is extremely beautiful glistening in the golden summer sun. I hope you can bring your precious daughter, the Queen, here to witness this. And, too, so that I can see you again." He gently took her hand into his. "I would so much like to see your sweet daughter."

Demeter reflected for a moment and said, "Queen Persephone is in Phlegethon now being Queen but I do carry a likeness of her with me. It is a statue of her likeness my brother God Hephaestus made for me. He cast me many little images of her. They are made of Orichalcum. A precious metal, you know."

"I did *not* know! How wonderful! May I see it or is it too great for my eyes to behold?"

She squeezed his hand. Just a little. "Yes, you may see it. It is in my quarters. I carry it everywhere. Actually, I have several."

He rose and pulled Demeter to her feet. "Let us go to your quarters right now, sweet Demeter. I must see this great object before the night is out. It excites me greatly."

Demurely, she replied, "Very well, although the twins may be there."

"Nonsense, Selene will keep them out dancing all night. There will be only me and your own beautiful, tragic self. Now, let's hurry back and idolize this great image of your precious daughter." He led her back to her room in the traveler's inn. He did not release her hand.

They entered her quarters. Only then did she remember to release her hand.

Demeter turned to face him. The oil lamps were burning. - *he is more kind than even Dionysus -- more sensitive -- he understands my suffering -- I have not even told him of my brutal rape by my own brother -- that would probably be more than he could bear -- he is handsome --*

Iasion allowed her to release her hand from his. She turned to face him with her sad little smile. *-- she is a ghod -- Selene said that is the highest of all ranks -- if I could couple with her then my career would know no limits -- if she didn't have me killed -- she is rather pretty -- so vulnerable -- she makes me feel useful – needed --*

He held out both hands to her and with a pained voice said, "Demeter?"

She took his hands.

After they had finished, Iasion said, "If you asked it of me, Great Demeter, I would hold back the moon, the sun, even the morning tide but I could no longer hold back my desire for you. You are too beautiful, too desirable, too sensitive, too wronged. I had to have you. Please understand and forgive my unforgivable weakness and forwardness."

"Silly boy. I forgive you. You are just a man wanting what men want. But look on the table beside you. You did not even notice the statute of Queen Persephone in your great passion to have me."

Iasion turned his head and looked at the statue looking back at him. He was shocked by its realness. "My Ghod Demeter! She looks so lifelike! Like she is looking out over a field of golden wheat! You have more of these likenesses?"

OCEANIDS: Metis, Tyche, Clymene, Eurybia, Amphitrite, Philyra, Rhodos.
TELCHINES: Dexithea, Makelo, Halia.
EAST: Azura, Seth, Typhon, Iasion, Endymion.
OTHER: Centaur Chiron, Charon, Hotep, Petra, Persephone.

"Yes, I have three. They are my company after everyone has deserted me!"

With one hand, he gently pressed her head into his shoulder; with the other, her breasts into his chest. -- *I must have one of these things -- it is so lifelike -- it would tie Demeter to me in some way -- it might raise my standing in Urfa -- with Endymion -- with Selene -- she looks down on me, now -- how do I get a statue? --*

"Great Ghod Demeter, would you consider placing a statue of Queen Persephone in Valki's Einkorn field? We could place it so that Queen Persephone looks over the golden fields of wheat all day long. She could help the wheat to grow; rejoice when it first peeks from the soil. And it would be like you being here all the time. After all, it would be you who placed the statue there and you are the Queen's mother. I cannot hold you like this forever but at least it would help me remember this moment." He squeezed her a little tighter.

Do women's hearts really flutter? Who can know these things? Demeter's heart fluttered. "Of course, you can, you sweet man. You may have anything you want." Her hips gently ground into his.

40. Tallstone Check-In

The Graikoi party arrived at Tallstone two days before the festival was to begin. Port Olympus retained a prime building to host receptions and meetings. The port also reserved three smaller buildings for the use of their guests. Urfa was retained to keep the buildings stocked with food and refreshments. Dionysus had Seilenos stock the buildings with wine, a commodity not usually available to the eastern tribes.

Amphitrite assisted Prince Periphas settle his entourage into the largest of the three Tallstone guest houses. Kaptara had by far the largest delegation.

The prince had begrudgingly spent the previous day and night touring the city of Urfa. As interesting as the prince found the large, cosmopolitan city, he was far more interested in observing the intricacies and planning which went into this festival of overwhelming proportions.

Today, he watched as the Scholars and elder women busily prepared their workshops, lectures, gaming fields, bread and grain tables, and toilet facilities. No one wished to take time to talk to the prince. A retired chief from the Urfa Council of Chiefs was always ready to visit but they knew little of actual preparation requirements and their talk quickly reverted to "when-I-was-chief." Prince Periphas grew frustrated.

It was his co-host, Telchine Dexithea, who saved the day. She volunteered to find the prince a knowledgeable, enthusiastic mentor.

Dexithea walked with Periphas through the early morning festival grounds observing the preparations. She noticed many women wearing red belts running up to an older woman wearing both a red belt and a red headband, speaking to her, and then hurrying away. "Let's stand here and watch, Prince. We may learn something."

The prince stood silently as Dexithea watched the women talk. She heard the older woman say "... entertainment right over there." Dexithea had no idea of the context, meaning, or purpose of the comment but Dexithea was a Telchine, and Telchines jump right in.

Dexithea waited until no one was approaching the woman, said to the prince, "Wait here," walked up to the woman, and said, "I can provide the best entertainers in the world! Are you interested?" Dexithea had no idea of what the woman was interested in.

The woman looked at her and replied, "Perhaps. What tribe do you represent, Sweet? What is their talent?"

"I represent the Great Kingdom of Graikoi, the most sophisticated and culturally advanced country in the world. And my prince just happened to bring his best entertainers with him to your Festival. They just left a triumphant tour in Port Olympus. Their talents are unlike any you have ever seen. Are you interested in meeting my prince?"

"It's a little late to schedule new talent. The festival begins tomorrow but perhaps." The woman waved across the field to another older woman with a red belt and called out, "Take over for me, Edna. I'm going to take a break." The woman waved back in acknowledgment. "All right, Sweet. I am Abigail. Introduce me to your prince."

Dexithea left her prince talking with Abigail as she scurried off to find some Graikoi entertainers wandering around the gaming fields.

In a short time, the prince looked down the street and said, "Here come three of our entertainers now!"

OCEANIDS: Metis, Tyche, Clymene, Eurybia, Amphitrite, Philyra, Rhodos.
TELCHINES: Dexithea, Makelo, Halia.
EAST: Azura, Seth, Typhon, Iasion, Endymion.
OTHER: Centaur Chiron, Charon, Hotep, Petra, Persephone.

Abigail looked in the direction the prince was pointing. Her eyes widened. The Tumblers were coming side-by-side down the street performing Round-offs, Flicks, Whips, with Double, Triple, and Twisting Somersaults. They greeted Abigail as the largest tumbler nailed a twisting somersault directly in front of her, the next tumbler, landed directly on his shoulders, and the third, a petite female, scampered up the back of the first two to stand on the second gymnast's shoulders, her arms triumphantly in the air.

The prince asked, "They are our gymnasts. What do you think?"

Abigail replied, "I think I need to sit down."

Meanwhile, Amphitrite spent the morning at her guest houses awaiting the next delegations. Soon, Halia arrived with Chief Kemet and his small delegation. After warmly greeting the chief and getting his people settled into the second guest house, Halia briefed Amphitrite on the two delegations that should be arriving in the late afternoon, Makelo's Kaptara Delegation and Nerite's Ghod delegation with a centaur; but Ghod Demeter had wished to remain another night in Urfa.

"Dung!" Amphitrite said. "I have Ghods to deal with!"

Amphitrite expected Dionysus to arrive in a few days but until then she was the host. Amphitrite decided that the Kemet delegation and Kaptara delegation could be housed in one building and that Ghods Demeter, Athena, and Apollo could be assigned to the third unit. Keeping the dignitaries away from the Ghods was of paramount importance. -- *well, at least it's only Demeter and the twins -- I should be able to handle the three of them -- a centaur? -- what is that? --*

She went to Chief Kemet and explained her problem.

Kemet exclaimed, "Of course, we would be delighted to share quarters with those Kaptara people. But they are so serious! Maybe we from Port Kemet can loosen them up a bit! I understand these Ghod people prefer to remain to themselves! We shall do our part to make that happen!"

"Wonderful, Chief Kemet. Don't tell anyone but you are my favorite chief!" She gave him a bear hug, hesitated, and gave him a second one. She then successfully settled the Kaptara delegation into their new quarters shared with the Kemet delegation. The two delegations mixed amicably; Amphitrite made sure the wine flowed freely.

ELDER OLYMPIANS: Hestia, Demeter, Hera, Hades, Poseidon, Zeus
OLYMPIANS: Apollo, Ares, Artemis, Athena, Aphrodite, Dionysus, Hermes,
Hephaestus, Heracles. LIVING TITANS: Oceanus, Tethys, Selene, Elder Oceanids.
DECEASED TITANS: Queen Kiya, Iapetus/Piercer, Cronus.

Makelo and her wards arrived in the early afternoon. She said to Amphitrite, "The Ghods are staying at least one more night in Urfa. Their Mother Azura met with us and is extremely interested in the Ghods. Titanide Selene and her friends have taken up with them. I don't know what's going on, and I don't know when to expect them. I'm tired, Mother Amphitrite. It's been a long quarter moon."

Amphitrite lovingly embraced the Telchine. "It's difficult, my child, being a weapon of war."

41. Winter Solstice Festival 75
< Year 101, WSF >

The crowd gathered in front of the stage. Colorful flags flew. Seth stood with Azura and elderly Chief Vanamtwo in the back surrounded by their assistants. Azura had arrived this morning for the opening ceremony.

A horn blew a deafening sound. The crowd grew larger.

Three vibrant young women dressed in knee-length red dresses ran onto the stage, hands high in the air. They shouted in unison, "Are you ready to have a festival?" They danced wildly. Each of the 'Color Girls,' Daphne, Leah, and Rebecca, then picked up a megaphone and repeated, louder, in unison, "We said, are you ready to have a festival?!"

The crowd responded with a roar. The Color Girls milked it.

Finally, with practiced hand and body motions, they quieted their audience.

Daphne shouted into her megaphone, "Everybody be quiet as a mouse now so they can hear us in the back. Can you hear me in the back?" There was a scattered response.

Leah shouted into her megaphone, "Here are your hosts for this wonderful event!" She waved toward the hosts standing at the back of the stage.

Rebecca shouted into her megaphone, "The great Elder Mother Azura of Urfa..." She did not pause for a response from the crowd as Azura stepped forward. "... the high-powered Seth of Tallstone and the exceedingly handsome Chief Vanamtwo representing the Council-of-Chiefs!" The two also stepped forward as their name was called.

OCEANIDS: Metis, Tyche, Clymene, Eurybia, Amphitrite, Philyra, Rhodos.
TELCHINES: Dexithea, Makelo, Halia.
EAST: Azura, Seth, Typhon, Iasion, Endymion.
OTHER: Centaur Chiron, Charon, Hotep, Petra, Persephone.

Over the polite applause, Daphne screamed, "Tell them all -- THANK YOU!" The other two held their arms high in the air and prodded the crowd for even more noise. Much more. Again, they milked it for a while and then again quietened them.

Leah shouted, "We have a new learning field just for women, 'The Art of Self Defense.' Look for the signs. Remember to use the toilets, wash your hands, and take a piece of Sweetbread, some have nuts."

Rebecca, with a quieter voice, said through her megaphone, "And let us remember those who created this yearly Festival seventy-five years ago, Great Mother Valki of Urfa, Master Littlerock of Tallstone, Chief Nanatan of the Clan of the Lion, and Chief Vanam of the Clan of the Serpent."

Daphne then shouted into her megaphone, "And they all want you to go out and have a fabulous time!" The crowd responded.

The three young women dressed in red screamed as they ran from the stage, "Let's go have ourselves a Festival!"

The great horn blew. The seventy-fifth Winter Solstice Festival began.

Most of the crowd began retiring to the gaming fields and festival tables but a few stayed near the stage to watch the ceremonial "Gathering-of-the-Chiefs."

Chief Vanamtwo walked to the right-side stage entrance to greet his grandson, who was leading half the active chiefs onto the stage. Enosh walked to the left side to greet Clan-of-the-Lion Chief Nanamulla as he led the other half of the current chiefs onto the stage. Abigail coordinated two dozen retired Color Girls to serve refreshments.

Vanamtwo gave his grandson a bear hug. "Great Chief Vanamfour, it is wonderful to see you again!"

The stage filled with chiefs. Nanamulla and Vanamfour, the traditional hosts, met in the middle, exchanged bear hugs, and greeted one another.

Abigail began introducing each chief to his peers on the stage. Around a stone table at the south of the stage, the elderly Urfa 'Council of Chiefs' members stood exchanging memories and admiring their replacements strutting upon the stage.

ELDER OLYMPIANS: Hestia, Demeter, Hera, Hades, Poseidon, Zeus
OLYMPIANS: Apollo, Ares, Artemis, Athena, Aphrodite, Dionysus, Hermes, Hephaestus, Heracles. LIVING TITANS: Oceanus, Tethys, Selene, Elder Oceanids. DECEASED TITANS: Queen Kiya, Iapetus/Piercer, Cronus.

Far away, at the edge of the crowd, two imposing figures stood observing the ceremonies. One of the two imposing figures, the male, demanded of a passing older hunter, "What is happening on the stage? Who are those men? What are they doing?!"

The hunter looked at the man, obviously of high rank. "That is the gathering of all the chiefs, Great Master. They meet to be seen and to visit one other."

"These men are of some local importance?"

"Yes, Great Master. They are the chiefs. The most powerful men in the land."

Ares said nothing to the man. He merely stood staring at the stage, considering what he saw.

The hunter stood there, waiting to be dismissed.

The woman glanced at the hunter with annoyance and waved her hand at him to go away. The hunter hurried away.

Ghod Ares said to Ghod Athena, "I will go inspect these 'chiefs.' Come to me when I am finished."

They strode purposely toward the stage; oncoming people automatically parted to make way for them.

Ares was met at the stage by an older woman in a red dress at the foot of the stage stairs. "I'm sorry, but this is a gathering of chiefs. I'm afraid you must be a chief to go up there."

Ares spat out, "I am a Ghod!" brushed past the woman, climbed the stairs, looked around for someone who might be of significance, and locked onto two men who stood at the center of the group. -- *most appear to fear those two* --

He walked to the two, physically running over those in his way, faced the two men, and commanded, "Who are you?!"

Chief Vanamfour and Chief Nanamulla looked at the interloper and then at one other. Without warmth, Nanamulla responded, "I am Chief Nanamulla. Who are you?"

OCEANIDS: Metis, Tyche, Clymene, Eurybia, Amphitrite, Philyra, Rhodos.
TELCHINES: Dexithea, Makelo, Halia.
EAST: Azura, Seth, Typhon, Iasion, Endymion.
OTHER: Centaur Chiron, Charon, Hotep, Petra, Persephone.

"I am Ghod Ares, an Olympian Ghod! What do you rule?"

Nanamulla was taken aback by the man's rudeness and would have admonished him to the point of physically throwing him off the stage.

But Vanamfour responded before Nanamulla could speak. "You are an Olympian, you say. An Olympian who destroyed the Titans?"

Ares answered, "Yes, Sister Athena killed the last Titan-loving Gigante that was murderously attacking the peaceful Olympians in our Port Olympus home. Ghod Hestia was outraged at Titan Queen Kiya's insurrection and in order to maintain peace in the future, Hestia sent two cadres of Hecatoncheires into the Titan lair at Tartarus and killed every abominable war-loving Titan they found. The Ghods have maintained peace in the land of Tartarus ever since."

Vanamfour replied, "That Great Bitch Kiya murdered my namesake, the greatest chief to ever live, Chief Vanam of the Clan of the Serpent. The story is told at every campfire, how Vanam went to greet Kiya on the Riverport dock with outstretched arms, how she approached him with a smile and then drove a dagger into his unsuspecting heart, how the world grieved the loss of Chief Vanam, how Bitch Kiya then strutted with self-importance across the land. I must thank you and all Olympians for ridding the world of this bitch."

Ares looked at Vanamfour with interest. Nanamulla looked upon both men with disgust, grunted, and left the two to themselves.

Ares said to Vanamfour, "Ghod Athena is nearby. Would you like to meet her?"

"It would be an honor and privilege to meet one such as Ghod Athena!"

Ares said, "I will introduce you to her. You may introduce yourself as Lord Vanamfour.' If asked, say that Ghod Ares made you a Lord. All lower classes must now do as you command. Come, I will introduce you to Ghod Athena."

Vanamfour said, "Thank you, Ghod Ares. I shall always endeavor to uphold my title. I look forward to meeting Ghod Athena. Does she happen to be that striking woman wearing the suit of armor?" -- a *lord? - - all lower classes must obey me? -- not just my tribe? -- even Nanamulla?! -- I don't know what a lord is! -- I don't know what a ghod is -- but it sounds important —*

ELDER OLYMPIANS: Hestia, Demeter, Hera, Hades, Poseidon, Zeus
OLYMPIANS: Apollo, Ares, Artemis, Athena, Aphrodite, Dionysus, Hermes,
Hephaestus, Heracles. LIVING TITANS: Oceanus, Tethys, Selene, Elder Oceanids.
DECEASED TITANS: Queen Kiya, Iapetus/Piercer, Cronus.

~

Standing beside the tall stone on the hill looking down upon the stage, General Typhon and his apprentice, Amazon Otreta, watched.

He said, "So it begins."

~

Strolling through the festival, Amphitrite and the three Telchines decided to inspect the gaming fields where muscular, half-naked men competed in games. They stopped to ask for directions. "Follow that path until you come to statues of naked athletes somebody placed at the intersection. Turn left and you will be at the men's playing fields."

They strolled on and saw the statues in the distance. When they arrived, they stopped to observe three young women puzzling over a strange phenomenon. "I just stroked his thing for good luck. It was little when I first touched it but look at it now. Touch it. It feels like a real one ready to mate!" The three young women continued to touch and study the Greek Statue with amazement. One exclaimed, "Let's go try another one!"

The Telchines exchanged glances. Amphitrite turned left but Dexithea pointed to the right as she said, "Wait. Look. There is a field of women doing something!"

They turned right, quickened their step, and stopped in front of a field of women performing slow movements in unison. The post contained an icon of a female figure standing on one leg with arms extended gracefully above her head. "What's going on?" Makelo asked a woman in a white dress with a red sash.

The woman answered, "This is one of our few fields for women; our 'Synchronized Dancing Field.' Color Girl Daphne – she's the one in the red dress -- is teaching them the art of the 'Graceful Dance.' Color Girls teach six different dances throughout the day. Would you like to join them?"

Amphitrite replied, "Thank you, but not today. What other activities do you have for women?"

"Well, tomorrow in this field, Amazon Otreta -- she is one of the Tallstone Scholars of War -- will teach a class on self-defense. How to fend off an

OCEANIDS: Metis, Tyche, Clymene, Eurybia, Amphitrite, Philyra, Rhodos.
TELCHINES: Dexithea, Makelo, Halia.
EAST: Azura, Seth, Typhon, Iasion, Endymion.
OTHER: Centaur Chiron, Charon, Hotep, Petra, Persephone.

attack by lions and even a male. She will base her instruction on a combination of the 'Fast Dance' and the 'Balance Dance' which the Color Girls teach. But Amazon Otreta will incorporate handling a five-foot wooden pole into their dances. She will train the women in how to use the pole both as a synchronized team and in individual defense. This is the first year it will be taught. We are excited to add another opportunity for women. They have so few. The men have so many."

Dexithea snorted, "Men need it!"

Amphitrite asked, "So you look for instruction and gaming that you can provide the women?"

"Physical instruction, yes. The Scholars teach the Common Language, reading, and writing to those who wish to learn."

"I see. Can women compete in skills of archery?"

"What is archery?"

Amphitrite's face brightened. "I will make you a list of activities for women. Who do I present it to?"

"Any Color Girl can assist. The three in the red dresses are our initiates. The rest wear white dresses with red sashes. Leader Abigail also wears a red headpiece. I am Color Girl Edna. I assist at the women's playing fields."

A woman riding a horse acknowledged Edna as she rode past the group.

Makelo inquired, "Who was that?"

Edna replied, "That was Amazon Myrene. She is a scholar in the art of war."

Amphitrite said, "You have an interesting place here."

Edna laughed. "Yes, it is. Stand here long enough and you will see every woman in the world pass by."

Halia pointed down the pathway. "Look at that!" Tumbling toward them was a petite young woman performing nonstop aerial cartwheels. Following her with enthusiasm were three dozen young loud girls.

Amphitrite laughed. "You simply must add that to the list!"

Before they departed, Dexithea handed Edna a coin. "Here is a gift from my sisters and me. It has an engraving of our faces on the front and an engraving of us dancing naked in the rain on the back. It will help you remember us."

~

Meanwhile, Otreta had her assignment. She was to become the interlopers' friend. -- *who are they?* -- *what do they want?* -- *how can I help?* --

She strolled down to the stage, found Chief Nanamulla, and said, "I am Scholar Otreta, Great Chief. I saw you and Chief Vanamfour talking on the stage. Who was the man who joined you immediately before you left?"

Chief Nanamulla, as always, was gracious. "Ah, Scholar. I hope I did not appear rude, but Chief Vanamfour sometimes becomes carried away with his memories. The person whom you inquire about introduced himself as Ghod Ares. He appears to be a man of great self-importance. He claimed to be an Olympian involved in the western Titan wars and the killing of the Titans; a subject dear to Chief Vanamfour. This Ghod Ares is of interest to a scholar of war?"

"I have heard of Ghods, but I have never met one. Was he pleasant enough?"

"As pleasant as a striking serpent. He appeared to expect shameless adulation."

Otreta laughed. "Tallstone is fortunate to have such an insightful, powerful chief such as yourself dedicated to maintaining friendship between all tribes."

"Yet, this chief wonders why the Scholars of Tallstone study the art of war."

"The chief already knows the answer. So there will not be one." She paused. "Where did Chief Vanamfour and Ghod Ares go?"

"I believe there was a commotion on the other side of the stage; one involving a woman dressed in armor. Find a woman dressed in armor. You will find your man of interest."

Otreta stared at Nanamulla and struck her chest with her right fist, a sign of great respect. -- *a woman in armor?* -- *how interesting!* --

OCEANIDS: Metis, Tyche, Clymene, Eurybia, Amphitrite, Philyra, Rhodos.
TELCHINES: Dexithea, Makelo, Halia.
EAST: Azura, Seth, Typhon, Iasion, Endymion.
OTHER: Centaur Chiron, Charon, Hotep, Petra, Persephone.

A woman wearing armor was not difficult to track. Otreta found her at the 'Spear Throwing Accuracy' competition field. She stood beside the 'Ghod' and Chief Vanamfour, who was now their guide. *-- here we are -- two ghods and a powerful chief --*

She took a position away from them but close enough to hear their conversation.

Otreta picked up on the names 'Ghod Ares' and 'Ghod Athena' and that belittling the capabilities of the competition participants were expected. The Ghods appeared to be interested in the fighting capabilities of hunters in general. Her guild discussed Olympian Ghods in the abstract. Beside her, stood two Ghods in the flesh; a rich trove of knowledge to be gained. *-- general Typhon's instincts were correct -- know your enemy! – and I am his spy! -- now, how do I proceed? --*

Otreta sidled up to the edge of Athena's comfort zone and waited until a particularly inept participant was widely off the mark with all three of his attempts. She then said to Athena, "Disgusting! These hunters are simply disgusting, don't you think?"

Athena looked at Otreta without expression.

"What a magnificent sword you have! Is that Orichalcum? I have heard rumors of a wonderful metal but have never seen it. May I?" Otreta said as she reached to touch the sword without permission and leaned in for a closer look.

Athena snorted, "I suppose. Yes, you are correct, and you have nothing like it here because Orichalcum is reserved for the Ghods."

Otreta ran her hand over the hilt with great appreciation. "Is it well balanced? Does it fit your hand well? The scroll work is so detailed; obviously made by a master craftsman."

The questions and comments went straight to Athena's vanity. Athena removed the sword and, with some irritation, handed it to Otreta. "You know of such things? A woman!"

Otreta took the sword, tested it with a rapid series of aggressive thrusts using both hands separately, then together, and ended up holding the sword at its balance point. "Nice. A magnificent sword. Yes, I do, a woman. I am Scholar Otreta. You appear to be a person of great rank and

ELDER OLYMPIANS: Hestia, Demeter, Hera, Hades, Poseidon, Zeus
OLYMPIANS: Apollo, Ares, Artemis, Athena, Aphrodite, Dionysus, Hermes,
Hephaestus, Heracles. LIVING TITANS: Oceanus, Tethys, Selene, Elder Oceanids.
DECEASED TITANS: Queen Kiya, Iapetus/Piercer, Cronus.

importance." Otreta tossed the sword upward, caught it by the hilt, and ceremoniously presented it back to Athena.

Athena accepted the sword with a look of open amazement. "You have such a sword?"

"Oh, no. A person such as I am not worthy of such a sword, but I do have a wooden sword with a sharp stone blade. It is not as desirable as a sword of Orichalcum, but it's all I have." Otreta continued the conversation ingratiating herself into Athena's goodwill. She established their common interests in war and combat techniques. "Come with me. I will show you the sporting fields of greatest interest."

By now, Athena was interested in Otreta. -- *proper servitude -- respect for ghods -- a little higher class of person -- appreciates greatness and great things* --

Athena said, "Yes, show these fields to me," and turned to Ares. "I am going to inspect other fields of battle. I will find you later."

Ares turned to glare at Otreta and asked Athena, "Who is that person?"

Athena replied, "Her name is Otreta. She is a Scholar."

Otreta quickly cut in, staring at Ares without fear, "And you are Ghod Ares; a man who is said can teach a woman of submission and respect." She did not blink.

Ares stared at her and eventually said, "Yesss."

Otreta broke their mutual stare, looked at Athena, said, "Come, Great Ghod Athena, I will show you the nature of war," and with new familiarity took her arm and led Athena away to games of battle.

~

In Urfa, Selene and Melia sat on the bench facing Valki's grave.

Selene said, "That statue is disrespectful. This is Mother Valki's place; not a place for some likeness of a foreign monster."

"Mother Azura said to leave it. You and Iasion continue to provide wonderful information about these Ghods. That people such as these defeated Queen Kiya is unbelievable. Why we are to fear them is unimaginable. They are children. Simple children."

OCEANIDS: Metis, Tyche, Clymene, Eurybia, Amphitrite, Philyra, Rhodos.
TELCHINES: Dexithea, Makelo, Halia.
EAST: Azura, Seth, Typhon, Iasion, Endymion.
OTHER: Centaur Chiron, Charon, Hotep, Petra, Persephone.

"The report indicates nine more of them. Those nine are the more dangerous." She paused. "I made a mistake the other night when I set Nerites up with Artemis; I should have encouraged my sweet Endymion, instead. I don't know what I was thinking. Well, yes, I do, but I should have encouraged him, anyway. I could have told him, 'She is high-born, you know. I will be looking somewhere else if she tries to seduce you.' Men like that sort of thing. I could have retrieved a lot of information about Artemis. Come to think of it, I could have gained a lot of information from Apollo. Hmmm. He is cute. I will think about that."

~

Eventually and belatedly, Nerites and his delegation arrived at Tallstone. Demeter had remained behind in Urfa with Iasion. Amphitrite settled the group into their private quarters.

Evening came.

Campfires burned. Chiefs held their tribal council meetings. Western trading delegations gathered in Amphitrite's meeting house to be fed and entertained.

Chief Vanamfour held his tribal meeting. His Skywatcher organized the campfire and gathered the hunters and gatherers to surround it. He lit the fire as the sun set and nursed it to be a suitable council fire. Chief Vanamfour appeared and took his place between his Skywatcher and Elder Woman. Vanamfour went through routine tribal matters and had his Skywatcher present his concerns with weather, tracking, and the sky. Vanamfour recognized his elder woman to present women's concerns.

The elder woman went through the routine reports and ended with "Great Chief Vanamfour, you have brought great and distinguished guests to visit your great tribe. Tell us who honors us."

The tribe grew silent; they waited.

Chief Vanamfour stood and said, "Standing before you are those who ended the shame the Great Bitch Kiya brought upon our tribe. Before us stand those who avenged the treacherous murder of our great Chief Vanam." Vanamfour talked on and on.

Ares watched. -- *these fools are of no consequence -- our hecatoncheires will destroy them in moments -- Hestia was wrong to worry about these imbeciles -- they will not*

ELDER OLYMPIANS: Hestia, Demeter, Hera, Hades, Poseidon, Zeus
OLYMPIANS: Apollo, Ares, Artemis, Athena, Aphrodite, Dionysus, Hermes,
Hephaestus, Heracles. LIVING TITANS: Oceanus, Tethys, Selene, Elder Oceanids.
DECEASED TITANS: Queen Kiya, Iapetus/Piercer, Cronus.

even make good slaves -- their intestines and gore upon the ground will be a thing of immense beauty --

Athena watched. -- *I and Ares own these people -- why fight them when they are eager to do our bidding? -- I can train the men to fight with spears -- turn the women into archers -- arm the children with knives to slash the legs of our enemies -- if they will not fight here in the east, they will certainly fight in the west -- Hestia can subjugate the land without finding more hecatoncheires or gigantes -- and until that glorious day of war, they could provide labor to grow our crops -- muscle to build Olympus towers -- they wish to belong to us -- sister Hestia, here are your slaves --*

Athena quietly said to Ares, "Act as I act." When Vanamfour paused for breath, she held her sword high in the air and shouted, "Long live the Clan of the Serpent! Long live the great Lord Chief Vanamfour!"

The tribe stood as one and erupted with enthusiasm.

Athena turned to Vanamfour and said, "Bring your great tribe and settle in the land of Tartarus. Help the Olympians lay waste to the filth the Titans brought forth. Be part of our great effort to bring glory to the Ghods and humiliation to the memory of Titans." She went on. But Vanamfour already belonged to the Ghods.

Otreta was impressed. -- *you use us against ourselves -- good thinking, Athena -- your brother only imagined us as slaughter -- you, however, are a worthy enemy --*

~

Walking the deserted streets of Tallstone in the late evening, Apollo and Artemis saw and joined Athena and Ares. The two young Ghods were thrilled. The older two, not so much. But Ares was interested that Demeter had traveled to Urfa and remained there with a man she had met. -- *frigid Demeter met a man? -- did they couple? --*

"Did they couple?" he asked Artemis.

"Why, Uncle Ghod Ares, I do not ask such questions but from the sounds coming from her quarters, I would say with great enthusiasm!"

"Hmph." -- *she rejected me -- many times -- I will have to look into this change in Demeter -- with great enthusiasm?! -- "*

Ares commanded, "Athena and I will stay with you in your quarters. We will leave for Port Olympus the morning after the quarter moon. We must

OCEANIDS: Metis, Tyche, Clymene, Eurybia, Amphitrite, Philyra, Rhodos.
TELCHINES: Dexithea, Makelo, Halia.
EAST: Azura, Seth, Typhon, Iasion, Endymion.
OTHER: Centaur Chiron, Charon, Hotep, Petra, Persephone.

return early because we have much to discuss with Hestia. Inform Lord Nerites. We will pick up Demeter on our way back if she does not come here." -- *with great enthusiasm?!* --

42. The Idol

The festival raged on for another quarter moon.

Ares coupled with Otreta three times. He was always left with a vague feeling that he had not dominated her as completely as he intended. That, plus she had a way of making him talk more than he usually did.

The western leaders forged their own alliance, independent of Port Olympus. They agreed that port negotiators wanted to repair the damage done by the Olympians, but they were uneasy about the future. General Achaeous of Port Kaptara privately shared his suspicion that any words heard by Makelo or the other Telchines were repeated directly to Titanide Amphitrite and then on to Chief-of-Chiefs Philyra. He was unsure if this was to their advantage or disadvantage. But it was agreed that it was in their best interests to maintain private communications and form some type of council. Perhaps Port Spearpoint would join them. They agreed that they would visit Urfa after the Festival ended and return to the port in one caravan. If Amphitrite would agree to be their host on the way back, then the Telchines would be free to enjoy freedom from responsibilities.

Urfa had a problem with young girls drifting to Riverport and becoming Oceanids. There was little in Urfa to interest them. The new art of gymnastics enthralled them. The scholars had no interest in creating a Gymnastics guild, but the Color Girls saw a rich opportunity for their girls. The petite Port Graikoi acrobat needed little persuasion. She saw the fire that her art instilled. She knew her teaching would be received with earnest intensity. She requested and received leave to immigrate to Urfa. She challenged the Port Graikoi gymnasts to a competition at the 76th Festival.

The Centaur was the hit of the festival. The children flocked to him. He reveled in the memory of his youth when he taught the arts to the children and then rode them upon his back. Dexithea pointed out to Amphitrite that Chiron was a master of archery; an art in which the young women of Urfa might be interested. The Color Girls were delighted when Chiron agreed to stay at Urfa for a year and instruct the young. They would have an archery competition at next year's festival.

The Telchines were thrilled to be released from duty – "that's hard work" -- and were eager to return to their roots, Urfa, to see what was happening. Maybe dance in the fields. Make it rain. Do a little wrestling. Maybe this time with males. On the morning after the quarter moon, they begged a ride to Urfa with Nerites and the Ghods. The Telchines were so gregarious that the senior Ghods simply ignored their existence. Artemis laughed a lot.

"I miss my good friend, Ghod Hephaestus. He's so talented."
"Do you think Ghod Persephone is getting enough cave mushrooms? She doesn't like to leave Phlegethon, you know, because that's the only place she can get them."
"My special friend, Philias -- he isn't a dactyl, but he is almost as good -- makes these amazing lifelike Marmaros statues -- he made the little one of Queen Persephone that Ghod Heph used to cast the Orichalcum statues -- he is going to make Marmaros statues of all the Ghods."
"I love those little Orichalcum statues Ghod Heph made of Queen Persephone. They are so lifelike!"
"Ghod Demeter carries three of them with her everywhere she goes, you know, just to keep her company."

Finally, Apollo said, "Telchines, sing me a song of silence."

The Telchines looked at one another, shrugged, and began lip-syncing a traveling song; making no sound.

After a while, Ares said to Apollo, "Tell me about Demeter coupling with this commoner. She is sworn to celibacy."

Apollo laughed. "*Was* sworn. She seems to have discovered a new talent. One much to her liking."

Ares grew more angry than usual. "Did this commoner get her drunk or feed her cave mushrooms?" -- *bitch -- she refused to couple with me -- a ghod -- why would she possibly couple with scum? --*

Apollo answered. "All I know is that Iasion is solicitous of Ghod Demeter's suffering. He is always saying things like, 'How horrible it must have been to be raped by your own brother' and 'You have suffered so

OCEANIDS: Metis, Tyche, Clymene, Eurybia, Amphitrite, Philyra, Rhodos.
TELCHINES: Dexithea, Makelo, Halia.
EAST: Azura, Seth, Typhon, Iasion, Endymion.
OTHER: Centaur Chiron, Charon, Hotep, Petra, Persephone.

greatly but still you go on and try to find joy in life.' Those kinds of things. She must like it. At least she's loud."

Ares fumed. -- my frigid big sister Demeter? -- coupling? -- with great enthusiasm?! -- loud? -- and she rejected me -- a ghod! --

Their carriage approached the gates of Urfa.

~

Within Urfa, Melia's informant had arrived long before and told Melia the names of the Ghods who had left Tallstone that morning. Melia quickly conferred with Azura and Selene. They read and reread their dossier on Ares and Athena.

"The feared ones come at last," Selene offered. "What shall we do?"

Azura said, "Our dossier has grown nicely but we must gather even more information. Feed them. Entertain them. Get wine into them; especially the two new ones. See what happens." She spoke to Selene. "Iasion has requested that he be allowed to return with Demeter. He actually cares for the woman. Will Endymion allow it?"

"Iasion is uncomplicated, but he masters the horses with great skill and knowledge. He would be a great loss to Endymion."

"Urfa shall make it up to him. In the meantime, make sure the Ghods spend at least one night in your company. Use whatever resources you need. Valki's field has been ceremonially plowed and planted in her honor to coincide with the new year. Maybe use that in some way. But regardless, find out what you can. When Portmaster Clymene, General Typhon, and I meet after the festival, our shared knowledge will greatly enrich us. So far, I am well pleased."

That evening the restaurant was closed for a private party. And what a party! There was a feast, drummers, aulos players, flute players, singers, dancers, and wine. The event, with its dignitaries and festivities, attracted the hidden eyes of the curious, the busybodies, and the gawkers. They were smart enough to stay out of sight so that they would not be visited by the wrath of Azura.

After the guests had eaten and wine-drinking had begun in earnest, Selene whispered to Endymion, "That Athena is a real woman, really high ranking. It would raise your desirability to all women if you seduced her.

ELDER OLYMPIANS: Hestia, Demeter, Hera, Hades, Poseidon, Zeus
OLYMPIANS: Apollo, Ares, Artemis, Athena, Aphrodite, Dionysus, Hermes,
Hephaestus, Heracles. LIVING TITANS: Oceanus, Tethys, Selene, Elder Oceanids.
DECEASED TITANS: Queen Kiya, Iapetus/Piercer, Cronus.

"Do you want me to seduce her? Who will *you* be seducing Shining One?"

Selene laughed and playfully slapped his shoulder. "You are my only seducer, Endy. You know that! I just want you to show your animals to Athena; especially Iasion's horses. She would like that kind of thing. But if she can't keep her hands off you, I will understand. But only with her and not with that Artemis hussy, do *you* understand?! I just want to be a good host to these Ghod people. They are exceptionally important!"

"Just don't *you* be too accommodating, Moon Child!"

"I will remain sweet and innocent just for you." She slapped his shoulder again. "You're the only man I want, Endy!" -- *would you be worth it, Apollo? – maybe -- but certainly not you, Nerites --*

The air grew heavy, and clouds gathered. Dexithea exclaimed, "Let's go make it rain, Sisters. Mother Valki's field has been plowed and planted. It needs some rain. Let's go do a rain dance. You men come watch us. We can wrestle once we make it rain hard."

Neither Ares nor Athena intended to do more than drink their wine and then leave the commoners as soon as feasible.

But Endymion approached Athena. "Great Ghod Athena, I am told that you appreciate animals that provide useful services. I have developed three different types of horses. One breed to be ridden upon with great speed, one breed to pull heavily loaded wagons, and one breed perfect for pulling chariots. It would be my great pleasure and honor to show these to you. And allow me to say that you look especially lovely tonight."

Athena glanced at Ares who shrugged with indifference.

She replied, "Horses to pull chariots? Yes, I would like to inspect such an animal." -- *I am not lovely, dunce -- I am commanding! --*

Selene approached the three and said to Ares, "Please join us great Ghod Ares. All the others are coming. I am told the Telchines put on quite a show; dancing naked, chanting, that kind of thing. Lord Nerites will bring more wine than even five Ghods can drink. Ghod Demeter and Iasion will be there. With enough wine, things might get loud."

Ares stared at her. – *loud! -- Demeter? -- that scum Iasion? – great enthusiasm? –*

He said, "Very well. I will join you."

OCEANIDS: Metis, Tyche, Clymene, Eurybia, Amphitrite, Philyra, Rhodos.
TELCHINES: Dexithea, Makelo, Halia.
EAST: Azura, Seth, Typhon, Iasion, Endymion.
OTHER: Centaur Chiron, Charon, Hotep, Petra, Persephone.

Melia asked Selene to bring some torches in case the moon disappeared behind rain clouds and then she hurried to retrieve a supply of blankets, towels, and rain-repellant tarps for the Ghods. *-- a plowed field will be dirty enough -- if the Telchines do make it rain, the mess will be horrendous -- great fun for the young -- unbearable for my high-class targets --*

The Telchines improvised a hands-in-the-air traveling dance as they led the party to the plowed field overlooked by the graven image where the rain would be summoned. Untold hidden eyes followed in the darkness.

They arrived at Valki's field. Dexithea told her audience, "You all stay here at the edge of the field. My sisters and I need to go out there and find the perfect place to dance." With that, the three shed their garments, faced their audience, wiggled their hips, and ran into the fresh-plowed field.

Melia, with her load of blankets, arrived quickly. She laid a blanket upon the plowed ground three paces in front of the watching statue of Persephone. "Great Ghod Demeter, you sit here and watch. There is room for Iasion to sit beside you if you like."

She said to Nerites and Apollo, "Keep their wine cups full."

Ares fumed as Demeter, sipping her wine, called Iasion over to sit beside her on her blanket. *-- you fornicate with that scum with great enthusiasm?! --*

Fast-moving, heavy clouds were beginning to obscure the quarter moon. It grew darker.

Selene lit and placed some slow-burning torches in the ground including two bright ones to light the dancing Telchines and a smaller one for Ghod Demeter. She kicked her shoes off. *-- these shoes are ruined --*

The Telchines danced; their movements became synchronized and sensual; their chant mesmerizing. They slowed. All eyes were on them. After a long time, they began moving a little faster. Lightning flashed behind them. They were no longer of this earth. Thunder washed over the land. Faster. Hands in the air. Demanding. Faces toward the sky. Imploring. Faster. "The rain must come if the seed is to grow. We demand it!" All knew the earth must be nourished if it was to provide sustenance for its creatures. "We implore you, rain. Come to us."

Selene caught up in the magic of the ceremony and wishing the moon to reappear from behind the dark clouds, walked to the far side of the

ELDER OLYMPIANS: Hestia, Demeter, Hera, Hades, Poseidon, Zeus
OLYMPIANS: Apollo, Ares, Artemis, Athena, Aphrodite, Dionysus, Hermes, Hephaestus, Heracles. LIVING TITANS: Oceanus, Tethys, Selene, Elder Oceanids. DECEASED TITANS: Queen Kiya, Iapetus/Piercer, Cronus.

dancing Telchines, shed her tunic, faced the sitting Demeter on the other side of the Telchines, raised her arms to the sky, and threw back her head to stare at where the moon was hidden behind the clouds. She commanded, "Come back, moon! It's too dark without you! I, Selene, command you to come back!"

Demeter, hearing Selene and immersed with the warmth of the wine within her, loosened her tunic, let it slip from her body, stood with raised arms, and, too, stared at where the moon would be.

Between the raised arms of the two naked, high-born women, primeval forms danced. The five implored – demanded -- that the rain come -- that the moon return. Lightning split the heavens. Thunder answered. Torrential rain came; drenching the people and turning the plowed field into rich, life-giving mud.

Melia watched in stunned silence as did untold unseen watching eyes.

The scene continued for another few minutes. The quarter moon began to appear through the fast-moving clouds, but the five women were mesmerized. Heavy rain pounded their bodies. Cleansing rain. Nurturing rain. Erotic rain.

Then it was over. By command of Selene and Demeter, the quarter moon once more shined between the clouds, its light filling the night sky, its light reflected off the rain-drenched glistening bodies of the supplicant women.

Suddenly, the Telchines fell to their knees and picked up hands full of mud which they plastered on their sister's bodies. Halia stood up and shouted, "Lord Nerites, Ghod Apollo, come over here! We want to show you something!"

Apollo and Nerites, both drenched, looked at one another, shrugged, pulled off their boots and tunics, and ran into the field of mud.

The Telchines greeted them by tackling them. The five wrestled wildly in the oozing, slippery mud. Dexithea blindly reached, searching for a penis to play with. She found an erect one, but someone's hand already claimed it. She searched to find who had beaten her to it. It was Nerite's, and it was Apollo who claimed it.

OCEANIDS: Metis, Tyche, Clymene, Eurybia, Amphitrite, Philyra, Rhodos.
TELCHINES: Dexithea, Makelo, Halia.
EAST: Azura, Seth, Typhon, Iasion, Endymion.
OTHER: Centaur Chiron, Charon, Hotep, Petra, Persephone.

Selene slowly recovered her senses, looked around, and then down at her naked, drenched body. Embarrassed, she covered herself as best she could and made her way back to find her garments.

Demeter, still filled with the overwhelming fullness of joy, sat heavily upon her blanket, leaned back, and balanced herself by placing her hands behind her into the oozing richness of mud. She looked at Iasion and with the sudden passion of a once passionless woman, put both arms around him, and with muddy hands pulled him down on top of her.

Ares watched and could stand it no longer. He removed his clothes, walked to the wet entangled bodies of Iasion and Demeter, picked up Iasion, and threw him headlong into the muddy field beside them. He stood, naked and with a full erection, staring down at his surprised and confused sister. He said, "How horrible it must have been to be raped by your own brother. I have never forgiven Zeus for treating you, my precious sister, like that. You have suffered so greatly but still you go on and find joy in life. I wish to fornicate with you. May I?"

Demeter sat halfway up, hands in the mud. She was staring directly into Ares's erection. -- *my ghod!* -- *it's huge!* -- *that thing will not possibly fit inside me!* -- *he was angry with Zeus?* -- *he never told me that!* -- *the sweet man needs me to console him!* -- *he thinks I am precious!* -- *oh, sweet Ares* -- *how we both suffer* -- *we must console one another as best we can!* -- *you asked for my permission like a gentleman* –

She said, "Of course, you may have me, sweet brother. But be gentle."

Ares was not gentle. He expended his fury upon her.

After initial sharp pain, she acclimated and returned his fury. Head thrown back, hands clenching mud, her gaze eventually turned toward Iasion, sitting in the mud, watching her and Ares. -- *poor sweet boy* -- *I had forgotten about you* -- *do you mind?* -- *you look upset* -- *hurt* -- *are you mad because Ares is plowing my field and you have to watch him do it?!!* –

She whispered to Ares, "You are plowing my field, Ares. I like the way you plow me, but I think Iasion may be jealous."

Ares heard only the last phrase. -- *Iasion -- jealous?* –

He looked toward the forlorn figure sitting in the mud. Watching. He laughed, picked up Demeter, placed her on her hands and knees facing Iasion, and returned to his work with greater vigor.

ELDER OLYMPIANS: Hestia, Demeter, Hera, Hades, Poseidon, Zeus
OLYMPIANS: Apollo, Ares, Artemis, Athena, Aphrodite, Dionysus, Hermes, Hephaestus, Heracles. LIVING TITANS: Oceanus, Tethys, Selene, Elder Oceanids. DECEASED TITANS: Queen Kiya, Iapetus/Piercer, Cronus.

Demeter wasn't usually clever with words. She was pleased with herself and wanted to share her cleverness. She screamed, "Plow me, Ares! Plow me hard!"

Ares finished, remained still for a few moments, stood, and stared down at the forlorn Iasion. "You're scum."

Contented, Demeter sat up, leaned over to place the side of her face into Ares's groin, and said, "That was incredible, Ares. The best I have ever had." Her hands took his buttocks and pressed him into her face. Her eyes happened to catch the stare of Iasion. She smiled at him as she stroked Ares's penis. Ares responded.

For the first time, Ares became inventive in his fornication techniques. Demeter was his willing subject.

Selene, now dressed, watched with Melia from the shadows. -- *inhuman scum! -- both of you! -- 'sweet, innocent' Demeter -- I see you clearly now – Ares, it is not with passion that you do this -- it is with rage and revenge! --*

Melia said, "Our dossier thickens."

Selene replied, "Yes. We have added a great deal, but still..."

Again, Ares released himself into Demeter. He smugly rested for a moment and then asked, "Sweet Demeter, would you like to be plowed a third time?"

"Oh, yes. Again! Plow me again!"

Ares looked at the tortured Iasion, picked Demeter up, and carried her to Iasion. There he threw her on her back into the mud with her head landing in Iasion's lap. He knelt, took her ankles, raised her knees to her head, and commanded Iasion, "Hold her legs apart. Wide apart."

"Oh, Ares," Demeter moaned as Iasion obediently took her ankles.

Ares commanded her, "Look into his face while I plow you. Show him the ecstasy I give you."

She gazed up at Iasion with parted lips, half-closed eyes, and soft moans.

Ares finished, rose, said to Iasion, "You can have her," and left.

OCEANIDS: Metis, Tyche, Clymene, Eurybia, Amphitrite, Philyra, Rhodos.
TELCHINES: Dexithea, Makelo, Halia.
EAST: Azura, Seth, Typhon, Iasion, Endymion.
OTHER: Centaur Chiron, Charon, Hotep, Petra, Persephone.

Demeter's head remained in his lap, looking up at him. Dreamily she said, "You poor, sweet man. You had to watch Ares plow me three times. I hope you enjoyed watching us. But now, come to me, my sweet Iasion."

Disgusted, Selene said to Melia, "Wait here!" Selene strolled over to Ares as he finished dressing. "An impressive show, Ghod Ares. Can a Titan get some of that? I understand if you can't go a fourth time, but I'm told you consider yourself to be a superior man. Let me find out if that's so."

She fell to her knees, pulling his pants down as she went. She grasped his testicles as she began to fellate him. She did not get a significant response. She looked up at him and asked, "Problems, Master? Not up for it?" She returned to her task, but he did not achieve an erection. She stood and said, "It's all right. I understand." She stared at him without expression.

His pants were still around his ankles. "Pull my pants up!"

"No." She stared back.

He prepared to roar his command but realized that she was playing with his mind. He stooped, raised his pants, glared, and stormed off.

Melia walked over. "Something for the dossier?"

"Yes. He fears Titans."

The others began returning from their muddy frolicking. An unrecognizable Nerites commanded, "More wine for everyone."

From the field, Demeter called out, "We will be there in a moment!" After a few seconds, she giggled loudly and said "Make that many, many moments! Iasion hasn't yet finished plowing me!"

In the darkness, untold unbelieving wide and hidden eyes watched the spectacles with wonderment. -- *these were ghods and lords and high-ranking people -- did they make the rain? -- do they make the crops grow? -- what did it all mean? -- what powers do they have and how do they wield them? --*

Teumessian, self-proclaimed wisest of the Shaman scholars, tried to make sense of what had unfolded before him.

And silently, upon a grave, a graven image sat looking out over a plowed field, seeded, and rained upon. Overlooking the rites of life. Waiting for the birth of a field of color.

ELDER OLYMPIANS: Hestia, Demeter, Hera, Hades, Poseidon, Zeus
OLYMPIANS: Apollo, Ares, Artemis, Athena, Aphrodite, Dionysus, Hermes, Hephaestus, Heracles. LIVING TITANS: Oceanus, Tethys, Selene, Elder Oceanids. DECEASED TITANS: Queen Kiya, Iapetus/Piercer, Cronus.

43. A Meeting of the Ghods

Nerite's carriage arrived at Phlegethon two days after leaving Urfa, a record time. They were greeted by Dactyl Celmis. The two horses were near death.

The angry and excited Ares demanded, "Don't stop. Continue to Port Olympus. I must meet with Ghod Hestia immediately. Continue at full speed. I command you!"

Nerites said, "Yes, Great Ghod Ares. But consider letting Demeter, Athena, and Artemis relieve themselves. Do you Ghods need to stop for a moment?"

Artemis replied, "That would be delightful. Would you mind terribly, Uncle Ares?"

Ares snorted, "Do it quickly!"

Nerites exited the carriage and went directly to Celmis. He said, "Change out the horses immediately. They will die if they go farther."

Celmis said, "I don't have a set here, Master. I can get a set from Asphodel Meadows but that will take hours."

Nerites barked, "Send for them. Take these two and cool them down. Try to save them. Is Ghod Hephaestus or Ghod Hades here?"

"Ghod Hephaestus is working in the workshop. King Hades and Queen Persephone are visiting the Elysium Fields."

"Move quickly. Cooldown the horses before they die."

Nerites returned to Ares and said, "Celmis told me that I could cut an hour off the remainder of the trip if he washes the horses. They will be able to run faster. I commanded him to do whatever will get you to Hestia the fastest but to get the horses back before the women return. Women take forever, don't they? What is it they do in there? I think I will take a quick stop, too. I will be back before they are. Jump down and walk around. It will renew your strength."

Nerites and Iasion hurried off toward the dining hall where the women would be. He met them as they exited the toilet area. "Ghod Athena! How can you not share your tremendous triumph at the Festival with Ghod

OCEANIDS: Metis, Tyche, Clymene, Eurybia, Amphitrite, Philyra, Rhodos.
TELCHINES: Dexithea, Makelo, Halia.
EAST: Azura, Seth, Typhon, Iasion, Endymion.
OTHER: Centaur Chiron, Charon, Hotep, Petra, Persephone.

Heph? You received so much adulation wearing your armor made with such expertise by Ghod Heph! Would you deprive him of your glorious triumphs? Your own brother and great admirer? It would only take a moment to visit with him. He would adore a surprise visit by his glorious sister. He is in the workshop. I wonder what new spectacular things he has made that you would find exciting?"

Nerites said to Artemis, "Olympian Artemis, you could take this time to entertain Ghod Ares with your delightful presence. This would be a wonderful chance for you to entertain him but don't be too desirable. You know how men are!"

The two women excitedly hurried off in separate directions.

Nerites relieved himself, picked up cups of chilled fruit-wine for Ares and Artemis, and delivered it to them. *-- keep them distracted -- keep them entertained -- for a couple of hours -- dung! --*

But finally, the fresh horses arrived and were harnessed to the chariot. The horse master hurried to inspect the two that had been driven to exhaustion. All of this was unnoticed by the Ghods.

At last, Nerites climbed into the chariot, pounded his chest in silent respect to Celmis, and yelled as loudly as he could, "Where is everybody? These horses want to run fast. Let's leave for Port Olympus! RIGHT NOW!"

The Ghods heard him and suddenly Ares remembered that it was imperative that they get to Port Olympus immediately. All hurried over and boarded the carriage.

Iasion observed, but wisely did not mention, that the two horses had changed color.

~

Nerites arrived at the port Transportation Center with his entourage. Abas did not recognize the horses. *-- better to ask later --* He offered a sycophantic greeting to each of the Ghods and Nerites. To Iasion, he said, "I apologize for my inexcusable stupidity, Master, but I fear I do not recognize you. I am Abas, the lowly Transportation Center Manager."

ELDER OLYMPIANS: Hestia, Demeter, Hera, Hades, Poseidon, Zeus
OLYMPIANS: Apollo, Ares, Artemis, Athena, Aphrodite, Dionysus, Hermes,
Hephaestus, Heracles. LIVING TITANS: Oceanus, Tethys, Selene, Elder Oceanids.
DECEASED TITANS: Queen Kiya, Iapetus/Piercer, Cronus.

Nerites interrupted. "Stay behind and introduce yourself Shepherd Iasion. Ghod Ares requires an immediate meeting with Ghod Hestia. I will clear his way to the sixteenth floor."

Abbas said, "Very good, Lord Nerites. I will arrange for baggage to be delivered with undesignated items going to your office."

Abas always sent Hestia an 'Alert' each time a Ghod or Lord left or returned. He also shared this fact with Titan Dionysus, who received a similar note. Abas juggled his self-interests as best he could. -- *who knows who will do what to who?* --

He quickly scribbled a note and handed it to an assistant. "Deliver this Alert three times faster than normal!"

To another assistant, he said, "Find Titan Dionysus and invite him to join us."

To Iasion, he said, "A Shepherd, you say? Do you know anything about horses?"

Abas was excited to talk with Iasion. Abas learned of the exchange of horses at Phlegethon, of Iasion's work with horses at Urfa, and that Iasion was "a friend of Ghod Demeter's."

Abas took a calculated risk. They were, after all, united by their love of horses. He asked, "A, ahh, 'Special' Friend?"

Iasion laughed. "It is no secret, Friend Abas. I give joy to Ghod Demeter in her world of little joy."

Dionysus came strolling up.

Abas made his multiple quick calculations, considerations, and trade-offs. -- *who knows who will do what to who?* -- *when in doubt* -- *go with Dionysus* --

"Titan Dionysus, here is an Alert and this is our new friend, Shepherd Iasion of Urfa Ranch. You will want to share your best wine with him."

Dionysus took the note, read it, nodded thank you, and then slipped into his charming, ingratiating character. "Shepherd Iasion. I am honored and delighted. I have a wonderful table on the dock patio. Let's go drink some fine wine and see who can tell the greatest lies about themselves." He put his arm around Iasion's shoulder to escort him to the patio.

OCEANIDS: Metis, Tyche, Clymene, Eurybia, Amphitrite, Philyra, Rhodos.
TELCHINES: Dexithea, Makelo, Halia.
EAST: Azura, Seth, Typhon, Iasion, Endymion.
OTHER: Centaur Chiron, Charon, Hotep, Petra, Persephone.

Iasion thought -- *he is a titan like Selene -- I am consort to a ghod! -- by the ghods, my life is good! --*

At port headquarters, Hestia read the Alert she had just received. -- *why would ares want a meeting immediately? – plus, he is bringing Athena -- what's going on? --i have my hands full with the Olympus towers project and I haven't even seen the site yet -- they will be here in... --*

Ares burst into her office followed by Athena. "Greetings Sister. We bring great news! You need a plan! You have a quarter moon to prepare for the arrival of a hundred hunters with their women and children. We knew you would be excited! What are you going to do?" Ares waited with anticipation.

"Let's have a party for them. Will they be staying long?" -- *dung-headed brother! --*

Athena, more coolly, said, "An entire tribe is immigrating to our land, Aunt Hestia. They are now willing subjects of Ghod Ares because you killed Kiya, their avowed enemy. They want to move to Tartarus to help build our Olympus Towers. I think that they can all be used as construction workers alongside the Gigantes, and I can train them in the ways of war for our coming glorious day of domination over the eastern lands. What do you think?"

Hestia commanded, "Sit on the sofa." She called to Creusa, now her assistant, "Creusa, bring us drink!" She moved and sat in a chair adjacent to the sofa. "Now, let's hear what we have to work with and make a plan."

Creusa brought them each a cup of wine and remained listening nearby. In case Hestia needed anything.

44. A Meeting of the East

Azura was delighted to fete Amphitrite with her western trade delegations.

She was more delighted to later welcome her compatriots into the library where she held her important meetings. Portmaster Clymene, accompanied by Oceanid Melia, had already arrived with her report. Selene was there; her report had been submitted and reviewed. General Typhon, accompanied by Amazon Otreta, arrived and was closely followed by Titanide Amphitrite.

ELDER OLYMPIANS: Hestia, Demeter, Hera, Hades, Poseidon, Zeus
OLYMPIANS: Apollo, Ares, Artemis, Athena, Aphrodite, Dionysus, Hermes,
Hephaestus, Heracles. LIVING TITANS: Oceanus, Tethys, Selene, Elder Oceanids.
DECEASED TITANS: Queen Kiya, Iapetus/Piercer, Cronus.

Azura said, "We have much to share. Selene, you are an accomplished writer. Take notes on our meeting today and consolidate each of our reports into one master report. Have the scribes copy four duplicates. Keep the master in the library and transmit a copy to Tallstone, Riverport, Dionysus, and myself. I understand that Oceanid Melia just had an interesting crossing at Riverport. Tell us about it, Sweet."

Melia said, "The dead horses? Well, when we left Urfa, I told Ghod Demeter that I could ferry them across the river. She was thrilled that she would not have to be exposed to the filthy dock creatures. When we prepared to cross the river, Clymene told me they had found a dead horse floating down the river and another one farther upriver. They went to the Northern Dilation and found tracks made by two people on one side and tracks made by two horses on the other side. It appeared that the riders tried to cross on horseback and drowned their horses. Both bridles contained Orichalcum. Clymene asked me to find out if any of my party had lost a horse."

Melia looked around for questions, but everyone was listening intently. "Well, anyway, while we were crossing, I asked my passengers, 'Does anyone know anything about a lost horse? The woman on the dock said they found some dead ones.'"

She paused. "Athena did. It seems that she and Ares had traveled from Port Olympus on horseback. They didn't know the way and wound up at the Northern Dilations instead of Riverport. They rode their horses into the shallows but apparently when Athena's horse stepped into The Deep, it panicked and threw her off. She couldn't swim with her armor on so she grabbed the horse's head to hold her up but that kept the horse's head underwater. They moved through the deeps as the horse thrashed and when the horse quit moving, she grabbed onto the head of Ares's horse. Eventually, she and Ares made it out of The Deep onto the shallows. But the horses didn't. Athena wanted to know if you retrieved the bridles. She said that the horses were worthless, but the bridles are quite valuable. I said that Oceanids aren't that smart. I glanced at poor Iasion. He was horrified."

General Typhon said, "So, they now know of the Northern Dilatation. It takes a fool to drown a horse there, but Athena will certainly remember that there is a way from Tartarus to Tallstone that doesn't run through

OCEANIDS: Metis, Tyche, Clymene, Eurybia, Amphitrite, Philyra, Rhodos.
TELCHINES: Dexithea, Makelo, Halia.
EAST: Azura, Seth, Typhon, Iasion, Endymion.
OTHER: Centaur Chiron, Charon, Hotep, Petra, Persephone.

Riverport; especially if they suffer massive casualties here. Clymene, do you have any Oceanids interested in setting up a new port?"

"Well, they would have water, but it would be even more isolated than Riverport. They have little enough excitement or males to keep them entertained. How far away is it from the Scholars?"

"Close enough. I will start building a road."

Azura said, "Very good. Now, Titanide Selene, I hear we have a graven statue, an idol, sitting on top of Mother Valki's grave. I understand you had a party there. My gossips are saying many things and posing many questions. I'm sure it's all in your report but tell us what happened."

Selene and Melia looked at one another. Selene said, "Too much of it involves me. Let Melia tell of it."

Melia breathed deeply, exhaled, and told the events of the night in detail.

Azura said, "You probably know there were hundreds of eyes watching from the darkness. The stories I hear were variations of what you have just told but with more questions than answers. 'Did the three dancing women make it rain?' 'Did Titanide Selene really make the moon to shine down?' 'Will the Ghods mating make the wheat grow?' 'Does the statue of Ghod Persephone really watch out over the fertile fields?' 'If I touch her image, will she watch over me?' And on and on. I don't know what to make of these questions, but they aren't rational. I don't like it."

Selene offered, "My Oceanid friends tell me that the people talk favorably of the Ghods. They are impressed with their supposed high status and their total indifference to the working class. Rather than being upset, the people seem to admire being looked upon with disgust."

Otreta added, "That is exactly the response of Vanamfour and his tribe to Ares. They seemed to glow in his presence as he belittled them. They neither noticed nor cared of his disgust toward them."

Porphyrion said, "Vanamfour, at least, had reason to idolize Ares; his tribesmen not so much. His tribesmen do not think for themselves. They happily accept and follow their chief's pronunciations, no matter how perverse. The tribe seems to relish blindly following illogical reasons. The entire Clan of the Serpent tribe is soon immigrating and settling in Tartarus. They are sheep blindly following their shepherd."

ELDER OLYMPIANS: Hestia, Demeter, Hera, Hades, Poseidon, Zeus
OLYMPIANS: Apollo, Ares, Artemis, Athena, Aphrodite, Dionysus, Hermes, Hephaestus, Heracles. LIVING TITANS: Oceanus, Tethys, Selene, Elder Oceanids. DECEASED TITANS: Queen Kiya, Iapetus/Piercer, Cronus.

Clymene asked, "Could they be made to fight against their brethren?"

Selene said, "I think many Urfa citizens would not raise a finger to fight against the Ghods even if Urfa, itself, were under attack. I'm sure most would refuse to defend Riverport and Tallstone."

Porphyrion said, "I was confident in our defense when it was the east against the Olympians. But we have raised new issues. The east is not a united entity. Each community has its own identity and may not fight to defend the other communities. I had never considered this."

Azura said, "I will make a large Flag of the Festival and fly it above the Flag of Urfa and instruct my managers to refer to Urfa as a member of the 'Festival Nation.' Wherever we fly the Urfa flag we will fly the Festival flag above it. I will make many and suggest you fly above your own flags."

Porphyrion said with respect, "An attack on my flag is an attack on me!"

Azura said, "I propose Selene, Otreta, and Melia work together and develop a plan to make this happen. Include as many tribes as you can."

Porphyrion and Clymene concurred.

Selene offered, "The Gigantes were split in their allegiance to Titan or Olympian. Many died fighting on both sides. And not all Oceanids left the Olympian murderers. Many remained and are subservient to them. The Ghod's power over people lies in what? The needs of the person? What needs? A need to be told what to do? We are our own enemy."

Azura laughed and admonished Selene, "We know ourselves. We know our enemy. We cannot fail!"

Selene muttered, "Maybe."

They talked into the night.

~ Return Trip ~

Amphitrite's party toured Urfa for an additional day as the scribes transcribed the report.

Amphitrite led the delegations back to Port Olympus, carrying with her a copy of Azura's report.

OCEANIDS: Metis, Tyche, Clymene, Eurybia, Amphitrite, Philyra, Rhodos.
TELCHINES: Dexithea, Makelo, Halia.
EAST: Azura, Seth, Typhon, Iasion, Endymion.
OTHER: Centaur Chiron, Charon, Hotep, Petra, Persephone.

The Telchines had joined the delegation in Urfa and were excited to tell the story of how they had made it rain for Mother Valki's freshly plowed field. Halia opined, "None of the men wanted to mud-wrestle with me, Chief Kemet. I wish you had been there."

The chief laughed loudly. "As do I, Telchine Halia. As do I."

Later, Amphitrite overheard a remark about forming an alliance and trying to interest Oceanus at Port Spearpoint to join. She went into full charming combat mode and added much to the conversation. *-- it excites us so --*

"Of course, Oceanus will be interested ..."
"You should have done this years ago..."
"No need to mention this to anyone at the Port..."
"The Ghods certainly don't need to hear of this..."
"Let me know if I can be of assistance..."
"Oceanus is my father, in case you didn't know..."
"My sister, Oceanid Metis, could be a great help..."
"Metis is good at this sort of thing..."

Entertaining, informative, delightful, and exciting.

45. A Meeting at Port Olympus

Philyra begged Hestia for use of her party barge for an important meeting. "An informal gathering of my Lords and friends to formulate a plan for the few hundred people Ares has said will be joining us shortly; housing, food, work assignments, that sort of thing."

"Do it yourself, Sweet. What do you need them for?" Hestia purred.

"I'm not that smart, Great Ghod Hestia," Philyra said as she dressed. "But I surround myself with people who are."

Hestia said, as she stood and embraced Philyra from behind, "I think you are extremely smart. Come back with me to my sofa."

Philyra rolled her eyes but purred back, "Only if you will share your magnificent barge with me. It would make me feel all warm inside."

~

So now, on a glorious afternoon, on a decadent party barge, safe from prying ears, Philyra raised her glass of brown-wine and toasted, "To Queen Kiya!" Dionysus put his aulos aside as the guests raised their

ELDER OLYMPIANS: Hestia, Demeter, Hera, Hades, Poseidon, Zeus
OLYMPIANS: Apollo, Ares, Artemis, Athena, Aphrodite, Dionysus, Hermes, Hephaestus, Heracles. LIVING TITANS: Oceanus, Tethys, Selene, Elder Oceanids.
DECEASED TITANS: Queen Kiya, Iapetus/Piercer, Cronus.

glasses; each knowing this was their death sentence if Hestia heard of it. If anyone here betrayed them, it would mean untold riches for the betrayer, and agonizing death to all others. All knew that each person in the group had the power of betrayal.

"To Queen Kiya!"

Philyra then said, "We meet to bring everyone up to date on the events of last month. Amphitrite let's begin with you. What happened in the east?

"Oh, my! An Oceanid, the center of attention, whatever shall I do?! But I shall try." She told of Riverport and of new eastern alliances and of new western alliances and of rain dances and of the people's love of Ghods.

Charon told of the coming of the Clan of the Serpent and how he must build a village for them between Tartarus and Oursea.

Philyra told of the new scale models of Olympia Towers and how the Olympians were infatuated with theirs. "The model has brought me a great deal of time, but I still have the Poseidon-Oceanus problem. Hestia is infuriated that Oceanus ignores her command to come to Port Olympus and meet with Poseidon. As of now, they agree that Poseidon can go to Port Spearpoint and meet Oceanus there at the next full moon. So that's when I want the Ghod's tour of Olympus Towers. It will get Hestia's mind off her missing the Poseidon-Oceanus confrontation. The tour *must* be given then."

Charon said, "That's as good as I should expect. A year would be better, but the next full moon it will be."

Amphitrite said, "It's good for me. Hestia won't be placing as much pressure on my husband. I can keep him calmer."

Philyra said, "Good! Then that's the plan." She turned to Dionysus. "What do you have for us, Dionysus? You left on your way to Tallstone. You returned from Por Spearpoint. There's got to be a story there."

"Me? I brought the wine! Do I have to do everything around here?"

"Cut the dung! Give us your report!"

"All right. Amphitrite told you of her meeting with Atlas and Meoetius at Riverport and that they immediately turned around to get their report to Tethys. Well, our paths crossed as I was on my way to the festival, and I

OCEANIDS: Metis, Tyche, Clymene, Eurybia, Amphitrite, Philyra, Rhodos.
TELCHINES: Dexithea, Makelo, Halia.
EAST: Azura, Seth, Typhon, Iasion, Endymion.
OTHER: Centaur Chiron, Charon, Hotep, Petra, Persephone.

decided to go with them. We were met on the lower dock by Tethys. She now has complete knowledge of the situation. She thanked me and invited me to leave. I am welcome to return but only when I am prepared to pledge allegiance to Oceanus. That's the end of my report." He sipped his dark wine and was silent.

Philyra said, "Tell us the rest."

"Oceanus is not as helpless as we thought. I want to go pledge my allegiance to him. Please, let this be my report."

Charon said, "Strange things are happening. If I need to know or can help, send word to me."

Amphitrite walked over and embraced him. "My, my. Give my love to Mother and Father. Tell them I have postponed Poseidon coming to subjugate Father for as long as I can, but apparently, I and my beloved will come to humiliate him at the next full moon. I will see them at the humiliation."

Philyra said, " Who wants brown-wine? Who wants regular?"

Dionysus accepted the brown and walked to the far side of the barge.

Amphitrite accepted regular wine, knowingly glanced in Dionysus's direction, and looked at Philyra without speaking.

Philyra supplied Charon with his usual brown-wine and left him talking with Amphitrite.

She filled her own glass and walked across the barge to join Dionysus who was leaning against the rail.

Dionysus turned to meet her, stepped in, put his lips to hers, pressed in, backed off, and pressed in, again. He held his lips to hers.

She gasped with surprise and may have trembled a bit but otherwise, she neither accepted nor rejected his kiss. When he finished, she turned and leaned against the rail looking out over Oursea. "This will be over someday, Dionysus."

Dionysus again leaned against the rail. "In ten thousand years, this will not be over. This is forever."

They sipped their wine.

ELDER OLYMPIANS: Hestia, Demeter, Hera, Hades, Poseidon, Zeus
OLYMPIANS: Apollo, Ares, Artemis, Athena, Aphrodite, Dionysus, Hermes,
Hephaestus, Heracles. LIVING TITANS: Oceanus, Tethys, Selene, Elder Oceanids.
DECEASED TITANS: Queen Kiya, Iapetus/Piercer, Cronus.

46. Poseidon and Amphitrite

Poseidon stood looking from his fourteenth-floor southerly view. Amphitrite lounged on the sofa. Nerites sat on a nearby chair.

"Hestia has commanded me to subjugate and humiliate Oceanus."

"Hestia commands Poseidon? When did this begin?"

"Suggested. I suppose she suggested, rather than commanded, although it did sound like a command."

"Hestia does not command Poseidon. You will not let Hestia bend you to her will. Am I wife to a weakling?"

"No, Amphitrite. But I do not look forward to meeting Oceanus. There may be blood."

"Blood only if you desire it, husband. I have told you the nature of my father. You know the wise words which will make him wish to pledge his fealty to you without reservation. It is only your sister's weak character and desire to humiliate the last remaining Elder Titans that prey upon your mind. You alone will decide whether to humiliate him or to follow the wisdom of your mind. It is your nature, as it is Hestia's, to wish to subjugate and humiliate Oceanus but you both know that Oceanus is a Lord and should be treated as a Lord. Your mind tells you to bend Oceanus to your will with words of respect, but your nature is a powerful thing to overcome. Decide as you will, but decide because it is *your* will; not Hestia's." -- *will reason prevail? -- can you overcome your nature and treat Oceanus with respect? -- you must, husband -- you must!* –

She paused. "I am looking forward to sailing to Port Spearpoint with you for your meeting. Whatever shall we do to pass the time?"

She paused again, "Do you want to watch Nerites and I fornicate?"

"No. I wish you for myself tonight. You may go Nerites."

Nerites bid farewells and left them. Poseidon turned again to face Oursea.

Amphitrite rose and gently embraced him from behind. She lowered her hands to his hips, pressed her body firmly against his, and sent her hands out to explore. "Alone with my husband as he decides the wisest course to control Oceanus. I'm so excited!"

OCEANIDS: Metis, Tyche, Clymene, Eurybia, Amphitrite, Philyra, Rhodos.
TELCHINES: Dexithea, Makelo, Halia.
EAST: Azura, Seth, Typhon, Iasion, Endymion.
OTHER: Centaur Chiron, Charon, Hotep, Petra, Persephone.

47. Port Spearpoint

The approach to Port Spearpoint is formidable. One can travel by boat to the Low Dock at the base of the sheer cliffs and then be raised to the High Dock by one of the six transportation elevators or one can travel the long, treacherous, uphill path from Port Graikoi by foot or by packhorse. Either way is difficult. The settlement is unassailable by anyone intent on harm.

Dionysus sailed directly west from Port Olympus to Port Spearpoint. The ship he sailed upon carried figs, honey, and Marmaros. The ship docked at the floating Low Dock. Dionysus debarked and was happy to see the outdoor patio. He suddenly remembered -- *they drink beer here; not wine -- not as civilized but refreshing enough* -- He found what would become his favorite table, sat, and signaled for the server.

The server arrived. Dionysus ordered beer and nuts.

"Yes, Master. You appear to be someone of importance. Should I alert that we have a 'Distinguished Visitor?'"

"Do you have a 'Visiting Titan' flag?"

"A Titan! Most certainly. Immediately!"

The server quickly left but returned shortly with a beer and a bowl of nuts. "I believe Oceanid Metis will be arriving to greet you shortly, Master Titan. She usually arrives directly in front of you. She makes an impressive entrance."

Dionysus looked around for an elevator or stairway.

"From up there, Master. From her board."

Dionysus looked to the top of the cliff and saw a plank sticking out over the water. "Up there?"

"Yes, Master. From up there. Enjoy."

The server left Dionysus sipping his beer and looking 'up there.' – *looking for what? --*

Shortly, a figure appeared and walked out on the plank. The figure bounced once and dove out over Oursea far below.

With wide eyes, Dionysus watched the figure descend headfirst, arms extended. *-- in the name of Queen Kiya -- what? --*

The figure entered the water making a small splash, swam to the dock, emerged unclothed, dried her body with a nearby towel, and donned a tunic that was hanging there. She continued drying her long hair as she walked to Dionysus's table, sat down, and flashed him her smile. "Hello. Remember me? I am Metis. We were both in Tartarus when Grandmother and my aunts and uncles were slaughtered. You rode in with news that the Gigantes had been defeated. My family died a magnificent death, didn't they?"

He stared at the woman for a moment. "Of course, I remember you. Your sister, Amphitrite, is my hero. She does more in service of Queen Kiya than any other person and suffers the greatest abuse."

The server brought her a beer. "Yes, Mother told me what you said. I believe you spoke the truth. Grandmother Kiya was taken with you, you know. She lamented that she was late in knowing you; you and your wine and your general lack of direction. You wanted to be an Olympian and then wanted to be a Titan; a little boy lost in the wilderness. 'Destined to be a great one,' she said. Perhaps she was right. You're still trying to get done what Grandmother would want to be done. I admit I overreacted to the actions of my little sister. I'm just not as complex as she."

"You don't appear to be surprised to see me."

"I'm not. Mother said you would return. She showed you just enough to whet your appetite. Mother said that between what she allowed you to see and Sister's project you would be drawn to Port Spearpoint like a moth to a fire. It is your nature. So, what do you think?"

He sipped his beer. *-- there is more I haven't seen?! --*

He said, "There's been another development. The western leaders want to form an association to increase their trading power with Port Olympus. They intend to ask Port Spearpoint to join them."

She sipped her beer. "It's doubtful that will ever amount to much. They are a disparate group. Completely different interests and goals. Father must already juggle his relations with the Olympians, each of Oursea chiefs, the fishing settlements springing up on Oursea, the proliferation

OCEANIDS: Metis, Tyche, Clymene, Eurybia, Amphitrite, Philyra, Rhodos.
TELCHINES: Dexithea, Makelo, Halia.
EAST: Azura, Seth, Typhon, Iasion, Endymion.
OTHER: Centaur Chiron, Charon, Hotep, Petra, Persephone.

of settlements on Middlesea west of Spearpoint, and some other things, including operating the most complex port in the world; although Mother takes care of most of Spearpoint, and some of the other things."

"So, I shouldn't promote such a union?"

"Do as you wish. If asked, Father will say, 'What an interesting idea. Oceanid Metis, pursue this idea. See what becomes of it!' The leaders will be excited but it's just one more thing for me to oversee."

"What are the other things?"

Metis laughed out loud as she held her beer in the air. "To Queen Kiya!"

Dionysus chuckled and held his beer up in response. "To Queen Kiya!"

They finished their beers. Metis insisted they take the stairs to the main level but paused beside some black boxes and ran her fingers across one of them. After finishing, she talked as they climbed. "Mother said that if the Titan was you, to bring you to her quarters. She doesn't want you wandering around unattended plus you can help her prepare Father for his meeting. You shared Sister Ampi's goals with Poseidon, but her exact words would reinforce Father's message when they meet. They will meet and then both men will be -- 'men.' Disgusting, sometimes."

They neared the top of the stairway. Dionysus winded; Metis still going strong. "Mother and Father have separate quarters; hers overlooks Oursea; his overlooks Middlesea. They quarter together when they are both in Port. Let's go to Mother's. I told her we are on our way."

"You told her that we are on our way?"

"The Messagebox at the base of the stairs, I sent her the message."

"Oh. The Messagebox. I see." – *things of which we could never dream* --

They emerged from the stairwell into the bright afternoon sunlight, walked to a small building overlooking Oursea, and entered.

Metis called out, "Mother, I have Titan Dionysus with me."

A voice called back, "Show him around, Sweet. We need not keep secrets from our new friend."

Metis led Dionysus to a table containing three black boxes. "Mother has three of these Messageboxes; one connected to the lower dock that I used to tell her we are on our way, one connected to the upper dock, and one connected to Father's quarters. She taps on this lever and a sound can be heard on the other end. The tapping codes are becoming quite descriptive."

Dionysus stared at them in silence.

She then walked over and patted a large urn. "Mother said that you saw Roomlites when she met you on Low Dock. Well, this is the power source for it. If I place this rod into the stuff in the urn, then the Roomlite will turn on. No oil lamps, no candles, no burning wood; just good old, cool light illuminating the room. Mother said that she thought you might have been impressed with this on Low Dock."

Dionysus touched the rod. -- *the Olympians will be amazed -- I am amazed! --*

Metis led him across the room to stare out into Oursea. "It doesn't look quite right, does it? And there is absolutely no wind. Reach out in front of you."

Dionysus reached out but his hand was stopped by something that wasn't there. -- *what? --*

"We call it a window. It's made of glass; the same material that contains the light from the Roomlites. It's like invisible rock, but I'm told it's invisible sand. You are looking through the most perfect window our lab could produce; made especially for Mother's view of Oursea. It's easy to make drinking vessels, beads, and Roomlites out of it but not big, smooth sheets like this. Those are three of the bargaining chips Father will use to conquer Poseidon. Unfortunately, Father is not much of a negotiator. Fortunately, Mother is world-class, and Father humors her."

"Any one of the three is more than enough distraction. Plus beer, don't underestimate the beer. Olympians are like little children, somewhat simple children, attracted to and impressed with bright and shiny things. Unfortunately, they are also greedy, violent, and bloodthirsty. Just keep them distracted and entertained."

Metis dryly replied, "So we understand."

At that, an imposing, older woman entered the room carrying a tray of refreshments. She set the tray on a table and walked over to greet Dionysus. "I am happy to see you again, Titan Dionysus. These

OCEANIDS: Metis, Tyche, Clymene, Eurybia, Amphitrite, Philyra, Rhodos.
TELCHINES: Dexithea, Makelo, Halia.
EAST: Azura, Seth, Typhon, Iasion, Endymion.
OTHER: Centaur Chiron, Charon, Hotep, Petra, Persephone.

circumstances are less stressful than the last time we met. I continued my wonderful visit with Atlas and Master Menoetius after you left. They argue whether your Olympus Towers is good or bad but either way, Atlas may immigrate to Tartarus to help build it or maybe to destroy it. They agree that you remain a disciple of Mother Kiya. A powerful and busy disciple who is also a confidant to Amphitrite and Lord Philyra and the peoples of the east. So welcome to Port Spearpoint and your 'western frontier.' I wish to hear every word my daughter Ampi has said to you about her husband meeting my husband. Her exact words as best you can remember them." She led him to sit on the sofa in front of her window and served him a beer in a large, heavy mug made of glass. "Now, every word!"

Dionysus sat, collected his thoughts, and repeated every word he remembered Amphitrite saying and then shared his observations on the control she had over Poseidon. Metis stood listening in the background.

Tethys said. "Oceanus will return with the full moon. I must train my husband with the proper response for every possible thing Ghod Poseidon might say plus have a memory prompt for his response. I will update his training based on what you tell me. You and I will review everything after evening's meal. Poseidon arrives with the full moon, you say? That will give us just enough time to prepare. In the meantime, Metis, take Dionysus out and show him Northport. Tell him everything that he needs to know."

"Not Northport, Mother! That will make his little brain explode."

"We cannot keep such knowledge to ourselves much longer. Show him Northport and tell him what he need know."

Dionysus listened to the exchange in complete silence. -- *Northport? -- little head explode? -- all he need know? --*

As he left with Metis, Dionysus turned and asked, "Do you dive, Great Titanide?"

She laughed, "My word. No. I am not an Oceanid. Only their mother. But thank you for asking."

Metis walked with Dionysus toward the north until they came to a stable with a collection of carriages. "A carriage for Northport, please."

"Yes, Great Metis. Immediately."

ELDER OLYMPIANS: Hestia, Demeter, Hera, Hades, Poseidon, Zeus
OLYMPIANS: Apollo, Ares, Artemis, Athena, Aphrodite, Dionysus, Hermes,
Hephaestus, Heracles. LIVING TITANS: Oceanus, Tethys, Selene, Elder Oceanids.
DECEASED TITANS: Queen Kiya, Iapetus/Piercer, Cronus.

The attendant brought them a nicer carriage than Dionysus anticipated. "It's Mother and Father's. They often visit Northport but it's remote so visitors won't accidentally find it." She drove down what appeared to be a small, secondary road but which passed a large storage building and then turned into the widest, firmest road that Dionysus had ever seen. "This is the road connecting Port Spearpoint to Northport."

They rounded a corner and were stopped by two Gigantes armed with impressive weapons. The larger one approached Metis.

"I am Oceanid Metis. This is my guest, Titan Dionysus. We travel to Northport. No farther."

"You are on my list Oceanid. The Titan is not."

"He is my guest. Let him pass on my word."

"My report shall so indicate. Oceanid. You may continue to Northport."

Dionysus said, "I am losing control of this situation rapidly, Metis."

"Dionysus. You were never, nor will you ever be, in control of any situation at Spearpoint, Northport, or Southport. Stay quiet. Don't be afraid."

-- Northport? -- Southport? -- don't be afraid? --

They rode on in silence; the vast panorama of Middlesea on their left, a tall peak appeared in the far distance.

Metis spoke. "I am going to show you a large red egg. You will not see a yellow egg or a blue egg or a green egg or a white egg. There is only one such egg in the world. It is red. No others exist nor did they ever exist. There is only enough material to make one such egg. It is red. Seth has told you the secrets of the Scholars. You may not discuss their secrets. So, I tell you secrets of the west. You may not discuss anything you see here but the red egg."

"I understand."

They rode on.

The building appeared in the distance. It was huge. They rode on. The building grew even larger. In front of the huge building stood a huge red

OCEANIDS: Metis, Tyche, Clymene, Eurybia, Amphitrite, Philyra, Rhodos.
TELCHINES: Dexithea, Makelo, Halia.
EAST: Azura, Seth, Typhon, Iasion, Endymion.
OTHER: Centaur Chiron, Charon, Hotep, Petra, Persephone.

egg. It was balanced on five rods on its smaller side. The rods were fixed into what appeared to be a large basket.

-- what in the name of the ghods is that? -- what is this place? -- the building is huge --

He asked, "Northport?"

"Northport."

The Guard at the entrance stopped them. "Oceanid Metis and Titan Dionysus?"

Metis replied, "Yes. I am here to show the Titan the Red egg."

"Excellent. Be careful, Oceanid. Keep your guest near you."

Metis said to Dionysus, "This is the farthest distance Master Prometheus can make a Messagebox operate. His people continue to work on the problem. They believe it may someday be possible to messagebox from Port Spearpoint to Port Olympus. I'm sure you understand that I know nothing of a Prometheus."

"I understand."

An attendant at the gate led the horse away to be tended to.

Metis walked with Dionysus to the red egg. It grew larger as they approached. *-- that thing is impossibly huge -- it's supported by nothing but slender rods that look like rope -- how does it stay balanced? --*

A gentle wind blew in from Middlesea. The red egg seemed to tremble. A man walked out of the huge building.

"Metis the Great! Good to see you girl! Who is your friend?"

"Pilot Icarus! Keep your hands to yourself! Don't embarrass me in front of my important guest! His name is Dionysus. He has many distinguished titles but, most importantly, my grandmother liked him."

Icarus struck his chest in respect. "I am Icarus, Master Dionysus. Don't be afraid. Few die on my watch!"

Metis said, "He does not know what awaits him, Pilot Icarus."

Icarus hesitated. "I see." He became attentive. "This way, Master Dionysus."

ELDER OLYMPIANS: Hestia, Demeter, Hera, Hades, Poseidon, Zeus
OLYMPIANS: Apollo, Ares, Artemis, Athena, Aphrodite, Dionysus, Hermes,
Hephaestus, Heracles. LIVING TITANS: Oceanus, Tethys, Selene, Elder Oceanids.
DECEASED TITANS: Queen Kiya, Iapetus/Piercer, Cronus.

Icarus led Dionysus and Metis to the basket directly under the Red Egg. They climbed five steps and entered the basket through its gate. In the center of the basket a hot oven burned; fueled by black rocks. The exhaust of the oven fed into a narrow neck leading into the gigantic Red Egg precariously balanced directly above them. Icarus took black rocks from the nearby pile and threw them into the oven.

Dionysus was uneasy. The basket shifted under his feet. -- *don't be afraid - - is that what they both said? -- don't be afraid --*

Icarus asked Metis, "Ready?"

She nodded, "Yes."

To Dionysus, he said, "Either hold onto the railing or else ask Metis to hold your hand."

Icarus yelled out toward a man standing nearby, "All systems clear, Iapyx!" With that, Iapyx untied three ropes and the Red Egg jerked into the waiting sky.

Metis allowed Dionysus to grasp her arm as the Red Egg rose toward the clouds.

"It's serene, isn't it?" Metis asked in quiet wonderment as she finally disengaged his hand. "I thought nothing could be as serene and loving as the sea but the sky, too, embraces me. You can see forever." She paused. "Its technical name is an Airboat. This is Airboat 313."

Icarus remained silent letting Dionysus drink in the wonder of what lay before him.

"I have no words."

They flew silently across an endless sky. Icarus turned an unseen propeller and rudder beneath the basket to control the Airboat's direction.

Eventually, they returned to Northport. Icarus released hot air from the Red Egg and the Airboat gently lowered itself to the ground. Iapyx ran from the building to pull the Airboat and tether it to its mooring pad.

Metis helped Dionysus exit the Airboat's basket. "Let's unwind in the hangar with a beer." She took Dionysus to a small eating area inside the

OCEANIDS: Metis, Tyche, Clymene, Eurybia, Amphitrite, Philyra, Rhodos.
TELCHINES: Dexithea, Makelo, Halia.
EAST: Azura, Seth, Typhon, Iasion, Endymion.
OTHER: Centaur Chiron, Charon, Hotep, Petra, Persephone.

hangar. They walked past a yellow egg and a blue one. "The other Airships must be out on missions. Let's get a beer and I will show you the world!" An attendant gave them each a large, heavy glass of beer.

Metis took Dionysus to a wall containing large markings. "This is a map - - THE map. This is a map of the known world. Our white Airboats, which don't exist and are impossible to notice from the ground, have sailed over every mile of the known world within two quarter moons sailing distance of Northport. Our map makers take note of the land, water, streams, vegetation, hills, valleys, and mountains. Titan Atlas records all these notes onto his maps; this one he shows, he has many he doesn't show, I'm told. Notice the shoreline of the great Ocean bounding our most western land. There are rumors and stories of Airboats crossing over the great Ocean and returning from some far shore. But this is the limit of the knowledge that Scholar Helios will share. In the meantime, trade develops around Middlesea. People and tribes meet and come together. Civilization grows little by little. And amidst all this, Father must deal with a Ghod."

Dionysus asked, "None of this simply appeared at Port Spearpoint one day. Who? When? How?"

"There are things you don't need to know, Dionysus. But so that you will not ask inopportune questions at inopportune times in front of inopportune people, know that Piercer's projects did not die with Piercer. nor did Littlerock's projects die with Littlerock. We deny the existence of Deep Lab. Those two words are never uttered together. We maintain that there is only one Red Egg, and it was given to Oceanus by an appreciative tribe from beyond our borders. If Oceanus gifts the Red Egg to a Ghod, then the Ghod will have the only Red Egg in the world. Did you see any other Red Eggs today?"

Dionysus laughed. "No. I didn't. Helios is Theia's son, isn't he?"

"I believe he was. It's late. We need to get back. You and Mother have work to do. Father does not have a negotiating bone in his body; he commands. Fortunately, he obeys Mother without question. Your little plan has a good chance of working. Sister Ampi will have done everything she can on her side. She is an Elder Oceanid, you know."

Dionysus laughed a weaker laugh. "Yes. Oceanids, especially Elder Oceanids, are not to be trifled with."

ELDER OLYMPIANS: Hestia, Demeter, Hera, Hades, Poseidon, Zeus
OLYMPIANS: Apollo, Ares, Artemis, Athena, Aphrodite, Dionysus, Hermes, Hephaestus, Heracles. LIVING TITANS: Oceanus, Tethys, Selene, Elder Oceanids. DECEASED TITANS: Queen Kiya, Iapetus/Piercer, Cronus.

48. Olympus Towers

The Ghods gathered on the dock to bid Poseidon farewell.

Hestia lamented, "I regret that I will not see you humiliate Oceanus, but Creusa will report on every detail. Always stay alert. These Port Spearpoint people are even lower than the common people here. Don't let your wife distract you from your birthright. Humiliate the Titan even if he *is* a Lord! The Ghods will wish to hear about it. And while you are gone, I will make sure the Lords are building us a proper Olympus Towers. Remember, you are the Ghod of the Sea and Oceanus is your insignificant vassal!"

Amphitrite brashly interrupted. "Ghod Poseidon is a Ghod among Ghods. He is more than capable of commanding everything he wishes to command, aren't you, Dear? Creusa, start getting your boat loaded. We must be off now!"

Hestia thought -- *the moment Poseidon tires of you, you will die a slow, painful, horrible death, bitch!* --

Telchine Halia helped Creusa finish loading the ship. The two women were assigned as assistants to Poseidon and Amphitrite. They had no sailing experience but were experienced in dealing with a Ghod. A lone sailor commanded the vessel. He could ask for help from the two women if required.

The vessel set sail under the flag of Port Olympus and the flag of Ghod Poseidon. The sea was calm.

A full moon would come soon enough.

~ First Viewing ~

Few Ghods cared about wishing Poseidon well. They were happy to be rid of him so they could now receive their first viewing of their magnificent Olympus Towers.

Acmon drove Hestia and Philyra's chariot which was followed by a caravan of Ghods in carriages. They set off to Olympus Towers. Attendants walked with the carriages in case a Ghod needed something.

At Tartarus, CoM3 Charon and Petra reviewed the plan for those now on their way. Should they, or should they not, allow all the Ghods to visit the

OCEANIDS: Metis, Tyche, Clymene, Eurybia, Amphitrite, Philyra, Rhodos.
TELCHINES: Dexithea, Makelo, Halia.
EAST: Azura, Seth, Typhon, Iasion, Endymion.
OTHER: Centaur Chiron, Charon, Hotep, Petra, Persephone.

scaffolding of the first level or only Hestia and Zeus? Zeus was the most excitable. They needed to overload his senses while keeping Hestia pleased with the progress. The first goal was achievable; the second would be more difficult.

Hotep added more scale model trees around the wooden model of Olympus Towers which had been placed on the patio. A functioning scale model river flowed from the direction of Overlook Point, under the model, and on toward Oursea in the south. -- *creating the river is now a wasted effort since Poseidon won't be here – but maybe not -- I can show Hestia how Poseidon's river completely obliterates Kiya's patio -- we can talk about turning Kiya's residence into the sewage treatment plant -- Charon says that ghod Hestia loves that kind of talk -- just make her happy – then we can then do whatever we want to do –*

He completed his puttering and turned his attention to the Gigantes working in the far distance. They continued their work on building the settlement for the soon-to-be-arriving Clan of the Serpent.

Lord Charon was a master at instilling excitement in the Ghods. He would guide Ghods Hestia, Ares, and Athena through the construction. He would also get Hestia to realize that building the settlement slowed work on Olympus Towers considerably.

The three current resident Oceanids had called reinforcements from Urfa. They had prepared a mid-day feast for the Ghods. After the afternoon tour, there would be copious celebratory wine.

The four primary load bearing Marmaros pillars, located at the four corners of the patio, soared fifteen paces into the air; approximately one-third of their ultimate height. The load-bearing pillars for the entire first floor were in place. Staircases on both the west and east sides led from the ground floor to the first floor. The walkway around the perimeter of the first floor had been completed, exterior walls for the rooms were going up, interior walls stubbed in, and steps from the first floor to the second floor on the north and south sides were taking shape. Temporary first-floor flooring allowed walking over the entire first floor with a view of the emerging center atrium.

Today would be Philyra's first viewing of the real thing. She had only Charon's assurance that she and the Ghods would be pleased with what they would see today.

ELDER OLYMPIANS: Hestia, Demeter, Hera, Hades, Poseidon, Zeus
OLYMPIANS: Apollo, Ares, Artemis, Athena, Aphrodite, Dionysus, Hermes,
Hephaestus, Heracles. LIVING TITANS: Oceanus, Tethys, Selene, Elder Oceanids.
DECEASED TITANS: Queen Kiya, Iapetus/Piercer, Cronus.

So came Acmon driving the chariot of Ghod Hestia and Lord Philyra. So followed the carriages of the Ghods. So, they all saw, in the distance, four Marmaros pillars rising upward toward the sky and upon the top of each pillar, the flags of the Olympians waved. So, upon the signal of Acmon, attendants began drumming their drums. So, began the soft melody of the female attendants punctuated with the repetitive marching sounds of the male attendants. Farmer women had been commanded to appear and strew Asphodel petals in front of the chariots and add their voices of praise. 'Bursting into flame' had been suspended for this event.

The closer the caravan came, the louder the drums, the louder the voices.

They arrived. Acmon held up his hand for the caravan and all music to instantly stop. The Oceanids ran out and placed red carpets for the Ghods to step upon.

King Hades of the Underworld and Queen Persephone of the Colorful Fields greeted their brethren. "Welcome to our Olympus Towers where the Ghods reign supreme!"

The Oceanids supplied each Ghod a necklace of flowers and wine in an Orichalcum cup.

CoM3 Charon greeted Hestia. "Welcome, Great Ghod Hestia. I hope you will add your magnificent suggestions to what I show you today."

A particularly beautiful and articulate Elder Oceanid was Zeus's escort, charged with keeping him excited and enthusiastic. Clymene, attending Tartarus specifically for this event, flashed her most charming smile to Zeus. Her skin crawled with revulsion. She took Zeus by the hand, saying "Everyone loves you so much! Come, look at these stairs. This will someday take you to the sky!" Clymene had been warned, "Zeus is charming and powerful. Beware!" Turn your hatred into revenge. -- *just continue to love them as you kill them --*

An attractive Oceanid took Heracles by the hand and said to Hera, "Come with me. I know where they hide the good wine. Let's get Heracles drunk and then take advantage of him!" Hera squealed with disgusted delight.

Another Oceanid escorted Demeter to introduce her new friend Iasion to Queen Persephone and King Hades.

OCEANIDS: Metis, Tyche, Clymene, Eurybia, Amphitrite, Philyra, Rhodos.
TELCHINES: Dexithea, Makelo, Halia.
EAST: Azura, Seth, Typhon, Iasion, Endymion.
OTHER: Centaur Chiron, Charon, Hotep, Petra, Persephone.

Hotep introduced himself to Ares and Athena and insisted that they inspect and criticize the new settlement being built for the Clan of the Serpents. "This tribe is going to be of tremendous help in building your glorious Olympus Towers and being trained to kill your enemies. Are there any more tribes you could recruit?"

A handsome Gigante and an attractive Oceanid found Aphrodite, Artemis, Apollo, and Hermes. "Come. Let us show you places where you can frolic by the river. It's quite romantic and secluded."

The attendants began providing background music. The wine flowed freely. The Ghods were given personalized tours of their someday-to-be magnificent Olympus Towers.

Toward evening, Ghod Hephaistos arrived in a wagon driven by Dexithea. They were greeted by Charon who verified that they carried Hestia's 'surprise.' Charon found Philyra and said, "Chief-of-Chiefs, the delightful surprise you ordered for your favorite Ghod has arrived. Take her to the first floor, wait until you see the atrium torches burning, and then take Ghod Hestia to the atrium. I hope she likes it!"

Hestia, mellowed by the constant flow of wine, looked at Philyra with excitement and said, "You have a surprise for me? Whatever can it be?"

Philyra, with feigned rapture, said, "Just a simple gift from a simple admirer. I think you will like it."

Hestia was almost giddy as the two climbed the stairs and walked to a bench beside the potted plants lining the walkway. Philyra sat down close to Hestia; their knees touching as they each sipped their wine and chatted about the glorious building. After a while, after the sun had set, Philyra saw the light from the atrium torches. "Well, let's see if you like your gift!"

They rose, walked to the atrium, and looked down to where Kiya's fire pit had once stood. There, illuminated by the torches, slowly rotating on a pedestal turned by the surrounding stream, stood a life-size, life-like painted Marmaros statue of Hestia -- head thrown back looking upward in triumph, hands raised toward the sky -- dominating all! Hestia's knees went weak. She grabbed Philyra to keep from falling.

Hestia clung to her Lord as they watched 'Hestia Triumphant' slowly turning below.

ELDER OLYMPIANS: Hestia, Demeter, Hera, Hades, Poseidon, Zeus
OLYMPIANS: Apollo, Ares, Artemis, Athena, Aphrodite, Dionysus, Hermes, Hephaestus, Heracles. LIVING TITANS: Oceanus, Tethys, Selene, Elder Oceanids. DECEASED TITANS: Queen Kiya, Iapetus/Piercer, Cronus.

~ Poseidon at Sea ~

Meanwhile, on a calm and full moon sea, Amphitrite said, "You have calmed the raging waters, my husband, but you have inflamed me! Do you wish to watch me pleasure sweet Halia while the sailor plows me from behind?"

Poseidon sat naked on the deck, sipping wine. "Yes, and the other female can pleasure me as I watch."

Creusa shuddered with revulsion as she removed her tunic and proceeded to her assigned task.

49. The Conquest of Poseidon

High Dock always spotted Oursea incoming ships before Low Dock. The signal went down to Low Dock and across to Tethys, "Olympus Class One flying Ghod flag."

Metis and Dionysus sat at their favorite table on the Low Dock patio drinking beer.

"All right, Titan. Give a good performance. I, myself, refuse to breathe the same air as an Olympian, other than my daughter Athena and maybe her father Zeus. I will go up and help with preparations and then go on a Red Egg ride. Give my regards to Sister Ampi. Maybe we can get together when the cretin isn't around."

"Your sister is a hero and a patriot, Metis. She needs you."

Metis stared at him, thought, rose, and said, "Very well. Give her my love. Tell her that I will see her soon." Metis left to trot up the stairs.

Dionysus quickly finished his beer, stood, walked to the Low Dock railing, leaned against it, and watched the boat sail into the dock. -- *I get along well with Poseidon -- Amphitrite, I believe you and your mother may pull this off - the most powerful ghod of all subservient to a titan -- Hestia isn't going to like this -- Queen Kiya, may your will be done!* --

Dionysus walked to the gangplank and called for two mugs of beer. Upon providing them, the server whispered to Dionysus, "Metis will arrive a few moments after they are on the dock."

OCEANIDS: Metis, Tyche, Clymene, Eurybia, Amphitrite, Philyra, Rhodos.
TELCHINES: Dexithea, Makelo, Halia.
EAST: Azura, Seth, Typhon, Iasion, Endymion.
OTHER: Centaur Chiron, Charon, Hotep, Petra, Persephone.

The ship arrived and was tied to the dock by the sailor. Creusa led the way from the vessel, followed by Poseidon who was greeted by Dionysus. "Great Ghod Poseidon! Welcome to our little Port." He took the beer from the server and handed it to Poseidon. "Try this! Local stuff. Not wine but fairly good. Let me know what you think!"

"Lord Dionysus," Poseidon said. "I am so glad to see you. I thought there would be no one here but the lower classes! It will be good to have someone of consequence to drink with."

Dionysus laughed. "You have Ampi with you and sweet Telchine Halia, and that pretty woman who led you off the boat. But, come over here! Everybody! Come over here, stand by the railing, and look up!" He led the group to the rail and slipped in behind Amphitrite. "All right, everyone. Look up at that person standing on the board!"

He waved to the figure. The figure waved back. The group looked up in confusion. The figure was motionless for a moment, then bounced on the board, and dove headfirst toward the waiting sea. Dionysus took Amphitrite's hand and whispered, "She brings you her love and admiration!" He felt Amphitrite tremble. He released her hand and stood back as the figure entered the water without making a splash.

Dionysus then put his hand on wide-eyed Poseidon's shoulder, "Everybody loves the sea around here. They are excited that the Ghod of the Sea has finally found time to introduce himself to Oceanus. Come on. We can beat the others to the elevator. We will have it just to ourselves." He led Poseidon to the elevator, tapped on a Messagebox in passing, listened to sounds returning, signaled 'ready' to the elevator operator, and turned back just in time to see the women on the dock greet Metis emerging from the sea.

The freight elevator rose. They were surrounded by solid rock, an unfamiliar and unsettling experience for Poseidon. "I signaled that you were on your way. You caught them by surprise. Great negotiating tactic. No one had any idea that the Great Ghod Poseidon, himself, would be arriving at the Port. I hope Oceanus is in residence. I would hate for you to sail all this way and then miss him. Oh well, if nothing else, this unexpected visit will give your wife time to visit her mother. They get together so seldom. I'm glad you didn't make the sea angry, back there. You were insightful and merciful to keep it calm. The locals like that sort

ELDER OLYMPIANS: Hestia, Demeter, Hera, Hades, Poseidon, Zeus
OLYMPIANS: Apollo, Ares, Artemis, Athena, Aphrodite, Dionysus, Hermes, Hephaestus, Heracles. LIVING TITANS: Oceanus, Tethys, Selene, Elder Oceanids.
DECEASED TITANS: Queen Kiya, Iapetus/Piercer, Cronus.

of thing and will take note of it." The elevator reached the upper level. "Well, here we are. It will probably take a while to get the women up here. In the meantime, I will show you around while your hosts prepare your reception."

"They know that I am here?"

"Yes. I used their Messagebox to signal ahead. They know everyone who just arrived. They told me they would have a reception for you at evening's meal at High Dock. So, anyway, this place is remarkably interesting. Oceanus was inventive back in his day. Those two parallel straight pieces of metal on the ground are called 'rails.' The freight on the Low Dock is placed on the freight wagons, raised to the upper level, and is then pulled by a donkey over these rails to High Dock, two stades away. The freight is stored there until it's shipped out to the various ports. As I understand it, operating this place takes a lot of time. Oceanus will be relieved that a Ghod is willing to take on the responsibility of controlling the sea."

"They can talk to each other two stades away?"

"Yes. They do it all day long. Come on. Let's jump on this wagon. The donkey to take us to High Dock on the other side of the Port. This wall of rock we will cross is the only thing keeping Middlesea from spilling into Oursea."

They climbed onto an empty wagon sitting on the rails. Dionysus took the reins and commanded the donkey forward. He continued, "Remove the wall and the level of Oursea would rise higher than the roof of Port Olympus. The coastal villages would be wiped out. Fortunately, the wall cannot be removed."

They rode on. Dionysus rambled on but Poseidon was no longer listening. *-- they can talk to each other two stades apart! --*

The large storage building loomed in the distance. The closer they came, the larger the building became. The rails ran directly into the building. The two men were greeted by an attendant who took the reins from Dionysus. "Welcome Great Ghod Poseidon and Titan Dionysus. I will Messagebox Titanide Tethys that you have arrived. She commanded I tell you that she and her guests will leave immediately for the reception of our honored guest. In the meantime, Oceanus awaits you on the High Dock. Just stay on this sidewalk. It goes directly there."

OCEANIDS: Metis, Tyche, Clymene, Eurybia, Amphitrite, Philyra, Rhodos.
TELCHINES: Dexithea, Makelo, Halia.
EAST: Azura, Seth, Typhon, Iasion, Endymion.
OTHER: Centaur Chiron, Charon, Hotep, Petra, Persephone.

Dionysus was shocked. He blurted out, "Oceanus awaits us? Tethys and Amphitrite are on the other side of Port Spearpoint?!" -- *no, no, no!* -- *their wives must be with them when they meet!* -- *that is the entire plan* --

Poseidon began walking down the sidewalk to the pier. He turned to Dionysus and asked, "Are you coming with me?"

"Oh, yes, certainly." -- *I can't let them meet without their wives* -- *Poseidon will lose his catastrophic temper* -- *Oceanus will stare at him like he is a stupid fish* -- *all is lost!* -- *Amphitrite* -- *what happened?* -- *did I misunderstand?* -- *what am I going to do?* -- *I don't have wine or beer or anything!* --

He breathed deeply and calmed himself. -- *so much work and planning come down to this* -- *Amphitrite* -- *Tethys* -- *be with us now and in the moment of their meeting* -- *stay calm!* --

In the distance, they saw the figure leaning against the railing and staring out over Middlesea.

Dionysus breathed in and breathed out. He noticed that Poseidon, upon seeing the figure, had almost imperceptibly slowed his gait. -- *fear is a bad thing* -- *he will lash out!* --

He said, "That must be our friend, Oceanus, contemplating the glory of Middlesea while he awaits the Great Ghod Poseidon that he has heard so much about. He may be a little anxious. Know what I mean?"

"No." They walked on toward the figure.

Dionysus coughed as the two men began crossing the dividing road.

The figure, hearing, turned to face the men, drew to his full height, and stared noncommittedly at the two men. The two giant men glared at one another; both tall, broad-chested with powerful arms; both men-among-men; men who commanded without hesitation fully expecting their commands to be instantly obeyed.

Dionysus held his breath. -- *Amphitrite* -- *Tethys* -- *be with us!* --

Oceanus spread his arms wide, smiled broadly, embraced Poseidon in a bear hug, picked him up off his feet, swung him around, released him, stood back with his hands tightly holding Poseidon's shoulders, and said, "Ghod Poseidon, you are more glorious and powerful than my beloved daughter told me. She did not do justice to your commanding presence. I

ELDER OLYMPIANS: Hestia, Demeter, Hera, Hades, Poseidon, Zeus
OLYMPIANS: Apollo, Ares, Artemis, Athena, Aphrodite, Dionysus, Hermes, Hephaestus, Heracles. LIVING TITANS: Oceanus, Tethys, Selene, Elder Oceanids.
DECEASED TITANS: Queen Kiya, Iapetus/Piercer, Cronus.

am so glad that you have come to take on the terrible responsibility of commanding the sea. I shall assist you to my fullest capability."

Dionysus opened his eyes and watched intently. -- *were those your words, Ampi? – or yours, Tethys? -- by the ghod -- I wish I had some wine!* --

An attendant walked up and said, "Here is the wine you ordered, Oceanus; our finest wine in our finest glasses for your powerful guest. Titanide Tethys messageboxed that she and her daughter are on the way."

The attendant served wine to the two men but not to Dionysus. The attendant glanced at him and shrugged with a touch of sympathy.

Oceanus said, "My wife had demanded to meet you, Ghod Poseidon. Lord Dionysus, go and escort her to us."

Dionysus nodded acquiescence, then turned and walked to the storage building to await the women. Arriving, he asked, "Can I get a beer, now?"

Soon enough, a trolley arrived; hand-powered by the sailor. It carried the sailor, Creusa, Amphitrite, and Tethys.

"Well?" Tethys asked after dismounting the trolley.

Dionysus raised his just-received beer in salute, took a drink, and said, "When I left them, they appeared to be best friends. You two may be on your way to being replaced."

Tethys was not amused. "It was my husband's doing. Amphitrite and I have been terrified since Oceanus told us he would meet Poseidon alone. We were commanded to stay in my quarters while he met Poseidon at the dock. He told the high-side captain to send you alone with Poseidon to the High Dock."

Amphitrite curtsied and said, "Thank you, Dionysus. After I heard no thunder nor saw roiling skies, I had hope that your plan worked. Mother and I did everything we could to prepare our husbands for this meeting. Father said he would do what needed doing and assumed his women had trained him well."

Creusa snorted, "That's just like a man! The men get the credit after the women do the work. And we get the blame if things don't work!"

OCEANIDS: Metis, Tyche, Clymene, Eurybia, Amphitrite, Philyra, Rhodos.
TELCHINES: Dexithea, Makelo, Halia.
EAST: Azura, Seth, Typhon, Iasion, Endymion.
OTHER: Centaur Chiron, Charon, Hotep, Petra, Persephone.

Amphitrite laughed. "Such are our natures, but it is not over yet. We must ensure they remain best friends until we can get our husbands back into our beds and reinforce their glorious triumphs."

Tethys commanded, "Dionysus, you, Creusa, and the sailor go get the reception moving. Our resident Oceanids are busy at Southport preparing our evening meal. Our dock workers seldom host a reception. They aren't sophisticated in these matters. I will depend on you three to guide the workers along." And to Amphitrite said, "Well, Daughter. Let's go join our husbands. We have a reception to attend."

The night came. It was not an Olympian party, but Poseidon was not entirely bored. The Creusa girl kept bringing him a beer and touching him on the shoulder. Tethys had told him, "I am mad at you, Ghod Poseidon. You leave my husband to deal with all of these lower-class people while you are out commanding the sea!" The sailor had said, "I look forward to sailing on the powerful sea which you command! All the sailors do!" Amphitrite took him aside and whispered, "The Titans are a higher class than even your Lords at the port. We simply need to remember to treat them with the respect that we do our Lords. That way, the glorious Olympians won't have to deal with the lower classes. The Lords and Titans will do it for us!"

At sunset, two carriages pulled up outside the reception. Tethys rang a bell and then addressed the entire reception. "My husband and I are so pleased to at last meet the Great Olympian Poseidon, Ghod of the Sea. Oceanus is honored and excited to assist the Great Ghod in whatever small ways he can. Let us all thank Ghod Poseidon for sharing his gracious presence with us, here, this evening." With that she turned toward Poseidon, clapping her hands together. The dockworkers knew what was expected of them. Each tried to applaud louder than the others.

Poseidon had never witnessed such a display, but he was sure that this was a good thing, acknowledging his superiority over everyone there. He uncharacteristically smiled at the crowd in recognition.

Tethys recognized this as a small fleeting victory. She nodded to the audience and with new familiarity, took Poseidon by his elbow and pressed him to turn toward the waiting carriage. "You must be famished after all the work you have had to do this afternoon. I understand my Oceanids have a bit of a feast waiting for us at our Southport location.

ELDER OLYMPIANS: Hestia, Demeter, Hera, Hades, Poseidon, Zeus
OLYMPIANS: Apollo, Ares, Artemis, Athena, Aphrodite, Dionysus, Hermes,
Hephaestus, Heracles. LIVING TITANS: Oceanus, Tethys, Selene, Elder Oceanids.
DECEASED TITANS: Queen Kiya, Iapetus/Piercer, Cronus.

Shall we see if a Ghod of your stature will find it edible?" She began walking him toward the carriages.

Oceanus took Amphitrite's arm and began escorting her toward the carriages. "Wait!" Oceanus suddenly commanded. All stopped to look at him. He commanded the High Dock Manager, "Messagebox Southport that we are on our way but don't send the closing signal!" To Poseidon, he said, "Come with me Ghod Poseidon. Let us do this together!"

The two men walked to a bank of Messageboxes. The Manager tapped on the one labeled Southport and then stepped away.

Oceanus said, "Ghod Poseidon, press down on that lever for one heartbeat; no more, no less."

Poseidon pressed the lever and then looked at Oceanus for an explanation of what he had just done.

"Tremendous work, Ghod Poseidon. You have just told Southport that you and I and our guests are on our way, and they had best be prepared for us! I have never seen anyone do it as well as you did! Congratulations!"

Amphitrite walked to her husband, took his arm, and said to Oceanus, "I told you that he was powerful and magnificent, didn't I, Father?"

"Yes, you did, Daughter. Yes, you did."

Poseidon was pleased with himself, people clapping their hands for him in awe, sending a command to people before he even arrived to command them. -- *Oceanus is turning out to be a useful lord -- even if he is one of those titan people that Hestia despises so --*

The four walked to the lead carriage. Dionysus, Creusa, the sailor, and the High Dock Manager followed. They entered their carriages and leisurely traveled southward along the coast of Middlesea. Tethys and Amphitrite assisted their husbands in their amicable chat to Southport.

The building at Southport was too large for the dock it serviced and there was a large flat field between the dock and the building.

Poseidon thought -- *a strange arrangement* --

The Oceanids had prepared two square tables for their guests. The tables were covered with white linen with a flower arrangement on each. The

OCEANIDS: Metis, Tyche, Clymene, Eurybia, Amphitrite, Philyra, Rhodos.
TELCHINES: Dexithea, Makelo, Halia.
EAST: Azura, Seth, Typhon, Iasion, Endymion.
OTHER: Centaur Chiron, Charon, Hotep, Petra, Persephone.

eight guests were seated. The visitors had a nice view of Middlesea and the large flat field beside it. Excellent wines had been brought in by Dionysus.

Poseidon said, "I am told that the strip of rock Port Spearpoint sets upon is all that keeps your Middlesea from raising the level of Oursea above the roof of Port Olympus."

Oceanus answered, "Yes, that's true. I watch for change constantly. The level of Middlesea can change up to a full pace depending on the time of day and the fullness of the moon. The change in the level of Oursea is always less than a pace. The scholars cannot tell me why this is so, but I know it to be true. Were it not for this wall of rock, Oursea would be the same level as Middlesea."

"Will the wall ever fall?"

"No. The wall is solid hard rock far into the earth. Chief Aeolus of Kaptara continually asks the same question. I believe he secretly wants it removed. He wishes to be a great seagoing nation and lusts for a direct sailing route from Kaptara to my ports on Middlesea. Were there no wall, he would have his direct route. He has suggested several times that I could create a magnificent waterfall if I cut a canal from Middlesea to the eastern side." Oceanus laughed again. "He plays upon my love of even the smallest waterfall. He also knows that the water level of Oursea would eventually be raised. The larger the waterfall, the quicker Chief Aeolus would have his direct sailing route. But no, the wall will not fall and, no, I shall never build a canal."

Concern flashed through Poseidon's mind. -- *Oceanus is the master of this rock wall* --

Both men, for the first time, found themselves to be brilliant conversationalists. The women interjected brief comments only when the men became inarticulate. The wine flowed. A wonderful meal was served. Sweet dessert followed. Conversation flowed as easily as the wine.

An Oceanid signaled Oceanus. He began his carefully rehearsed soliloquy. "Ghod Poseidon, I feel that you and I can work together to fulfill our individual destinies. I know that I can rely on you to command the sea and all waters while I continue my work managing the trade and the ports. You won't have to dirty your hands with the things that I do but there

ELDER OLYMPIANS: Hestia, Demeter, Hera, Hades, Poseidon, Zeus
OLYMPIANS: Apollo, Ares, Artemis, Athena, Aphrodite, Dionysus, Hermes,
Hephaestus, Heracles. LIVING TITANS: Oceanus, Tethys, Selene, Elder Oceanids.
DECEASED TITANS: Queen Kiya, Iapetus/Piercer, Cronus.

remains one great problem that I hesitate to mention but it may be insurmountable." He became silent.

Poseidon, softened by the effects of wine, felt magnanimous. "My dear Lord Oceanus, there is nothing we cannot work out together. What is your concern?"

"I will be blunt, Ghod Poseidon, as I know you command me to be. Your Sister, the senior Olympian, Ghod Hestia, wishes me and my kind ground beneath your foot like a slimy creature from a river. Hestia had my family killed. She cannot rest until I am dominated. She is neither strong enough nor smart enough to do it herself. She needs and wants you to do it for her. You are strong enough. I MUST, here, in this place, convince you that you are the leader of the Olympians; that they do your bidding, and that you WILL NOT be commanded by Hestia. Hestia is your older sister. This will be difficult for both of you. Both of you must KNOW that you are the master. Your bones must know this thing. I have long considered if I might be able to assist you in this matter. I believe that I can. I have decided to give you my most prized possession. The only one in the world. My Red Egg!"

"Red Egg!" Poseidon spat out. "I need no Red Egg. I don't need an egg of any color." Even through the haze of wine, a perfect evening, and Amphitrite's hand gently squeezing his knee, still, Poseidon's temper flared. -- *my sister brazenly criticized -- by a titan -- i, myself, accused of weakness -- the suggestion that a ghod requires the assistance of an inferior person! -- a red egg?! -- this insolence shall not be tolerated! --*

Oceanus did not break his cold stare. – *now I conquer you, cold-blooded murderer -- bow to me -- acknowledge my control over you -- I will not gloat! -- bow! -- now! --*

Poseidon, face reddening, too enraged to speak, prepared to explode.

When seeing the inconceivable, it takes the brain a moment to recognize it sees the inconceivable. A hot-air balloon glides through the air in complete silence; perhaps the sound of a small fire in the far distance but, otherwise, in silence. The large, red Airboat began floating into Poseidon's periphery view as he spat out the words 'Red Egg.' The object did not register in his brain because what his eye saw was inconceivable. But the red Airboat continued its slow, silent descent into Poseidon's full vision. To look directly at it was unavoidable. His eyes refocused from Oceanus

OCEANIDS: Metis, Tyche, Clymene, Eurybia, Amphitrite, Philyra, Rhodos.
TELCHINES: Dexithea, Makelo, Halia.
EAST: Azura, Seth, Typhon, Iasion, Endymion.
OTHER: Centaur Chiron, Charon, Hotep, Petra, Persephone.

to the red object hovering over the landing field directly behind Oceanus. Poseidon's eyes widened; his lips parted.

Creusa and the sailor had been warned to say and do nothing if they saw something unusual. They were too stunned to say or do anything, anyway.

Oceanus continued. "With the Red Egg, you will be the most powerful man to ever live. You will know this in your bones. You need not demonstrate or prove your power to any man. Hestia will bow to your power without your command to do so. You are now 'Poseidon -- Ghod of Ghods.' It is I, Oceanus, who make you so!"

Poseidon heard each word but had no mental facility remaining to process words; his mind was riveted upon the spectacle that unfolded before him.

Oceanus rose. He held out his hand to Poseidon, helped him up from his chair, and escorted him to watch the Red Egg complete its landing. -- *I have won!* --

Tethys and Amphitrite rose and followed behind the two men.

Amphitrite had been told what was to happen and how she should proceed. but being told did little to reduce the wonder of what was unfolding. -- I *wish my little Telchines could see this -- they would explode with excitement* --

The Red Egg landed. Iapyx threw out tethering ropes, jumped out of the basket, and tethered the Airboat to its pilings. He then walked up to Oceanus, thumped his chest in respect, and said, "She is all yours, Oceanus."

Oceanus nodded in recognition and said to Poseidon, "Airman Iapyx comes with the Red Egg. He is now your subject. He will take you and your guests aloft upon your command, Ghod Poseidon."

Oceanus walked to the basket, patted it, and said, "I will miss my Red Egg. Tethys and I have had many wonderful excursions in it. By the way, Airman Iapyx's total attention is always focused entirely on flying his craft. He has no idea of what else may be going on inside the carrier." Oceanus winked. "She is now all yours, Olympian Poseidon, Ghod of Ghods."

Amphitrite's words had been scripted by Tethys. Amphitrite walked up and took her husband's arm. "Take me for a ride, Sweet. Do you want Creusa to come with us?"

ELDER OLYMPIANS: Hestia, Demeter, Hera, Hades, Poseidon, Zeus
OLYMPIANS: Apollo, Ares, Artemis, Athena, Aphrodite, Dionysus, Hermes,
Hephaestus, Heracles. LIVING TITANS: Oceanus, Tethys, Selene, Elder Oceanids.
DECEASED TITANS: Queen Kiya, Iapetus/Piercer, Cronus.

His mind was not functional. He merely shook his head, "No." Iapyx held the gate to the carrier open for Amphitrite to enter leading her husband behind her. Iapyx entered, threw coals in the boiler, signaled to the High Dock Manager who untethered the Airboat, and said to Poseidon "You might want to hold the woman's hand, Master. So that she won't be too frightened." He forced hot air into the neck of the balloon. They slowly ascended toward the moonlit sky. The powerful, commanding, Olympian Ghod tightly held the hand of the Elder Oceanid beside him.

Oceanus and Tethys's watched the ascent of the Airboat. She whispered, "My husband can converse in 'Ghod-Speak' with the best of them!"

He snorted, "It is not my nature. I do it only for you, Tethys."

She squeezed his hand.

Dionysus approached Tethys, knelt before her, rose, and thumped his chest in respect. "You and your daughter have saved your lands from the cruel rule of the Olympians. I salute you!"

Oceanus broke in, "Well, I had something to do with it!"

Tethys laughed, "Yes, Dear. It was you and Dionysus who accomplished this. Dionysus made the plan, and you executed it. Well done, to both of you!" Tethys clapped her hands together as she laughed and cut her eyes to see if Creusa might be listening.

Dionysus said, "We must make a plan for his grand entrance into Port Olympus. All Ghods must witness his return in triumphant splendor. He must be accepted as Ghod of Ghods. Arriving under a full moon would be best but that is a long time away. I must meet with Amphitrite and the pilot to formulate a plan!"

Tethys took Dionysus's hands into hers and pressed their hands against his chest. She said, "Slow down, Titan. All in good time. Let us savor this moment for a while." She released their hands and leaned against Oceanus. "What next, Husband?"

"Poseidon is going to be talkative for a long time even without wine. I will bring up the subject of his triumphant return during the carriage ride back. He will talk nonstop. Amphitrite will be listening and can formulate a plan. Dionysus, you and your people help Iapyx get the Airboat into its hangar after they return. He can tell you what he can and can't do when landing.

OCEANIDS: Metis, Tyche, Clymene, Eurybia, Amphitrite, Philyra, Rhodos.
TELCHINES: Dexithea, Makelo, Halia.
EAST: Azura, Seth, Typhon, Iasion, Endymion.
OTHER: Centaur Chiron, Charon, Hotep, Petra, Persephone.

Losing Iapyx is a setback to my programs but you will find him trustworthy and competent. He understands that Poseidon is now his master but that you and Amphitrite will always counsel him wisely. He will serve you well enough. Now, excuse me, but I intend to savor the rest of my evening"

He asked Tethys, "Shall we inspect the hangar before they return? We need it to be spotless for the Ghod."

"Oh, Oceanus. You know how inspecting the hangar excites me! Let's!" The two walked off toward the hangar.

Dionysus looked at Creusa and the two men. "Let's go get a beer!"

50. Ghod of Ghods

Dionysus knocked on Philyra's door.

She answered the knock holding an oil lamp and wearing little. "It's late. Do you expect me to invite you in?"

"Come on, Philyra. I have been away on important business for two quarter moons. Aren't you even interested in a progress report?"

"All right. You know where the brown-wine is. Get us both one. I'll put on something more substantial." She let him in and went to her bedroom to change. She returned to find he had opened the shutters between the interior and the outside overlooking the docks.

He was standing in front of the opening staring outside. He handed her a glass containing the brown-wine.

She looked at the glass with amazement. "What am I holding? Is this from Port Spearpoint?"

"Yes. They manufacture it there. It's called 'glass.' They can make it any form they wish. I'll take measurements of the opening for your shutters and send them to Tethys. She will send you a sheet of glass that can replace these shutters. You will be able to look outside protected from wind and rain. The candles I just lit are obsolete now. I have a gift for you waiting on the dock. It's called Roomlites. They will deliver it in the morning, and I will install it for you. Do you ever invite Hestia to your place? I think that you might want to show this to her, yourself. Roomlites are unbelievable. Would you like a device to communicate with

Amphitrite when you are in your quarters and she is in hers? I can get you such a device."

He had not looked at Philyra. He simply stood staring out through the opening.

"These are the things of which I could never dream?"

"No. These are trinkets. Common Port Spearpoint trinkets. There is more." He shivered in the brisk gust of air.

Philyra almost reached out to touch him, to comfort him, but thought twice about it. "Tell me."

"Are any of the Telchines around?"

"I can't keep up with them. I assume they are with Hephaestus at his workshop. They are enthralled with making things with him."

Dionysus said, "Let's talk until sunrise then send for them. Charon, too. He is a talented planner. Amphitrite and Poseidon will arrive at high noon the day after tomorrow. We must prepare a proper reception for them. By the way, how was the tour of the Olympus Towers?"

"Fabulous. Better than I should ever hope for. The Ghods were overwhelmed. It bought us a great deal of time. Charon and Petra did an outstanding job both in planning and in execution."

"Good. I will ask Charon to plan a reception unlike any before. Can we sit on your sofa? I will tell you of things you have never dreamed."

They sat.

Dionysus talked on and on into the late night. Eventually, whether from the brown-wine or the stress of the past days, or the uncertainty of the coming days, he fell asleep; or perhaps passed out.

Philyra laid his body out on the sofa, covered him with a blanket, and retired to her bed. -- *maybe I can get a few hours of sleep before sunrise -- we will be busy tomorrow -- sleep? -- red eggs? -- flying machines? -- Poseidon and Amphitrite arriving on the roof of port Olympus? -- roomlites? -- glass windows? -- sleep? -- the world is changing much too fast -- Queen Kiya would already have given these wondrous things to all people -- I must use them as weapons against the ghods -- sleep? -- what is sleep? --*

OCEANIDS: Metis, Tyche, Clymene, Eurybia, Amphitrite, Philyra, Rhodos.
TELCHINES: Dexithea, Makelo, Halia.
EAST: Azura, Seth, Typhon, Iasion, Endymion.
OTHER: Centaur Chiron, Charon, Hotep, Petra, Persephone.

~

Sunrise.

Philyra rose, cleaned, dressed, and quickly prepared for her day.

Before she left, she shook Dionysus from his deep sleep. "My office within the hour." She passed Charon's quarters, knocked loudly, and greeted the groggy Lord with "My office within the hour." She walked to Admete's quarters, gently knocked, and said "We are going to have a busy day. Start with Travel Dispatch. Have him find and bring me the Telchines immediately. Tell them excitement awaits. Then come in. I have a meeting with Charon and Dionysus and may need to call in others. By the way, good morning."

She turned and continued to her office.

Meetings were held all day. Tomorrow would come all too soon!

~

Meanwhile, as soon as the Telchines arrived and were briefed, Dionysus and Dexithea, who wore her black leather dress with matching handbag, called upon Hestia.

After receiving Hestia's initial verbal abuse, Dionysus explained that she would host a special Olympian party on the roof all day tomorrow for Poseidon's triumphant return. Lords and commoners would also be invited. He gave many persuasive reasons for the party including "Poseidon declares himself triumphant. He wants a hero's welcome when he returns! His arrival will be a life-changing event."

Hestia glared at him in silence. -- *typical Dionysus dung!* –

She snapped, "Why should I invite random Lords and commoners to an Olympian party? I think not, Dionysus!"

Dexithea said, "Dionysus told me that if Ghod Poseidon's arrival goes badly that you will be mortified. I believe that the presence of commoners like me will keep things from going badly" Her lips smiled. Her eyes didn't.

Hestia stared at the two of them, considered, and said, "If this party will make Poseidon and my other brothers and sisters happy, I will allow it." -- *how bad can it be?* --

ELDER OLYMPIANS: Hestia, Demeter, Hera, Hades, Poseidon, Zeus
OLYMPIANS: Apollo, Ares, Artemis, Athena, Aphrodite, Dionysus, Hermes,
Hephaestus, Heracles. LIVING TITANS: Oceanus, Tethys, Selene, Elder Oceanids.
DECEASED TITANS: Queen Kiya, Iapetus/Piercer, Cronus.

They left with Dionysus silently relieved that he had neither lied nor involved Philyra in any way.

~

Tomorrow came.

The Ghods gathered on the rooftop in the late morning. They were going to have an all-day surprise party to welcome Poseidon back from his successful trip to dominate and humiliate Titan Oceanus. Poseidon would bring them presents and everything! They would wave to him from the roof as he sailed into port. It would be grand! The Telchines were going to pass out coins engraved with the image of each Ghod. It was rumored that Poseidon might bring back a new type of drink, like wine but different; called beer!

Dexithea had convinced Queen Persephone and King Hades to attend. Demeter was beside herself with joy that her daughter would join her and the other Olympians and that Iasion had been granted permission to join attend the roof party. She giggled at the thought that Ares might force her on the table and plow her in front of everybody. She mentally scolded herself for having such naughty thoughts and said to Iasion "Now, you protect me if Ghod Ares tries to plow me on that table when you are watching!"

Iasion dutifully grimaced.

Demeter had prepared a large urn of wine with the juice of fruits and berries mixed to make a lighter morning drink.

Dionysus had brought Zeus a keg of brown-wine "because I love you so much, Dad, and I don't want you drinking that fruity woman's drink. I think it makes your penis fall off."

A band with singers had been brought in. Their instructions were to keep playing their program regardless of what happened. Regardless! So now the band played, the singers sang, and the Ghods and their guests drank their fruit-wine drink.

Hestia looked over Oursea looking for the ship carrying her triumphant brother. She saw a ship on the horizon. -- *that's probably Poseidon -- greeting him from up here is going to be a complete failure -- but how bad can it be? --*

OCEANIDS: Metis, Tyche, Clymene, Eurybia, Amphitrite, Philyra, Rhodos.
TELCHINES: Dexithea, Makelo, Halia.
EAST: Azura, Seth, Typhon, Iasion, Endymion.
OTHER: Centaur Chiron, Charon, Hotep, Petra, Persephone.

She turned and saw, in a far corner of the room, Dionysus and his followers lost in deep conversation. She sipped her fruity wine. *-- yes -- how bad can it be? --*

Dionysus instructed the three Telchines, Charon, and Nerites, "Don't feel smug. Even though you know what's coming, when you see it, you will be terrified. Experience it and get through it as quickly as you can. When I say 'Begin,' then forget all else. Do your job! If you fail to secure the ropes properly, we will all be thrown down the atrium." He then addressed the Telchines. "All three of you are going to be extremely excited. Enjoy the moment but when I command, you will focus on nothing but your tasks. This will be the moment of Telchine glory. Do not fail!"

The five smiled at one another. *-- Dionysus is so dramatic, isn't he?! --*

Dionysus, because he was looking for it and knew what he was looking for, saw it first.

Charon, chatting with team members, turned to follow the path of Dionysus's gaze. *-- is that what he is staring at? -- the strangely shaped cloud? -- it appears to be red -- I have never seen a red cloud before -- one appearing to be coming straight at us -- a red cloud shaped like an egg -- a giant egg --*

He looked back at Dionysus focused intently on the red cloud egg coming directly at them. Charon looked back at the Red Egg growing larger as it approached. In a whisper, he asked, "Poseidon?"

Dionysus quietly responded, "Poseidon."

Nerites and the Telchines heard the exchange and followed the gazes of the two men.

Dionysus told them, "The Red Egg brings Poseidon and Amphitrite just as I described it. Prepare to do your tasks."

They stood and stared.

Dexithea muttered, "I'm wetting myself."

Dionysus looked at the urine running down her leg and puddling on the floor. He glanced at the other two Telchines and said, "Don't worry. I will take care of it. He quickly went to the food area and retrieved towels.

By then, everyone was looking at the Red Egg. It was too large in the sky not to see. No one else had been told what to expect. No one had a concept of what they were seeing.

Dionysus returned to the Telchines and cleaned their wet legs and then the puddles of urine on the floor. They continued staring at the unimaginable sight before them; none of them acknowledged his touch. "All right. You are all good, now."

Then, Hera dropped her fruity wine drink.

Hestia stood staring in horror. -- *what? -- how? -- Poseidon? -- what? --*

She began to tremble. Urine ran down her leg. -- *Poseidon? -- hero's welcome?! -- life-changing event?! -- what is that thing? -- does Poseidon really command it? -- father, I need you -- but I killed you and mother! -- is that you coming to take me? -- where will you take me?! -- Grandmother! -- that's **you**, isn't it? -- come to take your revenge on me! -- this is your backup plan!! !--*

She fell to her knees into her urine, staring at the inevitability of the arrival of an unknowable monster coming to devour her.

Zeus stared at the thing stunned and excited. He was not one to ponder the complexities of the universe. He was mostly about coupling and being loved. -- *what is that? -- does it bring me gifts? -- will I be able to touch it? -- this is exciting! --*

Hades stared at the Red Egg in cold anger. -- *what is that thing? -- how dare it approach the ghods without permission? -- I will ignore it until it goes away -- it will not frighten me! -- oh, my sweet Persephone! -- does it frighten you? --*

He turned to look at Persephone enraptured with the Red Egg. -- *the color is pretty -- like a red cloud in the sky -- it's beautiful --*

The Red Egg came. Some were beginning to realize the egg carried a huge basket beneath it. Some saw that within the basket were Poseidon and Amphitrite. Some saw Amphitrite waving to them.

Demeter fainted.

Still, it came.

It arrived at the corner of the edge of the roof and hovered there. A man threw down ropes from either side.

OCEANIDS: Metis, Tyche, Clymene, Eurybia, Amphitrite, Philyra, Rhodos.
TELCHINES: Dexithea, Makelo, Halia.
EAST: Azura, Seth, Typhon, Iasion, Endymion.
OTHER: Centaur Chiron, Charon, Hotep, Petra, Persephone.

Dionysus commanded, "BEGIN!"

The command brought his team back to reality. Charon and Nerites immediately ran to grab the ropes and tether the Airboat to the north and west side of the roof railing. The Telchines walked rapidly to stand beneath the carriage where they had been told the carriage door would open. The carriage floated a pace above their heads.

Iapyx steadied the Airboat as best he could. -- *it's hard enough maintaining a constant altitude -- this wind is not helping things -- hold those ropes as steady as you can --*

Finally, he was comfortable enough to open the carriage door and drop the ladder to the roof. He returned to his controls as he said, "It's all yours, Oceanid Amphitrite. Be careful. Stay focused."

She smiled at him, said, "It is my nature," and began her descent down the ladder to the roof. Makelo and Halia stood on each side of the ladder holding it as steady as they could. Dexithea took Amphitrite's hand as she stepped from the rope ladder.

They turned to face the dumb-struck crowd. Dexithea loudly announced, "Great Ghods, I present to you Elder Oceanid Amphitrite, Consort to Ghod-of-Ghods Poseidon, Ghod of the Sea, arriving by his personal Airboat from Port Spearpoint!"

Dionysus strolled up and handed her a glass of wine. "Welcome home, Amphitrite. Have you been well?" They chatted nonchalantly. Still, no Ghod spoke or moved.

Dexithea took a deep breath and walked to her assignment -- Hestia. "I am commanded by Ghod of Ghods Poseidon to escort you to the airboat. As the oldest Olympian, it will be your privilege to be the first to join Ghod-of-Ghods Poseidon for the coming flight."

Hestia, still on her knees, eyes wide with terror, said, "Get in that thing? No, I won't! What is that thing?!"

Dexithea did not speak. She reached down, took Hestia's hand, and forcefully pulled her to her feet. She whispered, "Do not embarrass me, woman! I will not have it! You WILL climb that ladder. You WILL join your brother." She pulled Hestia toward the waiting carriage. Halfway there, Dexithea snarled under her breath, "COWARD!"

ELDER OLYMPIANS: Hestia, Demeter, Hera, Hades, Poseidon, Zeus
OLYMPIANS: Apollo, Ares, Artemis, Athena, Aphrodite, Dionysus, Hermes,
Hephaestus, Heracles. LIVING TITANS: Oceanus, Tethys, Selene, Elder Oceanids.
DECEASED TITANS: Queen Kiya, Iapetus/Piercer, Cronus.

The word stopped Hestia in her tracks. Fear turned to hatred. She stared in fury at Dexithea. Dexithea returned the stare in kind and then let a wide smile slowly come across her face as her eyes widened with excitement. "You excite me, Ghod Hestia, but you are being a bad girl. You will need to be punished. But for now, go on a ride with your brother. We will discuss this tonight." She led Hestia to the ladder. Hestia hesitated, looked back into Dexithea's unyielding eyes, and climbed the ladder into the waiting carriage.

Halia then walked to face Zeus. She said, "I am commanded by Ghod of Ghods Poseidon to escort you to his personal Airboat. As the youngest and most beloved Olympian, it will be your privilege to be the second to join Ghod-of-Ghods Poseidon for the coming flight."

Zeus exclaimed, "I can touch it? Will it fall out of the sky? Where will it go? What is it?" He climbed the ladder still talking as he climbed.

Makelo then went to Hades and repeated the command. He refused. Makelo turned to Persephone and asked, "If your King held your hand in a Red Egg ride up into the sky would you be afraid?"

Persephone answered, "Oh, no. My king will always protect me. A ride in the sky would be such fun!"

Makelo turned to Hades with a quizzical look.

"Oh, all right. But only for my precious Queen Persephone."

Persephone and Hades ascended the ladder. They were then followed by Amphitrite who, upon entering the basket, turned, and waved to the gathering. She then said, "All are on board and secured, Pilot Iapyx."

Iapyx waved to Charon and Nerites to release the mooring tethers which they did. The Red Egg slowly ascended into the afternoon sky. Below, staring up at the impossible, were the unbelieving citizens and workers of Port Olympus. -- *what have the ghods wrought?!* --

Poseidon and Amphitrite were now experienced. "Due east, Pilot," he said.

Hestia gripped the railing with white knuckles. -- *he is taking me to Tartarus -- where I killed Father and Mother* --

Zeus was ecstatic. -- *I fly higher than the birds -- I am ghod of the sky* --

OCEANIDS: Metis, Tyche, Clymene, Eurybia, Amphitrite, Philyra, Rhodos.
TELCHINES: Dexithea, Makelo, Halia.
EAST: Azura, Seth, Typhon, Iasion, Endymion.
OTHER: Centaur Chiron, Charon, Hotep, Petra, Persephone.

Persephone was wide-eyed with wonder. "It's so beautiful, Husband Hades. I can see forever. I can reach out and touch the clouds. You are so wonderful to bring me here."

Hades was pleased with himself.

They sailed on. Toward Tartarus.

Poseidon asked, "I have not yet seen this Olympus Towers of ours, Hestia. Are we pleased?"

Hestia ignored the question. "Where did you get this thing, Poseidon? This is Dionysus's doing, isn't it? If he has betrayed me, I will personally throw him down the atrium one small piece at a time."

"No, you won't, Sister. I forbid it. You will treat him with the dignity we treat all Lords. Oceanus gave this airboat to me. It is the only one he had. He wanted me to have it to complete my journey to becoming Ghod of Ghods. I made him a Lord for it. I now command Oceanus as you command Philyra. No order goes to Oceanus except through me. He is my loyal subject."

"Did you make him grovel?"

"No. He is a Lord. Lords do not grovel."

"I see. So, you are taking over my job at the Port!

"No. I am taking over the Sea and all the waters. The Port remains under your control."

"Thank you, Poseidon," she said with slight bitterness knowing that Poseidon had just claimed leadership of the Olympians. "I have been a bad woman. I need to be punished."

"Nonsense, Hestia. You have brought the Olympians to the clouds. We are above all things -- all people. We are Ghods. You have done this thing. I rejoice at what you have accomplished."

She looked out forlornly over the vast panorama. *-- you did this, Dionysus and sadly, I don't even know what it is you did -- I need to be punished --*

Zeus was hanging over the edge of the basket looking straight down. "Take us higher, person! Take us as high as we can go!"

"Look, Husband! There is Elysian Fields. I can see all of it! I am so happy!"

ELDER OLYMPIANS: Hestia, Demeter, Hera, Hades, Poseidon, Zeus
OLYMPIANS: Apollo, Ares, Artemis, Athena, Aphrodite, Dionysus, Hermes, Hephaestus, Heracles. LIVING TITANS: Oceanus, Tethys, Selene, Elder Oceanids. DECEASED TITANS: Queen Kiya, Iapetus/Piercer, Cronus.

Tartarus came into sight. The outline of the Olympus Towers was obvious. It had taken shape. Initial work on the third level had begun.

Tartarus! Home to the incredible Olympus Towers! Tartarus! Where Kiya and her children died!

The Airboat circled Olympus Towers and then sailed back to Port Olympus. Debarking was repeated. Wine and excitement greeted the celebrants. Poseidon debarked last.

Dexithea greeted Hestia with a glass of wine. "Me or Philyra?"

"Both of you. I want Philyra to watch."

Dionysus reported to Poseidon. "Do you have a preference for where we build the hangar, Ghod Poseidon?"

"Yes. In Elysian Fields near Tartarus. The Persephone girl can watch over the Airboat. She will want to go up at every opportunity. Establish continuous fast transit between here and the hangar for my use and Zeus's. He is like a child in it. Take your people with you and securely anchor my airboat. Have Pilot Iapyx report to my office tomorrow. That is all."

"Your will be done, Ghod of Ghods Poseidon!" Dionysus rounded up his crew to be transported back to Tartarus by air.

Halia's eyes grew large. "You mean I am going to ride in that thing?!"

Dionysus laughed. They boarded the Airboat and set off for Tartarus, except for Charon who requisitioned a large carriage from Transportation.

The Airboat arrived at Elysian Fields. Iapyx directed the tethering. The team inspected the area and developed plans for housing the craft. It was decided where to build the hangar and that it would be safe enough, for now, where it was tethered. Planning complete, everyone boarded Charon's carriage and, exhausted, returned to Port Olympus.

~

Dionysus knew that Philyra would be with Hestia and Dexithea. He made his way to Amphitrite's quarters, instead. If she weren't there, he would force his way in and sleep on her sofa. He was beyond exhaustion.

OCEANIDS: Metis, Tyche, Clymene, Eurybia, Amphitrite, Philyra, Rhodos.
TELCHINES: Dexithea, Makelo, Halia.
EAST: Azura, Seth, Typhon, Iasion, Endymion.
OTHER: Centaur Chiron, Charon, Hotep, Petra, Persephone.

She answered his knock. "Come in, Sweet. Are you exhausted? Brown-wine? I will have one with you."

"Yes, and yes, and how are you doing?"

"Refreshed, actually. I have been with my husband for far too many nights. I look forward to being alone. I happened to mention to Aphrodite that if she were especially pleasing to Poseidon that she would undoubtedly be invited to ride in the Airboat and that no girl had ever really coupled until she had coupled sailing through big, fluffy clouds. I believe she will keep my husband entertained, probably until morning. Here's your brown-wine, Sweet." She sat down beside him on her sofa. "I expect Dexithea to come knocking on my door around sunrise. And poor, Philyra. I don't know how she handles all the demands required of her. We live in interesting times, don't we, Dionysus?"

He held out his wine to her in salute. She returned the gesture. They drank.

She said, "These glasses are exquisite. Wine tastes even better in a glass. I will make a big production when I gift the glasses to my in-laws. Maybe tomorrow or the next day."

"Philyra's Roomlites were delivered. Maybe I can install them tomorrow. I hope she can use them to her advantage with Hestia."

"Oh, about that, Sweet. There's been a slight change in our power structure. Poseidon and Hestia talked about things during their ride. Everything you hoped for has come to pass. Poseidon has taken his natural place as leader of the Olympians. Hestia can retain control of the Port. And the most delicious part is that he and she accept the concept that they are Ghods high above everyone. They don't have to control the day-to-day activities of the masses. That's what the Lords are for. Hestia has her Lord Philyra. Poseidon has his Lord Oceanus. That was your plan all along, wasn't it?"

Dionysus mumbled, "The west is safe for now. The east is safe for now. The Port is safe for now." He stared silently into his glass of brown-wine.

"For now, Sweet. You have given them many new playthings to excite them, distract them, and interest them. But for how long? Even a long time eventually passes. They will someday remember their ambitions to have everything, to dominate everyone, to command, to be obeyed, to keep their heel upon the masses. Ares delights in slaughtering living

ELDER OLYMPIANS: Hestia, Demeter, Hera, Hades, Poseidon, Zeus
OLYMPIANS: Apollo, Ares, Artemis, Athena, Aphrodite, Dionysus, Hermes,
Hephaestus, Heracles. LIVING TITANS: Oceanus, Tethys, Selene, Elder Oceanids.
DECEASED TITANS: Queen Kiya, Iapetus/Piercer, Cronus.

creatures. Zeus demands love or he will have Athena kill you. Hestia wants the end of all good things, but she hasn't found enough Hecatoncheires to carry out her will. All of them simply want, want, want! There is nothing you can do to change them, Dionysus. It is their nature."

"There *is* a way. I shall find it! Kiya was greater than any of them and she picked up all who had fallen, nurtured everyone around her, and loved all people, even those who would have her dead. What is it one has and the other doesn't? Is Hestia missing some basic truth about our kind? What did Kiya have that Hestia doesn't?"

"Kiya chose to think for herself and taught her children to do the same. She looked inward and understood the nature of others and that to help the least of them would ultimately benefit everyone, including herself. Hestia looks outward and neither knows nor cares about the lives of those around her nor understands that to help them is to help herself. She believes that if they have it, she doesn't! Kiya was enlightened and expanded her world. Hestia never evolved from belonging to a tribe, a somewhat evil tribe, I fear."

"I shall temporize and postpone their ultimate assault on civilization until I find deed or word to enlighten them; to save them; to save us all. I shall! The love of Kiya demands it!"

"Perhaps you will, Sweet. If you live ten thousand years, perhaps you will. In the meantime, I will take your glass. You lie on the sofa and put your head on my lap."

He did. Then he wept.

51. Building Olympus Towers
< Year 102 >

In the early morning, Airboat 313 hovered over the large block of Marmaros to be transported to Olympus Towers. Hotep directed the attachment of the carrying ropes as Iapyx carefully maintained the Airboat's position.

Queen Persephone saw Hotep and his crew arrive. She ran to them. "Builder Hotep! Builder Hotep! May I go with you?!"

OCEANIDS: Metis, Tyche, Clymene, Eurybia, Amphitrite, Philyra, Rhodos.
TELCHINES: Dexithea, Makelo, Halia.
EAST: Azura, Seth, Typhon, Iasion, Endymion.
OTHER: Centaur Chiron, Charon, Hotep, Petra, Persephone.

Hotep turned and smiled at the young woman as she approached. "The King approves?"

She replied, "The King is at Phlegethon inspecting his mines. I ate a lot of cave mushrooms last evening. I am still excited and want to return to the sky. The King doesn't like the sky. He prefers to stay underground! May I go? Am I allowed to command you to take me with you?"

Hotep called up to Iapyx. "She doesn't weigh that much. Can you handle the additional weight?"

Pilot Iapyx replied, "We only have four trips today. None of the loads are particularly heavy. She will be safe enough. If she dies, we all die with her, so why not?"

Hotep said, "Queen Persephone, I would be delighted if you were able to join us in our work today." He nodded to the site manager to indicate the Queen would be joining them.

She clapped her hands in excitement. "I know how to stay out of the way and just watch but it would be so exciting if I got to help you build my Olympus Towers!"

"We'll see."

The four climbed the rope ladder to the Airboats carriage and lifted off.

Persephone forgot there were others with her. She reached out to feel the wind, to touch the clouds, to stare in wonder at the land passing below. She sang a flying song.

They arrived at the site. Hotep said, "My men will be in extreme danger, Queen Persephone. You know to be quiet and not distract them. I, too, shall do as you do."

She nodded agreement with great seriousness.

Iapyx positioned the Airboat over the first of the central pillars. The two men descended from the carriage, attached harnesses around the pillar, then signaled Hotep, "Slight northeast."

Hotep relayed the signal to Iapyx who moved the Airboat slightly to the northeast. The signal was returned. "Good. Lower"

Hotep signaled Iapyx to lower the Airboat. He felt the Marmaros column contact the pillar, then moved the Airboat slightly up and down as the two workmen positioned the column perfectly onto the pillar. The "in-place" signal was given and the carrying ropes were released from the column. The "all-clear" signal was given, and the Airboat rose a pace into the air.

Hotep said to Persephone, "Queen, are you strong enough to pull the four carrying ropes back into the carriage? That would be a great help."

She was and she did.

Iapyx then lowered the carriage to be even with the workmen. Hotep handed an Orichalcum bolt to each workman and then a sheet of thin Orichalcum. The workmen matched the pre-formed holes in the sheet to the pre-formed holes in the Marmaros columns and inserted the bolts. Petra had argued against this step as being unnecessary. "The weight of the columns will keep everything in place."

Hotep had replied, "You are probably correct. How high did you say the pillars are to stand? What happens if you're wrong?"

The crew repeated this process three times. Another level was added to the central support columns. Tomorrow, they would attach heavy wooden cross members to the pillars.

After completing the installation in the late afternoon, Iapyx flew the two workmen to Vanamfour Village where the men were quartered. The reaction of the ex-hunters and gathers always brought Iapyx and Hotep delight. Persephone waved gaily to the tribesmen. The children yelled and waved back at the still unimaginable sight.

Iapyx detoured to the Marmaros site where both Persephone and Hotep debarked. Hotep said to Iapyx, "Take it back to the hangar. I need to speak to Ghod Heph. I'll walk back."

Iapyx saluted and piloted the airboat back to Elysian Fields.

Hotep said to Persephone. "Your assistance today was invaluable Queen Persephone. Your subjects admire you."

OCEANIDS: Metis, Tyche, Clymene, Eurybia, Amphitrite, Philyra, Rhodos.
TELCHINES: Dexithea, Makelo, Halia.
EAST: Azura, Seth, Typhon, Iasion, Endymion.
OTHER: Centaur Chiron, Charon, Hotep, Petra, Persephone.

Persephone was ecstatic. "Yes. I worked on my Olympus Towers today. I am extremely pleased with myself. I must tell the King!" She then left to find the king to tell him of her exciting day.

Hotep walked toward the workshop speaking to the dactyls as he passed. He entered the workshop. Heph worked at the furnace.

The three Telchines were busily scurrying around. Makelo looked up and saw him enter. She picked up a handful of small objects and walked to him. She held out a coin. "What do you think, Builder Hotep? This is my first batch of them. Do you think Ghod Poseidon will be pleased?"

Hotep took the coin and examined it closely. "This is incredible, Makelo. The detail in his face is amazing."

"It is, isn't it? My Marmaros sculpturer made the master engraving for me. She is getting better with each Ghod. I should have a full set before the Festival. I cast Zeus in Gold. I think it's the prettiest metal and it's so shiny. Zeus and Poseidon are going to the festival, you know. They are going to arrive in the Red Egg. It will be awe-inspiring. I want to make many Gold coins for Zeus to give to his admirers. I don't know which other Ghods are going but I will make coins with their likeness for them to pass out, too."

Hotep chuckled. "You are becoming one of them, Makelo."

She cast her eyes downward. "Thank you, Builder Hotep." Then returned to her work.

Hotep stood there for a moment. -- *thank you?* –

He waited until Hephaestus completed his task and then walked over to greet him. "Ghod Heph, the fixtures you created to hold the Roomlites are magnificent. They are in place on the first floor. The energy urns slip into the decor seamlessly. I am anxious for you to inspect them to see if you approve. Plus, the ground floor infrastructure is taking shape. The landscape designers have some innovative ideas on how Roomlites could be used to accentuate the beauty of the plants, walkways, and water features. I'll set up a team meeting for your convenience."

"Magnificent? I was expecting something better than 'magnificent.' I will come for tomorrow's noon meal. You can explain to me why the fixtures are not grandiose and majestic."

ELDER OLYMPIANS: Hestia, Demeter, Hera, Hades, Poseidon, Zeus
OLYMPIANS: Apollo, Ares, Artemis, Athena, Aphrodite, Dionysus, Hermes, Hephaestus, Heracles. LIVING TITANS: Oceanus, Tethys, Selene, Elder Oceanids.
DECEASED TITANS: Queen Kiya, Iapetus/Piercer, Cronus.

"Excellent. The Oceanids will prepare their finest mid-day meal for you and then we can inspect your majestic work. You are most Ghodly!" He excused himself and began walking back to Tartarus. -- *grandiose and majestic lighting fixtures? -- I thought magnificent was too much!* --

As he left Phlegethon, Hotep heard a woman's voice call out from behind him. "May I walk with you, Builder Hotep?"

He turned to see Halia following.

"You are Halia, are you not? Why are you going to Tartarus this late in the day?"

"I watch you direct the workmen picking up the Marmaros with the Red Egg. I find it exciting. You are building the greatest structure there has ever been. Sometimes I tremble just thinking about it."

Hotep laughed in appreciation.

I wanted to talk to you about Ghod Heph's fixtures. They are hideous!"

"Oh?!"

"The structure you are building deserves the finest of everything. Roomlites give off a hideous light. It is cold and uninviting. Placed in an appropriate Orichalcum fixture, the light would become warmer and more pleasing. The fixture could direct the light to where you want it rather than all over the place. Each space needs a different size and shape of fixture. Ghod Heph's craftsmanship is impeccable, but his design, in this case, is lacking!"

"That kind of talk could get us both killed, Halia."

"Are you going to betray us, Builder Hotep?"

"No. But you have made your point. Change your descriptions to be positive. I will understand what you mean."

"Yes, you will understand because you want beauty as much as I do. But you are like everyone else. You tell the Ghods how wonderful everything they do is. Hephaestus breaks wind and Makelo gushes about the smell of flowers in the room."

"That's dangerous talk, Halia. I require you to stop it."

OCEANIDS: Metis, Tyche, Clymene, Eurybia, Amphitrite, Philyra, Rhodos.
TELCHINES: Dexithea, Makelo, Halia.
EAST: Azura, Seth, Typhon, Iasion, Endymion.
OTHER: Centaur Chiron, Charon, Hotep, Petra, Persephone.

"They get inside your head, Builder Hotep. Being around them all day, you start to change. I'm frightened. I have been trained in how to handle them and how to talk to them by the absolute best. Still, I'm frightened, and I have no one to talk to about it. Certainly, not Makelo. And sister Dexi is changing. Darker in some way. I think she enjoys the things Amphitrite needs her to do. It's like she isn't on our side or on their side. It's like she is on her own side. But anyway, if you decide that you want your Roomlite fixtures improved upon, call me. I know what needs doing. Thank you for the pleasant walk and I won't talk this way about the Ghods anymore. I'll leave you to your walk home, now." She turned to return to Phlegethon.

"Halia! We are halfway to Tartarus!"

She turned, laughed, and said, "I lost track of time. Your work is so interesting and exciting, Hotep. I envy you so much. Have a nice night."

"Halia, they won't miss you. We have a lot of time before we go to bed. We can walk through Olympus Towers and discuss proper fixtures and things."

She stared at him for a long time. "Are you sure?"

"Yes, I'm sure."

She returned and they continued their walk to Tartarus. She said, "And the outside handrails are made of wood, but they would be so beautiful and impressive if they were made of Orichalcum. And we could hang bells to ring in the wind and metal urns to hold the plants."

~

Sunrise.

Petra arrived at the building site. The morning was cool and beautiful. A woman was moving things around on the ground level as Hotep watched.

An Oceanid brought Petra his usual Sweet Drink with fruit. Petra said to the Telchine, "Good morning. You are out working early!"

"Oh, Builder Petra, good morning. I'm Telchine Halia!" The woman had a warm glow about her. "Builder Hotep is allowing me to express my thoughts on how he can use Orichalcum in building your glorious structure. He told me that you wouldn't mind."

ELDER OLYMPIANS: Hestia, Demeter, Hera, Hades, Poseidon, Zeus
OLYMPIANS: Apollo, Ares, Artemis, Athena, Aphrodite, Dionysus, Hermes, Hephaestus, Heracles. LIVING TITANS: Oceanus, Tethys, Selene, Elder Oceanids.
DECEASED TITANS: Queen Kiya, Iapetus/Piercer, Cronus.

"Quite the contrary. The more heads and hands we have, the better. The Oceanid told me that Ghod Heph is visiting us for the mid-day meal to inspect the Roomlite fixtures." He spoke to Hotep, "Do you like the fixtures, Builder Hotep?"

"Do you like them, Chief?"

"It's not my job to like them or dislike them, Builder. That's your worry. That and keeping Ghod Heph happy."

Hotep said, "Telchine Halia is an expert in lighting fixtures, Chief. And an advisor to Ghod Heph!"

Petra looked at her. "As Lord Charon says, 'it's good to have a plan!'"

Halia offered, "Ghod Heph's fixtures are so majestic, they will be hard to improve upon."

Petra laughed, "Whatever! The Vanamfour men are transporting the lumber for the third-level floors today. We will have a roof over the second floor before the next quarter moon. You can start stubbing in the second-floor walls then. Chief Philyra wants to show off a completed first floor and a stubbed-in second floor by the new moon. She is talking about their moving into the second floor when we finish it. May the Ghods help us. How would that work?!"

Hotep responded, "The first floor won't be completed by the new moon, Chief. Even if we had more tribes. The Vanamfour men can provide muscle, but I need craftsmen for finishing the interior. Three hunters and two gathers are becoming adequate craftsmen, but it takes time to train them, and such work is not their nature."

Petra replied, "Lord Charon is aware of that. He is doing what he can."

Halia offered, "My old home, Urfa, has too many builders. They have built everything they need to build. When I left, they were busying themselves improving what was there and carving decorative patterns into buildings."

Petra became alert. "Too many builders? Carving decorative patterns? Where is this Urfa? Will they immigrate to Tartarus?"

"I don't know. Mother Azura of Urfa would decide things like that. Lord Dionysus obtained the release of me and my sisters. I suppose he could get some builders for you. Urfa is near Tallstone; a five-day walk due east."

OCEANIDS: Metis, Tyche, Clymene, Eurybia, Amphitrite, Philyra, Rhodos.
TELCHINES: Dexithea, Makelo, Halia.
EAST: Azura, Seth, Typhon, Iasion, Endymion.
OTHER: Centaur Chiron, Charon, Hotep, Petra, Persephone.

Petra became lost in thought. "Charon and Dionysus counsel with each other every day and it is a Telchine who solves my problems?" He called out loudly, "Oceanid!"

An Oceanid came promptly, "Yes, Builder Petra?

"I need expert builders. Expert builders are plentiful in the city of Urfa. Let Lord Dionysus or Lord Charon know of this as soon as possible."

"As you request, Builder Petra." The Oceanid disappeared into the morning.

The mid-day meal was one Oceanid short of perfection.

Makelo had wrangled an invitation to accompany her Ghod; after all, she was an expert craftsman with Orichalcum.

Halia offered to give a tour of the grandiose and majestic Roomlite fixture installations. Hephaestus grandly accepted, eagerly anticipating the lavish praise he would undoubtedly receive.

They toured. Makelo held onto Heph's arm as she, too, lavished praise upon the fixtures.

As the tour ended, Halia praised what they had seen, then said, "For you to make all these fixtures yourself will take untold hours, taking you away from the glorious objects you make for your brothers and sisters which thrill them so. Now that I have seen and been inspired by your glorious work, I believe that I could complete this project for you. After all, it is you, the greatest Orichalcum artist to ever live, who trained me. I believe I am ready to demonstrate what a glorious teacher you are! I would dedicate myself to this great project so that you will have time to make magnificent gifts for your family."

Halia surprised herself by how fluent and devious she had become. -- I *should have gotten some wine into him, first!* --

Hephaestus was reticent but Halia was accomplished in Ghod-handling. In the end, the project was hers. She glanced at Hotep with a look of triumph.

Wine was served to celebrate Heph's grandiose and majestic light fixtures.

Halia encouraged Makelo to return with Ghod Heph to the metals workshop to continue work on producing enough Ghod coins for the approaching Winter Solstice Festival. Whichever Ghods decided to attend, surely, they would want a supply of personalized Ghod coins.

At last, Makelo escorted Hephaestus to their carriage and they were off!

~

Dionysus and Charon rode in on fast horses soon after. The Oceanid jumped off from behind Dionysus and took the two horses away for proper grooming.

Charon said to Hotep, "I want you to go with Dionysus to Urfa immediately to interview builders. You know what you need. Select as many as that Mother Azura woman will let you have. Get them back here as fast as you can. We are already twenty years behind schedule. You have the Red Egg scheduled to pick up the main pillar cross timbers at sunrise tomorrow. Who have you trained that can take your place?"

Hotep replied, "Er -- no one Lord Charon."

Charon snarled, "NO ONE! Petra, I'm holding you personally responsible for this! Have Hotep train his backup during tomorrow's runs. Send him to Urfa after the cross-timbers have been delivered. While you are at it, Pilot Iapyx is our only qualified Airboat pilot. If he offends a Ghod, we won't have anyone to fly that thing. We need more pilots! Have him start training them!"

Dionysus put his hand on Charon's shoulder and said, "You have too much going on, my friend. Let's sit and talk." He led Charon to the table and signaled an Oceanid for Bitters. "Here's a plan. Tell me what you think. Postpone the cross-timber pick-up for four days. This will put you only twenty years and four days behind schedule. The Ghods don't want the Egg seen in the east before their triumphant entry to the Festival, but we can land it on this side of Riverport without being seen. Iapyx can start training another pilot. He can drop me, Hotep, and Halia off near Riverport. On the way back, his trainee can get in some flying time."

The Oceanid brought them each a Bitter in an earthen cup.

Dionysus said to her, "Oceanid, instruct your replacement sisters to bring a supply of drinking glasses when they start their rotation and tell me this, would you like to learn to fly an Airboat?"

OCEANIDS: Metis, Tyche, Clymene, Eurybia, Amphitrite, Philyra, Rhodos.
TELCHINES: Dexithea, Makelo, Halia.
EAST: Azura, Seth, Typhon, Iasion, Endymion.
OTHER: Centaur Chiron, Charon, Hotep, Petra, Persephone.

~ Oceanid Rhodos ~

Oceanid Rhodos would sing her song many times. "To rise into the sky -- surrounded by endless blue -- to glide effortlessly through endless blue -- to look forever into endless blue -- like the sea." And then when her Airboat first flew over Oursea, "Endless blue surrounding me in all directions -- no land to be seen -- only sky and sea -- endless -- I could see blue forever -- if I were to dive from the sky into Oursea, I could swim forever in any direction -- and remain in the sea -- in the eternal blue embrace of the sky and the sea."

But first, she must answer Dionysus. She said, "Thank you, Titan Dionysus, but I am an Oceanid, not a bird!"

Dionysus laughed. "Go with us so that Pilot Iapyx can have company on the flight back. He is shy. You will be safe alone with him. Let him teach you to fly or not, as you decide."

She glanced at Iapyx. -- *he is somewhat attractive* --

"Respectful, you say?" She hesitated. "All right, I will go. I will make arrangements with my sisters."

~ Pilot Rhodos ~

Iapyx set the airboat down near the gathering of five unbelieving beggar women. None of the Oceanids broke character but they did stand in awed silence trying to process what they saw before them. In the meantime, Rhodos descended the rope ladder first; Hotep and Dionysus followed.

Rhodos said to the beggars, "I am Oceanid Rhodos of Tartarus. These are friends of Queen Kiya. You are Oceanids!"

After a brief hesitation, one of the women answered, "I am Oceanid Melia. I am charged with bringing Portmaster Clymene advanced reports of those who travel to Riverport."

Rhodos and Melia engaged in intense conversation. Dionysus helped Hotep anchor the airboat and walked toward the two Oceanids, stopping a respectful distance away. He watched them converse. -- *there is more going on than the exchange of words -- it's how they stand and position their hands -- expressions on their face -- inflections and eye movement -- they have a language beyond what others understand -- what are they really telling one another?* --

ELDER OLYMPIANS: Hestia, Demeter, Hera, Hades, Poseidon, Zeus
OLYMPIANS: Apollo, Ares, Artemis, Athena, Aphrodite, Dionysus, Hermes, Hephaestus, Heracles. LIVING TITANS: Oceanus, Tethys, Selene, Elder Oceanids. DECEASED TITANS: Queen Kiya, Iapetus/Piercer, Cronus.

Finally, Melia turned to Dionysus and said, "Welcome Titan Dionysus. Portmaster Clymene speaks warmly of you. She will be pleased to see you. I'll escort you and your friends to Riverport whenever you are ready."

Dionysus, Hotep, and Halia said farewell to Iapyx and Rhodos. The three began walking with Melia to Riverport as Iapyx and Rhodos prepared the Airboat for the return flight.

Rhodos asked Iapyx, "Will I be allowed command of the airboat on the return flight? I will be comfortable piloting the vessel."

"First you must untether the boat by yourself. Then I will issue commands for takeoff. You will execute them immediately!"

She did, did, and did. Then Iapyx told her how to set a return course by way of Oursea.

Like all Oceanids, Rhodos learned quickly.

~ Riverport ~

Dionysus, Hotep, and Halia were warmly greeted by Clymene. They drank his wine on the dock that evening.

Clymene said, "I was told of the difficulty in finding a landing site close to Riverport from high in the air; that perhaps a structure which could be seen from a great height would be helpful in the future."

Dionysus did not recall anyone ever saying that, but Hotep responded, "Yes, that is true. Navigating in areas we are familiar with is easy but when flying over unknown terrain, we have no markers to guide us. We were fortunate to identify the river and use it to find Riverport."

Clymene observed, "Such structures would be advantageous to our friends but could also be used by our enemies. I will discuss this problem with General Typhon."

Dionysus sipped his wine. -- *weapons of war* --

The three departed for Urfa the next day.

They would pass through Riverport three days later; followed by three dozen master builders.

OCEANIDS: Metis, Tyche, Clymene, Eurybia, Amphitrite, Philyra, Rhodos.
TELCHINES: Dexithea, Makelo, Halia.
EAST: Azura, Seth, Typhon, Iasion, Endymion.
OTHER: Centaur Chiron, Charon, Hotep, Petra, Persephone.

52. Winter Solstice Festival 76
< Year 102 >

The 'Ghod Help Us' team, composed of Amphitrite, Charon, Dionysus, and Halia arrived for the 76th Winter Solstice Festival a full quarter moon before it would begin. They met with Clymene, Azura, Seth, and Typhon. The plans of the Ghods were revealed to the prey; a response formulated, and posturing established. "To prevent war, prepare for war!"

The great festival flag flew over the flags of Riverport, Urfa, and Tallstone.

The meetings were successful, and the team continued to Tallstone.

They settled into their quarters and were content that the principal parties knew what to expect and had appropriate responses planned. As they relaxed, their concern turned to Philyra back at the Port. They knew she would be overloaded. Three western delegations would soon be arriving for trade negotiations, building Olympus Towers was ongoing and never-ending, and dealing with Hestia was growing more difficult.

Amphitrite observed, "Poor Hestia is stressed over so many different things. Her brothers and sisters are leaving her behind while they make their grand entrance at the Winter Solstice Festival. Hestia never liked the eastern settlements because she can't control them, and now she is being abandoned by her family. She must bluster and be all imperial all by herself. The poor creature suspects that Philyra plays her like an aulos. Correctly, of course. Fortunately, Philyra has Creusa helping. Creusa has developed the skill to know whether to send Philyra or Dexithea to Hestia to console her."

Charon observed, "Creusa is becoming quite the company asset. She manages Hestia well and understands the intricacies of scheduling, communication, and meeting deadlines. If Nerites gets a promotion to Poseidon's full-time plaything, I have his replacement."

Amphitrite laughed. "Don't be dull, Charon. Nerites is there at my pleasure. Just be thankful that I don't get my beloved husband interested in you rather than Nerites."

Dionysus interrupted, "Don't be stupid, Amphitrite. Charon is too ugly. Maybe send in Demeter's Iasion. He is better looking than even Nerites."

Halia jumped in, "Men are so crude! Let each person find joy where they may and don't judge them. Let us worry about important things -- like my sister."

Charon, wrapped in the warmth of wine and his only friends, offered, "Makelo has gone to the other side, Halia. She is lost to the cause. She is now Heph's better half. That's not too bad, though. Heph is just Heph. Neither friend nor enemy. He just wants to forge things out of metal. How bad can that be?"

Dionysus suggested, "Yes. He and Hades live in worlds of their imagination. Whether the real world is ruled by Olympian, Titan, or Oceanid, they will be content if left to their private realities." He raised his glass of wine, "Let us drink to the future of our glorious world! May it be ruled by Oceanids and Telchines!"

They raised their glasses and drank.

Amphitrite looked contently at the two men without speaking. -- *silly uncomplicated men -- Grandmother Kiya planned for all eventualities of which she could conceive and yet -- ghods in flying machines?! -- we can only guide today into tomorrow as best we can -- the future will be of its own making --*

~ Arrival ~

Opening day.

The future made its way toward Riverport.

The flight plan was flawless. "Follow the white straight-line markers to Riverport." Rhodos knew that Clymene's 'white straight-line markers' would indeed be in place, visible from high altitudes, and directing the Airboat straight to Riverport. Clymene had said it would be so. It was so.

Clymene and General Typhon had conceived of the long, thin markers using reflective white linen attached to relocatable wagons. The wagons could be repositioned to direct an incoming airboat in any direction Clymene desired. In this case, straight to Riverport.

And in this case, Rhodos saw Riverport far below. Over Riverport, she began her controlled descent toward Urfa. Over Urfa, the airboat was low enough to be seen by bewildered observers on the ground which excited both Poseidon and Zeus who stood looking out over them. Demeter

OCEANIDS: Metis, Tyche, Clymene, Eurybia, Amphitrite, Philyra, Rhodos.
TELCHINES: Dexithea, Makelo, Halia.
EAST: Azura, Seth, Typhon, Iasion, Endymion.
OTHER: Centaur Chiron, Charon, Hotep, Petra, Persephone.

busied herself comforting Iasion who sat on the floor vomiting. Iasion was supposedly the co-pilot since Iapyx could not be included because of weight restrictions. Fortunately for Rhodos, she had discovered that Persephone was a natural co-pilot. Her sharp eyes could find the white markers and issue course adjustments. She was learning to read the terrain. A co-pilot was not mandatory but was helpful; especially on long flights such as this one. Persephone was pleased to be a useful person.

Over Urfa, Rhodos turned the propeller to put the airboat on a northeastward course straight to Tallstone. Her marker would be the tall stone located on top of the only hill. -- *so far -- so good --*

Iasion would be useless in debarking and securing the Airboat but, if all went as planned, Dionysus and Charon would be close to the stage and grab the tethering ropes and pull her in. If not, she always had anchors she could drop; dangerous and not desirable, but possible.

Her descent rate was an estimate based on the reported distance between Urfa and Tallstone. And now, in the distance, rose the tall stone.

"We approach too low, Pilot," Persephone announced.

"Slowing descent rate, Co-pilot." She smiled to herself. -- *excellent, Persephone! -- we were coming in far short of our target --*

Poseidon and Zeus could now see individual faces. Everyone at the coming festival was now looking up. Some fell to their knees. All were silent; stunned by what approached from the sky.

Persephone announced, "On target, Pilot."

"Do we have ground support, Co-pilot?"

"Yes. To the left of the target, Pilot. A second one to the right of the target. Both ground support crew are in place, Pilot."

Rhodos's last thought before she concentrated on the coming tricky landing was -- *Demeter, you should be proud of your daughter -- but you do not even understand your own kind --*

"Initiating final approach. Prepare Tethers Three and Four."

"Preparing Tethers Three and Four."

ELDER OLYMPIANS: Hestia, Demeter, Hera, Hades, Poseidon, Zeus
OLYMPIANS: Apollo, Ares, Artemis, Athena, Aphrodite, Dionysus, Hermes,
Hephaestus, Heracles. LIVING TITANS: Oceanus, Tethys, Selene, Elder Oceanids.
DECEASED TITANS: Queen Kiya, Iapetus/Piercer, Cronus.

"Hovering at landing altitude. Drop Tethers Three and Four to Ground crew."

"Tether Three dropped... Tether Four dropped... Tether Three received... Tether Four received."

"Signal ground crew to begin haul."

"Signal sent and acknowledged."

Dionysus and Charon began guiding the airboat down. To the credit of all involved, it would land on the stage as planned.

The Gathering of Chiefs had begun to wind down. Only Seth, Typhon, and Azura had known what was coming. Even knowing, the experience was overwhelming. Seth recovered enough to look around at the people remaining on the stage. He saw old Chief Nanamulla staring dumbstruck at the airboat. -- *I am sorry, old friend, that I could not warn you of what was to come* --

Dionysus and Charon signaled in unison, "Tether secure!"

Persephone relayed the signal. "Both Tethers secure, Pilot!"

Rhodos set the controls to maintain the current status and declared, "Airboat 313 Secure! Co-pilot. You have permission to debark!"

Persephone unceremoniously shoved her Uncle Poseidon out of her way at the carriage gate, opened it, positioned the wooden step ladder, stepped down upon the stage, and with an uncharacteristically loud and commanding voice announced, "All lower-class people, kneel to Olympian Ghod Poseidon!" She extended her hand to help Poseidon down the steps onto the stage.

Seth, not yet fully recovered from the shock of what he had just seen, stiffened. -- *kneel to him? -- that was not discussed! -- how I greet him sets precedent! -- kneeling must not happen!* --

Poseidon stepped upon the stage.

Seth, his mind in turmoil, rushed over and gave him a bear-hug, the standard greeting between chiefs. -- *I hope this isn't the obnoxious one!* --

Poseidon wasn't at all sure that this person should be touching him. -- *who is this person? -- is he of consequence? -- he had better be at least a lord!* --

OCEANIDS: Metis, Tyche, Clymene, Eurybia, Amphitrite, Philyra, Rhodos.
TELCHINES: Dexithea, Makelo, Halia.
EAST: Azura, Seth, Typhon, Iasion, Endymion.
OTHER: Centaur Chiron, Charon, Hotep, Petra, Persephone.

Seth stepped back, kept both hands on Poseidon's shoulders, and launched into his rehearsed greeting. "Welcome, Great Chief. I am Seth! The supreme master of all scholars. All scholars and all Chiefs obey my commands. I have more knowledge than any living person. You appear to be a person of the highest class. Who are you?"

Poseidon was taken aback. -- *this is not at all the reception I expected -- this person should be overwhelmed with doubt and wonder and the knowledge that he stands before a ghod -- a person above all classes - did he not hear Persephone command him to kneel before me? -- Hestia insisted upon this! -- this person considers himself to be my equal! -- I may have ares kill him! -- he did say that I appeared to be of the highest rank! -- at least he recognized that! -- and all chiefs obey his command?! –*

He said, "I am Olympian Poseidon, Ghod of the Sea. I and my brother Zeus and Sister Demeter have come to observe your Festival and let you look upon the glory of the Ghods!"

Seth replied, "Ghods, you say. Then you must know Ghod Athena and Ghod Ares who attended last year's festival. Delightful people in a class above all others. You say that Ghod Demeter is also with you? I understand she made quite an impression in Urfa last year. I am so happy she has returned. You all must simply stay in our highest-class guest house during your visit. You appear to be glorious! Will any of our scholars be allowed to go up in your flying machine? This would be of great interest. Ghods must be extremely accomplished to command one of these machines. Our absolute best scholars will wish to talk with you about how it operates." -- *have I said the things you need to hear? -- are we equal? -- at least for now? -- did I prepare well? -- kneel indeed! --*

"No one but Ghods and Lords may ascend in my great Red Egg, but I will allow all to look upon it in wonder. You say that you are of high rank in this land?"

"The highest rank, Ghod Poseidon. As a matter of fact, I seldom speak to the common people. Let me introduce you to one of my highest Lords, Lord Typhon. He and his trusted servant, Amazon Otreta, will be your host while you visit world-renowned Tallstone."

Seth waved Typhon over as he looked toward Persephone who was assisting a white-faced person down the airboat steps. Seth asked Poseidon, "Is that Queen Persephone of the Colored Fields that introduced you? I recognize her from her idols at Urfa."

ELDER OLYMPIANS: Hestia, Demeter, Hera, Hades, Poseidon, Zeus
OLYMPIANS: Apollo, Ares, Artemis, Athena, Aphrodite, Dionysus, Hermes, Hephaestus, Heracles. LIVING TITANS: Oceanus, Tethys, Selene, Elder Oceanids. DECEASED TITANS: Queen Kiya, Iapetus/Piercer, Cronus.

Poseidon replied, "Yes, Queen Persephone is also a Ghod. That is the Queen Mother Ghod Demeter with her. And that is Olympian Zeus, Ghod of the Sky, on his way over." Poseidon added, with a touch of slight disdain, "Ghod Zeus sometimes requires patronization."

Typhon and Otreta quietly joined Seth and began ingratiating themselves with Poseidon.

Seth conspiratorially asked Poseidon, "What greeting would most please Ghod Zeus?"

Poseidon replied, with a touch of superiority, "Just tell him how wonderful he is and how much you love him."

Seth turned to face the approaching Zeus, held out his arms, and, as he reached to embrace Zeus, said, "Great Olympian Zeus, Great Ghod of the Sky, I would recognize you anywhere. I love you so much!"

Dionysus ambled up to join Zeus. Amphitrite welcomed Demeter and Persephone. Charon ministered to Iasion. Azura identified which Ghod was Zeus and then found Chief Color Girl Abigail. Azura pointed him out to Abigale with instructions ending with, "No words of adulation a woman can say to him is too much and she should always end with 'I love you so much.' I will personally give a gorgeous red necklace to the Color Girl who is the most outrageous."

Iasion, not yet fully recovered from his airsickness, found Azura and requested an urgent private meeting with her after the evening meal.

Philyra and her three western trade delegations had arrived for the opening ceremonies and had witnessed the Ghod's arrival. Dionysus saw and joined the group. He lied that the arrival of Ghods in this extraordinary airboat was unexpected. In any case, the delegations should avoid contact with the Ghods to eliminate any possible confrontations. The heads of state needed no encouragement to make this so.

A great mass of humanity gathered to see the big Red Egg as it hovered over the stage. The masses parted to make way for two obviously important people strolling through them, Dionysus and Zeus. Bystanders took note every time a woman dressed in white with a red sash approached Zeus, told him how wonderful he was, and gushingly said, "I love you so much!" Zeus rewarded the adulation by giving the woman a

OCEANIDS: Metis, Tyche, Clymene, Eurybia, Amphitrite, Philyra, Rhodos.
TELCHINES: Dexithea, Makelo, Halia.
EAST: Azura, Seth, Typhon, Iasion, Endymion.
OTHER: Centaur Chiron, Charon, Hotep, Petra, Persephone.

gold coin with his image on one side and an engraving of birds flying on the other. As Dionysus and Zeus exited the crowded throng, three vibrant young women dressed in red rushed toward Zeus with arms outstretched. The things they said to Zeus brought a smile to Zeus and a blush to Dionysus. They ended with, "We are going to show you more love than you can stand!" and then ran off. Zeus was so excited he forgot to give them their gold coins.

Otreta sized up Poseidon as they toured the festival.

Charon and Persephone performed ground crew operations so that Rhodos could lift off and return to Tartarus to pick up and bring Ares, Athena, Artemis, Apollo, and Nerites to the festival. Charon and Iasion then escorted Persephone and Demeter through the festival.

All Ghods gave metal coins engraved with their image to people who were in proper awe of them. The Ghods were this year's hit of the festival and disruptive to the planned events. The Ghods were pleased with the reactions of the no-account but appreciative lower-class people.

The day drew to a close. The festival attendees were still excited by what they had seen. Those that had received Ghod coins showed them to their jealous friends. Everyone wanted one of their own. This phenomenon did not go unnoticed by Dionysus. They covet useless coins. He remembered the rock coin in his pocket that Kiya had given him. -- *Dexithea had asked me to give it to her -- I refused -- why? -- what value are these things? --*

As he had requested earlier, Iasion found Azura inside the reception building. She was sitting with Seth, her husband, and Enosh, their son.

Iasion said, "Excuse me, Great Mother Azura. I do not wish to interrupt. I can meet with you when you are ready."

She replied, "I had not forgotten you, Shepherd Iasion. Titanide Selene tells me that Chief Endymion misses your expertise with the horses greatly. Need this be a private discussion?"

"It involves the rain dance festivities of last year. Ghod Demeter fully expects this to be an annual event. She looks forward to this year's ceremony. I did not know if you have planned for this or not. I just wanted to make sure that you knew of Ghod Demeter's expectations."

Azura considered this bit of information. "Sweet Husband and Son, I will meet you later at Pumi's table. Shepherd Iasion and I must discuss a complex, sensitive issue."

The two men excused themselves.

"Sit, Iasion. Ghod Demeter actually wants to repeat last year's debacle?"

"Ghod Demeter was thrilled with the ceremony, Mother Azura. She fully expects the Telchines to dance and bring forth the rain and for Selene to make the moon reappear from behind the clouds. She has made Ghod Ares agree to come and, ah, 'plow her field' three times while I watch. That was the most exciting night of her life. She wishes it repeated. I am not included in the planning of such things but wanted to make sure you knew. I believe she plans for her daughter, Persephone, to come and witness the ceremony."

"She wishes her daughter to see her become a whore?" Azura thought in silence. "Thank you for the information, Shepherd Iasion. I shall make sure that you are told of any plan made for this matter. If and when you return to Urfa, you will be recognized as a citizen of the highest honor. Thank you for your outstanding service to our people. I will be in touch with you."

Iasion recognized dismissal, gave the proper response, and left. -- *citizen of the highest honor? -- outstanding service? -- maybe my suffering will turn out well --*

Azura considered this new information for a moment then walked outside into the crisp night air. She found a passing Oceanid and requested, "I am Azura. I will be visiting Master Seth and Enosh at Pumi's table. It would please me if Titan Dionysus and his friends were able to join us."

The Oceanid replied, "As you wish, Mother Azura," and scurried off to make it so.

Soon after, Dionysus, Amphitrite, and Halia joined Azura, Seth, and Enosh at Pumi's stone table. Deep discussions followed.

Elsewhere, Charon set up a table where Ghod Zeus greeted his adoring public.

Color Girls provided crowd control and explained proper protocol when meeting a Ghod. If the person did everything perfectly, said exactly the

OCEANIDS: Metis, Tyche, Clymene, Eurybia, Amphitrite, Philyra, Rhodos.
TELCHINES: Dexithea, Makelo, Halia.
EAST: Azura, Seth, Typhon, Iasion, Endymion.
OTHER: Centaur Chiron, Charon, Hotep, Petra, Persephone.

right words, and otherwise pleased the Ghod, they might be rewarded with a Ghod coin; not everyone, but many. It helped to be a gushing woman.

After Zeus eventually tired of the festivities, Ghod Poseidon, having seen the adulation given to Zeus, agreed to take Zeus' place at the table. He gave complimentary Ghod coins imprinted with his image on one side and the raging sea on the other.

The festival, like the imprinted sea, raged on.

~

Infatuation with the Red Egg and the Ghods began to wane on the third day. Attendees began returning to the usual playing and competition fields. Educational workshops resumed. A squad of all-age girls was seen traversing the walkways performing continuous somersaults and backflips. The festival had renewed its traditional vigor.

But now there were Ghods to contend with. And on the sixth day, the Red Egg returned bringing four more Ghods, each of whom had a good supply of Ghod coins.

After the Ghods had debarked, Rhodos, exhausted after seven days of continuous piloting the Airboat, was greeted by Philyra and Halia.

Halia told Rhodos, "Pilot Rhodos, we have a problem! You must immediately transport Chief Philyra and me back to Tartarus and exchange Chief Philyra for Telchine Dexithea. You must then transport all three Telchines to Urfa. We are to perform our rain dance under the full moon by command of Mother Azura."

Two days later, Rhodos landed the Airboat at its home field in Tartarus.

The boat was met by two Oceanids. Upon seeing the vacant, lifeless expression on their sister's face, they immediately led her over the Elysian Fields toward Oursea. "You have been in that thing for almost a full quarter moon, Sister. You are exhausted."

Philyra went immediately to Hestia. "I could not stand the thought of you being here with that Telchine woman. Send her back to the Festival in my place. I wish to remain here with you! I will do whatever you want."

ELDER OLYMPIANS: Hestia, Demeter, Hera, Hades, Poseidon, Zeus
OLYMPIANS: Apollo, Ares, Artemis, Athena, Aphrodite, Dionysus, Hermes, Hephaestus, Heracles. LIVING TITANS: Oceanus, Tethys, Selene, Elder Oceanids.
DECEASED TITANS: Queen Kiya, Iapetus/Piercer, Cronus.

Halia went immediately to find her two sisters. She exclaimed, "We are commanded to do our rain dance. It's all so exciting!"

It was Pilot Iapyx who carried the three Telchines to Urfa.

At Urfa, Azura placed Selene in charge of planning and overseeing Demeter's Fertility Ritual, now to be held annually at the original einkorn field and Persephone's Orichalcum statue.

As they walked to prepare the site, Selene said, "Dung! Endymion. I don't like doing this! Things may get a little wild and I may have to do some rather immodest things. Don't think badly of me, Sweet. Especially if one of those Ghod creatures is involved. Just remember, anything I might have to do is completely meaningless and disgusting to me, all right?"

Endymion replied, "I didn't ask, but you were a little immodest last year, weren't you?"

She flashed an embarrassed glance. "Yes, I did, Endy. But I tried to make it up to you in my own way."

He chuckled. "You are your own woman, Selene. Do whatever's right. That's the Titan way, isn't it?"

She took his arm and squeezed it.

They arrived with their supplies and equipment at the field long before sunset. They found the plowed, seeded field already surrounded by spectators. Most held a locally made carved wooden copy of Persephone's statue that Demeter had placed over Valki's grave this time last year.

Endymion said, "I knew a few people were having those things made to place over their fireplace 'to bring good fortune.' I didn't realize there were so many."

Selene walked to a spectator and engaged her in conversation. They talked for a long while. Selene finished with, "Thank you. I will see what I can do."

She returned to Endymion and said, "The woman watched last year's debauchery. She hopes that Ghod Demeter will touch her idol of Persephone and maybe speak to her. She will faint when she finds out that Queen Persephone, herself, will be here. And, she has not yet heard that these Ghods can fly through the air."

OCEANIDS: Metis, Tyche, Clymene, Eurybia, Amphitrite, Philyra, Rhodos.
TELCHINES: Dexithea, Makelo, Halia.
EAST: Azura, Seth, Typhon, Iasion, Endymion.
OTHER: Centaur Chiron, Charon, Hotep, Petra, Persephone.

"I don't envy you, Selene. You and Melia are going to have a difficult evening. Melia gave me a blow-by-blow, so to speak, report on everything that happened last year."

She hit his shoulder with her fist and said, "That bitch told you EVERYTHING?!"

"Melia was bursting with pride, Selene. She thought you to be the greatest woman to ever live. You intimidated one of those Ghod people and made him back down. She was so proud of you."

Selene sighed. "You may not want to stay and watch tonight, Endy. You are too innocent. I don't want to participate in the rain ceremony, but Seth and Aunt Ampi want me to, and Azura commanded me to. Aunt Ampi plans on being here to help make sure everything goes exactly like last year. She can't control the rain, but the Telchine women are sure they can. They do put on an impressive show. I will have to get naked, you know. You may be invited to play in the mud. Oh, Endy. What have I gotten us into?"

"Mother Azura wants a yearly fertility ceremony. It will entertain her staid subjects and maybe keep these Ghods out of Urfa's business. The stories we tell each other will grow more outrageous with each telling. And my sweet, innocent, proper Titanide Selene will melt into legend. Go get naked and call forth the moon, Sweet. Somebody has to do it!"

She leaned against him and murmured, "I will make this up to you, Endy. In my own way."

The day of the ceremony came.

~ Ritual ~

Selene wore sensible shoes this year. Instead of lighting torches, she prepared many small bonfires so that the gathered masses could witness the proceedings. She prepared a large bonfire near Demeter and Iasion so that Demeter's planned liaisons with Ares and then Iasion could be well seen by everyone.

Darkness fell. The crowd of onlookers grew larger. All were cautious not to step upon the field. The moon rose higher and higher into the night. Clouds began obscuring the moon.

The three Telchines arrived and bantered with the crowd.

ELDER OLYMPIANS: Hestia, Demeter, Hera, Hades, Poseidon, Zeus
OLYMPIANS: Apollo, Ares, Artemis, Athena, Aphrodite, Dionysus, Hermes,
Hephaestus, Heracles. LIVING TITANS: Oceanus, Tethys, Selene, Elder Oceanids.
DECEASED TITANS: Queen Kiya, Iapetus/Piercer, Cronus.

"Do you want to see us naked?"
"I like getting drenched with rain. Do you?"
"We will make it rain as soon as the moon gets high enough!"
"You are going to get awfully wet!"
"We hope you like our dance."

Selene greeted Amphitrite and Melia as they arrived with the Ghods. She did not acknowledge the cold stare of Ares. Selene escorted Demeter to her special location on a blanket in front of Persephone's statue permanently located over Valki's grave. Iasion obediently followed and sat down beside her. Demeter slipped a smile to Iasion and a leer to Ares.

Queen Persephone was given a chair directly beside her statue. A murmur ran through the crowd, "It's her. It's the Queen of the Colored Fields, herself." Many fell to their knees in awe.

The clouds grew darker. Selene signaled the Telchines to begin. They removed their clothes and ran to the center of the freshly plowed and seeded field. They danced.

Selene watched their orgiastic dance begin slowly and build to its crescendo. There was lightning. The thunder rolled. -- *this isn't possible -- they are going to do it! -- they are actually going to make it rain --*

The sky gave forth its bounty of water. All were drenched from the torrential rain. Selene saw Demeter directly across from the dancing Telchines. She watched Demeter remove her clothes, stand, and hold her arms up to the cloud-hidden moon. -- *if they can bring forth the rain, I can bring forth the moon! --*

Selene removed her tunic and mimicked Demeter's motions. The Telchines danced, Ghod Demeter and Titanide Selene beseeched the moon to return.

The scene continued for a while. The quarter moon began to appear through the fast-moving clouds as the heavy rain pounded their bodies. Cleansing rain. Nurturing rain. Erotic rain.

Then it was over. The quarter moon once more, by command of Selene and Demeter, shined between the clouds and filled the night sky. Its light reflected off the rain-drenched glistening bodies of the supplicant women.

OCEANIDS: Metis, Tyche, Clymene, Eurybia, Amphitrite, Philyra, Rhodos.
TELCHINES: Dexithea, Makelo, Halia.
EAST: Azura, Seth, Typhon, Iasion, Endymion.
OTHER: Centaur Chiron, Charon, Hotep, Petra, Persephone.

The Telchines summoned their male friends to come into the field and wrestle with them.

Selene put her tunic back on and made her way back to Endymion. He put his arm around her shoulder. She said, "Amphitrite advised me to disappear now. She fears for my well-being. She reminded me that Ghods are vindictive, especially Ares. He may seek revenge for my impertinence at our meeting last year. But I decided not to run away. As long as you can forgive me, I will face whatever humiliation may happen."

Endymion pulled her close, said, "You will do what's right, Moon-child," and gently squeezed her shoulder. They watched that which played out before them.

Demeter was more full of passion than she had ever experienced. She knew what was to come and it would be glorious. She turned and fell to her knees in front of Iasion as he sat on their blanket. Iasion, too, knew what was to come. Demeter grasped Iasion's head as she kissed him, her rear in the air. Ares came to her and entered her body. She continued to kiss Iasion as Ares coupled with her. Heavy moans began emanating from her as she continued to kiss Iasion. Ares ejaculated into her. He rose, rested, renewed, and twice more entered her. Finally, he rose, smirked at Iasion, and said, "She's all yours!" The nearby bonfire raged on, lighting up the night sky, for the gathered masses to witness the power of the Ghods.

Selene watched the proceedings with detached interest. She glanced at Ares after he had left Demeter to Iasion's custody. Ares was glaring at her. *-- oh, yes -- I have tried to forget about last year -- I suppose you remember --*

She broke his stare as her gaze returned to Demeter and Iasion. She involuntarily pressed more firmly against Endymion.

Ares stood naked beside Zeus and Poseidon who were laughing. Ares called Melia over and spoke to her.

Melia then walked to Selene and said, "Ghod Ares commands you to speak with him, Selene. Sorry."

"That's all right, Melia. I can handle him." She turned to Endymion and said, "I must do what I must do, Endy. Forgive me, if you can." She left and walked to the three Ghods standing together laughing. Selene prepared for the inevitable.

ELDER OLYMPIANS: Hestia, Demeter, Hera, Hades, Poseidon, Zeus
OLYMPIANS: Apollo, Ares, Artemis, Athena, Aphrodite, Dionysus, Hermes,
Hephaestus, Heracles. LIVING TITANS: Oceanus, Tethys, Selene, Elder Oceanids.
DECEASED TITANS: Queen Kiya, Iapetus/Piercer, Cronus.

Selene arrived, stared defiantly at Ares, and said, "I am here."

Ares said, "Do it! Do it quickly and without resistance and it will be over all the sooner. Take off your tunic. I want you naked while you do it!"

She looked at him and said, "All right." -- *Endy -- I do this for my people -- to prevent a horrible war -- because I am commanded by mother Azura, by Seth, by Clymene -- by the will of my Grandmother Kiya to do that which must be done without regret -- it is difficult only when you are unsure of what is right --*

She let her tunic fall to the ground, stared at him a moment, fell to her knees, and began to fellate him.

Melia had returned to Amphitrite's side. Amphitrite quietly commanded, "Do nothing. Do not speak. Do not move. You will do your duty, Oceanid!"

Ares enjoyed it for a moment and then nodded to Zeus. An extremely excited Zeus threw off his tunic, grabbed Selene's hips, pulled her off Ares -- her rear in the air, and slammed his large erect penis violently into her. She yelped in surprise and pain as Zeus continued to couple with her. Ares grabbed her head and tried to force his penis back into her mouth. She struggled against the assault and then Poseidon came and began constraining her. She struggled more violently.

Poseidon saw the man at the edge of the field pull his dagger and charge toward Zeus. Poseidon was ready as the man positioned his dagger to cut the copulating Zeus's throat. Poseidon's sword removed the head of the ungrateful scum.

Zeus continued his play. Poseidon said to Ares, "I don't think I would put my penis in her mouth. Wait until I am finished with her and then you can have her." Zeus climaxed, threw back his head in joy, and threw Selene hard onto the ground. Poseidon grabbed her, turned her over on her back, and violently entered her. Selene, drained of resistance, turned her head to look away from her violators. Endymion's separated head stared back at her. She tried to take the hand of his separated body, but she could not reach it. She could only gaze into his lifeless eyes. -- *I'm so sorry, Endy -- perhaps I will have good fortune -- perhaps they will kill me, too --*

OCEANIDS: Metis, Tyche, Clymene, Eurybia, Amphitrite, Philyra, Rhodos.
TELCHINES: Dexithea, Makelo, Halia.
EAST: Azura, Seth, Typhon, Iasion, Endymion.
OTHER: Centaur Chiron, Charon, Hotep, Petra, Persephone.

Ares saw Iasion rise from Demeter's side and rush, with knife drawn, toward Poseidon. *-- that's sister's plaything -- he is so disrespectful -- sister Demeter, I do this for you --*

He spilled the attacking Iasion's intestines to the ground. He smiled at Demeter as he did it and nodded to her as if to say, "This is for your enjoyment."

Poseidon finished plowing Titanide Selene.

Ares took his turn. Violently. He finished, slapped her hard across both cheeks, and then stood.

Untold unbelieving wide and hidden eyes watched the spectacles with wonderment. These were Ghods and Lords. *-- did they make the rain? -- do they make the crops grow? -- what does it all mean? -- look at what great power they have -- look at how they wield it --*

Among the wide, unbelieving eyes were Noam's who stared with wide-eyed wonder at the actions of the powerful Ghods. With her was Enosh who observed it all with the enquiring mind of a Shaman Scholar. *-- what power do they have? -- why do they wield it so? --*

Also, Master Shaman Teumessian watched and pondered; the self-appointed wisest Shaman of them all.

And, too, silently, upon a grave, a graven image sat looking out over a plowed field, seeded, and rained upon; overlooking the rites of life; waiting for a field of color. And, too, overlooking Selene, the Shining One, lying upon a muddy field with Ghod Ares towering above her, triumphantly glaring down at her beaten, naked body as she blindly sought the lifeless hand of her best friend, all illuminated by Demeter's gigantic bonfire that Selene had built.

~

The days passed.

The festival wound down.

The western trade delegations returned to Port Olympus by carriages and wagons hosted by Dionysus and Amphitrite.

The three Telchines returned to Tartarus by themselves and on foot. They were despondent. What should have been a triumph had turned into

ELDER OLYMPIANS: Hestia, Demeter, Hera, Hades, Poseidon, Zeus
OLYMPIANS: Apollo, Ares, Artemis, Athena, Aphrodite, Dionysus, Hermes,
Hephaestus, Heracles. LIVING TITANS: Oceanus, Tethys, Selene, Elder Oceanids.
DECEASED TITANS: Queen Kiya, Iapetus/Piercer, Cronus.

tragedy. They spent the first night in Riverport with Oceanids where everyone drank too much wine and sang songs of love and death and endless rain.

Iapyx piloted the return flight from Tallstone to Port Olympus with only the assistance of Queen Persephone. The craft was overloaded with Olympians and required all the skill and knowledge Iapyx could command All eight Olympians had demanded to be on the first flight back to Tartarus. As Dionysus told Iapyx, "May the Ghods help you!"

Artemis looked forward to the return trip. When Poseidon or Zeus or Ares became aroused on the long flight home, she was the only woman available to satisfy their passion. Demeter wasn't interested and Persephone was off-limits. Only she was available to sate the three of them. Or maybe her brother, Apollo. -- *oh, Apollo is available, too! dung!* --

The Ghods complained among themselves that Hephaestus had not made nearly enough Ghod coins for them to give to the slobbering masses. They would need untold Ghod coins next year. And statues of themselves.

Zeus opined, "Did you see those horrible wood carvings of Queen Persephone all over that city? There was not one engraved image of me, and they all love me so much. Hephaestus needs to make a life-size Orichalcum statue of me for the entrance to that city and make many small statues to give to the lower classes that love me most."

"And me, too, Father," Athena added. "An extremely impressive entrance into their city would be a statue of you on one side of the road and a statue of me in my armor on the other side."

Poseidon paid no attention to this exchange. Apollo, much to Artemis's envy, was busily sating him.

Ares, for most of the journey, stayed lost in happy reverie. -- *I watched Zeus fornicate with that Selene woman while Poseidon patiently waited his turn -- some random nobody attacked Zeus while Zeus was busy fornicating -- Poseidon ripped Iasion's intestines out for the viewing pleasure of Demeter -- and that Selene woman -- a titan no less -- my righteous revenge -- Hestia will be so pleased to hear it -- the titan's humiliation -- her degradation -- how she screamed as she burned in the raging fire --*

It had been a glorious trip.

The Ghods were in their heavens!

OCEANIDS: Metis, Tyche, Clymene, Eurybia, Amphitrite, Philyra, Rhodos.
TELCHINES: Dexithea, Makelo, Halia.
EAST: Azura, Seth, Typhon, Iasion, Endymion.
OTHER: Centaur Chiron, Charon, Hotep, Petra, Persephone.

53. The Fall of Philyra

Dionysus sat in silence at his table at the Port Olympus Cafe. He looked out over Oursea and sipped his brown-wine. Amphitrite sat with him.

Finally, she said, "Despite the bad, it was still a tremendous success, Sweet. You have accomplished all you set out to do. The west is safe, the east is safe, and the Olympians are completely distracted. Selene made a bad decision. I told her that Ares would return for revenge and with reinforcements; that she should not be there; to leave as soon as she could. She would have nothing to do with it. So unfortunate."

"Yes, so unfortunate. The moon is pretty tonight, isn't it? A good night to be alive. Philyra is having a hard time, isn't she?"

"Yes, she is. Hestia has lost control of her brothers and sisters. Since the 76th festival, each one has developed into a person with their own interests and none of them need or even listen to Hestia anymore. The only person Hestia has control over is poor Philyra. Dexithea cannot punish Hestia sufficiently to bring Hestia any peace. I don't know what to advise Philyra, but she cannot continue to suffer this abuse and pressure much longer."

"This brown-wine is good, isn't it? I discovered it on a whim. What happens if I distill wine that's already been distilled, I wondered. I was wild in my youth, you know. Let people live and die as they will, I thought. I seldom see Marsyas, anymore. Our friend Seilenos died; you know. A broken heart, I suspect. Our faithful donkey, Onos, had just died of old age. I never treated my donkey to any Red Nectar. We all die. Where do we go? Is anything really worth it? Heracles is one of them, now. Without Heracles, General Porphyrion would have killed Hestia. It was Heracles who saved her. Without Heracles, Queen Kiya's forces would have triumphed. I am the one who introduced Heracles to our father. The moon is pretty, isn't it? We all die. Where do we go?"

"When you get through wallowing, Dionysus, make a plan. You make excellent plans."

He looked at the woman across the table from him. He sat in silence for a long, long time, twirling and staring at his brown-wine. Finally, he asked, "You have Poseidon under control?"

ELDER OLYMPIANS: Hestia, Demeter, Hera, Hades, Poseidon, Zeus
OLYMPIANS: Apollo, Ares, Artemis, Athena, Aphrodite, Dionysus, Hermes,
Hephaestus, Heracles. LIVING TITANS: Oceanus, Tethys, Selene, Elder Oceanids.
DECEASED TITANS: Queen Kiya, Iapetus/Piercer, Cronus.

"Yes. Totally."

"So, my problem is how do I get Hestia under control?"

"That, and how do you save Philyra."

"Will Olympus Towers continue to grow without Philyra's management?"

"It appears to me that Lord Charon and his team are the force behind building Olympus Towers. Philyra spends her energy keeping Hestia away from the work being led by Charon. They keep constructing it one floor at a time. Slowly but consistently."

"Does Charon fear Hestia?"

"Once he did but he is now aware of Dexithea's relation with Hestia. She tells Charon of every encounter in detail. He has watched Philyra and Creusa deal with her. He is friends with Hades and Hephaestus. He is in a subservient but otherwise good relationship with Poseidon and Zeus and sometimes Athena. If Hestia told them to throw Charon off the atrium, they would not obey. She knows that. Charon knows that. So, no, he doesn't fear her. He is wary but not afraid."

"Is Philyra still an Oceanid in good standing?"

"Oh, yes. She returned to the sea after you forced her to face her misshapen son. She returned with a vengeance. It's the only way she keeps her wits about her."

Dionysus sat silently looking out over the harbor, sipping his brown-wine.

Amphitrite said, "Good boy, Dionysus. Don't tell me unless you need me to do something."

"Keep telling Poseidon what a good man Charon is and how he looks to Poseidon for leadership. Things might go even faster under his leadership rather than Hestia's. Maybe Dexithea can let slip that Philyra laughs at Hestia behind her back." He sipped his brown-wine. "You know everyone must die, Amphitrite. It's a rule."

She laughed, "The Ghods want to make a liar out of you, Sweet."

"Thank you for the words of wisdom, Amphitrite. Now, if you will excuse me, I must call on a friend."

OCEANIDS: Metis, Tyche, Clymene, Eurybia, Amphitrite, Philyra, Rhodos.
TELCHINES: Dexithea, Makelo, Halia.
EAST: Azura, Seth, Typhon, Iasion, Endymion.
OTHER: Centaur Chiron, Charon, Hotep, Petra, Persephone.

She raised her glass. "Do well, Sweet."

He walked up the stairs of the port building, forced her door open, and walked to her sleeping room. She lay on her bed, eyes wide open, staring out over Oursea. She wore her simple, white linen, translucent nightgown. She heard the door open and the footsteps approach. She continued to stare out over Oursea.

"Are you tired Philyra? You know not to be tired or ask for quarter. But are you so very tired?"

"Yes, Dionysus. In a just world, a loving, understanding, caring man would take me into his arms and hold me tightly. He would say, 'Poor Philyra. You try so hard, and you do so well.' He would gently remove my clothes and mount me, taking away the weight of the world, taking us both to the heights of paradise."

He walked to her, slid the nightgown off her shoulders and down her body, stared at the moonlight reflecting off the curves of her body, and said, "It is time, Philyra. Do you look forward to paradise?"

She turned her head to look at him. "You talk too much, Dionysus. Take this weight away."

~

The next evening, the formal Olympian party was well underway. The couple entered the room. He wore formal black accentuated with a wine-red cape; she wore a wine-red scarf. with a formal, bare-shoulder, form-fitting white dress designed to accentuate her curves. They were a striking couple. The man spoke to the Gigante butler.

Polybotes introduced them. "Great Ghods, I introduce Titan Dionysus of Everywhere and Chief-of-Chiefs Philyra of Port Olympus."

All eyes turned to them. She walked beside him, holding his arm, like a doe-eyed girl in love. Aphrodite took note as did Hestia. Dionysus joined his father Zeus standing with Heracles and Poseidon. "Ghods, you all know Philyra, I trust. She is off-limits, Dad. She is with me."

This made Philyra even more desirable. Zeus stared at her with lechery in his eyes. "Greetings, beautiful Philyra. I had forgotten how desirable you are. Where have you been?"

ELDER OLYMPIANS: Hestia, Demeter, Hera, Hades, Poseidon, Zeus
OLYMPIANS: Apollo, Ares, Artemis, Athena, Aphrodite, Dionysus, Hermes,
Hephaestus, Heracles. LIVING TITANS: Oceanus, Tethys, Selene, Elder Oceanids.
DECEASED TITANS: Queen Kiya, Iapetus/Piercer, Cronus.

"Hiding from you, Ghod Zeus. A girl would never get any work done if you were around distracting her."

Zeus moved a step closer to her. She instinctively tightened her grip on Dionysus's arm and pressed against him. "I am with Dionysus, great Ghod Zeus."

"My son loves me so much. He shares everything with me!"

Dionysus spoke, "Not tonight, Dad. But that Artemis girl has been eyeing you this evening." They bantered on.

Hestia stood with Demeter and Artemis, but her attention was on Philyra. *-- bitch! -- when did Dionysus start plowing your field? -- you should not have jumped on that thing -- it angers me! -- you have been looking haggard, lately -- lost your girlish beauty -- Creusa is much more desirable than you -- your work has been suffering -- you pretended to care for me while laughing at me behind my back! -- bitch! --*

Hestia walked over to Polybotes and spoke to him at length. Polybotes nodded and repositioned himself from the door to the atrium railing. Hestia returned to Demeter and Artemis with a smug look.

Amphitrite, standing with her two guests, Nerites, and Creusa, observed the transaction and waved an invitation to Dionysus and Philyra to join them. The couple disengaged themselves and drifted over to join Amphitrite's group. The five happily chatted.

Hestia watched them join Amphitrite who was directly on the other side of the atrium. *-- all right, bitch -- come to me! --*

Hestia caught Philyra's attention and waved for Philyra to join her.

Philyra said to Dionysus, "Hestia calls me," and stepped out to meet her. Dionysus roughly grabbed her by the nape of her neck, turned her face toward his, forced his lips onto hers, looked at her again, and then gently kissed her once more. They parted.

She looked at him like the doe-eyed girl, turned, and stepped away again. He slapped her rump. She jumped in surprise and cut her eyes back at him, coyly smiling. She then held out her arms to Hestia and walked to meet her midway across the floor.

OCEANIDS: Metis, Tyche, Clymene, Eurybia, Amphitrite, Philyra, Rhodos.
TELCHINES: Dexithea, Makelo, Halia.
EAST: Azura, Seth, Typhon, Iasion, Endymion.
OTHER: Centaur Chiron, Charon, Hotep, Petra, Persephone.

Philyra saw Polybotes step away from the atrium railing so that she would pass between him and the railing. -- *you are a good and faithful employee, gigante Polybotes -- I forgive you --*

Hestia approached her with outstretched arms and a smile.

Philyra drew even with Polybotes. He stepped toward her, picked her up by her hips, raised her over his head, their gazes met, his eyes were moist. He threw her over the railing to the center of the atrium. She did not scream as she disappeared into the darkness.

Hestia kept her pace as she joined Amphitrite's group. "Are you having a good time Dionysus?"

He smiled at her. -- *never let them see you unsure --*

"You Olympians throw the wildest parties, Hestia."

"I am a Ghod. You may call me Ghod Hestia."

"You may call me Titan Dionysus."

She smiled in amusement and turned to face Creusa. "Would you like a new position with the Port, Lord Creusa?"

Poseidon, who had observed everything, walked over to join the group. "Well, Hestia. Who will be our new Chief-of-Chiefs?"

She replied, "I was thinking of Lord Creusa. What do you think?"

"An excellent choice but I have been thinking that running the port and directing Olympus Towers construction are both full-time jobs."

Amphitrite cut in, "Yes, Husband. Did anyone else notice how haggard the last Chief-of-Chiefs looked? She was simply not up for both tasks. What can be done to correct this?"

Poseidon continued, "Appoint Lord Creusa as Chief-of-Chiefs of the port, Hestia. Lord Charon will now report directly to me. His sole duty will be to build Olympus Towers to my satisfaction. Creusa will not fail as the last one did. Charon can complete the Olympus Towers even faster. This will work out well."

Hestia stared at him. The realization of unintended consequences spread over her face.

Dionysus remained silent. -- *never let them see unsure, ghod Hestia --*

ELDER OLYMPIANS: Hestia, Demeter, Hera, Hades, Poseidon, Zeus
OLYMPIANS: Apollo, Ares, Artemis, Athena, Aphrodite, Dionysus, Hermes, Hephaestus, Heracles. LIVING TITANS: Oceanus, Tethys, Selene, Elder Oceanids. DECEASED TITANS: Queen Kiya, Iapetus/Piercer, Cronus.

Hestia stared coldly at Poseidon. *-- you usurp me as the leader of my own family -- I am undone -- did I not do well? -- did I not bring us to the heights of power? -- our father was weak and useless -- it was I who did these things -- and now I will be a useless remnant of the past -- with power over only one insignificant lord -- why did you laugh behind my back, Philyra? -- I thought you loved me. -- you never loved me, Philyra -- just like Father -- just like Mother -- you never loved me -- I am undone! -- Grandmother, did you know? --*

"Yes," Hestia replied. "This will work out well." She turned and rejoined Demeter and Artemis who both stood motionless as they watched the events unfold.

Dionysus spoke to Poseidon. "I have had a lovely time at your party, Ghod Poseidon. Don't hesitate to call me if I might be of assistance in your glorious endeavor. We simply must meet on the docks for drinks. Now, if you will excuse me, I think I will take a glass of your excellent wine and retire to my quarters."

Amphitrite said softly, "Thank you for everything, Dionysus."

He smiled, held her stare for a moment, said, "Good night, all," picked up a glass of wine on his way out, and nodded a pleasant goodnight to Polybotes. He then, rather than taking the elevator, slowly walked down the many flights of stairs to the pavilion.

He came to the pool at the base of the atrium. He did not see a body; only the white dress Philyra had been wearing. He retrieved it. It was smeared with blood. He took the dress and walked to transportation dispatch. Abas had left for the night. Dionysus did not recognize the night attendant. "Hello, anything happening tonight?"

"No, Master. All has been quiet."

"Good, good. By the way, I found a woman's body floating in the pool. It was thrown from the roof. I'll take care of it for you. Just make sure your records show that you threw it into the sea. That's the least paperwork and the least fussing from the top. Here, do you want her dress? It's a bit bloody."

"No, Master. Thank you. A woman's body, you say?"

"Yes. Fairly battered. She looked haggard."

OCEANIDS: Metis, Tyche, Clymene, Eurybia, Amphitrite, Philyra, Rhodos.
TELCHINES: Dexithea, Makelo, Halia.
EAST: Azura, Seth, Typhon, Iasion, Endymion.
OTHER: Centaur Chiron, Charon, Hotep, Petra, Persephone.

"Thank you, Master. I will enter the information right now."

Dionysus walked with the bloody dress and his wine to his favorite table in the outdoor cafe and seated himself. He sat down and sipped his wine.

A voice came from below the railing, "Can I have your cape, Master? I'm naked and cold."

"Do you want wine?"

"No, thank you. Just the cape."

He rose, jumped over the railing to the dock below, and placed his cape around Philyra's naked body. Her head was bloody. He daubed the wound with the dress. He then sat beside her and put his arm around her to protect her from the wind coming off the water.

"The water level of the pool was below specifications. It was too shallow. I hit my head on the bottom. I think it may scar."

"It will be a beautiful scar. One to tell your children about."

She snuggled against him.

He asked, "Now what?"

"You are going to take me to Kaptara. Eurybia is Portmaster at their main port. Between her and Metis, I will make do quite nicely, I think."

"Don't become their queen, or whatever. Hestia would find out that you're still alive and make trouble for you."

She laughed. "I need to pack a few things. Can I stay at your place tonight? I need to calm down. My heart is still racing. Here, can you feel it?" She took his hand and placed it under the cape and over her heart. "If Metis can dive from the top of Port Spearpoint, I can certainly dive eighteen stories. I'm an Oceanid, you know. And a good one! It's just that the pool was so shallow. I hope it doesn't scar."

They went back to his place. She worked off her excitement. After a few hours of rest but before sunrise, she packed her things, they stole to the dock, took a boat, and set sail to Port Kaptara.

His arms were wrapped around her as they stood in the front of the vessel looking away from Port Olympus and out over Oursea.

"Do you hear it, Dionysus? The music?"

ELDER OLYMPIANS: Hestia, Demeter, Hera, Hades, Poseidon, Zeus
OLYMPIANS: Apollo, Ares, Artemis, Athena, Aphrodite, Dionysus, Hermes,
Hephaestus, Heracles. LIVING TITANS: Oceanus, Tethys, Selene, Elder Oceanids.
DECEASED TITANS: Queen Kiya, Iapetus/Piercer, Cronus.

"The music?"

"The sky caressing the sea – the wind gently touching her – singing to her – the music they make together – I love it so -- I remember being a young woman -- lying on the beach – listening to the music of the sea -- thrilled with sassy little pieces of cloth covering my private parts -- then something happened – first Rhea -- then Cronus – then Chiron – then Hestia – then Chief-of-Chiefs – then horror -- I had forgotten the music -- I had forgotten life -- and yet here I am – here we are. Thank you, Dionysus. You have made me whole."

-- bring a little wine -- bring a little joy --

Oceanid Philyra, at last, had returned to the sea.

54. Olympus Towers

Charon stood atop the fifth floor looking out over the construction site. In the distance, Rhodos was delivering a load of Marmaros columns. Installation was always dangerous, but her team was well-trained and careful.

The Ghods had moved to their temporary quarters on the third floor after the fourth floor had been completed. Their presence did not slow construction too much. Charon felt that he was better equipped to handle the Ghods here at Tartarus than was Chief-of-Chiefs Creusa at the Port. Creusa was a competent manager, but she had neither the depth nor the breadth of experience as Charon, and Creusa was certainly not another Philyra. But with the Ghods out of her way and with space their leaving had freed up, the Port was again growing and claiming its role as the center of civilization.

The three Telchines kept the Ghods distracted. The Ghods seldom noticed them. They were fixtures, serving, directing, commanding, and entertaining. The Telchines were one of them; a useful, intelligent one of them. Dexithea had once confided in her sisters that the loss of Kiya's fire pit had depressed Dionysus and saddened Mother Amphitrite. They came up with a brilliant plan that would please so many people. Dexithea suggested to Hephaestus that he make a fire pit that burned an eternal flame that he could give to Hades as a gift over which Hades could install Hestia's rotating statue as a surprise for Hestia. "Hestia will love it and not even notice that the fire pit is still there. We can make three Ghods happy plus Dionysus and Mother Amphitrite. This will be so exciting!"

Technically, Hestia remained headquartered at the Port directing Chief-of-Chiefs Creusa. As a practical matter, she had relocated to Tartarus with the other Ghods. She had brought her two cadres of Hecatoncheires.

Hades had been thrilled to give his sister a fire pit in which burned an eternal flame over which he placed Hestia's rotating statue. He told Hestia, "This will be a glorious symbol of your triumphs and domination over all things. Plus, it will be a wonderful reminder that this is my land, over which I rule. Do you like it?"

Hestia had been thrilled. But, even with her superior intellect, she never considered other interpretations one might make of the work. So now, she would sit and stare at her rotating statue in the eternal flame work-of-art for hour upon hour. This is where she spent her time.

Dexithea had gifted Hestia with a bag of Ghod coins. On one side was the image of Hestia, on the other, a fire-lit hearth.

The atrium pool had been modified to become a continuous slow-moving river that ran from a man-made lake beneath Lookout Point, under the Olympus Towers, and on through the canal through Elysian Fields to connect to Oursea. Poseidon's boat stayed anchored near the atrium pool. He could sail through the canal to command Oursea whenever he wished.

Piercer's house had been enlarged with even more subterranean rooms and made suitable for the permanent living quarters of the King of the Underworld and his Queen of the Colored Fields. Hades considered the ground floor beneath the Olympus Towers to be his personal subterranean property. Hades' good dog Cerberus guarded the property. He seldom killed a trespasser; especially if he recognized the person.

Queen Persephone had grown to be quite imperial. Each morning, she left her abode and walked through Elysium Fields coloring the flowers. When finished, she returned to Olympus Towers and sat, in the workmen's way, on the highest completed floor monitoring the departure, arrival, and activities of the Red Egg. She would sometimes accompany the Red Egg assisting the Pilot. But as the excitement of flight dissipated, she grew to see such actions as beneath her.

ELDER OLYMPIANS: Hestia, Demeter, Hera, Hades, Poseidon, Zeus
OLYMPIANS: Apollo, Ares, Artemis, Athena, Aphrodite, Dionysus, Hermes, Hephaestus, Heracles. LIVING TITANS: Oceanus, Tethys, Selene, Elder Oceanids. DECEASED TITANS: Queen Kiya, Iapetus/Piercer, Cronus.

God Hades was thrilled to be living in Piercer's old house but rode Alastor back and forth daily to inspect his mines in Phlegethon. He was always delighted to see the joy in his queen's eyes when he returned with a gift of cave mushrooms.

Ghod Hephaestus had little interest in Tartarus and Olympus Towers. His permanent residence had been built adjacent to the great Phlegethon workshop. A trade route to a supply of Tinom had been established. This Tinom was combined with the locally available Kopar to make an endless supply of Orichalcum.

Hephaestus worked tirelessly to please his older sisters, Ghods Hestia and Athena, by making Orichalcum swords and armor for selected workers who continued to emigrate from the hunting lands of the east.

Ghod Athena held quarter-moon training exercises where all males learned how to take battle orders and attack a possible enemy. Those properly proficient were issued an Orichalcum sword. Of the ten swords issued, the best of the group would be issued an Orichalcum helmet. After ten helmets had been issued, the best of them received an Orichalcum breastplate. The sword, alone, proclaimed high status. The breastplate, in some way, elevated the recipient to a higher status than even his chief.

Ghod Demeter did not mourn the loss of Iasion. Poseidon had asked if she was pleased that he had ripped out the intestines of that disrespectful Iasion person; that he had done it for her honor and to please her. Demeter's eyes fluttered when she heard this. She gushed over Poseidon. She ended her gushing with "Now that I don't have that pretty little Iasion anymore, I will have to find a real man to plow me!" Again, she fluttered her eyelashes.

Demeter was displeased to hear that the misshapen half-man, half-horse upon whose back she had ridden long ago was no longer in residence at Asphodel Meadows. Halia explained that Chiron had immigrated to Urfa so that Demeter would no longer be offended by his misshapen body. She explained on, automatically framing her words to allow Demeter to decide what it was that Halia had decided Demeter should decide upon, which, in this case, was that Hades had a fine black stallion to ride upon, that Demeter would enjoy a fine white mare to ride upon. Demeter demanded, "Bring me a fine white mare to ride upon! I demand it."

OCEANIDS: Metis, Tyche, Clymene, Eurybia, Amphitrite, Philyra, Rhodos.
TELCHINES: Dexithea, Makelo, Halia.
EAST: Azura, Seth, Typhon, Iasion, Endymion.
OTHER: Centaur Chiron, Charon, Hotep, Petra, Persephone.

Later, as Halia lay quietly in Hotep's arms, she lamented, "I should have demanded a white stallion rather than a white mare. She could have trained it to plow her."

In the meantime, Demeter began riding her white mare along the Elysian Field canal chatting with Poseidon as he took his daily boat trip to Oursea to command the sea on what to do that day. Amphitrite was not pleased when word of this reached her. -- *you are my adoring, loving, obedient husband, Poseidon -- for you to become interested in a woman of rank is a bit of a bother!* --

Ghod Zeus could not be happier. He spent his days wandering the camps filled with the wives and daughters of the workers, accepting their adulation, usually accepting their invitations to couple, and giving the ones who pleased him a gold Ghod coin with his image. The coins were in high demand and imparted high rank to the recipients. The women fervently believed the words of endearment whispered in their ears as they coupled, as did Zeus. At least, until his next encounter. The women did their best to entice Zeus to call upon them at any time. Zeus always swore that he would come to them again. Zeus, in his wisdom, always began his day by giving his beloved wife, Ghod Hera, to whom he was always faithful, a large flask of wine.

The lesser Ghods had also settled into new routines.

Ghod Ares had taken an interest in Cerberus. They would walk among the workers. If a worker displeased Ares in some way, as would sometimes happen, Ares would command Cerberus - "Kill!" In this way, Cerberus stayed in training plus Ares could see the blood from the man's gnashed neck as his body was being ripped apart. It also had the advantage of instilling fear into those who looked upon Ares. Charon pointed out to Poseidon that these killings reduced the workforce. Poseidon pointed out that this made the remaining workforce work even harder.

Aphrodite and Heracles were a beautiful couple. Both were extraordinary specimens of their gender. Heracles was not 'pretty' like Nerites and Apollo. Heracles was all muscle, tall, and physically imposing. To watch them couple was a thing of beauty, a performance of art. They were vain about their appearance and their sexual performance. They knew that in each other, they had the most desirable partner one could have. And they put on a performance. They felt extremely alive performing on the great table where the carpenters prepared the lumber for final installation as the

ELDER OLYMPIANS: Hestia, Demeter, Hera, Hades, Poseidon, Zeus
OLYMPIANS: Apollo, Ares, Artemis, Athena, Aphrodite, Dionysus, Hermes,
Hephaestus, Heracles. LIVING TITANS: Oceanus, Tethys, Selene, Elder Oceanids.
DECEASED TITANS: Queen Kiya, Iapetus/Piercer, Cronus.

carpenters worked around them. They knew they had the intense interest of all the workmen who, if they showed any interest, would immediately be attacked by something -- a dog -- a Ghod. They didn't know exactly how they would die but die they most certainly would. The mental torture she knew she inflicted on the workmen drove Aphrodite insane with sexual ardor.

Artemis finally realized that with Aphrodite and Apollo around that she would always be the second or third choice. Zeus called upon her on occasion as did Heracles occasionally. But she was resigned that her twin brother, Apollo, would receive more sexual favors from the Ghods than she. She took to walking the grounds and practicing her archery. She began visiting the animal ranch in Asphodel Fields. She missed her friend and student, Chiron. She remembered the great peace she felt when she was around Chiron; totally unlike her frenzied desire to be accepted by the Ghods and her incessant need to receive their sexual invitations.

Her mother, Leto, never fully approved of her mingling with the Olympians. "Daughter, they are not honorable people." -- *well, Mother, here I am -- I just now realize, you never told me who my father was -- why was that? -- maybe you didn't want me to know -- well, I may be a third-rate sexual partner, but I can shoot an arrow true and far -- perhaps that is enough –*

When she was with the animals, she was at peace.

Pilots Iapyx and Rhodos were the force behind the significant progress being made in the construction of the Olympus Towers. They were efficient, careful, knowledgeable, and inventive. They worked with the builders at the Phlegethon facility to develop material transportation slings that could be preloaded with lumber or rock or metals or Marmaros. The Airboat need only arrive, lower the hoist, attach the sling, rapidly transport the load to the appropriate preparation site at Tartarus, then lower and release the sling. Loading and slowly transporting material by land was a thing of the past. Efficiency increased tenfold. They both worked with assistants and rigorously trained them in the art and science of piloting an airboat.

Rhodos was aware, but judiciously never enquired why, their airboat, presumably the only airboat in the world, was named 'Airboat 313.'

OCEANIDS: Metis, Tyche, Clymene, Eurybia, Amphitrite, Philyra, Rhodos.
TELCHINES: Dexithea, Makelo, Halia.
EAST: Azura, Seth, Typhon, Iasion, Endymion.
OTHER: Centaur Chiron, Charon, Hotep, Petra, Persephone.

Amphitrite was disturbed when she walked into her quarters and found Demeter loudly coupling with her husband. But Amphitrite merely walked to Poseidon, began massaging his shoulders, and placed her tongue in his ear. Later, Demeter gushed about what a good time she had with Poseidon, especially with Amphitrite watching her.

After Demeter had left, Amphitrite asked Poseidon, "Apollo developed into a nice looking Ghod. Do you think that I should let him plow me? You have had him, haven't you? Perhaps we could share him."

Poseidon thought that a fine suggestion.

Amphitrite smiled with relief. -- *I am still your whore!* --

55. Winter Solstice Festival 77

Demeter lay purring with her head in Amphitrite's lap. Poseidon had finished with her and had left to go command the sea or something.

Amphitrite purred back as she massaged Demeter, "Who will you be coupling with at the Fertility Rites this year, other than Ares, now that Iasion is gone? Nitrites might be nice. He is exceedingly pretty."

"I'm not going to the Festival. It just wouldn't be the same without seeing Iasion watch Ares plow me. I want to keep the precious memory of Iasion's tortured face. It excited me so. The memory still does."

"Oh? I am told the people of Urfa expect a Fertility Rite performed by the Ghods. You are the highlight of their year. They talk about how much better the crops have been since you first performed your rite. Not being there may cause problems for Urfa."

"Well, that is certainly not my problem, now, is it?"

"Of course not, sweet Demeter, of course not!" -- *that's my problem!* --

At port headquarters, Creusa met with Dionysus, Amphitrite, and the Telchines to prepare for trade negotiations with the western nations.

Creusa told them, "I see no indication that Ghod Hestia is interested in the negotiations one way or the other. She stays in Tartarus and appears to have withdrawn from commanding me to do her bidding. Maybe it's temporary, but for now, I foresee no problems."

Everyone agreed that 'she stays in Tartarus' was good news.

ELDER OLYMPIANS: Hestia, Demeter, Hera, Hades, Poseidon, Zeus
OLYMPIANS: Apollo, Ares, Artemis, Athena, Aphrodite, Dionysus, Hermes,
Hephaestus, Heracles. LIVING TITANS: Oceanus, Tethys, Selene, Elder Oceanids.
DECEASED TITANS: Queen Kiya, Iapetus/Piercer, Cronus.

Creusa continued, "But I did overhear her tell Poseidon that she wanted to go to the Festival in the Red Egg. She has been up in the egg only once and she has never been to a Festival."

"Oh, Good Ghod, NO!" Dionysus exclaimed. "Hestia at the Festival would be a disaster! Dissuade her from going at all costs! She would be offensive enough to Seth and Azura. If she accidentally encountered our Western Delegation, it could become war right there."

Creusa answered, "I can guide Hestia, but I can't change her course. Even Philyra would have had a difficult time keeping her from going. I miss Philyra, so!"

His only comment was, "Dung!"

The group discussed strategies. It was agreed that if Hestia suspected she was being pressured not to go then she would most certainly go. Creusa would do the best she could, and Amphitrite would work on Poseidon. But in the end, if Hestia did go, then it would fall on Dexithea to prevent Hestia from doing anything which would result in war.

"May the Ghods help me!" Dexithea said.

But Poseidon was not sympathetic to Hestia's request. "I don't have space available on my first flight. I and Zeus want Aphrodite, Artemis, and Nerites to accompany us. I can make space for you but not your two bodyguards. I think you would have a miserable time, but if you insist on going, I can make room on the second flight for you and both bodyguards."

"That will be acceptable, sweet little brother." -- *you worthless piece of dung* --

Meanwhile, Dionysus and the Telchines hosted each Western trade delegation in turn. All agreed that the delegations would remain at the Port until all negotiations were complete and then all would travel together to arrive at Tallstone the day before the festival began. Dionysus listened with interest as he learned of the evolving federation of seagoing nations. Oceanus, himself, had agreed that Port Spearpoint would join such a federation. Discussions were underway that the Great Oceanid Metis, herself, might accept the Presidency of the federation. Her only requirement was that Princess Ariadne of Kaptara is designated her Vice-President.

OCEANIDS: Metis, Tyche, Clymene, Eurybia, Amphitrite, Philyra, Rhodos.
TELCHINES: Dexithea, Makelo, Halia.
EAST: Azura, Seth, Typhon, Iasion, Endymion.
OTHER: Centaur Chiron, Charon, Hotep, Petra, Persephone.

Disparate statements always caught Dionysus's attention -- *princess Ariadne of Kaptara? -- who is she? --*

But he remained focused on his goal of bringing the negotiations to a satisfactory conclusion.

All parties were pleased with the final agreements and the three delegations, escorted by Dionysus, Amphitrite, and the Telchines set off for the Seventy-seventh Winter Solstice Festival.

On the morning of the opening ceremonies, the heads of the western sea-going nations were escorted to the premier viewing space in front of the stage, immediately behind the tribal chief's gathering area.

Noam, Mother Arura's chief assistant, was thrilled to be on stage assisting with Opening Ceremony preparations. As the time neared, she would be escorted by Shaman Enosh, Seth's son, to the premier viewing area.

Dionysus stood beside General Typhon and Amazon Otreta by the tall stone as they monitored the preparations.

Typhon mused, "It's still exciting to watch even though the center of civilization has shifted westward. Once, this was the place where all knowledge was shared among all people. Now, the tribes are not that significant. The real work is being done at Phlegethon and the labs of Port Spearpoint. Urfa is perfecting the art of city management. The Ghods have the only known airboat, but I noticed it's named 'Airboat 313.' It makes me wonder who has numbers one through three-twelve. Tallstone Scholars are unmatched in the fields of astronomy, mathematics, Shamanism, and, perhaps, the art of war but the tribes are unchanged since the beginning of time. The Festival celebrates that which was but not that which will someday be. I fear that it is no longer relevant."

Dionysus laughed. "They come for the excitement, not for any 'relevance.' It entertains and excites them, it's a change from their everyday, boring lives. Look at that mass of people out there. It's twice as many as I have seen before. Your little festival is the premier social event in the world, General. Look at the size of it!"

Otreta said, "Mother Azura told Seth that the people of Urfa have become interested in the festival since the Ghods began coming. The people are fascinated with Ghods and their escapades. They collect and trade Ghod coins. They talk of the yearly Fertility Rite endlessly. That's why the crowd is so large. All of Urfa has come to see the Ghods."

Dionysus replied, "I am told that Ghod Demeter is not coming this year. There probably won't be a Fertility Rite."

Otreta said, "Oh, no. That won't do at all. The people of Urfa will demand it! Mother Azura will demand it. Dionysus, you MUST ensure the rite is performed."

"I will see what I can do," Dionysus replied. -- *Aphrodite will be thrilled!* -- *she loves an audience* --

Opening time drew near. The crowd grew restless.

Finally, the great horn sounded. Three young, vibrant women dressed in identical red dresses ran onto the stage below the tall stone. Hands held high in the air, they shouted in unison, "ARE YOU READY TO HAVE A FESTIVAL?"

They performed. They cajoled. They quietened. They incited. They introduced. The crowd was their plaything. Amid their announcements were that Ghod Poseidon and the beloved Ghod Zeus would be arriving out of the sky later in the day. After the next quarter moon, Ghod Ares and Ghod Athena, his wonderful sister in her beautiful suit of armor, would be arriving. They were all rumored to have many Ghod coins to give to their adoring followers. And always remember, "Be extra-respectful to them! Bowing and kneeling never hurts."

Soon, the horn sounded again and the three young women in red dresses screamed, "Let's go have ourselves a festival, everybody!" The raucous crowd was dismissed to start the festival.

The tribal chiefs began gathering on the stage for reunions. All was good.

However, a few people in the masses asked anyone in a red dress, "When will Ghod Demeter arrive?"

Dionysus found Azura and Amphitrite. "We have a Fertility Rite problem, but I may have a plan." He presented his plan emphasizing Aphrodite's great beauty and lust. The two women were happy enough that the beautiful, accomplished Aphrodite would be replacing the loud, lustful

OCEANIDS: Metis, Tyche, Clymene, Eurybia, Amphitrite, Philyra, Rhodos.
TELCHINES: Dexithea, Makelo, Halia.
EAST: Azura, Seth, Typhon, Iasion, Endymion.
OTHER: Centaur Chiron, Charon, Hotep, Petra, Persephone.

Demeter in the rite. Aphrodite was, after all, one of the Ghods. A lesser Ghod, but a Ghod, nonetheless.

Later that day, the Red Egg was seen high in the sky. The crowd formed in front of the stage. From the Airboat, Zeus began waving excitedly to the people below. The boat was piloted by Iapyx rather than Rhodos. Poseidon did not care for Pilot Iapyx, but he certainly did not care for Oceanid Pilot Rhodos; she did not begin to bow enough and show proper deference. But he refrained from throwing the pilot over the side of the basket. He was not at all sure how to land his Red Egg and always decided to demonstrate mercy toward the Airboat Pilots.

Landing on the stage would require all Iapyx's skills and he had only Nerites to assist him. Two accomplished ground crew will be wonderful! Be there, Lord Dionysus!

The airboat drew closer to the stage. The crowd began waving wildly. Zeus waved back wildly. Dionysus and Oceanid Melia took their positions on either side of the stage. Melia had never been ground crew before, but Dionysus had explained what needed doing. -- *how hard can it be?* --

The faces of Poseidon and Zeus were now recognizable by the spectators! And each had his arm around a beautiful woman! And Zeus threw a handful of coins into the crowd below! Less than a dozen people were injured attempting to retrieve a coin. – *are the woman ghods? -- do they all have coins? -- oh, what a festival this will be!* --

The airboat landed without incident. The passengers debarked. Iapyx set flight again to return to Tartarus to pick up the second set of Ghods.

Seth and Azura were on stage to greet the arrivals. Proper words were exchanged; the Ghods considered Seth and Azura to be Lords and therefore to be respected. The Ghods also greeted the waiting tribal chiefs but with a touch of disdain. Dionysus patiently waited to talk with Aphrodite.

Finally, official duties over, Zeus hurried off the stage and into the crowd which parted as he walked through them. He would randomly choose someone to acknowledge, hold out his arms, and ask, "Do you love me?" The recipient, usually a woman, knew the proper words, "Oh, Great Ghod Zeus, I love you sooo much." Zeus was in his element. The person would usually receive a Gold Zeus Coin.

ELDER OLYMPIANS: Hestia, Demeter, Hera, Hades, Poseidon, Zeus
OLYMPIANS: Apollo, Ares, Artemis, Athena, Aphrodite, Dionysus, Hermes,
Hephaestus, Heracles. LIVING TITANS: Oceanus, Tethys, Selene, Elder Oceanids.
DECEASED TITANS: Queen Kiya, Iapetus/Piercer, Cronus.

Meanwhile, Dionysus approached Aphrodite and Artemis standing together on the stage. He held out his arms widely and said to them, "There is no beauty left anywhere else in the world for it all stands here before me."

Artemis gave him a warm smile. She surprised herself. It wasn't her 'invitation to couple' smile. -- *you don't want to lay with me, do you, Dionysus?* --

Dionysus said, "Sweet Aphrodite. I come with a request that may please you."

"Of course, I agree. I adore being pleased, Dionysus. What is it?"

"You must protect your virginity, at least in public, until the quarter moon. Then you will travel to a field in Urfa where you will couple at least four times with whatever males may please you. You must do this as hundreds of townspeople watch you with awe. It will add value if you scream 'Plow me! Plow me!' as you couple with them. What do you think?"

"How exciting! Yes! You will be my partner the first three times. I will put on an especially exciting performance. You can send in anyone you please after you have finished with me! Oh, Dionysus. I am so excited. I am finally going to get to couple with you. You have been so hard to get!"

"Dung, Aphrodite. Public displays of affection aren't of interest to me. Get Apollo or Heracles."

"No! You said any male that pleases me! That's you, Sweet! I expect you to keep your word!"

"All right." They bantered on for a while. He concluded their negotiation with a laugh and, "No, Aphrodite. We cannot go practice!"

Artemis laughed and said to Dionysus, "You poor put-upon male!"

The two women then left the stage to meet with the masses and pass out Ghod coins. Artemis's coin had her image on the front with a bow and arrow on the back. Aphrodite's had her image on the front with a phallus on the back.

Dionysus, Amphitrite, and Azura met on the stage.

OCEANIDS: Metis, Tyche, Clymene, Eurybia, Amphitrite, Philyra, Rhodos.
TELCHINES: Dexithea, Makelo, Halia.
EAST: Azura, Seth, Typhon, Iasion, Endymion.
OTHER: Centaur Chiron, Charon, Hotep, Petra, Persephone.

Dionysus told the two women of his successful conversation with Aphrodite. "Now, Amphitrite, if you can steer Poseidon away from my Western friends, we won't have any problems until Hestia lands next quarter moon. Then, if we can keep Hestia away from everybody of consequence and then get Aphrodite to perform at Urfa under the full moon, we will have another successful Festival."

Azura asked Dionysus, "Can you persuade that Artemis woman to perform the role that poor Selene played?"

"Probably, just don't let anyone tell Artemis what happened to Selene."

"I wish to meet with these two women to explain the importance of what they do for the people of Urfa. The Fertility Rite gives them confidence that the yearly crops will be bountiful. They suspect there may be no connection, but still, they are more comfortable when they know the Rite has been performed. The Rite gives them peace of mind and something exciting to look forward to each year."

Dionysus laughed. "Ghods care nothing of what pleases the masses, Mother Azura. They live for their own pleasure. I ask you not to meet with them. They know what they are to do, when they are to do it, and both look forward to doing it. Don't confuse them. They want only your adoration and your blind obedience; not appreciation or reason."

"I still wish to meet them and see what type of woman finds reward in public displays of nudity and animal behavior best left to the privacy of a single man and woman."

"That's exactly the type of talk I don't want them to hear, Mother Azura. No, it's best if you stay completely away from Aphrodite and Artemis."

"I insist, Dionysus. I will temper my words, but I insist on meeting them!"

"I will arrange a meeting, Mother Azura. You are a Lord. They almost respect the Lords. But always remember, never find fault with any Ghod for any reason. They expect and require deference. Artemis is likable. Aphrodite may ask you to perform sexual favors. Graciously decline because you are not worthy. But I will arrange your meeting." -- *may the ghods be merciful!* --

The next morning, Apollo attracted a crowd of admirers at the Archery Competition Field. He hit the center of the target one hundred times in succession before finally being off the mark. He retired with a sneer. "Let's see someone beat that record!"

One of the would-be competitors ran off the viewing area announcing, "I will go get the horse-man. He can beat that record!"

Apollo realized that the boy must be referring to Centaur Chiron. Apollo gave his Ghod coin to a bystander with instructions to retrieve Ghod Artemis who would undoubtedly be wandering around with Ghod Aphrodite giving out Ghod coins. "She will wish to greet her old student and watch him."

Chiron and Artemis arrived at the field at almost the same time. The three old friends enjoyed their reunion and then it was time for the centaur to fire his arrows.

Chiron missed the center on the one-hundredth arrow. "I fear no one can beat your record, Titan Apollo. You are the best archer in the world."

An irritated Artemis asked, "Is a woman allowed to compete on this field?" A large contingent of women had gathered by the time she fired her one-hundred-twentieth arrow without missing the center. No woman spoke. They stared at Artemis with reverent silence.

The quarter moon came.

The next morning, the Red Egg appeared in the sky. Dionysus, Dexithea, and Amphitrite met at the tall stone to watch the approach.

Dexithea muttered, "Hestia, Ares, Athena, and Heracles are all in the same airboat. May the Ghods be with us!"

Amphitrite added, "If it fell from the sky, all troubles would end."

Dionysus added, "Oceanid Rhodos would have made that happen if I had so commanded. I see now that I should have so commanded. The Oceanids would have sung the song of Rhodos forever."

Amphitrite said, "Too late for that, Sweet. We must rely on Dexithea to prevent Hestia from creating an incident. I have enlisted some sisters to keep us all aware of where Hestia is and where she might be going. If we can manage the situation for three days or so, Hestia will tire and command Rhodos to take her back home to Tartarus. All will be well!"

OCEANIDS: Metis, Tyche, Clymene, Eurybia, Amphitrite, Philyra, Rhodos.
TELCHINES: Dexithea, Makelo, Halia.
EAST: Azura, Seth, Typhon, Iasion, Endymion.
OTHER: Centaur Chiron, Charon, Hotep, Petra, Persephone.

Ghod Poseidon, Telchine Dexithea, General Typhon, and Amazon Otreta stood on the stage waiting to greet Hestia, Ares, and Athena. Typhon and Otreta were almost friends with Ares and Athena. The Ghods would be pleased with their greeting delegation. Hestia had never attended a Winter Solstice Festival and did not know one Eastern leader from another.

The craft landed. Ares was the first to debark. He almost smiled when he was greeted by Otreta. Typhon greeted Athena, the next to debark.

Then came Heracles followed by two Gigante bodyguards. The others gathered at to foot of the ladder to greet Hestia. Heracles shouted out, "You can do it, Ghod Hestia. You can do it!"

Finally, Hestia's head appeared over the staircase looking down at the three men. "If I fall and you don't catch me, I will have you killed," she said to Heracles.

Heracles comforted, cajoled, and coaxed Hestia down the flimsy steps; he took her in his arms when she stepped within his reach.

Hestia was livid, nauseous, disgusted, and ready to return to Tartarus, but not by airboat. "Kill the Pilot!" she commanded a Gigante. "No one should ever go up in one of those things again!"

Poseidon stepped up, laughing. "No. Don't kill the Pilot, Gigante. She is my property; not Hestia's." He then held out his arms to Hestia. "Welcome to the Festival, Big Sister. Do you have plenty of Ghod coins? The lower classes love them! They will love you if you give them one."

She looked at him in anguish. "Let the lower classes die in agony! No person has suffered as much as I, not even Demeter. I must return immediately to the comfort of our Olympus Towers."

Dexithea rushed over, arms extended. "Poor Ghod Hestia. You have been punished beyond what you deserve. Come with me to your quarters. I know how to comfort you. I will have someone arrange an immediate carriage to swiftly carry you back home. You can start back after I have sufficiently comforted you!" -- *it can't be this easy!* --

Hestia, not moving, stared at Dexithea. "No! I have come to see this festival! I will see it! Poseidon, show me what it is that I should see!"

ELDER OLYMPIANS: Hestia, Demeter, Hera, Hades, Poseidon, Zeus
OLYMPIANS: Apollo, Ares, Artemis, Athena, Aphrodite, Dionysus, Hermes,
Hephaestus, Heracles. LIVING TITANS: Oceanus, Tethys, Selene, Elder Oceanids.
DECEASED TITANS: Queen Kiya, Iapetus/Piercer, Cronus.

Poseidon laughed. "Come with me, Big Sister. There are at least two Lords in this place. I will allow them to see you!"

With that, Poseidon led Hestia into the animated reunion of Ares, Athena, Typhon, and Otreta. Typhon and Otreta were charming and friendly. Hestia not so much.

Dexithea was not asked to join them. -- *dung! I was so close!* --

Oceanids noted the direction and pace the Poseidon group began walking. Amphitrite was advised to lead her western delegations to visit the Urfa trade area instead of the men's gaming fields.

~

Azura found Dionysus. "I'm not accustomed to my requests being ignored, Titan Dionysus. I have yet to meet these two women who will perform the Fertility Rites and, I was surprised to be told that you, yourself, will be participating in their wanton acts."

"Oh, that. I must perform my duty, Mother Azura. No matter how disgusting. But I will have Aphrodite and Artemis at Pumi's table at sunset. I ask you to keep our accidental meeting as brief as possible with few words. Remember, they are not normal people." -- *I was hoping you would forget, Azura – you knew that I'm sure!* --

~

Dionysus met Aphrodite and Artemis at Pumi's table at sunset. Enosh and Noam were told to keep common people away but, as always, many eyes, especially male eyes, watched the two female Ghods incessantly.

~

Dexithea trailed behind Hestia and Poseidon as they walked the path to the men's gaming fields. The crowds always parted to make way for the Ghods. Oceanids watched everything.

~

Azura and Melia passed by Pumi's rock table at sunset. Melia called out, "Look, Mother Azura. There is Titan Dionysus. Let's speak to him."

The two women turned and walked toward the 'surprised' Dionysus.

OCEANIDS: Metis, Tyche, Clymene, Eurybia, Amphitrite, Philyra, Rhodos.
TELCHINES: Dexithea, Makelo, Halia.
EAST: Azura, Seth, Typhon, Iasion, Endymion.
OTHER: Centaur Chiron, Charon, Hotep, Petra, Persephone.

Dionysus called out, "Mother Azura, what a wonderful time to accidentally meet. I am visiting with the two magnificent celebrants for your upcoming Fertility Rites, the two most desirable women in the world, the incomparable Ghod Aphrodite and Ghod Artemis."

~

Nearing the men's gaming fields, Hestia said to Poseidon, "I am tired of this nonsense. Dexithea and I will return to my quarters." She motioned to Dexithea that they would now turn back. Oceanids noticed the change in direction and quickly discerned their probable destination and the probable path they would take.

~

At Pumi's rock table, Azura and Melia joined Dionysus, Aphrodite, and Artemis. "I am delighted to meet the two of you. I look forward to your great success at the Fertility Rite. I am told Titan Dionysus, himself, will partake in your event."

Dionysus said to the Ghods, "Mother Azura is the supreme Lord of Urfa, extremely high class."

The two Ghods relaxed. To be friendly to a Lord was quite acceptable. They were relieved to know that this was a person of extremely high rank.

Dionysus stood back and let the women happily banter on about the Rite and its importance to the people of Urfa. In the distance he noticed two Oceanids hurrying along the path surveying their surroundings as they hurried. He noticed the Oceanids notice *him*. The Oceanids stopped, looked at one another, and then doubled their pace in his direction. Their thumbs pointed in the direction from which they had just come.

Dionysus looked at the commotion far down the path. Oh, my Ghods! A Ghod must be coming this way! He nodded to the Oceanids and stared at them. One Oceanid pointed her thumb to the ground. -- *Hestia!* --

Dionysus said to Azura, "This has been a delightful surprise and a wonderful visit, but I am sure you have important business to attend to immediately! You must be going!"

Aphrodite said, "Nonsense, Dionysus. Lord Azura and I haven't even discussed what sexual positions she would like me to use. We have many details to work out."

ELDER OLYMPIANS: Hestia, Demeter, Hera, Hades, Poseidon, Zeus
OLYMPIANS: Apollo, Ares, Artemis, Athena, Aphrodite, Dionysus, Hermes,
Hephaestus, Heracles. LIVING TITANS: Oceanus, Tethys, Selene, Elder Oceanids.
DECEASED TITANS: Queen Kiya, Iapetus/Piercer, Cronus.

The Oceanids arrived, said to Dionysus, "Encounter is imminent," and kept walking.

The group looked at Dionysus with puzzlement. Dionysus said, "Melia, get Mother Azura to safety immediately. I can tell she is not feeling well." He looked sternly at Melia, who suddenly understood.

Melia said, "Come Mother. You must lie down immediately before you pass out. I insist!"

Azura neither understood nor was she prone to take orders. Precious seconds were wasted as she responded to the apparent insubordination. Aphrodite admired Azura's lack of patience with underlings.

The commotion drew nearer. Dionysus's mind raced. "Melia, attend to their needs. I believe an old friend is coming who I must speak with. Excuse me, all."

He hurriedly left to the approaching commotion.

Enosh and Noam stood with Master Shaman Teumessian as they listened and watched with confused silence. - *there appears to be a problem -- oceanid Melia is suddenly commanding mother Azura -- lord Dionysus is not acting normally -- where is he going? -- what is happening? --*

Azura and Aphrodite continued their delightful conversation.

~

Dionysus walked up to the approaching Poseidon, Dexithea, and Hestia with her two Gigante bodyguards.

"Great Ghods," Dionysus called out. "I hope you have sampled Urfa's bread-baking area. The different breads they make are delicious. Better, even, than what we bake at home. Come, Hestia, let me take you to taste their honey and nut bread. You won't be disappointed!"

Hestia did not slow her pace. "I am fed up with this Festival, Dionysus. Dexithea and I are retiring to my quarters. We are taking a fast carriage back to Tartarus in the morning! Leave us!"

Dionysus glanced a warning to Dexithea. Dexithea, aware of the fast-approaching congestion, said to Hestia, "Sweet Ghod Hestia, let's bypass

OCEANIDS: Metis, Tyche, Clymene, Eurybia, Amphitrite, Philyra, Rhodos.
TELCHINES: Dexithea, Makelo, Halia.
EAST: Azura, Seth, Typhon, Iasion, Endymion.
OTHER: Centaur Chiron, Charon, Hotep, Petra, Persephone.

the crowd up ahead. It will be a bit longer but much quicker." She gently took Hestia's arm to guide her to turn left.

Hestia was not to be deterred; she kept her pace. "Move this low-class scum out of my way," she barked to Dexithea. The crowd, seeing two more Ghods approaching, quickly parted to let them pass. The path passed near Pumi's rock table.

~

Poseidon was a head taller than most men and easy to see in a crowd. Artemis saw him. She gleefully called out, "Ghod Poseidon, come and meet the great Lord Azura of Urfa. She will be hosting our Fertility Rites under the full moon. She is telling Ghod Aphrodite what to do!"

Poseidon heard and glanced in Artemis's direction.

Hestia heard and became even more furious. She pivoted, told the Gigantes to move the scum out of her way, and headed straight toward Artemis. Hestia hissed to Artemis, "Scum does not tell Ghods what to do. Ghods tell scum whether they may live or will die! Do you understand me, Ghod Artemis?!"

"Yes, Ghod Hestia! I chose my words poorly. It will not happen again."

"See that it doesn't, Artemis!" Hestia then coldly glared at Azura and pivoted to storm off to her quarters.

Azura opened her mouth to respond but Dexithea thrust her face into Azura's and cut her off with "LORD Azura, I am so pleased to see you again. I must now clear the way for my Great Ghod Hestia to return to our quarters to recover from this festival. Perhaps we can visit tomorrow." Dexithea held her finger to her lips to indicate to maintain silence and then quickly turned to escort Hestia away from the gathering.

Hestia looked at Dexithea and said, "I forbid you to see this bitch scum again! Now, clear the path to my quarters."

Azura, Supreme Chief of Urfa, heir to the city of Great Mother Valki, proud keeper of the grains, leader of the most civilized city on earth, coolly replied, "So you are the great bitch Hestia that I have heard of. You are much less the person that I expected!"

Hestia froze. Her eyes were wide with disbelief.

ELDER OLYMPIANS: Hestia, Demeter, Hera, Hades, Poseidon, Zeus
OLYMPIANS: Apollo, Ares, Artemis, Athena, Aphrodite, Dionysus, Hermes,
Hephaestus, Heracles. LIVING TITANS: Oceanus, Tethys, Selene, Elder Oceanids.
DECEASED TITANS: Queen Kiya, Iapetus/Piercer, Cronus.

Time and space became a universe in which nothing moved. All was silence. There was no motion. All was frozen.

Dionysus spun to stand directly between Azura and Hestia. He spread his arms wide and said, "Poseidon -- Athena -- Hestia -- the Lord is mine. You will respect that she is mine. We will meet this evening for wine and discuss what actions are required in this matter."

Poseidon, too, was shocked with disbelief. His face reddened. He slowly reached for his dagger.

The two Gigantes went to high alert, awaiting Hestia's command.

Dionysus accessed his adversaries. Without emotion, he said "Know this, Poseidon. Hestia is within reach of MY blade. Attack and she will die by my hand. My blood will undoubtedly be the cost, but Hestia will undoubtedly be dead. Will the instant gratification of killing me be worth your sister's cut throat?"

Hestia. Livid. Commanded, "Gigante, kill the woman. Then Dionysus!"

Both Gigantes began raising their swords.

Before the swords even approached their striking positions, Dionysus had removed his dagger and had it pressed against Hestia's throat. He stared at Gigante Polypore and said, "Polypore, the Lord is mine. You may not strike her without MY permission. Understood?!!!"

In the background, an enraged Azura was trying to say, "I do not belong to any man!" Melia grasped Azura by her shoulders and whispered gently, "Mother Azura, *you* must be the wise adult here! Let the children play out their fantasies. This is difficult for all of us. I beg you to maintain your composure while those around you lose their minds!"

Azura was enraged and unsure but judiciously remained silent. -- *these people are not sane!* --

The Gigantes froze, waiting for clarity.

Poseidon said, "Polypore, find Ares, Athena, and Heracles. Tell them to prepare to bathe this land with blood and gore and bring them here!"

Dionysus quietly said to Enosh, "Sound your horn."

Enosh took a horn from his belt and blew it."

OCEANIDS: Metis, Tyche, Clymene, Eurybia, Amphitrite, Philyra, Rhodos.
TELCHINES: Dexithea, Makelo, Halia.
EAST: Azura, Seth, Typhon, Iasion, Endymion.
OTHER: Centaur Chiron, Charon, Hotep, Petra, Persephone.

Dionysus said, "Again."

Again, Enosh sounded his trumpet.

From the distance came galloping horses. Scholars began pouring from their dormitories holding daggers and Orichalcum swords. The horses drew near. Fear overcame the fascination of the masses. They scattered. Three horses arrived. Their riders, each with an Orichalcum sword, quickly dismounted and ran to Enosh.

Enosh said, "Mother Azura has been threatened with death. Protect her!"

The three women surrounded Azura immediately; crouched, swords ready, their backs to Azura.

Poseidon glared at Dionysus; face reddening; voice trembling as he commanded Polypore, "Do as I command! Find them! Bring them here prepared to kill!"

Dionysus removed his blade from Hestia's throat and laughed. "Yes, Polypore. They would have great sport before they, too, were cut into ribbons and fed to dogs. Remain here, Polypore! I, Olympian Titan Ghod Dionysus and firstborn son of Zeus, command it!"

Polypore remained frozen.

Amphitrite and the leaders of the Western delegations arrived at the scene. She had tried to dissuade them, but they were adamant that they investigate the commotion.

General Typhon and Amazon Otreta hurried toward the warrior-scholars who were already forming into attack formation. The Ghods, even with Athena, Heracles, Ares, and the two Gigantes, would be overwhelmed by sheer numbers.

Dionysus stared at Poseidon and calmly said, " Ghod-of-Ghods Poseidon, this is what you shall do. You shall leave these people as they are, then you will lead the Ghods back to Olympus Towers. You will complete your great building project. Athena can train whatever hunters may follow her in the ways of war. Hestia can search for more cadres of Hecatoncheires. The Ghods can discuss and decide how to react to this day. When you are properly prepared, you will have your day of blood and gore -- but not this day. You are wise enough to know that I am wiser than you. You are wise enough to accept my counsel. Are we in agreement?"

ELDER OLYMPIANS: Hestia, Demeter, Hera, Hades, Poseidon, Zeus
OLYMPIANS: Apollo, Ares, Artemis, Athena, Aphrodite, Dionysus, Hermes,
Hephaestus, Heracles. LIVING TITANS: Oceanus, Tethys, Selene, Elder Oceanids.
DECEASED TITANS: Queen Kiya, Iapetus/Piercer, Cronus.

Poseidon, his rage barely contained, spat, "I am a Ghod! No one tells ME what to do!"

Dionysus, allowing his features to melt into overwhelming anger, growled with venom, "I, too, am a Ghod! A greater Ghod than YOU. I DO tell you what to do and you SHALL do it! If you disagree with my words, then you and I shall fight to the death. Here! Now!" He paused for effect. He quietly continued, "So this is what you shall do, Ghod Poseidon, you will leave these people as they are, you will lead the Ghods back to Olympus Towers, and you will live to seek whatever future vengeance you may wish."

Polypore looked at Poseidon for orders.

The furious Poseidon glared at Dionysus; spittle oozing from his mouth. He opened his mouth to speak.

Dionysus calmly held his finger to his lips and said, "Choose your words wisely, Poseidon. Do as I say and let us all live another day. Your words will decide this thing! Choose life!"

Poseidon commanded Polypore. "Gather all Ghods to my Red Egg. We shall leave this accursed land tonight! One drop of Ghod's blood is more valuable than all the blood of all the scum who live in this land. Come, Hestia, let us remove our magnificent presence from these undeserving, abominable creatures."

Dionysus nodded to Poseidon as a sign of respect and said, "Good decision, Poseidon. Typhon would have ensured that no Ghod survived. All things would have ended here."

Azura remained silent during the altercation. -- *this isn't good! -- will they still perform the fertility rite? --*

Enosh and Noam heard every word as had the mass of mostly Urfa residents. -- *what did it all mean? -- who would make sense of it? -- would ghod coins still be given? --*

And so it was that Poseidon commanded Iapyx to pilot the overloaded airboat carrying only the eight Ghods back to Tartarus that evening. Heracles, Nerites, and the two Gigantes were commanded to find horses and return immediately without further contact with the worthless scum.

OCEANIDS: Metis, Tyche, Clymene, Eurybia, Amphitrite, Philyra, Rhodos.
TELCHINES: Dexithea, Makelo, Halia.
EAST: Azura, Seth, Typhon, Iasion, Endymion.
OTHER: Centaur Chiron, Charon, Hotep, Petra, Persephone.

Athena took notice of the Orichalcum swords and the precision with which the scholars had formed battle formations. -- *these people are well trained -- who do they prepare for? -- from where did they obtain those swords? --*

Zeus was upset that his wonderful trip had been ruined. -- *it was going so well -- so many women loved me -- but that scum had insulted ghod Hestia -- they are just so inferior! --*

Aphrodite was silently incensed. -- *the greatest performance of my life has been canceled -- and it was to be with Dionysus -- dung! -- and that Azura woman wasn't even being disrespectful! --*

Poseidon calmed down but was confused. -- *Dionysus is a ghod, but he sided with those lower-class people -- how can that be? -- he was probably correct about us being overrun and perhaps killed by the rabble, though -- I suppose he may have saved our lives -- he is clever -- I must think upon these things! --*

Hestia did not speak on the return journey. She merely stared out over the endless sky. -- *insulted by common scum -- powerless to kill her -- did you know, Grandmother Kiya -- that I would sink to this? -- Dexithea, come to me! --*

And so it was that Dionysus held counsel with Seth and Azura and the other principals. Dionysus and Amphitrite agreed that the insurmountable problem was Hestia. The other Ghods could be cajoled, distracted, and misdirected. But Hestia would forever be focused on her humiliation; she could not long tolerate it; she would have her revenge.

Azura was unrepentant of calling Hestia a bitch, "I am heir to Mother Valki of Urfa. I will not be insulted to my face by anyone regardless of the consequences!"

Dexithea offered to assassinate Hestia. "It would be easy enough. I might be far away before her body was discovered. There need not be blood; a potion, an accidental fall from a high place."

"One of their own kind -- dead?" Amphitrite mused, "Even if they thought it an accident, I am not at all sure how they would respond. Kill every living creature? Perhaps. I don't know."

Dionysus said, "We will discuss that possibility further if all else fails. In the meantime, do not even hint that such words were ever spoken."

Amphitrite and Dionysus agreed that their best strategy was to encourage the Ghods to postpone retribution until at least after the Olympus Towers was completed. This would give Athena time to build a fighting force of hunters and Hestia time to find more cadres of Hecatoncheires. They could then return and avenge the insult of a Ghod by the lowly scum.

Typhon, Azura, and Clymene would meet more often, double their security, and prepare for war sooner rather than later. Their military prowess had been revealed to Athena. When she came, she would not underestimate her adversary.

The Festival had gone badly but no blood had been spilled. Perhaps that was triumph enough.

After the Ghods had left, and having accomplished all he knew to do, Dionysus wandered to Pumi's stone table and sat down.

Seth joined him soon enough. "We knew this day would come. It went well enough, I think."

"For a complete disaster, I suppose so. Yet, why do we even try? My efforts have changed nothing. Kiya is still dead, Philyra is still gone. The taste of wine no longer brings me joy. Why are these things?"

Seth chuckled. "The chest that contains the Book of Pumi contains other wisdom including the teachings of Kiya to her children. Kiya is dead. Her words live on. What does that mean? The Shamans lose themselves in such questions. 'What is it all about,' they ask. I suspect they will find no answers but still, they look. The search makes my Scholar Shamans 'different.' They sometimes appear to live in a world different than ours."

He paused. "But, Friend Dionysus, let us go and retrieve the Book of Kiya from our Golden Chest of Life. My son, Shaman Enosh, would say that the words live so Kiya lives. A ridiculous statement to you and me, isn't it? But you will appreciate reading her teachings, dead as she may be. Let us make a Covenant. I will show you all the treasures in our chest if you will agree that if the Olympians destroy Tallstone, you will save our golden chest."

"Kiya wills it," Dionysus laughed. They rose and walked to the library where waited the golden chest of Tallstone.

OCEANIDS: Metis, Tyche, Clymene, Eurybia, Amphitrite, Philyra, Rhodos.
TELCHINES: Dexithea, Makelo, Halia.
EAST: Azura, Seth, Typhon, Iasion, Endymion.
OTHER: Centaur Chiron, Charon, Hotep, Petra, Persephone.

56. The Book of Teumessian

I. The Gods

1. And it was that the Gods wished to walk among men and to know their women. So, it was they suffered to leave the magnificent Olympus Towers and descend from the sky to walk among men.

2. The Gods' endless love for man is shown through Zeus, the Loving God of the Sky.

3. The Gods' endless passion for man is shown through Aphrodite, the Passionate God of Love.

3. The Gods' endless care for home and family is shown through Hestia, the Caring God of the Hearth and Fire.

4. The mighty anger and terrible wrath of Gods toward the unrighteous are shown through Ares, the God of War.

5. Demeter, the God of Crops, brings forth the endless bounty of the land each year after sacrifices are offered up to her.

6. God Persephone and God Hades, Queen and King of the Underworld, remain unseen by mortal men but wait patiently for them in their realm beneath the land.

7. The great God Poseidon rules over the Gods, men, and the Sea.

II. The Rite of Fertility

1. And so it was that the people gathered for the rites of fertility to honor and appease the Gods, but the Gods were not pleased and did not come forth. A great noise rose up from the people. "Where are the Gods? Why do they not come forth so that the fields will grow rich with grain and the earth give forth its bounty?" The people were sore afraid.

2. And a wise man said to the multitude, "We are of the image of the Gods and are their servants. They wish us to do these things ourselves. Let us choose the most desirable young maiden among us and our three finest young men. The three will then fornicate and leave their seed within the maiden. In this way, the Gods will be pleased, and the earth shall produce its bounty."

ELDER OLYMPIANS: Hestia, Demeter, Hera, Hades, Poseidon, Zeus
OLYMPIANS: Apollo, Ares, Artemis, Athena, Aphrodite, Dionysus, Hermes,
Hephaestus, Heracles. LIVING TITANS: Oceanus, Tethys, Selene, Elder Oceanids.
DECEASED TITANS: Queen Kiya, Iapetus/Piercer, Cronus.

3. And the maiden lay upon the plowed field where God Demeter had been thrice plowed by God Ares. The unwilling maiden was then mounted by each young man, each in his turn. And then, just as God Demeter had then been plowed by the mortal man, Iasion, then did the wisest of the men gathered there, plow the young maiden. And the people saw that it was good.

4. But then a cry again rose up from the people, "These three young men have left their seed within the maiden, but they will now go forth and fornicate with others and bring forth impurity which shall make the earth impure, and the earth will not bring forth its bounty. What do the Gods wish us to do?"

5. And the wise man among them said, "Even as God Poseidon purified the mortal men when he spilled their innards upon the ground and offered the good earth their bodies. So let us purify the three young men and offer the earth their bodies. Their bodies shall return to Great Mother Valki and show our great love for her." And the innards of the three young men were spilled upon the ground and the people saw that it was good.

6. But then another cry rose up from the people, "The maiden is filled with the seed of the four. Will not the seed become impure when another fornicates with her?"

7. And the wise man among them said, "Even as the three men join Great Mother Valki in the earth, then let the maiden join Great Father Pumi in the sky even as God Ares offered a maiden to the sky. In this way, all Gods and the Earth and the Sky shall be honored, and the earth will produce its great bounty."

8. And so a great fire was built, and the living maiden was thrown into it and burned, and her ashes rose to the sky to join with Father Pumi. And the people saw that it was good.

9. So it is that in this way, the Gods' will be done, and the people rejoice and praise the merciful Gods.

10. And so it is written, each year the people must so honor the merciful Gods so that the earth will bring forth its bounty and the people will know that it is good.

OCEANIDS: Metis, Tyche, Clymene, Eurybia, Amphitrite, Philyra, Rhodos.
TELCHINES: Dexithea, Makelo, Halia.
EAST: Azura, Seth, Typhon, Iasion, Endymion.
OTHER: Centaur Chiron, Charon, Hotep, Petra, Persephone.

57. Olympus Towers
< Year 116 >

~ Charon ~

It was late. Charon lay on his makeshift bed staring quietly into the star-strewn night sky. He maintained their living quarters on the highest uncompleted floor of Olympus Towers. He heard her soft footsteps as she exited the staircase and entered the top floor. He turned his head to watch her as she approached.

She was naked, carrying her tunic and little black bag over her shoulder. She let it all slide to the floor as she climbed in beside him to snuggle against his body.

"How did it go?" he asked.

Dexithea replied, "She will never find peace. I cannot punish her enough. How was your day?"

"Good. Petra is ready to add another level to the infrastructure. We will soon move our quarters another level higher. Hotep's workers are making good progress on building out the interiors. Halia comes behind them all. Her finishing touches make the area magnificent."

"I got back from the port this afternoon and went to Hestia on her orders. I need to continually assure her that Creusa manages the port operations well. I didn't tell her that Creusa is getting too close to Acmon; not wise for either of them. But all the easier for you to take over Port operations when the time comes."

"That won't be for a long time, yet. Her position is safe until this Olympus Towers project is finished. We will all be old by then. All ambition dead."

She laughed as she rolled over and began kissing his bare chest. She murmured, "Sure, we all believe that." Her kisses moved to his stomach.

~ Hotep ~

Hotep awoke from his sleep and gently moved Halia's head from the crook of his arm. He had almost a thousand workers to command. Even with Athena's continual demands that the workers train as fighting units, they still required unending supervision.

ELDER OLYMPIANS: Hestia, Demeter, Hera, Hades, Poseidon, Zeus
OLYMPIANS: Apollo, Ares, Artemis, Athena, Aphrodite, Dionysus, Hermes,
Hephaestus, Heracles. LIVING TITANS: Oceanus, Tethys, Selene, Elder Oceanids.
DECEASED TITANS: Queen Kiya, Iapetus/Piercer, Cronus.

The pressure on Hotep was almost unbearable, leading to many sleepless nights. -- I *am fortunate to have Halia even if she does siphon off my most talented workers -- to train them in how to make everything pleasing to the eye -- pleasing to the touch -- things of beauty -- she produces artisans -- not just builders -- her people turn my work into art -- yes -- I am most fortunate -- Halia makes me look good -- Charon recognizes the exquisite finishing touches -- he is pleased with me and my work -- even Petra's work with the gigantes and the pillars of great blocks of stone and great trees is not as demanding as my work -- Charon knows this -- yes -- I am most fortunate to have Halia at my side --*

~ Petra ~

Petra slept soundly. He, Iapyx, and the Gigantes would begin work on the ninth floor tomorrow. The building team had made great progress. Charon continually complained but, nonetheless, the progress was unbelievable. The first three floors were complete and finished with fine fixtures. Five more floors were in various stages of completion. Only four more floors remained. And, tomorrow, he would start building the ninth.

Olympus Towers would have fewer floors than the port building, but the height would be much greater. The ceilings in Olympus Towers were two to three times higher than the port building ceilings.

The Gods were quite happy that their building would be the tallest in the world. The concept of fewer floors was not something they easily comprehended because "their building would be much taller."

~ Hestia ~

The two Hecatoncheires cadre were stationed near Olympus Towers. No one entered Olympus Towers without their notice.

The incomplete fourth floor was currently the party and communal floor for the Gods and their nightly party.

All Gods save Hestia had living quarters on the third floor.

Hestia had established her living quarters on the second floor. She had asked Poseidon to command Charon to remodel the area adjacent to the atrium that overlooked her rotating statue on ground level. Charon so ordered and was impressed with what Hotep had created. Hestia merely grunted acceptance, but this immediately became her favorite place to sit.

OCEANIDS: Metis, Tyche, Clymene, Eurybia, Amphitrite, Philyra, Rhodos.
TELCHINES: Dexithea, Makelo, Halia.
EAST: Azura, Seth, Typhon, Iasion, Endymion.
OTHER: Centaur Chiron, Charon, Hotep, Petra, Persephone.

~ Entertainment ~

Dionysus suggested to Charon that some type of entertainment each quarter moon might help keep the Gods distracted and entertained. Charon passed this comment on to Dexithea who thought it a fine idea. For starters, the three Telchines could do a rain dance under each full moon. She hurried to find Halia to come up with events to fill in between their dances. They consulted with the twenty-four current Oceanids who rotated in and out of Tartarus from either Port Olympus, Riverport, or points unknown: like, perhaps, the far west.

Quarter-moon events grew into nightly events. The Gods would sit upon their balconies at sunset looking due east to the area between Tartarus and the hunter's settlement. Their guests could view the entertainment from the ground level beneath Olympus Towers. This was technically under Hade's dominion, but he permitted the nightly festivities because it thrilled Persephone so. Other workers jostled for viewing spots around the periphery. At first, there were only drummers and Aulos players playing for their audience. Singers were soon added along with additional stringed, wind, and reed instruments.

Melia had found fireworks the dactyls had stored away from the days of Piercer. The dactyls shot the fireworks as the Telchines performed their monthly rain dance. Rain sometimes came; sometimes not. But the fireworks made up for any lack of rain.

Athena, on her own, realized that a marching parade of her soldiers-in-training would be a morale booster for her warriors and provide excitement for the spectators, especially Hestia. Artemis observed how festive it would be if the troops performed synchronized sword movements and changes in direction on her command in front of the Gods. It might also help train the warriors to respond to her commands as a single unit during a battle.

The Gods, sitting on their balconies lighting up the night sky with Roomlites, drinking, and carrying on, made a significant impression on those gathered to watch not only the festivities but also to watch the Gods at play. Zeus sometimes showered the entertainers with golden coins. Most of the Gods watched from the first and second-floor balconies. Zeus always observed from the highest safe floor; he liked to have Roomlites spotlighting him so that the crowds could see and love him. He

ELDER OLYMPIANS: Hestia, Demeter, Hera, Hades, Poseidon, Zeus
OLYMPIANS: Apollo, Ares, Artemis, Athena, Aphrodite, Dionysus, Hermes,
Hephaestus, Heracles. LIVING TITANS: Oceanus, Tethys, Selene, Elder Oceanids.
DECEASED TITANS: Queen Kiya, Iapetus/Piercer, Cronus.

would sometimes let Aphrodite stand beside him and sometimes remove her tunic to expose her body to the adoring admirers. So much love.

Unknown to the Gods, despicable people from the East were often in attendance; notably, Noam, who was always accompanied by Enosh. He for the intellectual curiosity; she, because the Gods were so impressive and obviously so important and so wonderful.

With all the building and entertainment, the Gods were continually entertained and distracted.

Save one.

58. Hestia Revealed

Dionysus greeted Gigante Polypore at the entrance to the steps to the second floor. "Can I go up today, Polypore?"

"Your entry is not permitted, Titan Dionysus."

"Tell your mistress that I called on her, will you, Polypore?"

"I shall enter your call into my log, Titan Dionysus. But as you know, God Hestia watches you as we speak."

"May I wave at her?"

"I will be severely disciplined if you do, Titan Dionysus."

Dionysus glanced up at the stern-faced God Hestia glaring down from the floor above. "Have your log tell her that I love her and miss her."

Polypore almost smiled and uncharacteristically broke protocol when he responded, "A sentiment more gladly received by God Zeus than by God Hestia, Titan Dionysus."

"Yes! You are correct! I am here to see my father! May I go up?!"

Polypore almost made a look of resignation. "Wait here, Titan Dionysus. I will summon an escort to take you to the fourth floor." Polypore tapped into his guard station messagebox and summoned Zeus's personal Gigante guard.

Zeus's guard arrived. As Dionysus walked past Polypore, he whispered, "You are a good man, Polypore. The Queen is pleased."

OCEANIDS: Metis, Tyche, Clymene, Eurybia, Amphitrite, Philyra, Rhodos.
TELCHINES: Dexithea, Makelo, Halia.
EAST: Azura, Seth, Typhon, Iasion, Endymion.
OTHER: Centaur Chiron, Charon, Hotep, Petra, Persephone.

Polypore stared straight ahead as he trembled.

The two men entered the second-floor walkway-balcony and continued toward the stairway to the third and then the fourth floor.

Hestia intercepted the men at the foot of the steps to the next floor. "Why don't I just kill you, now, Dionysus?"

"Because I would be dead and you would still be alive, God Hestia. Nothing worthwhile would be accomplished. Will you speak with me? Please?"

She glared at him. "Dionysus says 'please?' This is not the arrogant, obnoxious, stupid, worthless piece of dung with which I am familiar."

"I brought my best wine!" He hesitated and then under his breath said, "But I'm not stupid."

She smirked a laugh. "All right. I will listen to your lies and insults and then I will kill you!"

"You are gracious and merciful, Great God Hestia. May you live forever!"

"I intend to!" she snapped as she turned to lead him to her quarters.

She led him to the chairs facing the table overlooking the atrium.

He said, "This place is magnificent Hestia. I have never seen a ceiling this high. The furnishings are exquisite."

"Yes. I know. What do you want?"

"I want to give you whatever it is you seek."

He removed the bottle of wine and two glasses from his backpack making a show of opening the wine and pouring it into the glasses.

Hestia watched his elaborate display in silence and then accepted the proffered glass of wine. He raised his glass to her in salute. She did not acknowledge his action.

"So, Hestia. I don't expect gratitude for saving your life at the Festival, but I *am* surprised that you will not even receive me. I truly do not understand why?"

He saw the cold fury building in her eyes. -- *come on, Hestia -- get it out!* --

"YOU DO NOT UNDERSTAND WHY?!!! NO MAN CAN BE THAT STUPID!"

"I saved your life, Hestia. And Poseidon's, along with your other relatives. No, Hestia, I truly do not understand why you are angry with me."

She glared at him, trembling with anger.

He remained silent for a long time and then quietly asked, "Are Poseidon and Father angry with me? What about my once friend, Heracles?"

She spat, "They are too stupid to still be angry! They do not understand what was done!"

"What *was* done, Hestia?"

"That intolerable scum Azura insulted me! She spoke to me as if she were my equal! As if I were inferior to her! As if I were not as good as her! She is lower than scum! She and her minions must die under the sword of Ares. She and her people must be cut to ribbons; their bloody flesh fed to carrion. I will not rest until this is done. Athena continually tells me that the time is not right. That I must wait. That she is building an army to do these things but that I must wait for my revenge upon this scum! I, a God, must wait?! It is intolerable! And it's all your fault!"

"I didn't realize."

"Yes! I was humiliated by that bitch scum in front of the world! And it is all your fault! You didn't kill her or anything! It looked like you took her side! It's all your fault, Dionysus!" She was almost screaming.

-- get it out, woman! get it out! --

"Yes, I can see that now. I should have seen it then. How Azura disrespected you. How I should have killed her! Can you ever forgive me for my inadequacies, Hestia? She should have been killed then. Not just killed, but humiliated, too. Can you forgive me?"

"BASTARD! ALL MEN ARE BASTARDS. JUST LIKE FATHER! HE LET MOTHER HUMILIATE ME AND HE DID NOTHING!"

-- father? -- mother? --

He said, "Yes. All men are bastards. Not protecting the innocent. The children. The loving. All men are unfeeling bastards!" He stood and held

OCEANIDS: Metis, Tyche, Clymene, Eurybia, Amphitrite, Philyra, Rhodos.
TELCHINES: Dexithea, Makelo, Halia.
EAST: Azura, Seth, Typhon, Iasion, Endymion.
OTHER: Centaur Chiron, Charon, Hotep, Petra, Persephone.

out his arms to her. She threw her glass of wine as hard as she could across the room; her body bending into the pre-natal position; clasping her arms tightly across her body.

Dionysus stooped and embraced the sobbing woman. "Yes. I understand." -- I *don't have a clue what this is about, Hestia* –

He said, "Look. Take some time. Compose yourself. Then let's take a nice walk. I haven't even seen your magnificent Olympus Towers. You have got to be pleased with yourself. You have single-handedly made this place the wonder of the world. You must be proud!"

She sobbed but said, "Yes, it is magnificent, isn't it? I have done most of it myself although Poseidon's airboat helped me, somewhat."

They continued their small talk. This was Hestia's first feeling of worth since Poseidon wrested control of the port, their siblings, and Olympus Towers construction on the evening that she had her only true friend, Philyra, thrown down the atrium. She showed Dionysus her quarters and then they toured the upper levels.

"Should I pay my respects to Father, Hestia? I haven't seen him since that accursed Winter Solstice Festival."

"Yes. I will show you to his quarters."

They were permitted entry into Zeus's quarters. Zeus and Aphrodite were busy coupling on his balcony. She, hanging halfway out over the balcony railing. Dionysus walked over and said, "Dad, I love you so much, Dad. Are you busy? Should I come back later?"

Zeus grunted, "Yes, come back later."

Aphrodite let out a few moans of unimaginable pleasure for the benefit of Dionysus.

Hestia and Dionysus continued to the ninth floor where work was just beginning. Hestia drew back; not liking the danger of heights. Dionysus walked over and spoke briefly to Charon and then returned to Hestia. He said, "I have had a great time Hestia. Let's go get drunk. I will plow you or go find Dexi and watch the two of you. Your choice."

She looked at him without expression. "I haven't seen Dexithea in a long time."

ELDER OLYMPIANS: Hestia, Demeter, Hera, Hades, Poseidon, Zeus
OLYMPIANS: Apollo, Ares, Artemis, Athena, Aphrodite, Dionysus, Hermes, Hephaestus, Heracles. LIVING TITANS: Oceanus, Tethys, Selene, Elder Oceanids. DECEASED TITANS: Queen Kiya, Iapetus/Piercer, Cronus.

He took her hand and led her back to her quarters where he had left a lot of wine. They arrived and sat back down on the opposing chairs. He said, "Share more wine with me. I will ask Polypore to summon her."

She nodded her consent.

He poured them each a glass and then took notepaper from his bag upon which he scribbled a long message. She watched with detached interest. He said, "Summon your Gigante for me, please!" which she did.

Polypore arrived. Dionysus handed him the note and commanded, "Give this to the first Oceanid you see. Tell her to ensure my instructions are properly relayed." He said to Hestia, "This shouldn't take long."

Hestia nodded and leaned back in her chair. "Your wine is good, Titan Dung."

"Thank you. It's what I do. Bring a little wine. Bring a little dung."

"I'm still going to have you killed. But I'll wait until after you witness the annihilation of the scum at Urfa -- and Tallstone, too, for good measure."

"You are kind and merciful, Hestia, always have been. That's why this magnificent structure is being built. I suggest you finish your Olympus Towers before you embark on your killing spree."

"Poseidon tells me the same thing. It's like you and he have common goals. Athena wants to wait until I recruit another Hecatoncheires, and she has time to build up her little army. But I want them dead! Now! I will keep insisting until they agree to my reasonable request."

He poured them another glass of wine. They talked on. He poured another. Hestia was becoming relaxed.

Dionysus said, "Dexi should be arriving soon." He stood, walked around the table, unbuttoned her blouse, and spread the garment open exposing her body. He walked back to his chair, sat down, sipped his wine, and stared at her exposed breasts. She made no recognition of what he had done, nor his stare.

"Nice," he said.

"Yes, they are."

OCEANIDS: Metis, Tyche, Clymene, Eurybia, Amphitrite, Philyra, Rhodos.
TELCHINES: Dexithea, Makelo, Halia.
EAST: Azura, Seth, Typhon, Iasion, Endymion.
OTHER: Centaur Chiron, Charon, Hotep, Petra, Persephone.

"Are you sure you prefer Dexi to me? I am told that I am quite accomplished."

"Don't even imagine it!"

They continued to drink and banter.

~

The Oceanid found Dexithea at Charon's quarters, delivered the note from Dionysus, and departed.

Dexithea read the note. "Hestia had a rough afternoon. She screamed 'Bastard! All men are bastards. Just like father! He let mother humiliate me! He did nothing!' We are now drinking wine. I offered myself. She wants you. As soon as possible. Do what's right. D."

She reflected a few moments, changed into her leather dress, and walked down the stairs to Hestia's. She remembered to take her cute little bag.

She entered Hestia's apartment without announcing herself and walked to the table overlooking the atrium where she knew Hestia would be. She stopped to consider the waiting scene. -- *what's going on here?* -- *Mother Amphitrite, how do I proceed?* -- *am I to be angry?* -- *offended?* -- *surprised?* -- *a threesome?* –

She decided to scream. "WHAT'S GOING ON?! WHAT ARE YOU DOING WITH THIS MAN, HESTIA?! ARE YOU EXCHANGING ME FOR A USELESS DUNG-HEAP OF A MAN?!"

Hestia sat upright immediately, set her wine on the table, and pulled her blouse together. She was inebriated and defensive. "No! Sweet Dexithea. I am just sitting here talking to God Dionysus. That's all!"

Dionysus jumped up and added, "She was letting me admire the view until you got here. Depriving me of the pleasure of her body excites her. She has been waiting on you, Telchine Dexithea."

"Get Out, Dionysus! Your kind is not wanted here! Hestia has been bad! She must be punished! GO! Leave us!" Dexithea stared ominously at Hestia as Dionysus hurriedly left. Dexithea shrugged and let her black dress slip to the floor. She opened her little black bag.

The two women played their drama. The last flick of the whip on Hestia's rear was more painful than normal. Dexithea said, "Your actions are unbelievably bad, Hestia. You must have disgusted your mother!"

Hestia rose and turned to face Dexithea. "Leave my mother out of this!"

Dexithea slapped Hestia so hard that Hestia fell back onto the sofa. "You have no respect for my authority. Your father did not raise you well."

Hestia rose and screamed "LEAVE MY FATHER OUT OF THIS. HE WAS WEAK! HE LET MOTHER HUMILIATE ME AND HE DID NOTHING! NOTHING!!!"

Dexithea pushed Hestia to the floor, sat wide legged across her chest, glared at her, bent over, put her face inches from Hestia's, and asked sweetly, "Humiliated you? How exciting! What did your mother do?"

"She told me that I was bad -- disgusting -- evil. Father watched and listened to her do it. I loved them both so much. I was so young. I didn't know anything. I would sneak and watch them wrestle together. I came to know they were doing something more than wrestling. I was so young. I didn't know anything. I loved Father so much. He was so powerful. Everybody obeyed him. And he could make his thing so big. It made mother so happy. She would moan with delight. He would grunt with pleasure. I loved Father. I wanted to make him grunt with pleasure just like Mother did. One night I waited until they had finished. They were both lying on their backs breathing heavily. I took off my clothes and went over and sat on Father's thing just like I had seen mother do. I moved my hips and felt his thing getting bigger. His hips began moving with mine. I was so happy, so filled with joy. 'I love you, Father! I love you, Mother! I am so happy that I know how to show Father love like a grown-up.'"

Hestia choked up, sobbed, and let the tears begin. "Father realized something was wrong. He opened his eyes, and his body went rigid. It woke Mother. She sat up and stared at me with horror. She screamed, 'Hestia, what are you doing? Get off your father!' She pushed me to the floor and glared down at me. I didn't know what I had done wrong. She told me that I was bad, that I was sick, and to never do that again. 'Now go back to bed, little girl. Now!' I looked at Father for guidance on what to do, for what I had done wrong. He said nothing. He made no move. I loved them both so much. I was so young. I didn't know. 'Get out of here,

OCEANIDS: Metis, Tyche, Clymene, Eurybia, Amphitrite, Philyra, Rhodos.
TELCHINES: Dexithea, Makelo, Halia.
EAST: Azura, Seth, Typhon, Iasion, Endymion.
OTHER: Centaur Chiron, Charon, Hotep, Petra, Persephone.

Hestia,' Mother screamed. 'I don't want you here.' I left them in their room together. I returned to my bed, lay down, and cried. It was the last time I ever cried until now. Silly, isn't it? Being a child? Not knowing? Wanting to be loved. Mother and I never spoke of it."

Hestia asked, "Well, Mistress Dexithea, do I excite you?"

Dexithea looked into Hestia's eyes. -- *do I show you love? -- compassion? -- pity? -- hope? -- do I punish you more? -- you are what you are, Hestia -- I'm so sorry --*

She said, "Extremely, God Hestia. You are the greatest God of all."

She leaned over to press her lips against Hestia's. She continued moving her hands and body over Hestia but with tenderness rather than domination.

After they had satisfied one another, Hestia lay with her head nestled in the crook of Dexithea's arm. Eventually, Dexithea rose, covered Hestia with a blanket, gently kissed her on the lips, and said, "I had a wonderful time this evening, God Hestia. You are the greatest god of all."

Hestia smiled sleepily and waved good night.

Dexithea usually walked back up to her makeshift room on the top floor without dressing. But tonight, she pulled her dress over her head and walked down the two flights of stairs to the ground floor.

Dionysus was there, as she knew he would be, staring into the fire pit, drinking wine. "How did it go?"

She sat beside him and accepted the glass of wine. She did not speak.

"That bad, huh? Sorry."

"Whatever it is you wanted, you got. Hestia is cleansed, at least a little. I need to talk with Mother Amphitrite. This 'Weapon of War' stuff grows burdensome. Hestia feels that I love her. She trusts me. When she understands that it is all a deception, she will be -- be -- I don't know what. I need Mother Amphitrite to forgive me for my deceptions and weaknesses and whoring and lies and existence." She held out her glass. More wine, please."

"Welcome to Enlightenment, Woman."

He poured the wine.

~ Charon sans Dexithea ~

Charon woke at sunrise. He did not find Dexithea by his side. -- *still at the port? -- playing with Hestia? -- who knows what trouble that woman is getting into --*

He rose and dressed; his day was planned. Iapyx would already be at work preparing the airboat. Petra would be at the Marmaros quarries preparing eight massive pillars for transportation to Olympus Towers. -- *the ninth floor -- I can't believe we are already preparing the ninth floor -- our progress is unbelievable -- just keep Hestia's rage under control -- the other gods want ruthless revenge, but they are perfectly willing to wait until their house is finished -- war will be their little victory celebration -- who knows what happens then? -- if the gods are all killed, maybe this will be my and Dexi's house -- it matters little -- what matters is that I built this place -- a wonder of the world! -- it will stand forever! --*

He took the elevator to the ground floor and exited. He saw the two soundly asleep on a blanket in the grassy area. She was nestled in his arms. Several empty wine bottles lay nearby. He walked over to watch them sleep and chuckled to himself. -- *hard night, Dexi? -- you're tough – you'll make it --I'm not sure about lord Dionysus, though -- help him as best you can -- I'm off to work, sweet -- I hope you feel well when you finally wake up --*

Charon left them; subconsciously pleased that she still had her clothes on.

~ Dexithea's Victory ~

Amphitrite snuggled against Poseidon. He had been unnaturally calm in bed after the party.

She and Dexithea had eavesdropped on the conversation between him, Hestia, Athena, and Zeus at last night's God party.

Poseidon was relieved that Hestia behaved so rationally. All Gods agreed that the low-class, scum Azura and her ilk must be destroyed and Tallstone burned to the ground; it was simply a matter of timing and time doesn't matter since Gods never die. Ares and Athena enjoyed the waiting; she to prepare for and plan an amazing war of destruction; Ares to savor the anticipation of the gore and the scraps of flesh their war would leave behind.

It had been only Hestia that demanded immediate punishment for the intolerable acts of Azura and her scum friends. And last night, Hestia had

OCEANIDS: Metis, Tyche, Clymene, Eurybia, Amphitrite, Philyra, Rhodos.
TELCHINES: Dexithea, Makelo, Halia.
EAST: Azura, Seth, Typhon, Iasion, Endymion.
OTHER: Centaur Chiron, Charon, Hotep, Petra, Persephone.

seemed more at peace, even patient. No one knew why; except Dexithea, then Dionysus, and now, Amphitrite.

Dexithea's only reward for her recent service was "Well done, Sweet!"

It was enough. The Great War of Retribution would wait until Olympus Towers challenged the very sky itself.

59. Ariadne Rising
< Year 121 >

The years progressed.

Winter Solstice Festivals were held and attended by delegations from the west. Dionysus and Dexithea hosted them. Amphitrite withdrew from Port activities in order not to attract the God's attention away from their precious Olympus Towers building project and risk one of them remembering the trade negotiations with the western cities. The Festival was never mentioned in front of any of the Gods. Without interference from the Olympians, the building went smoothly. Charon could begin to see the completion of his Olympus Towers.

Dionysus's heart was in a foreign land where he must not go; better a clean break than periodic clandestine visits always ending in separation. He did not allow himself to dwell upon love past, at least not too often. He spent much time in the east, studying with the Shamans in Tallstone, planning with Azura in Urfa, and then stopping off for pleasant diversions with Clymene of Riverport.

But mostly he assisted Creusa with Port Operations. On this afternoon, they met at his favorite table on the dock to conduct business and gossip about the Gods and especially Hestia; to whom Creusa must still sometimes provide 'special reports.'

Creusa enjoyed his company but insisted on leaving him when the Port Office closing bell chimed. "Company regulations prohibit our visiting after hours," Creusa would always tell him.

"I understand," he would always reply. But this day, Dionysus remained seated at his table after she left. He ordered another glass of wine.

After Creusa had departed and was out of sight, two Oceanids came and, without invitation, sat down beside him. "Greetings Titan Dionysus! We are commanded to tell you that Oceanus will be meeting with King Minos

ELDER OLYMPIANS: Hestia, Demeter, Hera, Hades, Poseidon, Zeus
OLYMPIANS: Apollo, Ares, Artemis, Athena, Aphrodite, Dionysus, Hermes,
Hephaestus, Heracles. LIVING TITANS: Oceanus, Tethys, Selene, Elder Oceanids.
DECEASED TITANS: Queen Kiya, Iapetus/Piercer, Cronus.

of Kaptara and King Theseus of Graikoi in Port Kaptara before the next full moon. They seek your wise counsel. Also, the adopted daughter of King Minos is being married to King Theseus. This will be a fortuitous time to meet and discuss matters of great importance to all concerned as well as participate in a social event of significance. You will attend."

Dionysus laughed and called for more wine and two more glasses. "That was a question, was it?"

"I'm sure it was," the Oceanid dryly replied. "Sister Metis fully expects you to escort her to the wedding. I am commanded to repeat her words to you. 'Everyone of importance will be here and I need someone to make me look good.'" She laughed. "Imagine, Mother Metis not looking good! Impossible, of course."

"Then attend I must!" Dionysus said as he raised his glass in salute.

~ Metis and Dionysus ~

The two Oceanids debarked their ship at Port Kaptara with Dionysus in tow. They led him up a primitive road to an almost elegant home on the right, overlooking Oursea.

Portmaster Oceanid Eurybia greeted them at the front door. "Welcome back, Sisters. I see you were successful. Welcome to Port Kaptara, Lord Dionysus. Sister Metis has been awaiting your arrival. I will announce you. You may sit in front of the window." She left them to find Metis.

The two Oceanids said their farewells to Dionysus and left him alone in the sitting room.

Metis strode into the room, arms extended, sun-bleached hair falling to her waist. She had aged well. She wore an almost opaque form-fitting, thin, linen dress. She exclaimed, "My Lord! We meet again!"

Dionysus rose, met, and returned her embrace. They exchanged pleasantries and then he asked, "How is Philyra?"

"Well enough. She easily melted into Kaptara. I'll share details of her life later, but for now, Dionysus, we must speak of important issues. There are matters under discussion that will change the shape of our world. My father is under constant pressure from both King Minos and King Theseus to raise the level of Oursea. He resists but their pressure is

OCEANIDS: Metis, Tyche, Clymene, Eurybia, Amphitrite, Philyra, Rhodos.
TELCHINES: Dexithea, Makelo, Halia.
EAST: Azura, Seth, Typhon, Iasion, Endymion.
OTHER: Centaur Chiron, Charon, Hotep, Petra, Persephone.

unending. The leaders of Kemet are ambivalent, but they agree that the advantages outweigh the disadvantages. Father needs your counsel in this matter. It is your land that would eventually disappear including Port Olympus and all of Tartarus, the ancestral home of the Titans; Father, Mother, Grandmother, all Oceanids; our home, underwater. Oceanus feels that you should have a strong say in the matter. It is a heavy decision."

"How, exactly, can Oceanus raise the level of Oursea?"

"Oh, that's easy enough. The questions are how high? How quickly? When? Father can construct a canal connecting the western shore of Port Spearpoint to the eastern shore. The waterfall into Oursea would be magnificent. Every Oceanid in the world would visit just to see and swim in this wonder."

She paused. Her eyes glazed over as she considered such a waterfall. Returning to the now, she continued. "If King Minos had his way, the level of Oursea would be raised to the level of Middlesea immediately. The Port Spearpoint Canal would become the crossroads of civilization. It would directly connect the primitive settlements of Middlesea to the civilized settlements of Oursea. Trade and travel would explode. Kaptara would be a major beneficiary. Their culture is sea oriented. They would suddenly be the greatest trading nation in the world; transporting goods across the connected seas. Graikoi civilization is developing far from Oursea. Raising the sea level a stade would move the water much closer to their population centers as it would for the land of Kemet. Port Olympus and the coastal cities, unfortunately, would be underwater. The kings argue for the two seas to become level in their lifetime. You are here to argue for the lands of Tartarus."

"I see. Now that that's out of the way. How is Philyra?"

Metis laughed. "Soon enough, Titan. The council meets at sunrise tomorrow. Collect your thoughts and prepare your arguments. That, plus Mother Tethys desires to visit you this evening. You are one of her few direct connections with Grandmother Kiya. She undoubtedly wishes to roll around in the mire of old memories."

"I'm good at that. And I will bring wine."

ELDER OLYMPIANS: Hestia, Demeter, Hera, Hades, Poseidon, Zeus
OLYMPIANS: Apollo, Ares, Artemis, Athena, Aphrodite, Dionysus, Hermes, Hephaestus, Heracles. LIVING TITANS: Oceanus, Tethys, Selene, Elder Oceanids. DECEASED TITANS: Queen Kiya, Iapetus/Piercer, Cronus.

~ Tethys and Dionysus ~

Tethys wore a necklace of colored stones and bear claws. She had not aged as well as Metis but remained a striking woman, nonetheless; Kiya's Red Nectar still performed its miracles on the Titans. Tethys sat down cross-legged across from Dionysus gaily sipping her wine. "You resolve the fate of the world tomorrow, Dionysus. Tonight, let us celebrate memories of the old one. Mother was enchanted with you. You were - are -- an Olympian. They call themselves Gods, now, as I understand it. Are you a God, Dionysus? No matter. Mother trusted your judgment. She said that you lived in all worlds. Her world was simple, 'I only have to do that which is right to do. What does one do when there is no right. When all decisions are wrong?' Tomorrow all decisions will be wrong, Titan. My husband will weigh your words carefully. Choose them well." She held out her glass to be refilled.

"Who am I to decide the fate of the world?" he asked as he poured her wine.

"You won't; Father will. You have only to say that which you believe to be best."

"Is Poseidon being consulted? He is God of the Sea, after all."

She laughed. "My husband's position is that if Poseidon happens to notice the sea level rising and is upset that he need only command the sea back to where it came. But no. Only you, Oceanus, and the two kings will meet. The leader of Kemet was invited but does not care what is decided. No advisors, not even Metis, me, or Princess Ariadne, will participate."

"Princess Ariadne?"

"She and King Theseus will marry under the full moon. An affair of state, I fear. It will solidify the union of two major Oursea States. But you need no distractions. You will have time enough for frivolous things after tomorrow's meeting."

Metis entered the room. "Will you be needing me this evening, Mother? Father wishes for me to join him on the precipice tonight."

"No, Sweet. Titan Dionysus is quite entertaining. But tell me, is Dionysus aware of Mother's final command to my husband?"

OCEANIDS: Metis, Tyche, Clymene, Eurybia, Amphitrite, Philyra, Rhodos.
TELCHINES: Dexithea, Makelo, Halia.
EAST: Azura, Seth, Typhon, Iasion, Endymion.
OTHER: Centaur Chiron, Charon, Hotep, Petra, Persephone.

Metis hesitated. "No, Mother. The fewer ears, the safer the world."

Tethys considered in silence for a moment. "He must be told, Metis. It will affect his words tomorrow. Oceanus will not tell him, but Dionysus needs to know all truth in this matter. Mother would wish it."

Metis said, "All right," and walked to sit on the floor at her mother's knee.

Metis said to Dionysus, "Grandmother eventually understood the depth and depravity of her Olympian grandchildren. She finally accepted that the sons and daughters of Cronus and Rhea were evil; that their lives, attitudes, and actions would infect the world; shape and corrupt the destiny of all people. She did all that she knew to do and waited until all hope was lost. But, in the end, if she were killed, I was to carry her last command to Father, 'Remove the wall.'" Metis became silent.

Dionysus sat in silence. – 'remove the wall'? --

Tethys continued. "Mother was Queen. Oceanus was not only her son but also her subject. Her command was to be obeyed. My tormented husband considered Mother's command a sleepless night looking over Oursea toward Port Olympus. He returned the next morning. His only words were, 'I will not do this thing.' Then he walked away. He disobeyed his Queen. We never spoke of it again."

Metis continued, "'The Wall' refers to the land bridge separating Oursea from Middlesea upon which Port Spearpoint was built. Grandmother had asked Master Littlerock if it were possible for anything to remove the wall because if it were removed, the resulting flood would submerge Port Olympus and Tartarus in a matter of days. She wished to know what or who might be able to do such a thing. It was then that Master Littlerock separated company with Piercer's Stone and Metalworks at Phlegethon. Littlerock took the brightest of their guild to Port Spearpoint and set up Deep Lab. They dedicated their lives to searching."

Dionysus muttered, "'Deep Lab' -- two words never spoken at the same time. They invented Airboats, glass, Roomlites, Messageboxes, fireworks, other things of which I know nothing."

Metis said quietly, "'Things to bring down a massive rock wall 'in the blink of an eye.'"

Tethys continued, "Back then they were just beginning their research. That which they had invented might, or might not, rupture the sheer rock. There was the likelihood that their powder would simply destroy the six Port Spearpoint elevators but not bring down the wall. Since then, Deep Lab technology has progressed to the point of knowing."

Metis said, "Not even the kings know this is a possibility. They think in terms of only a canal and equalizing the sea levels over a lifetime. Father will not mention it, nor will you, but in his mind remains his Queen's command: 'Remove the wall'!"

Tethys said, "And so, Sweet Dionysus, beloved of Queen Kiya, choose your words carefully when you speak. Know that which concerns Oceanus. Neither of you shall speak of it plainly. Speak only of the nature of the Olympians and their role in civilization. You know them better than anyone, perhaps better than Mother. Does Mother's command remain?"

Dionysus remained silent, staring into his glass of wine.

Metis rose, looked at Dionysus, and quietly said, "Yes, Sweet Dung-head, choose your words carefully." She turned and left to join her father on a precipice overlooking Oursea.

~

Sunrise.

The four men met. They chattered and bantered as each sized up the other three. Oceanids brought drink and food to them in the room overlooking Port Kaptara. Finally, Oceanus said to one of the Oceanids, "Close the door. Allow no one within hearing distance of us. We are not to be disturbed until I open the door."

They began. In the early afternoon, they still talked. King Minos addressed Dionysus, "Do I have your support in this matter. Your arguments are weak and ineffective. Will you give Oceanus your approval for a rapid rise?"

Dionysus replied, "Weak? Ineffective? I have forced all of you to agree that my land is the most fruitful, important, civilized, advanced, and innovative land that's ever been. You wish to put Port Olympus under a stade of water for your selfish purposes. No, King Minos. I do *not* give my approval."

OCEANIDS: Metis, Tyche, Clymene, Eurybia, Amphitrite, Philyra, Rhodos.
TELCHINES: Dexithea, Makelo, Halia.
EAST: Azura, Seth, Typhon, Iasion, Endymion.
OTHER: Centaur Chiron, Charon, Hotep, Petra, Persephone.

Objections were made. Words revisited. Concepts again presented. The good the world would experience against the loss of the ports and settlements on Oursea along with Port Olympus again weighed.

Dionysus studied Oceanus as the debate raged on. -- *I'm losing, aren't I? -- your only decision is how quickly -- what would Kiya want?* --

Finally, Dionysus capitulated, hopefully on his terms. "Once the level of Oursea is raised, it cannot be undone. But I am sure that Oceanus is clever enough to stop the water flowing through his canal upon his command. Build your canal with the capability to control the flow of water through it; from a slow trickle to a large volume to nothing at all. In this way, the affected people will have time to respond and adjust. Begin with the trickle. Give Port Olympus, and all affected lands, the opportunity to relocate as the water level rises. Oceanus alone will control the flow."

Oceanus asked, "You will support a slow-flowing canal rather than a rapid release of water?"

King Minos exclaimed, "The water should rise as rapidly as possible. Princess Ariadne insists that the Olympian evil must be dispersed as quickly as possible for the safety of the world."

Dionysus responded, "The damage the Olympians can do has been done. We cannot reverse it. We can only mitigate and direct their self-serving future actions." -- *he has a daughter who advises him on Olympians?* --

Oceanus asked, "So the destruction of the Olympians is not an issue?"

Dionysus answered, "It never was. Evil cannot be eliminated. Evil must be faced in its own time; each worthy person must be tested and become what they will become or be revealed for what they already are. To think evil can be eradicated is a foolish belief."

Minos injected, "Princess Ariadne is not foolish."

Oceanus stood and announced, "Great Kings, you have a wedding to prepare for. Ariadne is not one to be ignored. You each have presented forceful and well-reasoned arguments. Well done! I will announce my decision at the wedding reception. It will be my gift to you great Kings and your Kingdoms." He strode to the door, opened it, and left the meeting.

ELDER OLYMPIANS: Hestia, Demeter, Hera, Hades, Poseidon, Zeus
OLYMPIANS: Apollo, Ares, Artemis, Athena, Aphrodite, Dionysus, Hermes,
Hephaestus, Heracles. LIVING TITANS: Oceanus, Tethys, Selene, Elder Oceanids.
DECEASED TITANS: Queen Kiya, Iapetus/Piercer, Cronus.

The attending Oceanids saw him leave and rushed refreshments to the remaining three men. Dionysus took the proffered wine as did King Theseus.

The King smiled broadly at the Oceanid. "Do you come with the wine?"

The Oceanid responded professionally. "Tomorrow is your wedding night, King Theseus. I suggest you conserve your energy. Princess Ariadne does not gladly accept less than excellence in all things."

He and King Minos walked away both laughing at the rebuke.

The Oceanid said to Dionysus, "Mother Tethys is entertaining her daughters and the princess. You are commanded to pay your respect."

"Meet a real living princess. I would not miss the opportunity."

"We know."

Dionysus left the room, walked up the road to the almost elegant house, knocked, and listened to the approaching footsteps. The door opened. He looked at the Oceanid with complete surprise.

"Hello, Lord Dionysus. I am glad to see you!"

"Clymene?! What are you doing here? You're supposed to be in Riverport!"

She laughed. "I have come to a wedding, silly man. All of Mother's daughters are here. We are celebrating Ariadne's wedding. Metis said that you would want to meet the princess. Come in."

She led him toward a room filled with chattering Oceanids all wearing the standard Oceanid outfit; form-fitting almost-opaque white linen tunics that did little to disguise the fact that they were women.

Metis jumped up and announced, "Here he is, Sisters! A man!" A cheer went up.

From across the crowded room, Tethys loudly commanded, "Come meet our celebrant, Lord Dionysus: Princess Ariadne of Kaptara, soon to be Queen of Graikoi!"

Dionysus planted his professionally charming smile on his face and walked through the crowd of women parting for him. -- *all right, Princess*

OCEANIDS: Metis, Tyche, Clymene, Eurybia, Amphitrite, Philyra, Rhodos.
TELCHINES: Dexithea, Makelo, Halia.
EAST: Azura, Seth, Typhon, Iasion, Endymion.
OTHER: Centaur Chiron, Charon, Hotep, Petra, Persephone.

Ariadne -- your name keeps coming up -- you must be important -- self-important, anyway -- I, myself, am an Olympian -- a god -- but don't be intimidated --

She sat in a high back chair watching the crowd part for him. There was no emotion on her face. She was imperial. Tethys stood beside her, hand on the back of her chair. Dionysus stepped through the last of the gathering and stood before her. All chattering and giggling in the room stopped. All eyes were on Dionysus.

She spoke, "Are you well, Dionysus? I haven't seen you in a while."

He stood in silence. Staring. Remembering. Reliving. Feeling. Choking.

Finally, he said, "Princess Ariadne, I have missed your company. Your name is poetry. From where did it come?"

"Metis thought it an appropriate name for an Oceanid beginning a new life in a new country. It has served me well. Did Hestia ask of my dead body?"

"No. The name Philyra is no longer spoken in Tartarus." He walked to her, kneeled, put his face in her lap, rose, put on his professionally charming smile, and said, "So, you are being married tomorrow! To no less than a King."

"No less than the King of Graikoi. I will be his Queen. Jealous?"

His smile briefly disappeared. "Yes." He hesitated, then brightly continued, "We simply must get together after the madness settles. I am in need of wise counsel."

Tethys interrupted with, "Wise counsel she has. She advised King Minos on how to save his kingdom, how to grow it, how to advance it. She provided him with solutions to many of his vexing problems. She became part of the fabric of his kingdom. So much that he claims her as his daughter. Her marriage tomorrow binds two kingdoms together."

Dionysus asked, "Have you met your groom?"

She laughed. "Oh, yes. We have discussed affairs of state many times. He offered to couple with me after each meeting. I was forced to admit to him each time that I was a virgin sworn to chastity."

Dionysus stared at her. "I did not realize that. How impressive." They bantered on for a few minutes until Tethys interrupted, "I am so sorry

ELDER OLYMPIANS: Hestia, Demeter, Hera, Hades, Poseidon, Zeus
OLYMPIANS: Apollo, Ares, Artemis, Athena, Aphrodite, Dionysus, Hermes,
Hephaestus, Heracles. LIVING TITANS: Oceanus, Tethys, Selene, Elder Oceanids.
DECEASED TITANS: Queen Kiya, Iapetus/Piercer, Cronus.

that you must leave us now, Lord Dionysus. The princess wanted to see you before her marriage. I'm sure you understand."

"Yes. I understand. You are merciful and kind, Princess Ariadne. Thank you." He turned and walked away without looking back.

With a blank expression, Ariadne watched him walk away.

Metis joined his exit with a bottle of wine that she gave him. "Father is farther up the road looking out over Oursea, thinking. Don't go there. Maybe go down to the docks and join the men doing whatever it is men do whenever there are no women around to civilize them."

"Perhaps. But I had rather sit nearby and listen to the songs the Oceanids will soon begin to sing. Will they be happy or sad?"

She laughed. "Oh, they will be joyful. But maybe we will sing one sad song about a Titan and an Oceanid. Good night, Dionysus. We will meet tomorrow and then attend the wedding."

Dionysus found a solitary place to sit within hearing distance of the almost-elegant house. He drank his wine and listened to their songs. The next day, he dressed in his finest and met Metis who was dressed in her finest. They attended the magnificent wedding under the full moon. They said all the right things to all the right people.

Oceanus announced that he would build a canal, wide and deep, with gates to control the flow of water from Middlesea to Oursea. Only one part in ten of the water would be allowed through the gates during the first year. Two parts in ten the second year. He would access the results after the second year and adjust accordingly. All interested dependable partners would be consulted on how to proceed.

A wonderful time was had by all.

Dionysus then returned to Port Olympus and his table on the patio where he would periodically meet with Chief-of-Chiefs Creusa.

And then drink wine.

Alone.

OCEANIDS: Metis, Tyche, Clymene, Eurybia, Amphitrite, Philyra, Rhodos.
TELCHINES: Dexithea, Makelo, Halia.
EAST: Azura, Seth, Typhon, Iasion, Endymion.
OTHER: Centaur Chiron, Charon, Hotep, Petra, Persephone.

60. Noam and the Idols

The minutes became the hours became the days became the seasons.

The Olympians partied; their nightly entertainment grew ever more extravagant. They allowed visitors from other lands to observe their magnificence. They reveled in the adoration. Visitors were given commemorative God coins of their favorite God. Small statues of their favorite God were available.

Hunters and gatherers would sometimes attend the festivities, especially the Telchine Full Moon rain dance with mud wrestling following. A group from Urfa was always in attendance, notably Noam and Enosh. He for the intellectual curiosity; she, because the Gods were so impressive and so important and wonderful.

One evening, Hades, Persephone, and Demeter were returning from an excursion to Phlegethon in their oversized magnificent carriage of gold and purple when they decided to take part in the evening parade so that the lower classes could bask in their magnificence.

After completing the parade and as Demeter exited the carriage near the eternal fire pit, Noam lost control, broke through the surrounding people, prostrated herself upon the ground in front of Demeter, embraced Demeter's ankles, and exclaimed, "Powerful and merciful God Demeter, I am your most obedient and humble servant, Noam. The world does not deserve one of your greatness. You cause the bounty of the earth to burst forth. Your glorious coupling is celebrated every Winter Solstice Festival, the woman burned, and the men disemboweled in your magnificent name -- to make the earth burst forth with flowers so that your glorious daughter Queen Persephone may paint them with the colors of spring. Exalted is your name. Thank you for living and allowing one such as I to reflect in the glory of your being!"

Hades was preparing to kill the scum prostrated before his sister, but Demeter's warm giggle of delight made him hold back. Demeter led Noam to the back of her large carriage and opened the rear door to show Noam the many statues of herself and Persephone that the wagon-carriage always carried. The statues were in many shapes, sizes, and materials. "Take any one these you choose, whatever-you-said-your-name-is. And here, take a handful of my God coins, too. A person that genuinely appreciates the magnificence of the Gods should be rewarded."

Noam was overcome with emotion and wonderment.

None of the other Gods watching from their various balconies could hear the words being spoken but several looked at the proceedings with varying degrees of interest.

Ares had looked forward to seeing the insolent woman disemboweled.

Hestia was disgusted that lowlife scum was touching the feet of her sister.

Athena, however, looked on with different thoughts. She called to her Gigante attendant, "Give one of my God coins to that commoner accosting Demeter. Tell the commoner that I will meet her. She is to wait until I arrive."

The Gigante left on his errand.

Athena stood in silence for a few moments, lost in thought. She then walked down the stairs to Hestia's quarters and found Hestia looking out over the balcony at the activity below.

"Dear Sister, do you have a corner where we might talk in complete privacy; where none of our words can possibly be overheard by even the most inquisitive ears?"

Hestia was not especially close to Athena, but she recognized Athena to be one of the most competent Gods; perhaps the most competent. "Of course, Sweet Niece. This way." She led Athena to a remote corner where they sat down to visit.

Athena began. "Nothing we say here can be shared with anyone. Anyone! Not even Poseidon! Especially Poseidon! Every word into Poseidon's ear comes out his mouth into his bitch whore Amphitrite's ear and from there straight to Dionysus. They are always one step ahead of me. You and I will now take control of what they hear. They will hear what we want them to hear. We will prepare for your glorious day of revenge and my glorious day of triumph over that low-class general."

Hestia listened with interest. "What do I wish them to hear, Sweet Athena?"

OCEANIDS: Metis, Tyche, Clymene, Eurybia, Amphitrite, Philyra, Rhodos.
TELCHINES: Dexithea, Makelo, Halia.
EAST: Azura, Seth, Typhon, Iasion, Endymion.
OTHER: Centaur Chiron, Charon, Hotep, Petra, Persephone.

"Tell them that you are no longer interested in war or revenge or dealing with the lower classes in any way; that Olympus Towers is the only thing worthy of your attention; that you prefer good relations with the other lands. This attitude will become known to all our enemies. We will be patient and you will have your righteous revenge."

Hestia sat in silence, thinking. "Can you bring Azura to me still living, Athena?"

"Yes."

"Then this thing shall be. We will talk only in this room; only you and I; no one else. Bring her to me alive, Athena. Bring her to me alive."

Athena left Hestia and walked to the ground level where she found Noam standing with Enosh; both nervously waiting. Athena walked to them. "I am Ghod Athena. Here, take my God Coin. It is engraved with a wonderful likeness of me in my armor. I saw you with God Demeter. Who are you?"

Noam clutched tightly to her recently obtained statue of God Demeter, giddy with a mixture of extreme fear, excitement, and joy as she stammered out her introduction.

Athena said, "Your complete admiration and worship of the Gods is good and shall be appropriately rewarded. I wish to send statues and God coins to you in Urfa for you to trade with your people. Are you capable of this?"

Noam became faint. "You - you - you would allow me to trade the makings of the Gods? I -- I am not worthy of such a thing!"

"No, you're not. Nonetheless, I wish this to be done. You appear to be more worthy than the others. Are you capable of such a thing?"

Noam fell to her knees and embraced Athena's ankles. "My Lord -- my Lord -- that which you command, I shall do!"

"I will send someone to discuss arrangements, Noam. Do not fail me. I am not a forgiving God." Athena disengaged her feet and left Noam prostrated on the ground.

~ Captain Abra ~

And so, soon enough, Dactyl Captain Abra came to the river and stopped his great carriage-wagon of gold and purple. He suspected that the beggar

ELDER OLYMPIANS: Hestia, Demeter, Hera, Hades, Poseidon, Zeus
OLYMPIANS: Apollo, Ares, Artemis, Athena, Aphrodite, Dionysus, Hermes, Hephaestus, Heracles. LIVING TITANS: Oceanus, Tethys, Selene, Elder Oceanids.
DECEASED TITANS: Queen Kiya, Iapetus/Piercer, Cronus.

women he had encountered had already informed the port master that he would soon be arriving.

The Riverport Oceanids saw him, proper introductions were made, normal protocols were performed. Portmaster Clymene feigned nonchalance over the visitor in the great carriage. -- *what do we have here? -- this is not a normal traveler -- your carriage is a thing of the gods --*

Abra accepted Clymene's offer of hospitality. They sat at a table on the dock with refreshments. Clymene subtly plied him for information that Abra had already been well-trained to innocently provide. "I am just a dactyl with my God's command to deliver trading merchandise to Noam of Urfa. Do you know of her?"

"Why, yes, I do. She is a delightful person."

"Most of my trading items were made by Great God Hephaestus, himself. He delights in creating these things for the pleasure of his brothers and sisters. I am told that Noam is favored by God Demeter. The Gods seldom favor commoners. Noam must be special."

Abra was trained and practiced in being charming, the perfect companion, the perfect male. "I am told that I will make deliveries through your lovely port once each season." They bantered on into the evening.

~ Captain Cadabra ~

Meanwhile, toward the north, Dactyl Captain Cadabra and his squadron had risen early, loaded their wagon, and continued eastward marking the way they had traveled. Later in the morning, they came to the river. The random signposts had suggested turning north which they did. They soon came to the Northern Dilation, stopped, walked to the edge of the water, and gazed at the small buildings across the wide but mostly shallow river. They were noticed immediately by the in-resident Oceanids. Two jumped into a flat-bottomed barge and rowed across the shallows to greet them.

Reaching the other side, the two women exited the barge. "Greetings, I am Oceanid Tyche of Riverport. My sisters and I are charged with meeting and assisting travelers who find themselves at this place. We can direct you to your destination if you are lost."

"Greetings Oceanid Tyche. I am Dactyl Cadabra of Phlegethon. We are on our way to Tallstone to receive instruction from the Scholars. We will

OCEANIDS: Metis, Tyche, Clymene, Eurybia, Amphitrite, Philyra, Rhodos.
TELCHINES: Dexithea, Makelo, Halia.
EAST: Azura, Seth, Typhon, Iasion, Endymion.
OTHER: Centaur Chiron, Charon, Hotep, Petra, Persephone.

receive instruction for one season and then return through this place. The road is not well marked. Is this the proper path?"

There was much discussion.

Tyche told him, "We can direct you to Tallstone. But the southern route from Phlegethon to Tallstone through Urfa is well marked, unlike the path you came ..."

"Our masters have no wish for us to be exposed to the decadence of Urfa."

"We can transport you and your wagon across ...."

"You are as kind as you are beautiful."

"You are a gracious liar. You simply must let my sisters and I provide food for you and your company. Perhaps you could rest the night before you continue your strenuous journey."

"Yes. We also wish to learn what we may of your lovely countryside."

The men left late the next morning. They were not, however, well-rested.

~ God Merchandise ~

God Demeter had been thrilled to learn that her Fertility Rite was performed at the end of every Winter Solstice Festival. She was eager to have statues of herself and Persephone delivered to, admired, and worshipped by the Urfa commoners.

Ares had become interested in the Urfa trading proposal after he learned that the participants of the Fertility Rites were sacrificed to the Gods after every Rite; the living maiden was thrown into the fire just as God Ares had thrown the living Selene into the fire.

Hestia had given permission for her statues to be traded with Urfa.

Azura had been outraged at the human sacrifices and had made significant attempts to stop them, but Master Scholar Shaman Teumessian had explained the necessity of the sacrifices and how Azura, herself, would become a sacrifice if she continued her opposition. Azura continued trying to eliminate the sacrifices but with reduced visibility. She attempted, but failed, to stop the trading of God merchandise, especially the statues.

ELDER OLYMPIANS: Hestia, Demeter, Hera, Hades, Poseidon, Zeus
OLYMPIANS: Apollo, Ares, Artemis, Athena, Aphrodite, Dionysus, Hermes,
Hephaestus, Heracles. LIVING TITANS: Oceanus, Tethys, Selene, Elder Oceanids.
DECEASED TITANS: Queen Kiya, Iapetus/Piercer, Cronus.

The people of Urfa were infatuated with Gods. They were the sheep. The Gods were the shepherds or, perhaps, the wolves.

~ Tranquility ~

Dionysus often visited Tallstone and listened for hours to the Shaman's thoughts on the nature of death. He ate cave mushrooms with them, entering unimaginable worlds, and having unimaginable thoughts.

He always sought Queen Kiya.

She was never there.

The flow through the Port Spearpoint canal was now at four parts in ten. Dionysus noticed that the water level at the Port Olympus docks was higher than it had ever been. He began marking the level on the pier.

Every Oceanid felt duty-bound to swim under Spearpoint Falls. They would swim and look in awe at the diving board high above on top of the cliff from which Metis would dive at least once a day when she was in residence. "She can swim underwater for a full season, catch fish in her mouth, and eat them without coming up for air, you know."

The Olympians, including Hestia, no longer openly talked of revenge. The military training of the hunter-worker-soldiers continued, and Hestia finally recruited three more cadres of Hecatoncheires, but this seemed only something to occupy the time of the Olympians; no mention was ever made of actually using them.

Building Olympus Towers continued.

With the absence of perceived threat, the east grew complacent.

The seasons became the years.

61. Gods on Highest
< Year 126 >

Olympus Towers stood tall. Completed.

The two dozen Oceanids currently in residence at Tartarus were hosting an all-day, all-night party for the builders of the monumental structure to celebrate them and the completion of their work. All knew they were no longer of use to the Gods and, therefore, no longer welcome.

OCEANIDS: Metis, Tyche, Clymene, Eurybia, Amphitrite, Philyra, Rhodos.
TELCHINES: Dexithea, Makelo, Halia.
EAST: Azura, Seth, Typhon, Iasion, Endymion.
OTHER: Centaur Chiron, Charon, Hotep, Petra, Persephone.

~ Charon, Dexithea, Creusa, Petra ~

Charon sipped his dark wine. He was bitter. "This should be a month-long celebration surpassing all other celebrations. The people who built this thing are amazing; dedicated, hardworking, and talented. Each worker deserves their own celebration. It ends without acknowledgment by a single God. The workers deserve so much more than this."

Dexithea sat next to him, head against his shoulder. "Well, great Lord Charon, at least you will be free of the Gods. You can return to Port Operations and live a calm, uneventful life. Maybe have children or something like that."

Charon laughed. "Creusa. my returning to the Port is your decision. Do I have a future at Port Operations?"

Creusa, now the all-business professional, said, "Of course you do, Lord Charon. Chief Nerites is overworked. A liaison between his clerical work and a new Phlegethon Field Officer position would increase Port efficiencies ten-fold."

Charon replied, "That position would be perfect for Petra. He is originally from Phlegethon operations. I would be content with a mid-level desk job. It would give me more time to make babies."

"What's the chance of you quitting any time soon, Chief Creusa?" Dexithea asked.

Creusa looked at Dexithea with a raised eyebrow. "Why, whoever would replace me, Dexi?!"

Their banter continued as others passed through to pay their respects to the great, unflinching, demanding, dedicated Chief of Design and Construction of Olympus Towers; the great, indomitable Lord Charon.

~ Hotep, Halia, Kemet, and Guests ~

Ancient patriarch Chief Kemet sat between his son, Chief Nebka, and his young grandson, Djoser. They looked upon Hotep with pride and admiration.

Chief Kemet said, "The Titans would be impressed with what you and your friends have built Ho. I knew you would do well. I am proud of you."

"Yes," Nebka added. "What you have learned will be invaluable to your people. We are fortunate to have one with your experience and expertise returning to the land of Kemet. I have many building projects in mind and look forward to your return. You have been away too long!"

Kemet laughed a throaty laugh. "Maybe you can build a proper tomb to hold these ancient bones."

Halia laughed. "Your bones will still be dancing at the wedding of his children, Great Father Kemet.

Hotep pulled Halia close to him, put his hand on her abdomen, and said "*Our* children."

~ Iapyx and Rhodos ~

Iapyx and Rhodos walked the path from Tartarus to the Airboat hangar.

Iapyx was feeling philosophical. "Dung!"

"Dung?" she asked.

"It's over. All the excitement. All the building. Over. Now we will take the Gods on occasional sight-seeing excursions. God Persephone is the only one that appreciates what we command. Zeus likes to take Aphrodite up now and then for some in-sky frolicking. Poseidon just wants it for the status. Yes. Dung! It's over!"

Rhodos laughed. "Teach Persephone to fly it. She can get it off the ground, now. Maybe she can take Zeus and Aphrodite up with her. If she can't land it -- oh, well -- but they would probably land somewhere. You could return to Port Spearpoint. Maybe I could go with you. I need to swim under the falls, anyway. Maybe Airboat 314 is ready and needs a pilot. You would never tell me, where are the first three hundred and twelve airboats?"

"You don't have a need to know!"

She turned around to walk backward. She reached into his pants and grasped his penis. "I think I will work up a need for you to tell me." She felt him responding, stared at him defiantly, and demanded, "Tell me!"

Iapyx sighed, placed his hand on her shoulder, squeezed it, and said, "Many were lost over the great unending sea. A few returned. Many years

OCEANIDS: Metis, Tyche, Clymene, Eurybia, Amphitrite, Philyra, Rhodos.
TELCHINES: Dexithea, Makelo, Halia.
EAST: Azura, Seth, Typhon, Iasion, Endymion.
OTHER: Centaur Chiron, Charon, Hotep, Petra, Persephone.

later. Their stories were unbelievable. Only Oceanus, Atlas, and a few pilots know of their return. Pilot Icarus was the first. He is a legend. He was awarded the "Eagle Helmet," the only one ever awarded. To command an airboat such as that, on a mission such as that, is the highest honor a pilot can hope for. The reach of Oceanus is beyond your imagination. The future of this place is trivial compared to all that Oceanus commands."

"Could you get such an assignment?"

He considered the question as she continued providing incentive. "If you and I applied together, maybe. You, being an Oceanid and all, would be a strong asset if we applied as a team."

"Yes. You and I would make a good team. But I want an Eagle helmet, not that silly Falcon Helmet you wear!"

"Maybe. We can try."

His offering of love came to her.

~ Seth, Typhon, Otreta, Azura, Noam, and Enosh ~

The guests from the east sat together and apart from the others.

They had been invited by Dionysus and Amphitrite as observers. They came dressed as commoners. To attract the attention of the Gods would not be to their advantage; especially Azura's.

General Typhon observed, "It is now finished. Will their attention turn toward us, or will they be content to live in this monstrosity of a building?"

Enosh replied, "It is a work of art, General; the greatest structure people have ever built. If nothing else, it has served its purpose of distracting the Olympians from other civilized peoples. You have had time to plan and build defenses against them if they once more turn their gaze toward us. Let us appreciate it for what it is. Plus, sources indicate the Gods are no longer concerned with us. Perhaps it will remain so."

Amazon Otreta offered, "And perhaps at least one of them is more intelligent than one might think. Their apparent rancor ceased quickly. Too quickly. It did not merely die away with time. Their words of hatred simply ceased. Not a good sign."

Azura said, "They do not have long attention spans. Let us let them be."

ELDER OLYMPIANS: Hestia, Demeter, Hera, Hades, Poseidon, Zeus
OLYMPIANS: Apollo, Ares, Artemis, Athena, Aphrodite, Dionysus, Hermes,
Hephaestus, Heracles. LIVING TITANS: Oceanus, Tethys, Selene, Elder Oceanids.
DECEASED TITANS: Queen Kiya, Iapetus/Piercer, Cronus.

Noam gushed, "Well, I think they are wonderful. Great God Demeter sends me a supply of their statues and jewelry to trade every season. She is gracious, merciful, and kind."

General Typhon asked, "What do you give her in return, Noam?"

"Nothing. Nothing at all. I just visit with that delightful dactyl Abra. We gossip and share stories. He tells me that the Gods are extremely impressed with Urfa and only wish us the best."

Typhon and Otreta exchanged glances.

~ Tethys, Metis, Tyche, Clymene, Eurybia ~

Tethys, Metis, Tyche, Clymene, and Eurybia emerged from Oursea.

They walked to Tartarus through the village of hunter-gatherer workers where the wine flowed freely in celebration of the completion of their years of effort. Men whistled and made suggestive motions at the five women as they walked through the village in their soaked, clinging tunics.

Tyche wiggled her rear at them, Clymene waved to them; Tethys smiled at them; Eurybia ignored them, Metis did not notice them.

The women rejoiced in their reunion in the waters of Oursea But each knew, in her own way, that on this day, their world had changed.

~Dionysus ~

Dionysus bantered with the partygoers, an ingratiating smile on his face and wine in his hand. "Isn't this just the greatest day? Lord Charon and his people did such a magnificent job, didn't they? This is a wonder of the world, don't you think? I hear Hotep is returning to Port Kaptara and beyond. Halia's going with him. She's pregnant, you know. Dexithea and Makelo are angry with her, leaving them, and for a man at that. Who will dance naked with them to make it rain? Maybe Chief Creusa could fill in. How about God Hestia or Athena?"

He mindlessly bantered away. -- *Tethys and Metis are here but not Oceanus -- leaders from Kaptara are here but neither king Minos nor king Theseus -- trade negotiations are fast approaching -- will Hestia remember? -- will she interfere? -- Theseus could have at least sent Philyra – I mean Ariadne -- she is as responsible as anyone for building this thing -- they are probably in some great house in the middle of*

OCEANIDS: Metis, Tyche, Clymene, Eurybia, Amphitrite, Philyra, Rhodos.
TELCHINES: Dexithea, Makelo, Halia.
EAST: Azura, Seth, Typhon, Iasion, Endymion.
OTHER: Centaur Chiron, Charon, Hotep, Petra, Persephone.

Graikoi enjoying the better things in life -- are you enjoying Ariadne, Theseus? -- she is a better thing in life -- are you enjoying her right now? --

Dionysus suddenly shouted above the din, raising his glass high in the air, "Let us all now salute Lord Charon and his magnificent team for accomplishing the impossible!"

The crowd responded with an ovation.

The band played on.

~ The Gods ~

Zeus stood tall on top of the rooftop platform; the highest man-made structure ever built. He gazed across the sky, his kingdom, watching birds fly below him. All was good. He was Zeus, God of the Sky. His loving subjects were on the ground, a half stade beneath him, staring up hoping to catch a glimpse of him. Here, alone, at the top of the world. Zeus experienced some unknown emotion. His life had been an unending solicitation of absolute love and recognition from every living person. He reveled in their love. It gave him a boundless sense of worthiness, of superiority, of self-glory. He had also spent his life fornicating with every female he desired. Suddenly he felt, what? Melancholia? He wanted Hera by his side; his beloved wife to whom he was eternally faithful. Hera, mother to several of his children, the keeper of his marriage but who was sometimes furiously jealous of suspected infidelities. He went to the Messagebox he had finally learned how to use and called her to join him.

Hera was thrilled to be summoned by her husband. She was, after all, his queen, Queen Hera, God of Marriage and Birth. She was due his attention. She hurried to him.

Poseidon stood looking southward to Oursea. He could look across the Elysian Fields and, from this height, see the sea. It seemed easier to see now, like it was closer, somehow. His beloved wife Amphitrite stood behind him, pressed against him, her hands on his shoulders, whispering adulation into his ear. She could calm his rage when the sea did not immediately obey him, when Hestia was not as subservient as she should be, when the travails of the world conspired against him. -- *now that I have completed Olympus towers, I might go see Oceanus -- I could go in the red egg – a little adulation by Oceanus would be good -- what is Oceanus doing these days, anyway? --*

ELDER OLYMPIANS: Hestia, Demeter, Hera, Hades, Poseidon, Zeus
OLYMPIANS: Apollo, Ares, Artemis, Athena, Aphrodite, Dionysus, Hermes,
Hephaestus, Heracles. LIVING TITANS: Oceanus, Tethys, Selene, Elder Oceanids.
DECEASED TITANS: Queen Kiya, Iapetus/Piercer, Cronus.

Hades, God of the Underworld, was excited. Queen Persephone would soon be returning from Elysian Fields with her mother, God Demeter, and tonight was cave mushroom night. He basked in the cool darkness of the room reflecting on all the subjects within his kingdom. He considered all workers to be his and was jealous when they were called away from his domain. Athena told him the workers had one more task to accomplish then they would be released into the complete service of Hades.

He was pleased.

God Hephaestus, sat beside Hades in the darkness of the room beneath Piercer's original home in Tartarus; Makelo sat on his lap. They would all share mushrooms tonight. Hephaestus and Makelo admired the collection of artifacts from the days of Piercer; metals, stones, and jewelry of exquisite workmanship; rivaling that which Hephaestus, himself, could accomplish even with his advanced resources and tools.

Hestia met Athena in their private corner. They talked quietly about many things. Their meeting ended with the lifting of wine glasses toward one another in salute.

They were smiling.

62. Winter Solstice Festival 100

Creusa finished the trade negotiations with the delegation from Graikoi without incident. Hestia had offered no guidance on what the God's desired. The delegation joined the Kaptara and Kemet delegations who had already completed satisfactory negotiations.

Dionysus, Amphitrite, and Nerites would host the delegations in their yearly visit to the Winter Solstice Festival at Tallstone.

Although not the significant event it had been in its earlier years, the Festival still retained the aura of the place to be and to be seen. Winners of the various Festival competitions were acknowledged as the best in the world in that sport. Only Artemis could beat the centaur Chiron in archery. The Urfa tumblers could not be matched even by the best that Graikoi had to offer.

OCEANIDS: Metis, Tyche, Clymene, Eurybia, Amphitrite, Philyra, Rhodos.
TELCHINES: Dexithea, Makelo, Halia.
EAST: Azura, Seth, Typhon, Iasion, Endymion.
OTHER: Centaur Chiron, Charon, Hotep, Petra, Persephone.

It was a time for social gatherings and making contacts with those who might one day be of value. In short, when the days grew longer, Tallstone was the place to be.

Everyone came except the Gods.

No God had attended since, as the people of Urfa related, God Hestia was viciously attacked by Azura without provocation. God Hestia had forgiven Azura, of course, but still, justifiably, did not wish to be subject to such abuse again.

~

After the departure of Dionysus, Amphitrite, and the western delegations, Poseidon ordered Iapyx to prepare Airboat 313 to transport Gods to arrive at the Festival during the opening ceremonies.

Iapyx found this strange. – *that's interesting -- why the late notification?* –

"Rhodos, can you get word of this trip to Oceanus?"

~

And so, the western delegations passed through Riverport and Urfa. They arrived and settled into their guest houses sponsored by their Port Olympus hosts. They prepared to attend a festival.

~

And so, too, Captain Abra arrived at the river crossing in the gold and purple carriage carrying God items for Noam to trade. He was followed by another wagon of similar large size. He was greeted by Clymene who looked twice at the second wagon. Abra smoothly said, "It's for the festival crowds. God Demeter expects to do a brisk business with her wares; it's three times what she usually sends."

Clymene smiled and nodded her understanding. Nonetheless, Doris discretely looked under the tarps to check the contents of the wagons.

Abra said, "I would love to stay and partake of your hospitality Oceanid Clymene, but duty requires me to get my wares to Noam as quickly as I can so that she can prepare for the Festival crowds. Perhaps I can stay the night on my way back." He smiled and reluctantly bid her goodbye.

A half-hour out of Riverport the two pulled their wagons over to the nearby woods. They each raised their tarp and opened a door to a compartment beneath the false floor. Twenty cramped soldiers scrambled out of each wagon and into the woods.

Abra and the second driver closed their doors, replaced their tarps, and continued on to Urfa.

~

Captain Cadabra and his group came to the Northern Dilations and merrily waved across the river to Oceanid Tyche. The Oceanids came out to meet their old friends. They visited and had a little party with wine and everything. The men, as usual, decided to spend the night to keep the Oceanids company.

After the Oceanids had fallen asleep snuggling against their dactyl friends, the dactyls silently found their daggers and cut the throat of the Oceanid sleeping beside him.

After it was over, Cadabra returned across the Dilation and summoned the Gigantes and their accompanying five cadres of Hecatoncheires. The Gigantes brought a portable bridge. The deep portion of the Dilation was easily crossed.

~

Before sunrise, forty carefully trained soldiers surrounded the buildings at Riverport and encircled them with flammable oil. The oil was ignited. The soldiers waited patiently as each Oceanid burst through the wall of flame toward the river.

It was easy enough to kill each in turn. The Oceanids never knew what happened or why.

Only the last one realized and screamed, "Murderer" before her head was removed.

The bodies were thrown into the river.

~

The people of Urfa began waking and were excited about the opening of the festival. Few noticed the dark smoke rising in the west.

OCEANIDS: Metis, Tyche, Clymene, Eurybia, Amphitrite, Philyra, Rhodos.
TELCHINES: Dexithea, Makelo, Halia.
EAST: Azura, Seth, Typhon, Iasion, Endymion.
OTHER: Centaur Chiron, Charon, Hotep, Petra, Persephone.

~

General Typhon of Tallstone did notice the wisps of smoke. He nodded to Amazon Otreta and then nodded toward the smoke. She acknowledged his concern, called for her fastest horse, and set off to investigate.

~

The time for the opening approached. Finally, the sun rose to its highest point. The great horn sounded. Three young, vibrant women dressed in identical red dresses ran onto the stage below the tall stone. Hands high in the air, they shouted in unison, "ARE YOU READY TO HAVE A FESTIVAL?" Traditions carried on. All was well.

And then, high above them all, came the Big Red Egg; Zeus waving excitedly to the crowd far below. Both Pilots Iapyx and Rhodos would be required to land the craft. They could expect no ground crew to be waiting to assist them. Zeus was upset that there had not been room for Aphrodite to come with him. Athena had insisted that she be replaced with Heracles for some reason. Heracles was not fun like Aphrodite.

Hestia stood between Ares and Athena. Resolve on their faces.

Only they knew.

~

In the south, Otreta galloped past the woods on her way to the smoke coming from Riverport. She saw the twenty archers' step from the woods. She commanded her body to slip down so that the horse would be between her and the arrows. The arrows brought the horse down on top of Otreta. The swordsmen were upon her before she could escape the weight of the dead horse. The troops moved the two corpses into the woods, out of sight.

Further down the path at Riverport, hundreds of hunter-soldiers had already been transported across the river. Hundreds and hundreds more waited to be ferried across.

The bodies of five beggar women lay dead in the road where they had always begged.

All troops remained in hiding. Waiting for the sun to touch the horizon.

~

ELDER OLYMPIANS: Hestia, Demeter, Hera, Hades, Poseidon, Zeus
OLYMPIANS: Apollo, Ares, Artemis, Athena, Aphrodite, Dionysus, Hermes,
Hephaestus, Heracles. LIVING TITANS: Oceanus, Tethys, Selene, Elder Oceanids.
DECEASED TITANS: Queen Kiya, Iapetus/Piercer, Cronus.

Abra brought Noam to the Festival in the God's carriage of gold and purple. She was thrilled.

General Typhon was concerned. Otreta had had time to investigate the smoke and report back. -- *where is she?* --

He called an assembly of all Amazons. He sent three to follow up on Otreta, three to discreetly protect Azura, and three to watch out over Seth. He then began looking for Dionysus and his western friends. He assigned a dozen soldier-scholars to remain near him with their weapons hidden.

The Red Egg was landing on the stage to the cheers of the crowd. Zeus was beside himself with excitement; already throwing coins to the crowd.

On stage, Azura looked at Seth anxiously, unsure how to proceed. She looked up toward the tall stone and saw Dionysus standing there watching. She thought -- *all right -- let this thing play out as it will* --

Rhodos jumped over the side onto the stage and expertly pulled in and secured the Airboat to the moorings. She helped Poseidon triumphantly debark and then Zeus and Heracles. Hestia was the last God to debark. Hestia looked over those gathered on the stage and recognized Azura; the face indelibly etched into her mind. Hestia smiled a strange smile.

The arrival of the Gods was treated with pomp and joyous reunion.

"Meet me at sunset at that stone table," Hestia commanded Azura. "We will discuss resuming the God's participation in Urfa's respectful Fertility Rite which so greatly honors God Demeter."

Athena gathered Poseidon and Heracles together onstage for a private discussion. She told them what she, Hestia, and Ares would be doing at sundown; just so they would know. They could assist in this matter or not.

The Gods then resumed their tradition of letting the crowds adore them as God Coins and God trinkets were given to the select; old slights evidently forgiven and forgotten.

Dionysus and Amphitrite held a quick, spontaneous meeting. "Poseidon made no mention of this before I left, Dionysus. He could not have hidden such a trip from me. This was not planned until after we left with our delegations. At least, Poseidon was not aware of it."

OCEANIDS: Metis, Tyche, Clymene, Eurybia, Amphitrite, Philyra, Rhodos.
TELCHINES: Dexithea, Makelo, Halia.
EAST: Azura, Seth, Typhon, Iasion, Endymion.
OTHER: Centaur Chiron, Charon, Hotep, Petra, Persephone.

Dionysus replied, "As far as I know, Clymene has not alerted Typhon or Azura of any irregularities. Even Athena, Heracles, and Ares could not wage war against the east alone. I will consult with Typhon. You gather the Telchines and our western guests. Keep everyone near the edge of the festival so that you can lead them away if things go badly. Take the northern road."

General Typhon still waited on the return of any of his Amazons when Dionysus found him. Typhon listened to Dionysus's concerns. His response was "There was smoke from the direction of Riverport this morning. No Amazon has yet to return with a report. Safeguard your western delegations as best you can. I shall prepare for war."

The sun continued its descent toward the horizon.

Typhon found Azura. "We may have a problem, Mother Azura. I am informing my scholars to be ready to become warriors at the sound of my horn. I fear for your safety. I advise you to retire to the safety of Urfa and remain vigilant."

She replied, "Nonsense, General. I am meeting with God Hestia at sundown. She wishes to resume our talks about the yearly Fertility Rite. My people demand the Rites. The Gods can be of assistance. I look forward to working with them."

"Have you learned nothing of them, Mother Azura? Do not meet with her. It will be a trap. I urge you! I beg you!"

Azura laughed. "I know them well, General; of their cold disregard for everyone not a God. But they revel in the adoration of the masses. They need the lower classes to validate their useless existence. God Hestia wants the adoration that the people of Urfa can provide. I shall go to my meeting with Hestia. Trust me in this matter!"

They continued their discussion but, in the end, Azura was adamant. She left Typhon standing there. -- *Seth will have the scholars prepared -- the amazons were my cavalry -- they are evidently lost -- well, lord Centaur Chiron, we will see if you and your archers are loyal to the gods or to civilized peoples --* He left to find the Centaur.

The sun approached the horizon. Hestia stood talking with Heracles at Pumi's rock table. Athena and Ares stood talking together a respectful distance away.

ELDER OLYMPIANS: Hestia, Demeter, Hera, Hades, Poseidon, Zeus
OLYMPIANS: Apollo, Ares, Artemis, Athena, Aphrodite, Dionysus, Hermes,
Hephaestus, Heracles. LIVING TITANS: Oceanus, Tethys, Selene, Elder Oceanids.
DECEASED TITANS: Queen Kiya, Iapetus/Piercer, Cronus.

At Abra's suggestion, Noam and Azura arrived to greet Hestia in the carriage of gold and purple. After salutations and niceties, Hestia introduced Heracles. "Heracles would make a worthy male for the female in your rites."

The two women were excited with the thought of one such as Heracles joining the rites. "What a wonderfully successful Rite this will be!"

The sun touched the horizon.

~

Led by Polypore, five cadres of Hecatoncheires began a fast trot from the Northern Dilations toward Tallstone. In the south, a thousand warriors moved from their positions in the wooded area to begin their fast run to Urfa. The bodies of the ambushed Amazons remained in the woods.

~ The End of all Good Things ~

Polypore arrived at the festival site, walked to Hestia, and interrupted her discussions with Azura. "We are ready."

Hestia was delighted. She said to Azura, "Great Mother Azura, to celebrate our newfound friendship, I have arranged a parade of my finest Tartarus performers for you. They wish to demonstrate the precision and accuracy with which they can move together!" Without waiting for a response, she commanded Polypore, "Let the parade begin!"

Azura looked toward Polypore with concern and then looked for General Typhon. -- *something's not right! -- precision performers? -- what is that? --*

Abra prompted Noam to jump up and down and screech with excitement, "A parade! A parade!"

The five cadres of Hecatoncheires marched forth from the edge of Tallstone, where the traditional Clan of the Serpent campsite once lay. A group of drummers accompanied the cadres. There were banners and flags. It was all extremely festive.

Dionysus and Typhon observed the activity from beside the tall stone on the hill. Typhon blew his horn to initiate an attack by his scholar warriors and then hurried away to find Chiron to position him and his archers.

Dionysus ran down the hill toward where Hestia stood with Azura.

OCEANIDS: Metis, Tyche, Clymene, Eurybia, Amphitrite, Philyra, Rhodos.
TELCHINES: Dexithea, Makelo, Halia.
EAST: Azura, Seth, Typhon, Iasion, Endymion.
OTHER: Centaur Chiron, Charon, Hotep, Petra, Persephone.

Hestia loudly exclaimed, "This will be glorious!"

Athena and Ares nonchalantly ambled over to stand on either side of Abra and behind Azura and Noam. Heracles moved closer to Hestia.

Dionysus arrived, grabbed Azura's hand, and said, "Come Mother. We are leaving."

"I don't think so, Dionysus!" Heracles said as the Hecatoncheires marched past the gathering.

Rather than marching straight past the gathering, the cadre began circling and marched to encircle them; gold and purple carriage included.

Heracles had his strong grip sinking painfully into Dionysus's shoulder. Unable to free himself, Dionysus quickly removed his dagger and held it against Heracles's throat.

Hestia said, "Now, now, Sweet. I don't believe you want to do that. Kill Heracles and things would not go well for you and your friend, here."

Ares and Abra stepped forward and each took one of Dionysus' wrists in their firm grip.

The remaining four cadres of Hecatoncheires began moving to defensive battle formations.

Darker smoke began rising in the southern sky, from the direction of Urfa.

Hestia said to Azura, "Now, new friend Mother Azura, I want to take you on a carriage ride and show you my Olympus Towers." She nodded to Ares who physically picked Azura off the ground and threw her into the carriage. Hestia gracefully entered the carriage and asked Noam, "Would you like to ride with us, Sweet?"

Ares picked up Noam and threw her into the carriage. Polypore then entered the carriage and lowered the protective window coverings. Abra jumped into the enclosed driver's seat and raised protective shields. He urged the team of horses onward toward the Northern Dilations and then to Tartarus. The carriage was immediately surrounded by two dozen Gigantes whose sole assignment was to protect the carriage and to pull it back to Tartarus if a horse was brought down by sword or arrow.

Dionysus stared at the abduction and departure of Azura, then looked sadly at Heracles, and quietly asked, "Why, my brother, why?"

ELDER OLYMPIANS: Hestia, Demeter, Hera, Hades, Poseidon, Zeus
OLYMPIANS: Apollo, Ares, Artemis, Athena, Aphrodite, Dionysus, Hermes,
Hephaestus, Heracles. LIVING TITANS: Oceanus, Tethys, Selene, Elder Oceanids.
DECEASED TITANS: Queen Kiya, Iapetus/Piercer, Cronus.

Heracles answered, "Because I am a God!" He then raised Dionysus above his head and, with all the strength of Heracles, slammed Dionysus into Pumi's table of stone."

Blood seeped from the mouth, ears, and nose of Titan Dionysus.

The God's attack upon Tallstone began.

~

Directly over the stage, high above all things, in the colors of the sky, Reconnaissance Airboat 79 floated. Piot Icarus and his team observed the scene on the ground far below through a device with glass which enlarged the scene eight times over.

They observed with horror.

~

Time? What is time but the mind's attempt to separate all that happens into smaller sections which might be somewhat understood? Time passes? Time stands still? There is no time?

What do you think the nature of time, Dionysus? Here? In this place? Here in the darkness.

And death? What is death? What do you think the nature of death, Dionysus? Here, in the blackness.

Within the blackness that was the darkness of his mind, the white light formed and waited patiently in the center of his brain. Waiting to be acknowledged.

-- I have failed in all things -- all that I am and all that I have ever been -- useless -- meaningless -- accomplishing nothing -- I have failed all that trusted me -- respected me -- loved me -- I thought myself so smart -- so wise -- so clever -- so witty -- so much in control of all things -- I am nothing -- forgive me! -- I am not worthy of forgiveness -- but forgive me --

He saw the white light within the blackness that was the darkness of his mind. The light then began to grow larger. It grew larger than his mind and encompassed all that was. The white light was beautiful. Beautiful beyond knowing.

OCEANIDS: Metis, Tyche, Clymene, Eurybia, Amphitrite, Philyra, Rhodos.
TELCHINES: Dexithea, Makelo, Halia.
EAST: Azura, Seth, Typhon, Iasion, Endymion.
OTHER: Centaur Chiron, Charon, Hotep, Petra, Persephone.

The light spoke to him. "I am Kiya. Why do you despair, Dionysus? Do you not understand that all will be as it will be? Accept life for what it is. Experience it. Rejoice in it. Your experiences are like no other. How will I know this experience if not through you?"

Two other lights formed: there in the center of the brightness of the darkness of his mind. They grew. They were beautiful beyond knowing. The three lights merged into one, but still somehow separate.

Said one light as it grew, "I am Pumi. There is yet much more to be learned, much more experience to be gained, Dionysus. So much more."

The other light said to him, "I am Valki. You may join us if you wish. You have only to release yourself from your body. You will be free of the burden of your body, free from the burden of time. You will live as we live. Without time. With our experiences, sharing all experiences, knowing all things that are known, experiencing all things as one and as our own. Release yourself from your body, Dionysus. Join us. Become One with us and all things."

The light that was Pumi said, "You are strong, Dionysus. If it is your will, you can rise and continue living in the physical body which constrains your soul. But, too, you will continue to experience life. To learn. To add to our experience when you, at last, shed your physical body and become One with all things."

The light that was Kiya said, "Choose as your nature, Dionysus. If you choose to remain in that body, know this -- if you experience pain, the pain will pass away -- if you experience joy, the joy will pass away. Your physical body has only the Now. When you are released from that body, all pain and all joy pass with you, to be experienced by us, by all. Do not despair, Dionysus. All will be as it will be."

He tried to hold onto the light, but he was left with only the darkness in the blackness of his mind. -- I *can let go -- this thing will end --*

He considered letting go. -- *I will do that which is my nature --*

He willed himself to stand upon unsteady legs, to open his eyes, to look, to see. He stood, stoop-shouldered, covered with his and others' blood. He looked around at the carnage, heard the cries of bloodlust, cries of the dying. He saw pieces of bodies, gore, a red field of endless blood. The tall

ELDER OLYMPIANS: Hestia, Demeter, Hera, Hades, Poseidon, Zeus
OLYMPIANS: Apollo, Ares, Artemis, Athena, Aphrodite, Dionysus, Hermes,
Hephaestus, Heracles. LIVING TITANS: Oceanus, Tethys, Selene, Elder Oceanids.
DECEASED TITANS: Queen Kiya, Iapetus/Piercer, Cronus.

stone had been toppled. It lay upon the side of the hill toward the stage. The surrounding Guardian stones; toppled. Buildings were blazing.

He stumbled toward the main building -- the library. He entered through the flames and found the great chest covered in gold which contained the writings of the elders. He pulled it from the building just as the building collapsed behind him. He dragged the chest to the safety of the woods and hid it with brush as best he could. He turned and faced the madness unfolding in the distance. -- I *am Dionysus -- I shall do what I shall do!* --

He wandered across the battlefield; he stopped to comfort the dying; to bring water to their lips; to listen to their last words. The children were the hardest. They cried for their mother or their father who would be lying dead nearby and could not comfort their child. The air was heavy with the smoke that would contain the falling ashes of Urfa.

The scholars had fought well. Their corpses were surrounded by countless dead Hecatoncheire units. But in the end, battle is what Hecatoncheires had been bred for; it is what they did, and there were simply too many.

He found the dead archers; still clutching their bows; heads removed from their bodies. He saw the gentle Chiron; a swordsman had taken time to expertly cleave the hind portion of his body from his man-like portion.

-- you are now like other men, Chiron -- does this please you? -- would it please your mother? -- why am I not crying? -- or sad? -- or outraged? -- why is that? --

Near the archers, he found three women's torsos. They wore red knee-length dresses.

And, too, the mutilated body of General Typhon, still clutching a Flag of the Festival, surrounded by dead Hecatoncheires units.

In the far distance was the mostly silent sound of survivors being hunted down and killed. What lay in the south must be unimaginable. But he would go there. He would bear witness to that which is unimaginable.

-- and why is this, Hestia? -- because Azura would not bow down to you?! -- does the One appreciate evil? -- do they rejoice in the experience that is Hestia? -- yet how will the One know this evil -- this experience -- if not through Hestia? -- there is no good? -- no evil? -- only the experience? -- yes, Pumi -- I have a lot yet to learn --

OCEANIDS: Metis, Tyche, Clymene, Eurybia, Amphitrite, Philyra, Rhodos.
TELCHINES: Dexithea, Makelo, Halia.
EAST: Azura, Seth, Typhon, Iasion, Endymion.
OTHER: Centaur Chiron, Charon, Hotep, Petra, Persephone.

He began his slow walk to Urfa. He eventually stopped and slept fitfully for a few hours. He rose at sunrise, fashioned a walking cane, and continued his walk. The soldiers had finished their work and were probably now on their way back to Tartarus. They had been thorough but removing bodies was not part of their duties. The streets were strewn with bodies. Few buildings were left standing. They smoldered.

He stopped to place a baby in the arms of the woman most likely to be its mother. -- *you are insane, Hestia -- you and your brothers and sisters and the other gods — insane!* --

He knew he should cry, or at least be sad, yet there was no emotion within him. He looked for a horse and finding none, turned, and began his trek toward Riverport.

He arrived before noon. It was in ashes. He would rest here and hopefully find a horse. But at least rest and regain some of his strength. As he sat on the ground by the river, he turned his attention downstream. He noticed piles of white debris littering the bank.

He rose, walked to the first one, and found the body of the Oceanid. Each white pile of litter was the body of an Oceanid.

-- *sweet, competent, giving, nurturing, joyful, unassuming oceanids -- always ready to help — always ready to give —*

He continued walking downstream. He came to the pool of tranquility which he and Clymene would often visit with a bottle of wine. -- *Clymene taught me how to properly swing in a tree —*

He smiled and continued to the bench that faced the pond.

The Oceanid was still alive. Barely. She lay unconscious, half in water, breathing heavily. Half her face and body were severely burned. She had evidently crawled to this place and passed out. Dionysus gathered the limp body in his arms and looked into the disfigured face of Clymene. He carried her back to where the port once stood.

He retrieved a barge and filled it with leaves and grasses. He placed Clymene's still-living body carefully in it.

He found another barge and pulled it downriver. He gathered the Oceanid's bodies, and whatever heads he found, as he went. He removed their clothing and arranged their headless bodies in the barge in one

ELDER OLYMPIANS: Hestia, Demeter, Hera, Hades, Poseidon, Zeus
OLYMPIANS: Apollo, Ares, Artemis, Athena, Aphrodite, Dionysus, Hermes, Hephaestus, Heracles. LIVING TITANS: Oceanus, Tethys, Selene, Elder Oceanids. DECEASED TITANS: Queen Kiya, Iapetus/Piercer, Cronus.

another's arms. He then offered the barge to the swift current of the river. He washed most of the blood and gore from their apparel and lined Clymene's barge with the fabric.

He walked back up the road toward once-Urfa. He came to the wooded area and entered. He found what he knew would be there. The corpses of the horses were still saddled. *-- be there! -- be there! --*

He opened the first saddle. *-- yes! -- the supplies of a warrior! -- clothes, ointments, trail food -- all that's needed to wage a prolonged war --*

He retrieved six saddles and laid the remains of the Amazon warriors next to a steed and placed a sword across each of their bodies.

He knew little of ointments, but he found one that appeared as if it might be beneficial for wounds. Although unconscious, Clymene emitted small groans of pain. He applied the ointment to her burns. After a while, her groans seemed to subside a bit.

He patched and modified the barge so that he could use it to cross the river and then pull it like a sled down the road back toward Tartarus.

Nightfall came.

He ate from his supply of Amazon trail rations and then slipped into the barge to lay beside Clymene. He wet her lips with water through the night and kept ointment on her burns.

Sunrise came. Dionysus rose to stare into the forlorn eyes of two large horses; lost, without their Oceanid masters; without their comfortable stables; without human guidance.

-- I wish I could still feel joy! -- all will be as it will be -- I won't give you names -- Clymene will know who you are -- you will hear your names soon enough --

He took them to nearby fields to graze and found scorched remains of feed in their burned-out stables.

He spoke to the horses, "All right, you two, we have done all we can in this place. Pull us across this river and on to Tartarus!"

He harnessed them to the barge containing Clymene. Being horses of the Oceanids, they were quite accustomed to pulling barges across a swift river. They were content that they again had a human master.

OCEANIDS: Metis, Tyche, Clymene, Eurybia, Amphitrite, Philyra, Rhodos.
TELCHINES: Dexithea, Makelo, Halia.
EAST: Azura, Seth, Typhon, Iasion, Endymion.
OTHER: Centaur Chiron, Charon, Hotep, Petra, Persephone.

~ Hestia's Love ~

The war won, all Gods but Hestia returned to Olympus Towers by Airboat 313.

Poseidon had wanted Amphitrite to accompany him on his triumphant flight back, but she could not be found. He was concerned that one of the evil Tallstone soldiers might have callously killed his beloved Amphitrite.

Athena and Poseidon were beside themselves with excitement of victory. Heracles was allowed full God privileges for his services in the short war.

Ares walked around with a vacant look and saliva dripping from the edge of his mouth; lost in remembrance of things past.

~

The report Oceanus received from Icarus had been chilling. Horrifying. The status of the western delegations was not yet known but Oceanus expected the worse. He called for a full Council of the West. He dispatched Metis to Tartarus to gather as much information as she could.

Metis arrived in Tartarus and apprised her Oceanid sisters of all that she knew and suspected. "We must observe and gather what information we can." She then blended in with her sisters.

~

The purple and gold carriage carrying Azura, Hestia, and the others arrived at Tartarus three days after the ill-fated opening ceremony.

Hestia was festive as they arrived. "Come, Great Mother Azura. I will show you my Olympus Towers. This is where I live. Much grander than your hovel, I'm sure."

She exited the carriage, turned back to look inside, gaily laughed, and said, "Oh, yes, Polypore, unbind her arms and feet and take that silly gag off her. She is my honored guest."

For two days, Azura was treated like a God. Then the Hecatoncheires and builder-soldiers began arriving back to the island.

Hestia proclaimed, "We are going to have our own festival to honor the triumphant Gods and our returning warriors, Noam. It will be magnificent. Mother Azura will be our honored guest."

ELDER OLYMPIANS: Hestia, Demeter, Hera, Hades, Poseidon, Zeus
OLYMPIANS: Apollo, Ares, Artemis, Athena, Aphrodite, Dionysus, Hermes, Hephaestus, Heracles. LIVING TITANS: Oceanus, Tethys, Selene, Elder Oceanids.
DECEASED TITANS: Queen Kiya, Iapetus/Piercer, Cronus.

Noam had been in a state of complete confusion since Tallstone. She was not at all sure what was happening.

Oceanids, Gigantes, and servants began preparing for the great festival.

~

On the evening of the quarter moon, the God Victory Festival began. Hestia and Azura watched the festivities as they sat in front of the fire pit containing Hestia's statue rotating in the eternal fire. Azura no longer resisted but she said little. As the sun touched the horizon, Hestia called out, "God Ares, God Heracles, prepare our guest of honor to share the warmth I feel when low-class scum such as she dares insult me -- a God! Let all people see! Noam, come sit beside me as we watch the unfolding of the wrath of the Gods!"

Ares and Heracles roughly grabbed Azura and took her to a nearby table. They stripped her of her clothes, stretched her prone across the table, placed four long rods down the length of her body, and tied the rods tightly together. Ares was wild with joy as he carried one end of the rods and Heracles carried the other to its destination: two columns beside the fire pit upon which Azura would be placed and which would rotate the rods containing her; a spit for the roasting of Azura. She was placed over the eternal fire; the intensity of the fire was increased.

Azura tried not to scream and give satisfaction to her tormentors. She was a strong woman, heir to Mother Eve, wise, caring, brave, bold, determined, the supreme leader of the great city of Urfa. She screamed and screamed and screamed.

Hestia shouted to Ares, "When she is done, bring me a thigh!"

Ares was competent at keeping her alive as she was roasted.

Hestia sat beside the wide-eyed, panic-stricken Noam. Hestia said to her with some passion, "Do you understand, Lord Noam. The wrath of the merciful Gods! Do you understand what happens when you forget how great we are? How wonderful? How magnificent?!" Hestia's voice grew louder. "Always give us what we demand. Always love us!"

Azura's screams filled the night air as all looked upon the unfolding scene before them. The fires of Hades burned brightly yielding the smell of roasting flesh. Hades was pleased with the effectiveness of his pit of fire!

OCEANIDS: Metis, Tyche, Clymene, Eurybia, Amphitrite, Philyra, Rhodos.
TELCHINES: Dexithea, Makelo, Halia.
EAST: Azura, Seth, Typhon, Iasion, Endymion.
OTHER: Centaur Chiron, Charon, Hotep, Petra, Persephone.

Creusa looked on the unbearable horror.

She looked away from Azura screaming, rotating in the flames to look upon Hestia. Hestia was, Creusa was sure, having an orgasm.

~ Clymene ~

A quarter moon after leaving Riverport, Clymene regained consciousness. Her words: "I hurt."

Dionysus reached into the wagon-barge and took her hand. "We have herbs and potions. You will recognize them better than I."

He continued talking comfortingly to her as she cried soft tears of pain.

Clymene mumbled, "Doris screamed 'Murderer'... as I was preparing... to plunge... through the fire... that's how I knew... not to do it... Doris screamed... 'Murderer.'" She drifted back into unconsciousness.

On the seventh day of travel, they reached the way station that marked their arrival at Oursea. It was here where the two Elder Titan brothers had first beheld their great sea. The way station provided a rest stop for travelers either arriving at Oursea or departing to Riverport.

Dionysus settled Clymene as best he could and began to talk to her; as much for his benefit as hers. "Well, Clymene. Here we must decide what to do now; go marching into Olympus Towers demanding to know what they were thinking and demanding they correct the situation? Maybe set sail to Port Spearpoint and get you home to your mother and sisters? Maybe just stay here and swim in Oursea? What would most please you, Oceanid?"

She reached for his hand, found it, squeezed it, and squeaked, "Home, please."

"We start rowing at sunrise."

The next morning, he fed and watered the horses, pointed them up the road toward Tartarus, and said, "You are good horses, Bluewater and Whitewater. Safe travels!" He slapped their rumps.

He treated Clymene as best he could, drug the barge into Oursea, and began rowing the craft westward.

This would take many, many days.

ELDER OLYMPIANS: Hestia, Demeter, Hera, Hades, Poseidon, Zeus
OLYMPIANS: Apollo, Ares, Artemis, Athena, Aphrodite, Dionysus, Hermes,
Hephaestus, Heracles. LIVING TITANS: Oceanus, Tethys, Selene, Elder Oceanids.
DECEASED TITANS: Queen Kiya, Iapetus/Piercer, Cronus.

63. Home

Many, many days passed.

Dionysus stood scanning the horizon for land and the port flags. Blue flags would indicate a heading north of Port Spearpoint; three flags would indicate extremely far north; two would indicate far north; one, a little north. Red flags would indicate a heading too far to the south. Tall Green flags would stand on either side of the port, visible far out at sea.

Dionysus was exhausted. The noon sun beat down. Beat-beat-beat. Like drummers drumming. Beat-beat-beat. Wind accompanied the beat-beat-beat.

-- I *hear oceanids singing -- do you hear your sisters, Clymene? -- singing to us -- and the drummers, drumming? -- Beat-beat-beat. -- I'm tired, Clymene -- and the sun is so hot -- like it wants us to die -- here -- after we have come so far --*

Beat-beat-beat.

He tried to look directly at the sun, but it was too bright. -- *is that true, sun? -- do you wish us to die? --*

The sun said to him, "Die, Dionysus? Why, no. That is not of my concern. But I create the wind which carries you to your far shore. I have nurtured you. It is from me which all things come. I nourish the plants which sustain all things. But live or die as you will. It is not of my concern."

Beat-beat-beat.

He felt his knees begin to buckle but he grabbed the pole flying the white flag of distress. He scanned the horizon. There was neither land nor flags.

Beat-beat-beat.

The chorus sang louder, faster. The sun -- beautiful -- sometimes beautiful red -- sometimes beautiful yellow -- now beautiful blinding white.

Beat-beat-beat.

-- *it's the color of a beautiful white light I once saw -- where did I see that light? -- I don't remember -- but I remember it was beautiful --*

In his mind he heard "Am I that easy to forget, Dionysus? All of us? All will be as it will be. Do that which is your nature."

OCEANIDS: Metis, Tyche, Clymene, Eurybia, Amphitrite, Philyra, Rhodos.
TELCHINES: Dexithea, Makelo, Halia.
EAST: Azura, Seth, Typhon, Iasion, Endymion.
OTHER: Centaur Chiron, Charon, Hotep, Petra, Persephone.

Fortissimo: Beat-beat-beat.

Drifting in and out of reality. He felt himself drifting out.

-- dung, Clymene -- we almost made it -- we were so close --

Two Blue flags appeared: "Set course to SSW!" He did. He collapsed. His head landed on Clymene's stomach.

The pain caused her to jerk up from her sleep. She looked around and oriented herself. With what little strength she had, she pulled Dionysus to rest his head in the crook of her arm. The pain was almost bearable.

She closed her eyes but reached to place his hand into hers. *-- our flag waves in a different direction -- he has changed our course -- he knows our bearings -- the wind will carry us home -- you are my savior, Dionysus -- you are my friend --*

She returned to unconscious sleep.

~

Dionysus opened his eyes. He heard someone scurry away and say, "He is awake Mother Tethys."

He then saw a warm face standing over him. He heard gentle noises that sounded like, "Welcome, Lord Dionysus. You are safe, now."

He muttered, "How is she?"

"She is alive. She calls out to her dead husband, but we have applied ointments to relieve most of the pain. "

"Good. I think she may scar. I kept putting her eye back in when it tried to pop out. She screamed every time, but I think it was the thing to do."

"Yes. You did the correct thing."

"Do you know Philyra? She is my friend. Her son is dead. She will want to know. He was a Centaur, you know. He had this growth out his back -- half-man, half-horse. A gentle, loving person. Tell her that a swordsman cut her son in half. He looks just like a normal man, now. He died valiantly -- defending Tallstone -- he and his archers -- he was an expert archer -- he is dead now -- Philyra will want to know. She is my friend."

"Rest Dionysus. We will talk later."

"Yes. I will rest now." His voice trailed with, "I hope she doesn't scar."

ELDER OLYMPIANS: Hestia, Demeter, Hera, Hades, Poseidon, Zeus
OLYMPIANS: Apollo, Ares, Artemis, Athena, Aphrodite, Dionysus, Hermes,
Hephaestus, Heracles. LIVING TITANS: Oceanus, Tethys, Selene, Elder Oceanids.
DECEASED TITANS: Queen Kiya, Iapetus/Piercer, Cronus.

Tethys stared at the sleeping man for a moment and then said to the attending Oceanid, "Tell Oceanus that Dionysus will not meet with them today. Perhaps a few words tomorrow. Send word to Queen Ariadne of that which Dionysus has told us. As always, I would rejoice if she were my guest for a few days. I understand that her King is here and that she might be required to remain in Graikoi. But, still, she is invited. Tell Metis all that we have learned."

Tethys sat down to stare at the sleeping Dionysus. *-- your hopes will not come to pass, titan -- she will scar --*

Dionysus slept for three days.

Then he rose.

~

Metis entered the room. "Oceanus is on his way. He is angry."

Tethys sat at the head of the long table. Next to her, sat King Theus of Graikoi and his Queen Ariadne; then Ariadne's father King Minos of Kaptara and Chief Nebka of Kemet with his advisor, Hotep; once of Tartarus. Behind the seated counselors, against the wall, sat observers, Dionysus of Everywhere, Djoser -- the young son of Chief Nebka and brother of Hotep, Pilots Rhodos and Iapyx of Tartarus, Pilot Icarus, and Masters Helios and Atlas of Port Spearpoint Deep Labs.

The door opened. A haggard, red-eyed, Oceanus entered the room. There was no greeting, no preamble. "I am pleased to inform you that Metis has told me that all members of your trade delegations are safe. My daughter Amphitrite delivered them into Port Graikoi late last night. They are now resting and doing well. I thank Pilot Rhodos for her report. It was invaluable for our understanding of the situation. She is commended for remaining calm and observant under trying circumstances. Lord Dionysus's observations and my daughter Clymene's condition confirm what we were told."

He gazed around the room making eye contact with each of them.

"We have learned, deduced, debated, argued, discussed, ranted, raved, and sought consensus for a response to what has been done. We have discussed possible futures and possible responses and their effects. What is good, what is just, who and what will be affected, who will die when we

OCEANIDS: Metis, Tyche, Clymene, Eurybia, Amphitrite, Philyra, Rhodos.
TELCHINES: Dexithea, Makelo, Halia.
EAST: Azura, Seth, Typhon, Iasion, Endymion.
OTHER: Centaur Chiron, Charon, Hotep, Petra, Persephone.

do a thing. We have discussed all variations of all possible responses. That which remains is only this: What shall be done?"

He paused. "This is what shall be done. At sundown two days before the second full moon, I shall remove the rock wall upon which Port Spearpoint sets. This will be done in the blink of an eye. The resulting tsunami will place all current Oursea ports under a stade of water within days. Within a quarter moon, Oursea will be level with Middlesea. Metis will command all Oceanids to immediately tell all peoples what is to come, to move to higher grounds, to save whatever they may, to build boats for themselves and their animals. I cannot destroy the evil in the hearts of people, but I can punish and destroy the Olympians. If much of the civilized world is also destroyed, so be it!"

With that, he turned and left the room.

The room sat in silence until Tethys said, "That's going to an impressive waterfall."

Metis departed on her mission. Her words would spread through her Sisterhood as waves from a large rock thrown into still water. Within hours, nearby coastal people would hear of the coming flood. Within days, all people would know of it. The Oceanids in residence at Tartarus went into the Asphodel meadows and told those working the fields and caring for the animals that a flood was coming, and they should take their animals into the hills high above Phlegethon. The Oceanids would attempt to bring large boats to pick up survivors and drowning animals.

The Oceanids failed to mention any of this to the Gods.

But now, in the room of decisions, the kings of the west were ecstatic. They had received all they had asked for and more quickly. Who suspected that Oceanus could remove the sheer cliffs 'in the blink of an eye?' They invited everyone to the 'party room' where there would be beer, wine, and rejoicing.

Tethys shepherded everyone from the room save Dionysus and the woman now named Ariadne. It had been Ariadne, after all, who had grown Port Olympus to be the world power it now was, who had created the great Olympus Towers; a wonder of the world.

Tethys left the two to their sadness.

ELDER OLYMPIANS: Hestia, Demeter, Hera, Hades, Poseidon, Zeus
OLYMPIANS: Apollo, Ares, Artemis, Athena, Aphrodite, Dionysus, Hermes, Hephaestus, Heracles. LIVING TITANS: Oceanus, Tethys, Selene, Elder Oceanids.
DECEASED TITANS: Queen Kiya, Iapetus/Piercer, Cronus.

The man and woman sat in silence as the room emptied.

The man asked, "May I embrace you?"

The woman stood and nodded, "Yes."

Dionysus walked to her and took her in a gentle embrace. Then he lost all reserve and squeezed her body with his entire being. He felt her breasts pressing into his chest. He felt her breathe. She did not resist nor cry out.

He released her, stood back, and asked, "They told you of Chiron?"

Ariadne replied, "Yes. How foolish I was to wish him to be like other men. You opened my eyes."

"You will return to Graikoi, I suppose."

"Yes. My people are enthused with life. Most of the surviving Titans immigrated to Graikoi. With their support and guidance, the people pursue the arts, justice, governance, the joy of living. They will become a great nation, the center of world civilization. I have the organization and management skills necessary to establish the governments of the various settlements. I am fortunate to be their Queen and to have a husband that supports my endeavors. My marriage is one of state. My private affairs remain private with his blessing. Come to Graikoi with me. We could be a team once more."

"No. You are his wife. Send word to me if you ever dispose of him. I will come to you if I must crawl on hands and knees. In the meantime, I will be in Port Kemet. Chief Nebka has ambitious building plans. He has Hotep and plans to use his talents extensively. I must take a detour through Tallstone and retrieve a chest that I left hidden in the woods. The Djoser boy wants to accompany me. He is a smart, outgoing boy. He reminds me of me at that age." He laughed. "Shall we go to a party?"

She replied, "Let's!"

He suddenly reached over and kissed her on her lips.

She returned the kiss, then whispered, "I will be in the lands of Graikoi."

He replied, "I will be in the lands of Kemet."

He stared into her eyes. "I am Dionysus, you are Ariadne. In this story, we must build different worlds. Now, let's go get started building!"

OCEANIDS: Metis, Tyche, Clymene, Eurybia, Amphitrite, Philyra, Rhodos.
TELCHINES: Dexithea, Makelo, Halia.
EAST: Azura, Seth, Typhon, Iasion, Endymion.
OTHER: Centaur Chiron, Charon, Hotep, Petra, Persephone.

64. The Flood

Sunrise.

Oceanus walked into the Port Masters office and told the Gigante superintendent, "Close the port for maintenance. Divert all traffic to surrounding ports. Warn all that there will be extreme turbulence on both seas beginning immediately two days before the second full moon. There can be no ships at sea for a full quarter moon before and after. dismiss all dispensable employees from the port. Call a meeting of the Special Operation Team and review the Special Operations Plan. I shall attend and make sure that all are focused and dedicated to this project. Do you have questions?"

"No, Oceanus. I understand. It will be as you command!"

The Gigantes met.

Oceanus studied each of the thirty-six looking for signs of weakness, of nonchalance, for any sign that they might not be focused and dedicated to the task at hand. They knew what must be done and why and how.

For the remainder of the day, they laboriously began filling each Deep Well with untold amounts of rock and boulders. Upon each fill, they built a thick wooden divider. A Gigante would carry a large barrel of black powder as he carefully climbed down a rope ladder while holding onto a metal wire. He would carefully pour the powder on top of the divider. He would climb back up the ladder with the empty barrel while holding onto the metal wire. He would then repeat the process with a smaller barrel but mixing the new powder and the old with a wooden stick.

This process was repeated over and over in all six Deep Wells for a full quarter moon. After fourteen days of, even by Gigante standards, backbreaking work, the powder reached within the height of eight men from the top. Another thick, wooden platform was gently placed on top of the powder. Boulders were placed on these platforms. A thick watery mixture of sand and powders was poured around the boulders as more boulders were added until the boulders rose above ground level. The watery mixture filled every crack and crevice between the topping boulders. Finished, the Gigantes collapsed from exhaustion.

ELDER OLYMPIANS: Hestia, Demeter, Hera, Hades, Poseidon, Zeus
OLYMPIANS: Apollo, Ares, Artemis, Athena, Aphrodite, Dionysus, Hermes, Hephaestus, Heracles. LIVING TITANS: Oceanus, Tethys, Selene, Elder Oceanids. DECEASED TITANS: Queen Kiya, Iapetus/Piercer, Cronus.

The next morning, Oceanus called everyone together and surveyed the work. "It is the best that could be done. If we fail, then it was beyond the doing of men. We will wait three days to allow the filler rock to solidify."

He then said, "Well done, Gigantes. It has been an honor and a privilege to work with you. Whether a new world or the old world awaits, you will be needed to carry on. Take what you will from this place and immigrate to where you will. Regardless of the outcome, Port Spearpoint will be no more. The west will need you and your knowledge to continue its evolution. Extend my respect to all you meet who will listen. We have lived in interesting times. You are dismissed."

Each Gigante came and embraced Oceanus; several embraced Tethys and Metis who were standing nearby.

They kept one eye on Oceanus to make sure that this was appropriate.

For three days, there was little to do but wait.

The father, mother, and their four living Oceanid daughters celebrated their dead family including their beloved Tyche; murdered at the Northern Dilation.

The daughters pleased their mother by begging to again be told the story of the necklace Tethys always wore. "Tell it just one more time, Mother."

And Oceanus would tell the story of adopting his daughters. "I have never seen bigger eyes than the four little Oceanids had when they stood before me awaiting my reaction to the news that I now had four daughters. Older daughters but precious daughters. Mother was furious, but she grew to love each one."

The last two Elder Titans, old even by Elder Titan standards, talked of the new worlds they had discovered. Of the tribes, of the wonders, how much larger the world than he had imagined when he and Sagacity had left the Clan of the Serpents.

"That was a lifetime, ago," Tethys said. "We were children. Wild, savage children."

"We still are," Oceanus laughed. "You and I never fit in with genteel society. Our daughters are our stand-ins."

OCEANIDS: Metis, Tyche, Clymene, Eurybia, Amphitrite, Philyra, Rhodos.
TELCHINES: Dexithea, Makelo, Halia.
EAST: Azura, Seth, Typhon, Iasion, Endymion.
OTHER: Centaur Chiron, Charon, Hotep, Petra, Persephone.

~ The Last Day ~

They had lived their lives and lived them well. They were old and the world they would now create would be unrecognizable to them. It was time to join their mother, brothers, and sisters.

To maximize their chance of success, Oceanus would initiate the detonation command directly over the three southern Deep Wells; Tethys directly over the three northern Deep Wells. Long ago, Littlerock had strategically dictated the wells be placed near fault lines.

The time came. Oceanus and Tethys, who would die, said farewell to their daughters. Their daughters walked a safe distance beyond the wall and sat down to watch the finish of the penultimate chapter.

The metal wires from each set of three Deep Wells were joined together at a central location and attached to two metal rods. At the proper time, each Titan would insert metal rods into a vessel containing different chemicals. This would transmit the signal to the highly unstable powders in the six Deep Wells.

Nothing on this scale had ever been attempted but if everything worked correctly, which was expected, the wall would be shattered.

Oceanus would blow a whistle to signal Tethys to insert the rods. Everything was configured as planned; everything was done that could be done. The last two Elder Titans walked together to the spear, still where it had been originally placed.

They turned and waved in the direction of their daughters and then turned to look into each other's eyes. Tethys suddenly grabbed Oceanus, kissed him on his lips, his cheeks, his forehead, and then returned to his lips where she bit hard into his lower lip. She laughed, pushed him away, and said "Make it go boom! I'll meet you back here."

She turned, ran to her detonation position, and awaited the sound of his whistle.

Oceanus trotted to his detonation position, looked out toward Oursea, and, as the sun touched the horizon, quietly said, "Yes, you and I shall meet all things in the middle."

He picked up the two rods, blew the whistle, and inserted the rods into the vessel. The earth trembled. He ran toward the spear. He could see

ELDER OLYMPIANS: Hestia, Demeter, Hera, Hades, Poseidon, Zeus
OLYMPIANS: Apollo, Ares, Artemis, Athena, Aphrodite, Dionysus, Hermes,
Hephaestus, Heracles. LIVING TITANS: Oceanus, Tethys, Selene, Elder Oceanids.
DECEASED TITANS: Queen Kiya, Iapetus/Piercer, Cronus.

Tethys running toward him. The ground shook. He lost his footing but regained it and continued running. He saw Tethys, too, fall and get up to continue running. The ground fell away from beneath their feet. They flailed their arms trying to will themselves to each other in the middle. The wall of water from the upper sea engulfed them.

The four living Elder Oceanids stood on safe land to watch the granite wall give way. Water pushed the stone before it and cascaded through where the wall had once been. The immensity was beyond knowing.

Amphitrite watched their ending with sorrow and joy and resignation. --- *- Mother, do you forgive me for being a whore? -- I did what I had to do -- Grandmother said to never regret doing what you had to do -- I don't regret any of it -- it was all necessary for this day to come to pass -- the evil was that I enjoyed doing it -- can you forgive me for that? -- can anyone? -- but here -- in the end -- I need only the forgiveness of myself -- I am what I am --*

Clymene, wearing a headpiece that covered her scars, knew where the towering wall of water was going. What it would do. *-- revenge should be sweet -- I once longed for it -- with hatred in my heart -- with revenge in my mind -- and yet, now -- I love you Hestia -- I love all my Olympian brethren -- that you slaughtered my family is sad beyond bearing -- but in the end -- you are what you are -- at last, I understand and accept grandmother's words -- love everyone -- even the evil --*

Eurybia was overwhelmed with melancholia. *-- my parents are dying – everyone I know around Oursea will either be killed or displaced – father knew that whatever his decision, bad things would happen – will the good outweigh the bad, father? – will anyone ever know? – king Minos, get your ships to safe harbor – salvage what you can – your new world is coming – I am watching it happen – civilization is about to suffer a major setback -- grandmother, please make us do better this time --*

Metis stood watching the unimaginable. *-- mother and father are in that waterfall -- what a wonderful death for the water masters of the world -- extremely impressive -- you were the best parents ever -- we are the most fortunate daughters ever -- oh -- and Hestia – father and mother had to die to make it but they are sending you a gift -- it will be arriving soon – he timed it so that you will be having one of your fabulous parties -- Athena will be there – I'm sorry, Daughter -- at least you will die with your father -- I and Grandmother send our love --*

OCEANIDS: Metis, Tyche, Clymene, Eurybia, Amphitrite, Philyra, Rhodos.
TELCHINES: Dexithea, Makelo, Halia.
EAST: Azura, Seth, Typhon, Iasion, Endymion.
OTHER: Centaur Chiron, Charon, Hotep, Petra, Persephone.

~ Harvest ~

It was to be the greatest full moon party ever.

Even Hades, Persephone, and Hephaestus attended. The victory over the evil Urfa and Tallstone people was being celebrated. Also, the future subjugation of those arrogant western people had to be resolved. Athena was already coming up with wonderful plans to control the vermin.

Zeus stood looking over the moonlit sea beside his beloved wife, Hera, to whom he was always faithful. The sea looked so impressive tonight. Zeus then vaguely remembered he overlooked the sea at Port Olympus, but this was Olympus Towers sitting far inland on the carcass of Tartarus. His brother Poseidon, God of the Sea, must have changed something. -- *that Poseidon -- always busy --*

Hera giggled at what she saw. -- *how delightful! --*

Athena walked to stand beside Zeus and looked out. It took but a moment to consider and she understood that which she saw. She understood war. She understood death. She understood defeat. -- *so, Oceanus could remove the wall -- you will never know, father — there will be no pain --*

She took her father's hand and said, "Dad, I love you so much."

Poseidon, God of the Sea, was agitated. His beloved consort Amphitrite must have been killed at that Tallstone thing. If he found out who killed her, they would be tortured before they died. Without Amphitrite to calm him, Poseidon was usually agitated. He, too, looked out over the moonlit sea. -- *where did all that water come from? --*

Hestia, too, was agitated. Neither Dexithea nor Creusa had come to her. In this wonderful time of complete triumph, Hestia needed someone with whom to celebrate. -- *where are all the servants? —*

She would punish them later. In the meantime, she stared down the atrium at her beloved rotating statue many floors below. -- *something's different -- it looks like water or something around the fire pit —*

She continued to stare. The eternal flame flickered, then was extinguished. She was enraged. -- *this will not do! -- Hades will hear of this! -- he will relight my flame immediately! --*

ELDER OLYMPIANS: Hestia, Demeter, Hera, Hades, Poseidon, Zeus
OLYMPIANS: Apollo, Ares, Artemis, Athena, Aphrodite, Dionysus, Hermes, Hephaestus, Heracles. LIVING TITANS: Oceanus, Tethys, Selene, Elder Oceanids. DECEASED TITANS: Queen Kiya, Iapetus/Piercer, Cronus.

She turned to go find Hades but saw the Olympians standing at the window, staring out. Hestia joined them and froze. In the distance and rushing toward her, she saw the wall of water, taller than Olympus Towers. It took but a moment to comprehend. -- *Spearpoint!* -- *Oceanus!* -- *I accomplished everything and still you defeat me, Grandmother* -- *damn you!* -- *the gods are all-powerful* -- *we own the world and everything in it* -- *I have the power and you have nothing but your damnable love!* -- *still, you prevail* -- *how can this be?* --

Hestia whispered to Poseidon, "Brother, make it go away!"

The Gods watched as destiny came for them.

As the moonlit sea continued to rapidly rise.

As Olympus Towers began to tremble.

As a wave of unimaginable height washed over them.

~

So it was, beyond that which was in their minds and that which others freely gave them, the Gods had no power at all.

Yet, those who blindly follow the path of self-proclaimed Gods live on.

As do those who find and follow the path of the Titans.

OCEANIDS: Metis, Tyche, Clymene, Eurybia, Amphitrite, Philyra, Rhodos.
TELCHINES: Dexithea, Makelo, Halia.
EAST: Azura, Seth, Typhon, Iasion, Endymion.
OTHER: Centaur Chiron, Charon, Hotep, Petra, Persephone.

###

The Beginning of Civilization: Mythologies Told True
continues in
Book 4. *Isis and Osiris: Rise of Egypt*
that,
among other foundational narratives, including Djoser's,
continues the stories of
Dionysus, Ariadne, and Charon
-- the basis for
the greatest of all Egyptian mythologies,
the love story of Isis and Osiris.

ELDER OLYMPIANS: Hestia, Demeter, Hera, Hades, Poseidon, Zeus
OLYMPIANS: Apollo, Ares, Artemis, Athena, Aphrodite, Dionysus, Hermes,
Hephaestus, Heracles. LIVING TITANS: Oceanus, Tethys, Selene, Elder Oceanids.
DECEASED TITANS: Queen Kiya, Iapetus/Piercer, Cronus.

###

OCEANIDS: Metis, Tyche, Clymene, Eurybia, Amphitrite, Philyra, Rhodos.
TELCHINES: Dexithea, Makelo, Halia.
EAST: Azura, Seth, Typhon, Iasion, Endymion.
OTHER: Centaur Chiron, Charon, Hotep, Petra, Persephone.

APPENDIX

AUTHOR'S NOTES

The word "Titan" was originally defined by the Greek writer, Hesiod, who gave a double etymology. He derived it from titaino, "to strain" and tisis, "vengeance." He wrote that Ouranos gave them the name Titans "in reproach; for they strained and did a fearful deed, and that vengeance for it would come afterward."

The word "Olympus" is a pre-greek word and is generally thought to have originally meant "mountain" or "high place." In this work, the etymology "high place" is assumed.

My fictional Tartarus lies in the location of a proposed site for Atlantis as described by Robert Sarmast in his book *Discovery of Atlantis, the Startling Case for the Island of Cyprus* by Origen Press. Sarmast maintains that in 10,000 B.C.E. the plains of Cypress were not submerged by the Mediterranean and that this now-submerged landmass matches Plato's description of Atlantis in all respects.

The location of my fictional Tallstone is the Gobekli Tepe archeological site in southeast Turkey. My fictional Urfa is located fifteen miles away in the modern Turkish city of Sanliurfa, which claims to be the oldest city in the world.

My fictional Port Spearpoint lies over the Strait of Messina, the submerged narrow strait between eastern Sicily and Calabria, Italy. It is less than two miles wide at its most narrow point.

GREEK MYTHOLOGY PRIMER

The Earth gave birth to the Sky, the Mountains, and the Sea. These four gave birth to everyone else.

Anthropomorphically, Gaia gave birth to Ouranos, Ourea, and Pontus. Then it got complicated.

By Ouranos, Gaia gave birth to the twelve Elder Titans, the three Cyclops, and the three Hecatoncheires.

By Pontus, Gaia birth to Nereus, Thaumas, Phorcys, Ceto, and Eurybia. These children gave birth to myriad sea gods, goddesses, and nymphs.

ELDER OLYMPIANS: Hestia, Demeter, Hera, Hades, Poseidon, Zeus
OLYMPIANS: Apollo, Ares, Artemis, Athena, Aphrodite, Dionysus, Hermes, Hephaestus, Heracles. LIVING TITANS: Oceanus, Tethys, Selene, Elder Oceanids.
DECEASED TITANS: Queen Kiya, Iapetus/Piercer, Cronus.

By his splattered blood, Ouranos gave virgin birth to the Giants, the Erinyes, the Meliads, and maybe Aphrodite.

By Oceanus, Tethys gave birth to the many Oceanids who were Ocean and River Goddesses, and to the many Potamoi who were River Gods.

By Coeus, Phoebe gave birth to Leto and Asteria.

By Crius, Eurybia gave birth to Astraeus, Pallas, and Perses.

By Hyperion, Theia gave birth to Helios, Selene, and Eos - the Sun, the Moon, and the Dawn.

By Iapetus, Oceanid Clymene gave birth to Atlas, Prometheus, Epimetheus, and Meoetius - the Fathers of Mankind.

By Cronus, Rhea gave birth to Hestia, Demeter, Hera, Hades, Poseidon, and Zeus - the six Elder Olympians.

By Zeus,
Olympian sister Hera gave birth to Olympians Ares and Hephaestus
    and to mortals Hebe and Eileithyia,
the rape of Olympian sister Demeter gave birth to Persephone,
Titanide Aunt Mnemosyne gave birth to the "Muses,"
Titanide Aunt Themis gave birth to the "Horae" and "The Fates,"
Titanide Leto gave birth to twin Olympians Apollo and Artemis,
Oceanid Metis possibly gave birth to Olympian Athena,
the mortal Theban Princess Semele gave birth to Olympian Dionysus,
the mortal woman Alcmene gave birth to Heracles,
Pleiades Maia gave birth to Olympian Hermes.

~

The twelve Elder Titans were Oceanus, Coeus, Crius, Hyperion, Iapetus, Cronus, Themis, Mnemosyne, Phoebe, Tethys, Theia, and Rhea.

~

The twelve Olympians were the six children of Cronus and Rhea including Hestia, Demeter, Hera, Hades, Poseidon, and Zeus plus six of the many children fathered by Zeus including Apollo, Ares, Artemis, Athena, Demeter, Aphrodite, Dionysus, Hermes, and Hephaestus. The names of the last six vary within different traditions.

OCEANIDS: Metis, Tyche, Clymene, Eurybia, Amphitrite, Philyra, Rhodos.
TELCHINES: Dexithea, Makelo, Halia.
EAST: Azura, Seth, Typhon, Iasion, Endymion.
OTHER: Centaur Chiron, Charon, Hotep, Petra, Persephone.

GLOSSARY OF NAMES

biy = "born in the year" is referenced from the birth of Vanam.
cf = "contracted from" is the source name etymology.
IGR = "In Greek Mythology"

Abra was a highly trained Dactyl who rose to become a Captain in the Olympian Army. He led the Southern Army in the war against the east.

Aeolus was the first elected chief of Port Kaptara. See Kaptara.

Achaeous was the general of Port Kaptara.

Abas was the Port Olympus transportation dispatcher.
IGM there were several by the name Abas; a centaur, a companion to Perseus, and more.

Achelous was the first son of Oceanus and Tethys. Tethys gave birth to him in a river and called him a Potamoi.
IGM Achelous was a son of Tethys, a river god, father of the Sirens, nymphs, and others.

Acmon was Executive Assistant to Charon in M3.
IGM Acmon was a Dactyl, named "The Anvil."

Admete was Philyra's Executive Assistant.
IGM Admete was an Oceanid and companion to Persephone when she was abducted. Admete represents unwedded maidens.

Alastor was the black horse that pulled Hades' chariot.
IGM Alastor was the black horse that pulled Hades' chariot.

Alcyoneous was the great Chief of the Gigantes. He led the battle of the Gigantes against the Olympians attempting to regain control of Port Olympus for Queen Kiya.
IGM Alcyoneous was a Giant and the opponent of Heracles during the Gigantomachy.

Alpheus was the second son of Oceanus and Tethys. She gave birth to him in a river and called him a Potamoi.
IGR Son of Oceanus and Tethys. A river god.

Amazons were female scholars in the Art of War who were named Otreta, Myrene, and Hippolyta.
IGM Amazons were the daughters of Ares and nymph Harmonia and were originally from Libya. Queen Otreta was consort to Ares. Hippolyta wore a magic girdle. Myrene invented the cavalry.

Ambrosia was a potion that increased life expectancy by a factor of five. Hestia discovered and improved upon Kiya's recipe for Red Nectar.
IGM Ambrosia was the nectar of the Gods served to them by Hebe.

ELDER OLYMPIANS: Hestia, Demeter, Hera, Hades, Poseidon, Zeus
OLYMPIANS: Apollo, Ares, Artemis, Athena, Aphrodite, Dionysus, Hermes,
Hephaestus, Heracles. LIVING TITANS: Oceanus, Tethys, Selene, Elder Oceanids.
DECEASED TITANS: Queen Kiya, Iapetus/Piercer, Cronus.

Amphitrite *(am-fih-TRI-tee)* was the biological daughter of Oceanus and Tethys. She became wife to Poseidon, mentor to the Telchines, and confidant to Philyra.
IGM Wife of Poseidon and Queen of the Sea.

Aphrodite was a party girl who would do anything to be an Olympian and was everyone's favorite partner. BIY 47.
IGM Aphrodite was the daughter of Zeus and Oceanid Dione (in one tradition). She was consort to all the male Olympians and many others. Goddess of love, beauty, and sexuality.

Apollo was the son of Zeus and Titanide Leto and twin to Artemis. He was born a Titan but gravitated toward the Olympian lifestyle. BIY 47.
IGM Apollo was the son of Zeus and Leto, father of many children, and God of many things.

Ares was the Olympian son of Zeus and Hera. He was brutal and sadistic.
IGM Ares was the son of Zeus and Hera. He fathered many children. One of his consorts was Aphrodite. He was the God of War.

Ariadne was the name Oceanid Philyra took after exiling herself from Port Olympus. See Philyra.
IGM Philyra was a Cretan princess associated with mazes and the Minotaur. She may have been the wife of Dionysus.

Artemis was the daughter of Zeus and Titanide Leto. She was twin to Apollo, born a Titan but gravitated to the Olympian lifestyle BIY 87.
IGM Artemis was a daughter of Zeus and Titanide Leto. She was the Goddess of the Hunt and had no consorts or any children.

Athena was a daughter of Zeus and Oceanid Metis; possibly from Zeus's third ejaculation. She was a loud and dominating Olympian who dressed in armor and maintained that hers was a virgin birth directly from her father's mouth. BIY 84.
IGM Athena was the firstborn and favorite child of Zeus. She sprang fully grown from his head in full armor. She had no consorts or children. She was the patron of Athens and other cities. Goddess of wisdom and battle strategy.

Atlas was the son of Titane Iapetus and Oceanid Clymene. He was the keeper of the Deep Lab world maps. BIY 47.
IGM Atlas was one of the four fathers of mankind.

Aulos was a musical wind instrument much like a flute but with a reed. Often two were played simultaneously as a double aulos.

Azura succeeded Valki as the leader of Urfa. She was the wife of Seth and the mother of Enosh. As the leader of Urfa, she was the executive

OCEANIDS: Metis, Tyche, Clymene, Eurybia, Amphitrite, Philyra, Rhodos.
TELCHINES: Dexithea, Makelo, Halia.
EAST: Azura, Seth, Typhon, Iasion, Endymion.
OTHER: Centaur Chiron, Charon, Hotep, Petra, Persephone.

director of the Winter Solstice Festival. BIY 80.

In Judaic tradition, Azura was the wife of Seth.

Brown-wine was the common name for Brandy.

Cadabra was a Dactyl who rose to become a Captain in the Olympian Army. He led the Northern Army in the war against the east.

Calpeia was a local woman who befriended Tethys and Oceanus at what is now the Strait of Gibraltar.

In archeology, this name is given to the remains of a woman who lived in 7500 B.C.E. and whose DNA is identical to a modern-day woman.

Cave Mushroom was a local mushroom containing psilocybin that, when ingested, caused a psychedelic response in the brain.

Celmis was a Port Olympus M3 Department Manager.

IGM Celmis was a Dactyl named "The Smelter."

Clan of the Serpent was the second tribe to be designated "Clan" and was a founding member of the Winter Solstice Festival. Notable members include Chief Talaimai, Hunter/Chief Vanam, Moonwatchers Karan and Nilla, Elder Women Panti and Palai, Hunters Cirantatu, Valuvana, Maiyana, Master Stonecutters Pumi and Kattar, Gatherer Amma. Notable members acquired from other tribes include Kiya, Valki, and Skywatcher Voutch. The tribe was originally Chief Talaimai's and then Chief Vanam's.

Chief Vanamtwo was the retired chief of Clan of the Serpent, successor to Chief Armstrong, and namesake of the original Great Chief Vanam. He became a member of the Urfa Council of Chiefs and a director on the Winter Solstice Festival Committee.

Chief Vanamfour was the current Clan of the Serpent Chief, grandson of Chief Vanamtwo, and bitter namesake of Great Chief Vanam. He became enamored with the Olympians because of their role in killing Queen Kiya.

Charon *(KEH-run)* was a cafe server who became a powerful Lord and Chief of Mines. He managed the building of Olympus Towers. BIY 86.

IGM Charon was a psychopomp, the ferryman of Hades who carries souls across the rivers Styx and Acheron that divided the world of the living from the world of the dead.

Chiron *(KAI-run)* was the deformed son of Oceanid Philyra and Elder Titan Cronus. Biy 76.

IGM Chiron was a beloved Centaur.

ELDER OLYMPIANS: Hestia, Demeter, Hera, Hades, Poseidon, Zeus
OLYMPIANS: Apollo, Ares, Artemis, Athena, Aphrodite, Dionysus, Hermes, Hephaestus, Heracles. LIVING TITANS: Oceanus, Tethys, Selene, Elder Oceanids.
DECEASED TITANS: Queen Kiya, Iapetus/Piercer, Cronus.

Clymene *(cli-MEH-nee)* was the adopted daughter of Rivermaster and Tethys and the third of the Elder Oceanids. She married Elder Titan Piercer and gave birth to four sons. Biy 33.

IGM: Iapetus and Clymene gave birth to Atlas, Prometheus, Epimetheus, and Meoetius; the Fathers of Mankind.

Coeus aka Sagacity. See Sagacity.

Color Girls were the corps of women who hosted, or had once hosted, the opening ceremonies of the Winter Solstice Festival. They became the entertainment guild responsible for providing entertainment both for the festival and quarter moon Urfa public entertainment. The newest members were Daphne, Leah, and Rebecca. The oldest member, and chief, were Abigail. Also, Edna.

CoM3 was shorthand for "Port Olympus Chief of Metals Mining and Manufacturing."

The **Common Language** was the language spoken by most Neolithic tribes within the Levant. It evolved as tribes traded young women for mates to the men in other tribes. The women of their new tribe would learn the words of the new member's tribe and their expanded vocabularies would be passed on to their children. Different levels of sophistication evolved as the tribes moved from a nomadic lifestyle, without possessions, to a sedimentary lifestyle, with possessions. It should be recognized that by the Neolithic period, people were at least, if not more, as intelligent and forward-looking as we.

Creusa was an assistant to Philyra, then a Lord, then an assistant to Hestia, then Chief-of-Chiefs of Port Olympus.

Crius aka Starmaster. See Starmaster.

IGM Elder Titane Crius and Oceanid Eurybia gave birth to Astraeus, Pallas, and Perses.

Cronos was the sixth son of Kiya and her only son by Pumi. Because of his parentage, he was driven to be successful in all things. He became the Chief-of-Chief of Port Olympus and eventually became King of the Titans. He married Elder Titanide Rhea in the first true marriage. The two gave birth to six children who would become the Elder Olympians. By his executive assistant, Philyra, he fathered Chiron, who was physically deformed.

IGM Elder Titan Cronus and sister Elder Titanide Rhea gave birth to all Elder Olympians. See Elder Olympians. Cronus also fathered the first Centaur by Oceanid Philyra.

OCEANIDS: Metis, Tyche, Clymene, Eurybia, Amphitrite, Philyra, Rhodos.
TELCHINES: Dexithea, Makelo, Halia.
EAST: Azura, Seth, Typhon, Iasion, Endymion.
OTHER: Centaur Chiron, Charon, Hotep, Petra, Persephone.

A **Dactyl** was a specialist working with metals in the Port Olympus Metals Mining and Manufacturing (CoM3) department. They were Acmon, Celmis, Damnameneus, Idas, Paionios, Epimedes, Lasios, among others. IGM Dactyls were metalsmiths and metal workers.

Damnameneus was a Dactyl and CoM3 Department manager. IGM Damnameneus was a Dactyl called "The Hammer."

Deep Lab was the remote research facility established by Littlerock with the original intent of researching Queen Kiya's question of "how would one remove the granite wall which Port Spearpoint sits upon?" It evolved into a research center for advanced technology.

Deep Well was one of six elevator shafts drilled through the cliff upon which Port Spearpoint sat and used to transport goods between Oursea and Middlesea.

Demeter *(dee-ME-ter)* was the second child of Cronus and Rhea. She was an Olympian and a Ghod. Biy 62.
IGM Demeter was raped by Zeus and bore Persephone. The birth order of the Elder Olympians is convoluted. Goddess of the harvest, fertility, and law.

Dionysus *(dai-uh-NAI-suhs)* was a son of Zeus by Princess Semele; possibly from Zeus's first ejaculation. Dionysus was the inventor and bringer of wine. Initially spurned by his father, he adopted the Titans as his real family. In his youth, he was a party animal and drinking buddy with his half-brother, Heracles. He became an Olympian, a Titan, and a Ghod. Biy 84.
IGM Dionysus was an Olympian in some traditions but not an Olympian in other traditions. His mythology is great, complex, and important. He was God of Wine among other things.

Einkorn was a wild grain domesticated into wheat by Valki.

Elder Olympians were the six children of Cronus and Rhea. They were Hestia, Demeter, Hera, Hades, Poseidon, and Zeus.

Elder Titans were the six sons and six adopted daughters of Kiya. The Titanes were Oceanus aka Rivermaster aka Mutal, Coeus aka Sagacity aka Iran, Crius aka Starmaster aka Manar, Hyperion aka Watchman aka Nan, Iapetus aka Piercer aka Ain, and Cronus. The Titanides were Themis, Mnemosyne, Phoebe, Tethys, Theia, and Rhea. The Titanes were all children by Vanam except for Cronus who was fathered by Pumi. The Titanides were all adopted.
IGM the Elder Titans were all children of Gaia by Ouranos.

ELDER OLYMPIANS: Hestia, Demeter, Hera, Hades, Poseidon, Zeus
OLYMPIANS: Apollo, Ares, Artemis, Athena, Aphrodite, Dionysus, Hermes,
Hephaestus, Heracles. LIVING TITANS: Oceanus, Tethys, Selene, Elder Oceanids.
DECEASED TITANS: Queen Kiya, Iapetus/Piercer, Cronus.

Enceladus was a Gigante faithful aid to Kiya. He immigrated from Urfa after being brought there to presumably die as a child.
IGM Enceladus was one of the Giants and opponent of Athena during the Gigantomachy.

Enosh was the son of Seth and Azura and a Shaman Scholar.

Elysium Fields was the southern area between Tartarus and Oursea.
IGM Elysium Fields was one of the areas of the underworld and it was reserved for heroes.

Epimedes was an M3 research management dactyl.

Erinyes.
IGM Erinyes, "The Furies," were female, underworld deities who punished evil. Their names were Alecto, Megaera, and Tisiphone.

Eurybia was an adopted daughter of Rivermaster and Tethys and the fourth of the first four Elder Oceanids. She married Titane Starmaster.
IGM Elder Titan Crius and Oceanid Eurybia gave birth to Astraeus, Pallas, and Perses.

Giants, in this work, are conflated with Gigantes. See Gigantes.
IGM Giants were a race of extremely strong, aggressive extremely large people. They were the bane of the Olympians.

The **Gigantomachy** was the battle whereby the Olympians defeated the Gigantes and gained complete control of the lands of Tartarus.
IGM the Gigantomachy was the great war whereby the Olympians defeated the Giants.

Gigantes were a tribe of exceptionally strong but otherwise normal-sized people who befriended the Titans.
IGM see Giants.

Ghod was a title invented by Dionysus to separate the Olympians from the rest of humanity. Ghods were not a "social class" and therefore did not compete, or deal with, the lower classes. They were above everything and owned everything. All people would, in theory, fulfill their every desire. With the writings of Teumessian, the word morphed into "Gods."

Hades was the third child born to Elder Titane Cronus and Elder Titanide Rhea. He abducted and married his niece, Persephone. He eventually became the God of the Underworld. Biy 65.
IGM, the same.

Hebe was the daughter of Olympian Zeus and his sister-wife Olympian Hera. She was the cupbearer for their Ambrosia.
IGM Hebe was the daughter of Zeus and his sister Hera. Consort to Heracles. Cupbearer for the Olympians. Goddess of Eternal Youth.

OCEANIDS: Metis, Tyche, Clymene, Eurybia, Amphitrite, Philyra, Rhodos.
TELCHINES: Dexithea, Makelo, Halia.
EAST: Azura, Seth, Typhon, Iasion, Endymion.
OTHER: Centaur Chiron, Charon, Hotep, Petra, Persephone.

Hephaestus *(heph-A-stus)* was the son of Zeus and his sister Hera and was an Olympian. He worked in the Port Olympus Metals Department and became a master working with metals.
IGM Hephaestus was a son of Zeus and Hera, God of fire and metalworking. Aphrodite and Aglaea were his consorts. He had several children.

Hera was the third child of Cronus and Rhea and an Elder Olympian. She married her brother Zeus and was insanely jealous of her husband's affairs. She was not as bright as her siblings and loved her wine. Biy 63.
IGM Hera was the wife of her brother Zeus, Goddess of Marriage and Birth, and was insanely jealous and vindictive of his many liaisons. She gave birth to Olympians Ares and Hephaestus and non-Olympians Hebe and Eileithyia.

Hecatoncheires *(hek-a-TAHN-keh-rees)* was a cadre of 50 fighting men trained to fight together as a fierce single unit. The men did not have individual names, only the name of their cadre. The three cadres initially retained by Hestia were Briareus, Cottus, and Gyges.
IGM the Hecatoncheires were three giant extremely strong creatures with 50 heads and 100 hands. Their names were Briareus, Cottus, and Gyges.

Helios was the son of Hyperion aka Watchman and Theia and older brother to Selene. He became 'Master Scholar of Flight' at Port Spearpoint Deep Lab and reported to Oceanus.
IGM. God of the Sun

Heracles was a half-brother of Dionysus through Zeus. His exceptional strength was instrumental in assisting Athena to defeat the Gigantes at the battle of Port Olympus. He was eventually accepted as one of the Ghods. Biy 85.
IGM, a son of Zeus who became an Olympian.

Hermes was a son of Zeus by a distant relative. He became an Olympian and was a chief messenger at Port Olympus.
IGM Hermes was the son of Zeus by Pleiades Maia. He had several consorts and several children. He is considered the herald of the gods.

Hestia was the firstborn child of Titane Cronus and Titanide Rhea. She became the dominant member of her family and Chief-of-Chiefs of Port Olympus. She made and unmade kings, initiated the ouster of the Titans, and was victorious in the war with the Gigantes Biy 60.
IGM Hestia had no consorts or children, remained a perpetual virgin, and was Goddess of Hearth, Home, the State, and Virginity. The birth order of the Elder Olympians is convoluted.

Hotep was a builder and stonemason from Port Kemet and Chief Kemet's grandson.
In Egyptian history, Imhotep was a deified architect and builder.

ELDER OLYMPIANS: Hestia, Demeter, Hera, Hades, Poseidon, Zeus
OLYMPIANS: Apollo, Ares, Artemis, Athena, Aphrodite, Dionysus, Hermes,
Hephaestus, Heracles. LIVING TITANS: Oceanus, Tethys, Selene, Elder Oceanids.
DECEASED TITANS: Queen Kiya, Iapetus/Piercer, Cronus.

Hyperion aka Watchman. See Watchman.
IGM Elder Titane Hyperion and his sister Elder Titanide Theia gave birth to the Shining Children. These were Helios the Sun, Selene the Moon, and Eos the Dawn.

Iapetus aka Piercer. See Piercer.
IGM Elder Titane Iapetus and Oceanid Clymene gave birth to Atlas, Prometheus, Epimetheus, and Meoetius. They are considered the Fathers of Mankind.

Iapyx was the commander of Airboat 313.

Idas was an M3 Dactyl.
IGM Idas was one of four Idaean Dactyl's, called "the little finger."

Inachus was the third son of Elder Titane Oceanus and Elder Titanide Tethys. Tethys gave birth to him in a river and called him a Potamoi.
IGM Inachus was a son of Titane Oceanus and his sister Titanide Tethys. He was a river god. And, maybe, the first King of Argos.

Kaptara. See Port Kaptara.

Kemet, the man, was the leader of a tribe encountered by Titane Starmaster and Oceanid Metis during their circumference of Oursea. See Port Kemet.

Kemet, the lands, was the lands of Chief Kemet which eventually became the land of Egypt.

Kepten was the Port Olympus café patio chief of servers.

Kiya *(KEE-ya)* was the high-born, intellectual daughter of Chief Irakka and Elder Woman Naman of the Tribe of Irakka. In year 18, she was charged to Vanam of the Tribe of Chief Talaimai. In year 43, she and her children were banished. She founded Tartarus, directed the building of Port Olympus, and became Queen of the Titans. BIY 4, DIY 99.
IGM Gaia was the Earth. See Greek Mythology.

Kopar was copper. See Metals Workshop.

Lands of Tartarus was the island of extant Cypress including Tartarus, Port Olympus, Phlegethon Mines, Overlook Point, et al. Renamed Olympia by the Olympians.

Lasios was an M3 research management dactyl.

Littlerock was Clan of the Serpent Stone Cutter for Chief Vanam's tribe and a one-time apprentice to Pumi. Late in life, he became an apprentice to Piercer in geology and, with Piercer, founded Metallurgy.

OCEANIDS: Metis, Tyche, Clymene, Eurybia, Amphitrite, Philyra, Rhodos.
TELCHINES: Dexithea, Makelo, Halia.
EAST: Azura, Seth, Typhon, Iasion, Endymion.
OTHER: Centaur Chiron, Charon, Hotep, Petra, Persephone.

Littlestar was an apprentice to Vaniyal, Clan of the Lion Skywatcher. He developed the concept of using shadows cast by Tallstone to better understand the motion of the constellations. He eventually became Master-of-Masters at Tallstone.

Lords were the Port Olympus Managers with offices on the 14th floor. They were the buffer between the Olympian Ghods above them and the working classes beneath them. Well paid and powerful, they were treated with deference by the Olympians.

Marmaros was a white rock found in massive quantities at the cliffs of Tartarus near Overlook Point. i.e., marble.

Marsyas was a follower and aide to Dionysus.
IGM Marsyas was an aulos musician who challenged Apollo to a contest and lost.

Messagebox was a rudimentary telegraph developed at the Port Spearpoint 'Deep Labs.'

Metals Workshop was the workshop built by Piercer and Littlerock to experiment with Piercer's 'colored rocks.' It was built to explore the properties of the plentiful nearby rocks that were easily melted and could then be hammered into flattened shapes. These rocks -- blue azurite, bright green malachite, and red cuprite -- contained 'Kopar', i.e., copper. Littlestar then worked with 'Tinom,' i.e., Cassiterite, a tin oxide that can easily be reduced to tin. Littlerock discovered that mixing copper and tin yielded a more versatile metal he named 'Orichalcum,' i.e., bronze.

Metis was the dominant of the four daughters adopted by Tethys and Rivermaster and was the first of the Elder Oceanids. She was influential and powerful and influential in founding new civilizations. She was the mother of Athena by Olympian Zeus.
IGM Metis gave birth to Athena by Zeus but there are several different traditions.

Middlesea was the body of water between Port Spearpoint and the Atlantic Ocean and separated from the lower Oursea by the sheer wall upon which Port Spearpoint is located.

Mnemosyne *(neh-MOZ-eh-nee)* was the second adopted daughter of Kiya. She was an Elder Titanide and third in power among the Titans after her mother and older sister. She was a consort to Zeus and mothered several of his children. IGM by Zeus, Mnemosyne gave birth to the Muses. Their names were Calliope, Clio, Melpomene, and possibly six others.

Moirai.
IGM the Moirai were the three goddesses of destiny who controlled the fate of everyone. Their names were Clotho, Lachesis, and Atropos.

Mouflons were wild sheep native to Cypress and eastern Turkey and ancestors of domesticated sheep.

Nerites was Port Olympus Chief Dispatch.
IGM Nerites was the only brother of the 50 Nereids sea-nymphs, a beautiful boy, a boyhood friend of pre-Olympian Aphrodite, and Poseidon's charioteer and lover.

Noam was the Executive Assistant and adopted daughter of Azura. She was a special friend of Enosh.

Northport was hot air balloon port to the northeast of Port Spearpoint.

Oceanus aka Rivermaster. See Rivermaster.
IGM Elder Titane Oceanus and his sister Elder Titanide Tethys gave birth to the Oceanids and the Potamoi. They were water goddesses and river gods.

Oceanids were a sorority of unrelated, free-spirited women who learned to love and live off the sea independently of any traditional lifestyle. Their founders were Metis, Tyche, Clymene, and Eurybia who were adopted by Titans Rivermaster and Tethys. Their influence and attitudes spread to other young girls without families who collectively called themselves Oceanids. They taught one another all arts including reading, writing, and sexuality. They were nurturing, helpful, and intelligent.
IGM Oceanids were the 3000 water nymphs who were the daughters of Oceanus and Tethys.

Olympians were the six Elder Olympians (see Elder Olympians) plus six more fathered by Zeus with various women. The second-generation Olympians were Apollo, Ares, Artemis, Athena, Demeter, Aphrodite, Dionysus, Hermes, and Hephaestus. The names of the last six vary within different traditions.

The **Olympus Towers Report** was the report containing the Olympian's specifications for their new extremely tall residence.

Olympus Towers was the ziggurat step pyramid home to the Olympian Ghods. It was built over the Titan settlement of Tartarus.

Onos was the donkey that pulled the wagon of Dionysus and his followers. Etymology: "donkey."

OCEANIDS: Metis, Tyche, Clymene, Eurybia, Amphitrite, Philyra, Rhodos.
TELCHINES: Dexithea, Makelo, Halia.
EAST: Azura, Seth, Typhon, Iasion, Endymion.
OTHER: Centaur Chiron, Charon, Hotep, Petra, Persephone.

Orichalcum *(ori-CAL-cum)* was a yellowish-brown metal made from copper plus tin, i.e., bronze. See Metals Workshop.

Otreta. See Amazon

Oursea was the sea discovered by Rivermaster and Sagacity on their scouting expedition. It surrounds the island containing Tartarus. It is the western portion of the Mediterranean from the Strait of Messina to the shores of Syria. The western bank was delineated, at the time, by the sheer cliffs rising from the Strait of Messina.

Overlook Point was the entry point into the land of the Titans. It was located at the end of the narrow neck of land connecting the mainland with the almost island.

Pace. One pace is approximately 60 inches.

Palai was an original inhabitant, and the first Elder Woman, of Urfa. When younger, she was the Clan of the Serpent Elder Woman.

Panti was Kiya's successor as Clan of the Serpent Elder Woman. She was originally in line for the position rather than Kiya.

Paionios was a CoM3 research management dactyl.

Periphas was a Prince and subsequent King of the Graikoi frontier.

Paravi was a senior Urfa Elder Woman. When younger, she was the Clan of the Aurochs Elder Woman.

Persephone *(per-SEPH-o-nee)* was the daughter of Demeter by Zeus. She was abducted by Hades and became his wife. She eventually ruled Tartarus as "Queen of the Colored Fields."
IGM aka Kore. She was the wife of Hades with whom she ruled the Underworld. She was an important figure, along with her mother, in the Eleusinian mysteries which predate Greek Mythology. She had several children including, in some traditions, Dionysus.

Petra was Port Olympus Chief of Rock Operations.

Phidias was a Marble sculptor artist specializing in sculpting the Olympian Ghods.
In Greek history, he was the Sculpturer of Zeus.

Phlegethon was the camp near Overlook Point that housed Piercers mines and workshops.
IGM Phlegethon was "Fire Flaming," one of the six rivers of the Underworld running parallel to the river Styx.

ELDER OLYMPIANS: Hestia, Demeter, Hera, Hades, Poseidon, Zeus
OLYMPIANS: Apollo, Ares, Artemis, Athena, Aphrodite, Dionysus, Hermes,
Hephaestus, Heracles. LIVING TITANS: Oceanus, Tethys, Selene, Elder Oceanids.
DECEASED TITANS: Queen Kiya, Iapetus/Piercer, Cronus.

Philyra *(phil-EE-ra)* was an Oceanid who became Executive Assistant to Port Olympus Chief-of-Chiefs Hestia and then Hestia's replacement. After leaving the Port, she took the name, Ariadne. See Ariadne. Biy 52.
IGM Philyra gave birth to the first Centaur, fathered by Cronus, and may have become the wife of Dionysus.

Phoebe was an adopted daughter of Kiya and an Elder Titanide She married Elder Titan Sagacity.
IGM Phoebe and Coeus gave birth to Leto and Asteria.

Piercer was the fifth son of Kiya by Vanam. He became the first geologist and metallurgist. He and Elder Oceanid Clymene parented Atlas, Prometheus, Epimetheus, and Meoetius. His original name, Ain, was later changed to Iapetus by direction of Port Olympus management.
IGM See Iapetus.

Porphyrion was a Gigante extremely skilled in warfare who trained Kiya and her children in the intricacies of hand-to-hand attacks which was not widely known at the time.
IGM Porphyrion was one of the Giants who fought in the Gigantomachy.

Port Graikoi was the third seaport founded by the Titans. It was the second founded by Oceanus and Tethys. Graikoi evolved into Greece.

Port Kaptara was the second seaport founded by the Titans. It was the first founded by Oceanus and Tethys. Kaptara evolved into Crete.

Port Kemet, founded by Starmaster and Metis, was the fifth seaport founded by the Titans. Originally, it was only an obelisk marking a rendezvous spot for Titans and Chief Kemet. It evolved into Egypt.

Port Olympus was the first port built by the Titans. It contained the great step pyramid Port Olympus office/resident building.

Port Olympus Building was the step pyramid Port Olympus office/resident building.
Atrium: shaft running the height of the building ending into a pond at ground level. Being thrown down the atrium was an expression of Olympian displeasure.
Ground Floor: Atrium pond, Port dispatch, cafe with an outdoor patio.
Tenth floor: CoM3 residence. Olympus Towers model.
Twelfth floor: Philyra's residence.
Thirteenth floor: Executive offices for the management Lords.
Fourteenth floor: Olympian quarters, dining hall.
Fifteenth floor: Offices of the Olympians.
Sixteenth floor: Office for the reigning chief and then the Olympian Ghods.
Roof: View of the harbor. Party place.

OCEANIDS: Metis, Tyche, Clymene, Eurybia, Amphitrite, Philyra, Rhodos.
TELCHINES: Dexithea, Makelo, Halia.
EAST: Azura, Seth, Typhon, Iasion, Endymion.
OTHER: Centaur Chiron, Charon, Hotep, Petra, Persephone.

Port Spearpoint was the third seaport founded by the Titans. It was the third founded by Oceanus and Tethys. Initially, it was first only a spear marking a spot. It then became an Outpost then the major seaport connecting Oursea to all land west of the great granite seawall.

Poseidon was the fifth child, second male, born to Elder Titane Cronus and Elder Titanide Rhea. He eventually usurped Hestia as the dominant Olympian. He was an adversary of Elder Titane Oceanus.
IGM Poseidon was God of Sea, Storms, Earthquakes, and Horses.

Potamoi were male children of Tethys and Oceanus. They were each born in a different major river.
IGM the Potamoi were gods of rivers and streams.

Prometheus was the son of Titane Iapetus and Oceanid Clymene. Biy 48.
IGM Prometheus was one of the four fathers of mankind. Known for his intelligence and for being a champion of humankind. Author of the arts and sciences.

Pumi was Clan of the Serpent Stonecutter and the premier stonecutter in the known lands. He founded the Tallstone Camp and Urfa Camp. He was mate to Valki and he adopted sons Breathson and Putt. BIY 10, DIY 97. He was the biological father to Replaceson. cf "Earth."

Red Nectar was a drink developed by Kiya which reduced the aging process by 50%. The recipe was shared with her daughters upon their reaching maturity. The Titanides were tasked with surreptitiously providing the drink to only their own family members and sharing the recipe only with their own "worthy" daughters upon their maturity.

Rhea was the last daughter adopted by Kiya, the youngest of the Elder Titans, and "the wild child" of the family. She married Elder Titane Cronus and was the mother to the six Elder Titans.
IGM Rhea, by Cronus, gave birth to Hestia, Demeter, Hera, Hades, Poseidon, and Zeus. The tradition concerning the order of their birth is convoluted.

Rhodos was an Oceanid who became an accomplished airboat pilot.

Rivermaster was the first-born son of Kiya and Vanam. He was an elder Titane and married Elder Titanide Tethys. They adopted four girls who became the Elder Oceanids, and she gave birth to several sons and daughters. Rivermaster was fascinated with the nature of water. He and Tethys explored the lands surrounding Oursea and the great Middlesea.

ELDER OLYMPIANS: Hestia, Demeter, Hera, Hades, Poseidon, Zeus
OLYMPIANS: Apollo, Ares, Artemis, Athena, Aphrodite, Dionysus, Hermes, Hephaestus, Heracles. LIVING TITANS: Oceanus, Tethys, Selene, Elder Oceanids.
DECEASED TITANS: Queen Kiya, Iapetus/Piercer, Cronus.

Originally named Mutal, Tethys eventually renamed him Oceanus.
IGM. See Oceanus

Riverport was a river-crossing dock established by Rivermaster on the banks of a wide, raging river five days westward run from Urfa. It was the primary entry point into the eastern lands from Tartarus and was the scene of Kiya and Vanam's final challenge.

Sagacity was the second son of Kiya. He was an Elder Titane who married Elder Titanide Phoebe. They were parents of Leto and Asteria. Sagacity was an intellectual fascinated with the power of words. Originally named Iran, he was renamed Coeus by the direction of Port management.
IGM See Coeus.

Season was the basic unit of measuring time as measured from one full moon to the next. Tribes tended to camp at one site for one season and then migrate to another camp for the next hunting season.

Seilenos was an older aide, mentor, and wagon driver to Dionysus.
IGM Seilenos was the oldest of the Satyrs. He was a father, teacher, and companion to Dionysus.

Selene was the daughter of Elder Titane Hyperion and Elder Titanide Theia and became an influential resident of Urfa.
IGM Selene was one of the three children of Hyperion and Theia called "The Shining Ones." Selene drove her moon chariot across the heavens and was Goddess of the Moon."

Seth was the only biological son of Pumi and Valki. He eventually joined the Tallstone Skywatcher Guild and became Master-of-Masters at Tallstone. He was originally named Replaceson. Biy 47.
In Judaic tradition, Seth was the third-born son of Adam and Eve.

Stade. One stade is 607.2 feet. Ten stades are 1.15 miles.

Starmaster was the third son of Kiya by Vanam. He was an Elder Titane jack-of-all-trades. He married Elder Oceanid Eurybia. They parented Astraeus, Pallas, and Perses. Originally named Manar, he was renamed Crius by direction of Port Olympus management.
IGM See Crius.

The **tall stone** was the stone obelisk four times the height of a man placed in the center of the hill marking the location of Tallstone Camp. The site could be easily seen from a distance.

OCEANIDS: Metis, Tyche, Clymene, Eurybia, Amphitrite, Philyra, Rhodos.
TELCHINES: Dexithea, Makelo, Halia.
EAST: Azura, Seth, Typhon, Iasion, Endymion.
OTHER: Centaur Chiron, Charon, Hotep, Petra, Persephone.

Tallstone Camp, or Tallstone, was a hilly site Pumi selected as a potential campsite favorable to his tribe's gatherers. He manipulated his elders into accepting the site as a recurring camp and relocated his Rock Table from his favorite source of stones, Rockplace Camp. He then erected a tall stone obelisk on the hill so the site could be easily seen from a distance. Circumstances caused him to surround the tall stone with Guardian stones and personalize Sitting Stones for each chief that attended a Winter Solstice Festival. Tallstone cast shadows which helped the Skywatchers understand the motion of the sun and constellations.

Tartarus began as the small encampment where the Titans settled and which became the center of Titan life. It contained the ceremonial fire pit, an entertaining patio, and Titan residences. My fictional etymology is "Land of the Titans."
IGM while Tartarus is not considered to be directly a part of the underworld, it is described as being as far beneath the underworld as the earth is beneath the sky It was reserved for the worst people which, according to Ouranos, included the Titans. Zeus cast the Titans along with his father Cronus into Tartarus after defeating them.

Telchines *(tel-CHEE-nee)* were three companions to various dactyls and powerful people. Their names were Dexithea, Makelo, and Halia.
IGM Telchines were cultivators of the soil, demons with destructive eyes who could assume any form and bring rain, hail, and snow. They were also artists in brass.

Tethys was an adopted daughter of Kiya. She was an Elder Titanide who married Elder Titane Rivermaster. The two adopted Metis, Tyche, Clymene, and Eurybia who became the first Oceanids. She gave birth to a daughter, Amphitrite, and then to the Potamoi brothers who she named Achelous, Alpheus, and Inachus. She was an explorer and, like her husband, was fascinated with the power of water.
IGM Tethys, by Oceanus, gave birth to the Oceanids and the Potamoi who were water goddesses and river gods.

Teumessian was the Master of the Shaman Scholars and considered himself the wisest of the Shamans.
IGM the Teumessian Fox was sent by the gods, possibly Dionysus, as punishment to humans.

Theia was an adopted daughter of Kiya. She was Elder Titanide who married Elder Titane Watchman. They had three children, including Selene. Theia was the first and premier seamstress of her time.
IGM Theia, by Hyperion, to the Shining Children. They were Helios the Sun, Selene the Moon, and Eos the Dawn.

ELDER OLYMPIANS: Hestia, Demeter, Hera, Hades, Poseidon, Zeus
OLYMPIANS: Apollo, Ares, Artemis, Athena, Aphrodite, Dionysus, Hermes, Hephaestus, Heracles. LIVING TITANS: Oceanus, Tethys, Selene, Elder Oceanids. DECEASED TITANS: Queen Kiya, Iapetus/Piercer, Cronus.

Themis was the first daughter adopted by Kiya. She was the oldest Titanide and second in power among the Titans after her mother. She was a consort to Zeus and bore him several children.
IGM Themis, by Zeus, gave birth to the "Horae" and "The Fates."

Tinom was tin ore. See Metals Workshop.

Titans were Kiya, the Elder Titans, the children of the Elder Titans, plus those accepted into the Titan family.
IGM the Greek writer, Hesiod, gave a double etymology for "Titan." He derived it from titaino, "to strain" and tisis, "vengeance." He wrote that Ouranos gave them the name Titans "in reproach; for they strained and did a fearful deed, and that vengeance for it would come afterward."

Titanes were male Titans.

Titanides were female Titans.

The **Titanomachy** was Hestia's successful project to remove all Titans from positions of power in Port Olympus.
IGM the Titanomachy was the war between the Titans and the Olympians.

Tyche was an adopted daughter of Rivermaster and Tethys. She was the second of the first four Elder Oceanids. She assisted her parents in founding new civilizations Biy 32.
IGM there are several traditions as to Tyche's parents. None suggest a consort or offspring.

Typhon was the Master Scholar in the Art of War.
IGM Typhon was a monstrous, serpentine god who attempted to overthrow Zeus.

The **Underworld** was the land under the control of Hades.
IGM the Underworld consisted of the following areas:
Asphodel Meadows, a place for ordinary or indifferent souls,
Mourning Fields, a place for souls who wasted their lives on unrequited love,
Elysium, a place for the especially distinguished who could choose to live there or be reborn,
Isles of the Blessed, Elysium islands for souls who made it to Elysium three times, Eternal Paradise, and
Tartarus, a deep abyss used as a dungeon of torment for the wicked and as a prison for the Titans.

Urfa was the first city that evolved from a hunting camp founded by Pumi but developed by Valki as a "Last Camp" for the elderly and other cast-offs. Valki domesticated einkorn in her fields at Urfa. Building trades and animal domestication also evolved at Urfa.

Valki was a foundling by Vivekamulla, Clan of the Lion Elder Woman. She became the mate of Pumi and grew Urfa from a camp for the

OCEANIDS: Metis, Tyche, Clymene, Eurybia, Amphitrite, Philyra, Rhodos.
TELCHINES: Dexithea, Makelo, Halia.
EAST: Azura, Seth, Typhon, Iasion, Endymion.
OTHER: Centaur Chiron, Charon, Hotep, Petra, Persephone.

elderly and tribal misfits into the major city of its time. She domesticated Einkorn into wheat. She developed the Winter Solstice Festival into a major event. She adopted sons Breathson and Putt and was biological mother to Replaceson. BIY 13, DIY 65. cf "Valkkai" or "Life."

Vanam was the ambitious successor to the great Clan of the Serpent Chief Talaimai. He was mate to Kiya, fathered five sons, and adopted six daughters. BIY 0. DIY 44. cf "Uyar-Vanam" or "High Sky."
IGM See Ouranos, "The Sky."

Watchman was the fourth son of Kiya by Vanam. Elder Titane Watchman married Elder Titanide Theia. The two parented Helios, Selene, and Eos. Originally named Nan, he was renamed Hyperion by order of Port Olympus management.
IGM See Hyperion.

Winter Solstice Festival was a festival held at Tallstone Camp each Winters Solstice. The first Festival was the first planned Encounter between two tribes, the Clan of the Lion and the Clan of the Serpent. The festival grew larger each year. It solidified the position of Tallstone and Urfa as the cultural and scientific center of the world and was the catalyst for the beginning of civilization.

Zeus was the sixth child, the third male, born to Cronus and Rhea. The Olympian was flamboyant, gushing, overpowering, and a womanizer. He required ongoing and universal love from everyone. He eventually became God of the Sky. Biy 72.
IGM Zeus was King of the Gods. His wife was Hera who gave birth to Olympians Ares and Hephaestus and non-Olympians Hebe and Eileithyia. He mated with most females and fathered many children including Olympians Athena and Dionysus plus Greek Hero Heracles. The birth order of the Elder Olympians is convoluted. Zeus was the God of Sky, Lightning, and Justice.

ELDER OLYMPIANS: Hestia, Demeter, Hera, Hades, Poseidon, Zeus
OLYMPIANS: Apollo, Ares, Artemis, Athena, Aphrodite, Dionysus, Hermes, Hephaestus, Heracles. LIVING TITANS: Oceanus, Tethys, Selene, Elder Oceanids. DECEASED TITANS: Queen Kiya, Iapetus/Piercer, Cronus.

PUBLISHING SCHEDULE
as of 12/01/2022, subject to change.

Book 1. *Tallstone and the City: Foundation*
ISBN 979-8-9860246-0-8
194 pages; 74,928 words.
September 1, 2022

Book 2. *Kiya and Her Children: Rise of the Titans*
ISBN 979-8-9860246-1-5
288 pages; 103,362 words
December 1, 2022

Book 3. *Dionysus and Hestia: Rise of the Olympians*
ISBN 979-8-9860246-2-2
368 pages; 130,300 words
February 28, 2023

Book 4. *Isis and Osiris: Rise of Egypt*
ISBN 979-8-9860246-3-9
364 pages; 120,598 words
May 30, 2023

Book 5. *The Pharaoh and the Gods*
ISBN 979-8-9860246-4-6
August 29, 2023.

Book 6. *The Patriarch and the Lord*
ISBN 979-8-9860246-5-3
November 28, 2023.

OCEANIDS: Metis, Tyche, Clymene, Eurybia, Amphitrite, Philyra, Rhodos.
TELCHINES: Dexithea, Makelo, Halia.
EAST: Azura, Seth, Typhon, Iasion, Endymion.
OTHER: Centaur Chiron, Charon, Hotep, Petra, Persephone.

CPSIA information can be obtained
at www.ICGtesting.com
Printed in the USA
BVHW052107070223
658071BV00011B/198